Rudolph Leonard Tafel

Emanuel Swedenborg as a Philosopher

and man of science

Rudolph Leonard Tafel

Emanuel Swedenborg as a Philosopher
and man of science

ISBN/EAN: 9783337734619

Printed in Europe, USA, Canada, Australia, Japan

Cover: Foto ©Andreas Hilbeck / pixelio.de

More available books at **www.hansebooks.com**

EMANUEL SWEDENBORG

AS A PHILOSOPHER, AND MAN OF SCIENCE.

BY

RUDOLPH LEONARD TAFEL,

PHILOSOPHIÆ DOCTOR.

CHICAGO:

E. B. MYERS AND CHANDLER,

87, WASHINGTON STREET.

1867.

TO THE READER.

To remove the stigma cast upon a great and honorable name, to vindicate a true and holy cause, is a duty with the just, as it is a privilege to the generous mind. That his readers may be enabled to perform this duty, and enjoy this privilege, the editor of the present work has undertaken to place before them EMANUEL SWEDENBORG, and the cause which he advocated, in the light in which they appear to those who are entitled, by an honest and faithful study of his writings, to express the judgment which such study alone could render them competent to form.

For more than a hundred years the world has freely heard, and readily accepted, the testimony of men who knew neither Swedenborg nor his work,—and has judged him according to this testimony. Now, it is asked to give ear to the witness of those who do know him and his work, and who, from knowledge, are capable of speaking truly and wisely of one of the greatest and best, if not the greatest and best, of mortal men.

It is time that this simple act of justice should be done; that the imaginary picture of Swedenborg, painted by men who never saw him, and who, if they had looked upon him, would still not have seen him, should be exchanged in the world's eye, for another and truer one; which, however defective in its representation of the whole man, is yet faithful to as much as has been seen of him,—and, possibly, as could be seen of him,—by minds so far removed from the majesty of his intellectual proportions. To this end the editor has endeavored to bring together, and arrange in order, the separate and distinct portraitures of Swedenborg in his great and immensely varied mental activity and labors, as a reformer of science and philosophy,—which have been drawn by men here and there, who have had visions more or less distinct of his noble form and magnificent outlines. And he freely declares his belief, that the scientific mind of the age, however sceptical it may be, when it looks upon him as here portrayed, cannot fail to recognize his great importance to its own work; nor escape the conviction,—on evidence which only wilfulness can reject,—that a vast deal of the superior light of this enlightened century is contained, *in nuce*, in his writings, published in the early part of the eighteenth century.

He is well aware that the larger number of the men of science of this day, are not prepared for the science of Swedenborg. But he is equally well aware that they will never be prepared so long as they remain in bondage to their senses, and prefer to be instructed by dumb facts, rather than that higher reason by which alone the human understanding can be enlightened. The unmeaning objections, the perversions, and prevarications, which have thus far succeeded in preventing the superior light of Swedenborg's philosophical teachings from reaching the facts of the day, surely cannot avail much longer to hide it from the eyes of men,—confirmed as it is by the thoughtful, sober wisdom of a century, engaged in examining and scanning the claims of this illustrious philosopher.

The fact must be palpable to every unprejudiced reader of the Second Part of this work, that many of the most notable discoveries of modern science, which constitute the boast and glory of our present century, are found not only foreshadowed, but even distinctly announced in Swedenborg's scientific writings. And all real and earnest seekers after truth must be convinced that Swedenborg's philosophical and scientific theories are a new quantity, which henceforth must enter into the calculations of scientific men, if they wish to keep pace with the movement of the age. If science refuses to acknowledge the claims of Swedenborg, a new rival school will inevitably arise, which, untrammelled by the cumbrous apparatus and learned formulæ of a merely sensual science, will carry facts to that higher rational level, where Swedenborg has unfolded his systems and theories.

To the men of progress especially, who are willing to follow into a new world of principles, disclosed by the rational inductions of this truly great man, we would recommend a careful study of his philosophical and scientific works. They will find there some of their noblest aspirations realized.

Our object in preparing the present Volume, was not so much to urge upon the learned the claims of Swedenborg as the first expounder of theories that have since been adopted by science; but rather to enable them to share our conviction that his philosophical and scientific writings are indispensable to any further advance towards a rational induction of those principles which underlie all true science. These works come before the learned not as those of Leibnitz, Kepler, Bacon and Newton. Theirs are merely works of reference, and have only historical value—their use in science has already been fulfilled; for the principles and theories established by these men have long since been absorbed by the sciences, and have entered into their composition. But with Swedenborg the case is essentially different. Not one of the principles laid down by him has been adopted by science, or, if adopted, has been credited to him. It is astonishing how carefully men have avoided even the mention of him; so that his scientfic writings may be said to come before the learned of this day as though they had been written but yesterday. And yet they come ushered in by that very same science which more than a hundred years ago had spurned them; and which is now compelled to acknowledge that many of the leading theories and principles established within the last hundred years by the combined labor of all the scientific men of the world, are for the most part literally contained in them, though published more than a hundred years ago. Shall we wait until, at the expiration of another hundred years, the twentieth century, gathering up the theories and principles developed by the nineteenth, declares that all these theories were propounded *two hundred years* before, in the works of an illustrious Swedish philosopher, Emanuél Swedenborg? Struggle as it may to bring forth something new, science cannot go beyond the theories already indicated by him. They rest on principles which are firm and immutable, because they are true; and the more of truth there is in science, the nearer it draws to these principles. So long, however, as it ignores his work, and plods on in its old, beaten track, refusing his light and assistance, so long will he remain immeasurably in advance of it. There is no ratio given between the sensual and the rational; and while the sensual declines to be imbued with and adjoined to the rational, there must be between them a great gulf fixed.

No doubt some degree of resolution is requisite to enable one to shake off the illusions of the senses, and to place faith in the reality and existence of rational principles in science; but men of science are not without resolution, and it cannot but be that many will be found, who, when the question is distinctly presented for decision, will have the courage to give their belief to reason rather than to the senses.

For such the scientific works of Swedenborg are written. With a firm faith in the rationality of our age, we call upon its representatives to consider the scientific writings of Swedenborg, trusting that such will be the use which will be made of them, that at the expiration of this century, the next will not rise up in judgment to condemn it for having " bound up its talent in a napkin," when it should have put it out to usury.   R. L. T.

St. Louis, January 29, 1867.

TABLE OF CONTENTS.

PART I.

EMANUEL SWEDENBORG AS THE PHILOSOPHER.

PART II.

EMANUEL SWEDENBORG AS THE MAN OF SCIENCE.

I.

Swedenborg's Theories of Form.

II.

Swedenborg's Physiological Theories, and Anatomical Discoveries.

III.

Swedenborg's Chemical Theories.

IV.

Swedenborg's Magnetic Theories.

Page

V.

Swedenborg's Astronomical Theories.

PART I.

EMANUEL SWEDENBORG AS A PHILOSOPHER.

I.

SWEDENBORG IN ADVANCE OF HIS AGE.

1. " EVERY new age has distinctive scenery, features and views, with prominent aspirations and hopes uprising above the ordinary level, and dimly undulating the distant horizon, thereby forming the culminating point of man's intellectual progress. He, therefore, who first approaches and attains this summit, is in advance of his age, and can behold therefrom the distinctive features, views, and scenery, beyond and appertaining to the next age ; but which will be presented to and cover the forthcoming field of view. Such a one, *in advance of his fellows*, was EMANUEL SWEDENBORG. We need not wonder, then, at his having sketched out so faithfully the religious and scientific views of the *new era* now dawning upon us: we need not wonder that, waiting our approach to the same eminence, he calmly sat down (*Principia*, Part III. Appendix *) to record the *new views* on the next field of vision, *then* never dreamt of, but now familiar to us, and to sketch out that new horizon for mankind which ere long, as we advance, will loom into being."—SAMUEL BESWICK, *the Commentator of Swedenborg's " Principia," in "Intellectual Repository," for 1850, p. 213.*

2. " One hundred years ago EMANUEL SWEDENBORG lived, wrote and died. He made no noise in the world ; he did not thrust himself prominently forward ; he labored quietly, firmly,

---

* This extract will be found at large in our n. 60.—*Editor.*

1

unremittingly. . . . The truths he taught, unheeded in
a former century, are re-appearing now in the leading
men of England's Church—Trench, Maurice, Kingsley,—
and the light that lonely man kindled amid the snows of
Sweden has sprung from mount to mount, from height to
height : and it shall live, for there is peace upon its brow, and
in its eye the love which liveth, and which dieth not—the love
which is the sole fulfilling of the law—the love which riseth
high above both faith and hope, and is the primal element of
God Himself."—J. W. FLETCHER, *the author of* "*The Battle
of the Alma*," "*Cloud-Shadows*," &c., in his lecture on
" *Swedenborg*," 1859, p. 1.

3. "' *Truth is strong and will prevail.*' There are always a
few candid and earnest minds in the community, anxious for
the truth, and ready to seek it wherever it is to be found, and
to follow whithersoever it leads. Such there were, even in
Swedenborg's lifetime,—men, too, of high character, intelligence, and education, — who perceived the truth of the
principles he taught, received them with delight, and sought to
make them known to others. Since his death, the number has
been steadily increasing, in all parts of the world. And within
a few years past, many of the profound and original thinkers
of the age have repaired to his pages, as their chief source
of instruction, and have acknowledged that they could find
there satisfactory answers to their inquiries, that could be
found nowhere else, in the whole range of moral, theological,
and philosophical writers. The signs of the times are now
giving token of a change, and a great change, in the view generally. entertained of this author. As he becomes more known,
surprise and admiration take the place of neglect and contempt ; the earnest searchers for truth wonder that they had
not been directed to this light before,—the intellectual and the
learned are astonished that they had passed by a thinker and
writer, who far excels them both in intellect and learning ; and
the admirers and collectors of great names are beginning to
admit his into their list. And we venture the prediction that,
as years roll by, and these writings are examined, explored,
understood, more and more thoroughly—as the world grows

wiser and better—as the darkness of old error passes off, and the light of truth increases—the name of SWEDENBORG will shine the brightest in the whole galaxy of great names, and his memory be revered as that of the most powerful and most useful of all human instruments whom heaven has raised up, to communicate truth, goodness, and happiness to mankind."
—*From a Memoir* by the REV. O. PRESCOTT HILLER.

4. *From the "Intellectual Repository,"* London, March, 1857.

"It has been the fate of all great and original minds to suffer obloquy and contempt from the people of their own generation, and of several generations after them. Galileo, Newton, [Kepler,] and others have had this obloquy cast upon them, and have for a time been treated with oblivious contempt. But now such names shine in the horizon of science and literature as stars of the greatest magnitude. Swedenborg, it was, *a potiori*, from the extraordinary originality of his ideas, to be expected, would be treated in a similar manner. Swedenborg himself well knew this, and therefore prefixed to his 'Economy of the Animal Kingdom' the following from Seneca :—

"'Paucis natus est, qui populum ætatis suæ cogitat: multa annorum millia, multa populorum supervenient: ad illa respice, etiamsi omnibus tecum viventibus silentium . . . [aliqua causa] indixerit: venient, qui sine offensa, sine gratia judicent.'

"Which, being interpreted, means that 'the author is born but for few, who considers only the people of his own age. Many thousands of years and generations of people will come in succession. Let him look to those ; although some cause or other should impose silence upon all who live in the same age with him. Generations will come who will judge without offensive prejudice, and without prejudicial favor.' How truly this old saying of Seneca is coming to pass in respect to Swedenborg ! Many are now inclined to judge of him 'without offensive prejudice, and without prejudicial favor.'"

5. "I have often thought of writing a work entitled, 'A Vindication of Great Men Unjustly Branded,' and at such

times, among the names prominent to my mind's eye, have been . . . . *Emanuel Swedenborg.* I remember nothing in Lord Bacon superior, few passages equal, either in depth of thought, or in richness, dignity and felicity of diction, or in the weightiness of the truths contained in these articles. I can venture to assert, that as a *Moralist, Swedenborg is above all praise;* and, that as a Naturalist, Psychologist, and Theologian, he has strong and varied claims on the gratitude and admiration of the professional and philosophical faculties." —*Samuel Taylor Coleridge, Literary Remains,* Vol. IV. p. 423.

6. " I have gone through some parts of ' The Animal Kingdom,' which have interested me specially ; and I have been surprised to find how the mind of Swedenborg *has preceded* the present state of knowledge, writing his work at the time when he did. I hope the anatomists and physiologists of our day will profit by this work, both for the sake of extending their ideas, and of rendering justice to the genius of Swedenborg."—*Berzelius, in a letter to Dr. Wilkinson, of London.*

In another letter he says,—"I am surprised at the great knowledge displayed by *Swedenborg* in a subject that a professed metallurgist would not have been supposed to have made an object of study, *and in which, as in all he undertook, he was in advance of his age.*"

7. *From Douglas Jerrold's Magazine,* 1845.

" Slow as is the world to receive new revealments in science, and quick to brand as absurd any contradiction of received opinions, it is yet surprising that Swedenborg's 'Principia,'—a work declared only very lately, by one of the highest professors in Europe, not unworthy of being placed by the side of Newton's ' Mathematical Principia of Natural Philosophy,' —should have been utterly disregarded in all philosophical discussions, and that his great works on ' The Animal Kingdom ' and its ' Economy,' should never have been referred to even by Cuvier. Such ignorance must make us humble in our estimate of the state of human philosophy. It is probable that the grossness of judgment universally indulged in has led to this neglect; and because his theological works were esteemed visionary, his scientific were thrown by as rubbish. How false this decision is may be proved by the slightest reference to his scientific works (now in course of able translation) ; and the exactitude and mathematical clearness of his reasoning powers must be acknowledged, when it is known that he introduced to his country the first knowledge of the differential calculus."

8. *From Fraser's Magazine,* Feb. 1857.

" It is impossible, in the present state of mental science and religious philosophy, to arrive at any quite satisfactory theory of Emanuel Swedenborg. This inexplicability would, of itself, render him an interesting phenomenon in an age which understands so well as ours does, that the proper study of mankind is man ; but there are other and better reasons why all persons professing to be ' well informed,' should have given at least a passing glance at this extraordinary personage—the ' man of ten centuries,' as Coleridge has called him, and has thereby made unexamining ridicule of his life and writings simply impertinent.

" Probably not one in fifty of our readers has ever read a book of Swedenborg's. One of the advantages of anonymous writing is, that ' we ' may confess to having done queer things. For example, we admit that we have carefully read and re-read some six or seven of the fifty or sixty of Swedenborg's octavos, each of which is a good week's work. The result has been a conviction that far more of our modern light has come from Swedenborg than the world, which enjoys it, has in general any idea of. In this, as in many other cases, the light which has notably helped to change the face of the moral and intellectual world, has not reached it directly at all, but only by reiterated reflection and refraction, like the rays of the sun in a clouded spring.

" A few of the most original of recent great men—Words-worth, Coleridge, Flaxman, and Blake, among others—have admitted openly, or betrayed in their works unmistakably, a direct acquaintance with the Swedish mystic's writings."

9. *From Boston Medical and Surgical Journal,*
for April, 1846.

" From the evidences presented in this great work, ('Animal
Kingdom,') it is clear that Swedenborg was neither understood nor appreciated in his own age, and he certainly is not
in our own.   His researches in Vol. II. are exceedingly profound.   Teeming, as the elementary works of anatomy do,
with curious and striking descriptions of individual organs,
and physiological deductions, we have seen nothing superior to
this learned author.   He has laid all nature under severe
contribution, and left nothing of much importance to be
detailed in regard to the subjects discussed in this bibliographical monument of personal industry, and truly scientific
research."

In a later number we read,—" Without fear of contradiction, we honestly say that Swedenborg, as a physiologist and
natural philosopher, is either not known or appreciated by
those who have access to his works, or a studied injustice still
keeps him from being acknowledged, universally, one of the
most extraordinary men that have appeared since the dawn of
true science."

10. *Mr. George Dawson, M.A.,* of Birmingham, who is,
or was, reckoned about the best of the English lecturers, had
been lecturing on Swedenborg, in the Manchester *Athenæum,*
one of the first literary institutions in Great Britain, over
which, at successive anniversaries, Mr. Dickens, Mr. Sergeant
Talfourd, Mr. D'Israeli, and Lord Morpeth have been pre-
siding.   The following notices of his lectures on Swedenborg
appeared in the *Manchester Guardian*, January 16 and 23,
1847 :—

" In commencing his first lecture, *Mr. Dawson* observed
that in this instance he had some advantages over those he
possessed in considering the other characters.   It might be
said of the lectures he had already delivered, (on Carlyle,
Cromwell, etc.,) that he was merely adding his small meed
of praise to some men who had been already praised ; but the
man whom he was to consider that night was one of whom

almost total ignorance prevailed. He met in society with few men who knew anything of Swedenborg, except those who honor him, and bear his name. Indeed, he remembered no case where a man had written works so important, or exercised an influence over the chosen few so great, of whom the people were so entirely ignorant. Having given a brief notice of the life of Swedenborg, Mr. Dawson proceeded to a consideration of his writings, observing that, in all his works, there would be found a resolute attempt to press into the unknown, laying this down as one of the distinctive marks of true wisdom in a man. His aim appeared to be to use his insight into nature, that he might penetrate thereby nearer unto the Maker of nature, and by the contemplation of the pure, not only as it exists in nature, but in the Divine mind, be elevated into that morality which Pythagoras calls divinity. The great effort for which he struggled was to make science religious. Philosophy and religion had been too long separated, and made distinct. Swedenborg turned to natural science, to metallurgy, chemistry, anatomy, and various other sciences, to see whether they were not one with religion. . . . The 'Principia' of Swedenborg might be ranked with the works of Des Cartes and Leibnitz, making for themselves a new theory of cosmogony. . . . This book had received the honor of being placed in the *Index Expurgatorius* at Rome.

"At the close of his second lecture, *Mr. Dawson* observed that all he had done was to rescue a man : neglected, because he was not known, abused most by those who knew him the least ; and to show that this man, denounced as a mere dreamer and enthusiast, ought to be reconsidered by every thoughtful and studious man."

11. *From The Critic, 1847, p. 133.*

"Few know that Swedenborg was a patient and comprehensive investigator, a bold innovator, a great discoverer in almost every science, before he appeared as a theological reformer. It was only in his fifty-seventh year that those fertile religious fantasies began to stir within him, which he regarded as the divinest of revelations, whatever the opinion that others might form respecting them. And this alone should lead to much caution in pronouncing on his theological tenets; for it cannot be supposed that a man, comparable to Leibnitz in scientific acumen, and far surpassing him in scientific variety, should sink into a dreamer of foolish dreams, the moment he ventured on the noblest subject of human inquiry. In speaking thus, we are pronouncing neither for nor against Swedenborg's theology, with which we are very imperfectly acquainted, and which, from the excessive voluminousness of the works containing it, does not incite to study. We merely contend that Swedenborg's theological pretensions deserve a serious and thorough examination, on the ground of his scientific eminence, if on no other; and that so philosophic a mind should not be brushed contemptuously aside as a visionary that stuffed ponderous folios with his hallucinations. At all events, whatever the treatment that his theological system meets with, *the time is come when his scientific experiences and theories must be viewed as something more and something grander than cumbrous incongruities.*"

12. *From the Monthly Review, for 1844.*

" Men of slender pretensions, and even those taking high rank among the *peritissimi* of the day, have been accustomed to dismiss with a sneer, or condemn with a scowl, all mention of, or reference to, Emanuel Swedenborg. The enthusiast, visionary, monomane—the man who affected to converse with beings of another world—the cabalistic, mystic *qui naviget Anticyram dignus*—in short, ' the madman dreamy.' ' A person,' say they, ' who pretended to enjoy intercourse with invisible beings, who affected to be able to converse with the spirits of the departed, and who indulged in the delusive fancies of a heated, if not distempered brain, can surely lay no claim to the title of a man of science, or pretend to be expositor of the all but hidden laws of nature. It is not consonant with the views which we entertain of the sanity of men's minds, to admit Swedenborg among the penates of our literary mythology. We can have no feeling in common with a man who assumes the possession of such superior gifts, that were he indeed possessed of them, or did we admit his pretensions, we must immediately abandon all, or nearly all, the principles which have hitherto guided us in the contemplation and study of nature, for such a man would be only not a god because he is, or was, a creature.'

"This, or something like this, is the opinion either expressed or implied of most persons with whom we have conversed respecting Swedenborg and his works; and it is not derogatory to us to say, that until we perused some of his works—such is the influence of early academic prejudice—that we were just as much inclined to unite in the general censure, as are those to whom we have just alluded. That Swedenborg was really a learned, scientific, studious, and highly gifted man, few seem to know, and fewer stop to inquire. That he was of a high'y respectable family, his father being Bishop of Skara, and his mother, Sarah Behm, the daughter of Albert Behm, Assessor of the Board of Mines; and that he filled some of the most honorable offices in his own country, and retired only to London to devote himself to his theological pursuits, are facts little known even to those whose business is literature. Let it, therefore, be our duty on this occasion to put these facts fully before our readers, and in the light in which we think they ought to be placed, with a view to attract that attention to the work, the title of which ('The Animal Kingdom') is placed at the head of this article, which we think its importance demands, and its merits secure."

After giving a very lengthy sketch of Swedenborg and the work before him, the reviewer says: "In conclusion we record our opinion, positively, and not relatively: wholly, and without reservation, that if the mode of reasoning and explanation adopted by Swedenborg be once understood, *the anatomist and physiologist will acquire more information, and obtain a more comprehensive view of the human body, and its relation to a higher sphere, than from any single book ever published;* nay, we may add, than from all the books which have been written, (especially in modern times,) on physiology, or, as it has been lately named, transcendental anatomy.

"Swedenborg reasons not on any hypothesis, not on any theory, not on any favorite doctrine of a fashionable school, but on the solid principles of geometry, based on the immutable rock of truth: and he must and will be considered at no distant period the Zoroaster of Europe, and the Prometheus of a new era of reason, however, at present, the clouds of prejudice may intervene, or the storms of passion obscure the coruscations of his intellect."

13. *From Monthly Magazine*, for May, 1841.

"We would not conceal that Swedenborg's merits have been ridiculously underrated. Too long has there been a fashion, at once unphilosophical and irreligious, of branding with the epithets of fool, madman, impostor, a man of blameless sanity and undoubted genius,—who, if he lost anything for himself by not taking another path than that he followed so perseveringly, yet made the world a gainer, at once, by putting it in possession of his own remarkable case, and by achieving the consummation of all Scientific Theory,—perhaps, we might add, of all inductive science whatever."

14. "Hitherto I have known nearly nothing of Swedenborg; or indeed I might say less than nothing, having been wont to picture him as an amiable but inane visionary, with affections quite out of proportion to his insight; from whom nothing at all was to be learned. It is so we judge of extraordinary men. But I have been rebuked already; a little book, by one Sampson Reed, of Boston, in New England, which some friend sent hither, taught me that a Swedenborgian might have thoughts of the calmest kind on the deepest things; that, in short, I did *not* know Swedenborg, and ought to be ready to know him."—CARLYLE *in a letter, quoted by Dr. Wilkinson.*

15. *From the Southern Quarterly Review*, October, 1843.

"There has been a singular timidity evinced, even by bold thinkers, in respect to the very perusal of Swedenborg's works. They have been read by stealth, away from company—free from the curiosity of the prying eye. Persons have been afraid, as if they were engaged in some necromantic orgies, to breathe a word to their friends of their peculiar and forbidden occupation. They have come to their teacher, as Nicodemus came to the Saviour, in the night-time,

and have listened to his instructions with equal incredulity
and equal wonder. The ridicule levelled at the celebrated
Swede, by Dr. Southey, more than a quarter of a century
ago, in his 'Espriella's Letters,' has led many to turn with
indifference and contempt from his works—works full of light
and consolation—lest they, too, if detected in their perusal,
should come in for a share of the sarcasm of some lively and
witty satirist. The style in which these compositions are
clothed—in some degree eccentric and unique—but deriving
its singularity rather from the elevated character of the
subjects treated of, than from any want of tact and skill in the
writer, has deterred others, who have commenced the examination of them, from proceeding much beyond the threshold.
Prescriptive authority—educational biases—pride of opinion
—of opinions imbibed in other schools—long entertained, and
mistaken for truth—these have stood in the way of others."

16. *From the Journal Encyclopédique*, Sept. 1, 1785,
Vol. VI, Part 2.

" As Swedenborg, to a profound and universal knowledge,
joined the purest virtue and the sweetest manners, he might
be expected to meet with detractors; he accordingly has had
them, and he has them still. I have often heard him publicly
decried, but always from one of the three following motives,
and with the intention of preventing his works from being
read. Some attributing everything to chance, and believing
in nothing but nature, are afraid that the luminous works of
the greatest naturalist, and the sublimest theosophist that has
yet existed, would give the last blow to their tottering system.
Others having borrowed from him without acknowledging it,
are apprehensive that if his works should obtain more notice,
their plagiarisms would be detected.* The third class, enjoying
a reputation founded on a false opinion of their knowledge,
but being unable to conceal their incapacity from themselves,

---

* One of the modern poets of England (Patmore) being upbraided
for borrowing from Swedenborg without acknowledging it, we are
told, excused himself on the plea, that " Where there was so much to
take, he did not consider it a crime to help himself to a little."

dread the appearance of this polar star, because it will infallibly eclipse them, and soon reduce them to their just estimation."—Marquis de Thomé.

17. In a work entitled "*Swedish Seers and Bards*," by P. B. Atterbom, himself a celebrated modern Swedish poet and professor, occur the following passages :—

"Several decades have now flown by, since the period when voices, not proceeding from the circle of Swedenborg's followers, were first heard to pronounce his name with distinguished commendation. During this time, the manner in which he is generally regarded and spoken of is pretty generally changed, and this to his advantage. Among those who, in judging of literary matters, possess any standing, or are entitled to give an opinion, there are now few, if any, in whose estimation he does not rank as a great and venerable genius, infected with many oddities, but not with insanity.

"One thing is certain, namely, that the more we examine his writings merely with reference to philosophy and æsthetics, the more decided becomes our conviction, that they contain, mixed with much dross,* still more massive gold. Is it not, then, time to apply the apostle's advice,—' Prove all things; hold fast that which is good'? The holy frame of mind in which he conceived his views of the Word, the lofty method in which he exhibited all the essentials thereof, are fully worthy of a divinely inspired seer; his 'visions,' or his so-called *memorabilia*, not unfrequently vie in beauty with their Biblical prototypes; and many of them, if they had been found in the works of Dante, or Milton, would long since have been trumpeted forth over Europe with the most rapturous plaudits."

18. "The time has come when every enlightened man and woman ought, for their own sakes, to know Swedenborg and his pretensions.

"For consider the case. Here was an author, flourishing

---

* See note to No. 62 of the present volume.

in the last century, whose principal works were written from
1721–1772, and who, enjoying at first a good reputation as a
scientific and practical man, saw that reputation gradually
expire as his own mind unfolded in his works, until at length
he was only known as a visionary, and the fact of his early
career was scarcely remembered by his few surviving contemporaries. There was every reason why his works died to that
age. He had a firm faith, from the first, in the goodness of
God, in the powers of the mind, in the wisdom and easiness
of creation, and in the immovable firmness of revelation;
later on, a belief, too, in spiritual existence, in a sense intelligible to all mankind. In his case, there was a breaking of
shell after shell,—a rolling away of delusion after delusion,
until truth was seen to be itself real—to be the true creation,
the world above and before the world, of which mortal
creatures are made. How could so substantial a personage—
a man whose spirit and its relations were a body and a force
—be seen at all in the last century, when the public wave ran
in spring-tides towards materialism, frivolity, and all conven-
tionalities? The savage might as easily value a telescope or a
theodolite as Europe estimate a Swedenborg at such an era.
Accordingly, in proportion as he transcended brute matter and
dead facts, he vanished from its sight, and was only mentioned
with ridicule as a ghost-seer — the next thing to a ghost.
But how stands the matter now? The majority, it is true,
know nothing of Swedenborg. . . . But the vast majority
of those who *do* know—and the number is considerable in all
parts of the civilized world—regard him with respect and
affectionate admiration; many hailing him as the herald of a
new church upon earth; many as a gift of the same provident
Deity who has sent, as indirect messengers, the other secular
leaders of the race,—the great poets, the great philosophers,
the guiding intellects of the sciences; many also still looking
towards his works in order to gain instruction from them, and
to settle for themselves the author's place among the benefac-
tors of his kind. We ourselves are in all these classes,
allowing them to modify each other; and perhaps, on that
account, are suitable to address those who know less of the

subject, for we have no position to maintain, but the facts of the case.

"Now whence this change in public opinion? It has been the most silent of revolutions, a matter almost of signs and whispers. Swedenborg's admirers have simply kept his books before the public, and given them their good word when opportunity afforded. The rest has been done over the heads of men, by the course of events, by the advance of the sciences, by our own new liberties of thought, by whatever makes man from ignorant, enlightened, and from sensual, refined and spiritualized. In short, it is the world's progress under Providence which has brought it to Swedenborg's door. For where a new truth has been discovered, that truth has said a courteous word for Swedenborg; where a new science has sprung up, and entered upon its conquests, that science has pointed with silent-speaking finger to something friendly to, and suggestive of, itself in Swedenborg; where a new spirit has entered the world, that spirit has flown to its mate in Swedenborg; where the age has felt its own darkness and confessed it, the students of Swedenborg have been convinced that there was in him much of the light which all hearts were seeking. And so forth. The fact then is, that an unbelieving century could see nothing in Swedenborg; that its successor, more trustful and truthful, sees more and more; and strong indications exist that in another five-and twenty years the field occupied by this author must be visited by the leaders of opinion *en masse*, and whether they will or no; because it is not proselytism that will take them there, but the expansion and culmination of the truth, and the organic course of events."—J. J. GARTH WILKINSON, *Life of Sweden-borg*, 1849, Americ. edit. pp. 1–3.

II.

SWEDENBORG'S GREATNESS.

19. "WHEREVER you cast your eyes — to the blue starry heavens above, or the hard rocky earth beneath, to its atmospheres, magnetic, electric or aërial; to its waters or its minerals; or to the arcana, abundant as they are, of that best and most perfect organism in creation — the physical constitution of man; on each of these departments of physical creation this unwearied and devout Christian philosopher has left the foot-prints of his presence, and has handed over a legacy of truth, that even now has enriched human society to a degree that has oftentimes called forth our admiration, though that legacy be not announced in the name and under the acknowledged seal of EMANUEL SWEDENBORG."— SAMUEL BESWICK, *the Commentator of Swedenborg's " Principia," in " Intellectual Repository,"* for 1850, p. 372.

In another place he says: "During this philosopher's day it was universally believed that both *air* and *water* were elemental substances, having nothing in common but the general characteristics of fluidity. His penetrating sagacity, equal to all subjects in the wide field of human inquiry, and blessed as it was with suggestive capabilities of a higher and happier kind than mortals are ordinarily endowed with, not only broke through the spell of ages, and pictorially exhibited the twofold nature of each, but also proclaimed the identity of one of their elements. World-wide as is the just fame of many distinguished chemical philosophers, it is a non-entity compared with that which awaits the venerable Swede. As yet no monumental inscription has been raised to mark the spot where his bones are laid: better it is that an everlasting memorial should be deeply inscribed on the hearts and memory of men."— *Id.* p. 301.

(15)

Speaking of Swedenborg's contributions to astronomical science, he says : —

" Before Swedenborg's time, creation was considered a globular universe, bounded by the visible heavens. Beyond this there was no creation, but the spiritual heavens — the theological universe. Within this the material universe was inclosed, in the centre of which our solar system was placed ; whilst its interior surface was our visible heaven, over whose ethereal vault were strewed in unnumbered myriads the glimmering lights of other worlds.

" Swedenborg was the first intellectually to break through the inclosure of the heavens, and with powerful arm to burst asunder its confines, to draw aside the dark curtain of ages, to overthrow the barriers raised by ancient prejudices, and advance to some distance, though with cautious steps, over the uncertain ground beyond. With unwearied labor he had essayed every probable path, and having found the right one, proceeded along to the very gate of truth. Wonderful indeed were the results. At once, by a single effort of his genius, worlds innumerable, in congregated spheres, were beheld in harmonious operation, without end or limit — the boundaries of the universe, so to speak, became to man at once illimitable ; and the scattering goodness of the Divine Hand, strewing mercies and blessings amongst unnumbered worlds, hitherto unseen, unknown, and unconjectured, was a scene worthy of the Almighty — a prospective into a field so entirely new and unprecedented, that admiring millions are struck with awe at the Mighty Power and Infinite Love and Wisdom of that Being who moves, provides for, and supports the whole. It was a *Revelation* of the attributes of his Being and the Resources of his Power, infinitely beyond anything which the wildest imagination of the Atheist could ever have conceived, in demand for evidence of his existence. Literally, the heavens were opened — that most glorious and magnificent region in the material universe, the *Heaven of Heavens*, formed, as Swedenborg expresses it, of innumerable heavens, in congregated spheres, beyond or outside our own — was displayed *first* to the intellectual, and subsequently to the ocular vision, when one universal blaze of glory burst forth on the astonished world. 'Behold!' says Swedenborg, on drawing aside the dark curtain of ages, which had intercepted creation from the view of mortals, 'behold these new walks of the Almighty! Lift up your heads on high, and behold Him traversing the innumerable spheres with the same flowing richness, beauty, and care as is so conspicuous on this atom of a world on which we dwell.'"

"Listen to Swedenborg's own words: * "If all the spheres, if all the heavenly hosts are not even a point in respect to the infinite; if the whole visible sidereal expanse, which to our eye appears so immense, be only as a point in relation to the finite universe; if our solar system form only a part of the sidereal expanse, and our own world only a part of the solar system; truly we ask, 'What is man? Can he be such a one as he feigns himself to be? Vainglorious mortal, why so inflated with self-importance? Why deem all the rest of creation beneath thee? Diminutive worm! What makes thee so big, so puffed out with pride, when thou beholdest a creation so multitudinous — so stupendous around thee? Look down ward upon thyself, thou puny manikin! behold and see how small a speck thou art in the system of heaven and earth; and in thy contemplations remember this, that if thou wouldest be great, thy greatness must consist in this — in learning to adore Him who is Himself the Greatest and the Infinite." — *Principia*, Part iii. chap. i. n. 11.

Mr. Beswick continues: " This humble and devout philosopher was the first happy mortal on whom the high duty devolved of developing these mighty truths for the benefit of mankind. He was a suitable instrument for so glorious a Revelation. When the immensity of God's work, beyond or outside the visible starry heavens, had thus been opened to him, and, for the first time in human history, he had gazed mentally on the peculiar mechanism of our own immediate universe; had watched and measured the play of its mighty forces; had proclaimed, after geometrical measurement, the precise system or cluster of stars to which our sun's system belongs; yea, had placed his finger on the very spot in that

---

* Inserted by the Editor.

2*

cluster *five years* before Herschel was born; all of which we have proved in our articles not to be questioned. (See Chap. V. of our Second Part.) When they had been accomplished, nothing more, as to universal principles and universal mechanism, could be revealed to or made known by him, to be useful to mankind now. To progress further, the opening of the inner universe to mental vision must needs follow. For, as to *universal principles* and *mechanism,* he had seen all that man could *now see* where man doth dwell. He stood betwixt the darkness of the past and the light of the present, a humble instrument, holding in his hands the germs of those extraordinary discoveries and revelations which even now astonish the world. . . . .

"One thing is clear to all who may have carefully studied his voluminous writings,—as a child writing down his thoughts and experience, so has he been with regard to his opinions, and discoveries, and his almost universal experience. But it is equally clear ' the world knows him not.' "—*Intellectual Repository,* 1850, pp. 90–91.

In another place, where he speaks of Swedenborg's discovery of the "Translatory Motion of the Stars in the Milky Way," and on comparison proves his theory to be identical with that now held by modern astronomy, Mr. Beswick exclaims: "This contrast presents the two extremities of an age. At its commencement all is negation. It exhibits the Swedish philosopher in bold and striking relief. Behold him! he stands alone in an age of darkness. In the back-ground, the past is black as night. It brings him out like the sudden apparition of a new star bursting with glory and brilliancy, outshines the whole heavens, as if in advance thereof. It enables us to perceive that the genius of Swedenborg had traversed an unknown path and explored an unknown region,— had watched intellectually the stars in their magnetic courses, and followed them in their revolutions, and had grasped, with almost superhuman intelligence, the whole sum of this vast starry universe, to make it subservient to his thoughts, long before other men even suspected the existence of such translatory phenomena. With the striking theoretical discoveries present before the mind, who can doubt the transcendency of his genius, or object to his claims for the highest order of anticipative originality?"— *Id*. pp. 46–7.

20. "Beginning at the smallest facts — the humblest appearances of nature—he worked his way up to the crown and coping stone, and bowed with adoration in the outer courts of eternity. He swept the circle of the sciences with a patient, unflagging energy. . . . . In his own day he was the leader of his age — the captain of the free lances who fought their way into the citadel of truth. He is the representative man of that century — the shaft that was shot the farthest from the bow: he was the culmination of all past truth; and in him were shadowed forth the flashing glories of the future. He is the keystone of the arch that connects the coming with the gone: and every advance in art, every discovery in science, every new phase of truth, every additional development of nature, as it rises in orbed beauty to fill its place in God's great plan and universe, bears silent witness to the truth and power of him who is one of earth's master-spirits — adds one other stone to the arch of glory which the ages are rearing round the memory of Emanuel Swedenborg."—J. W. FLETCHER, *in his Lecture on* "*Swedenborg*," p. 9, 1859.

21. "In what way are we to regard this wonderful man? Look at him long — look at him most cautiously, most suspiciously; try him by any standard, and still he remains—the Wonderful. No man whose name biography has treasured demands a more careful study than he. For do but consider him: his Learning was boundless; in Science his knowledge was imperial on almost every subject; in Mathematics he was able to take the highest post both in the practical and theoretical worlds; in Languages he was erudite. Who can deny him a reach and stretch of thought capable of measuring all subjects, and amplifying and illustrating all. Is not his Fancy amazing in its play? His poems — for by this title you must style his Memorable Relations, if you cannot call them Visions — do they not kindle with the true light of genius, and flash with image and description? This is a Cyclopædic man, his shoulders are Atlantean. Does he not even dwarf giants by his side?

"And yet you say he is a Fanatic. . . . . What, then, is a Fanatic? One of the profoundest Mathematicians of his age; a deep and acute thinker; a subtle logician; a various and versatile scholar: above all, a calm and most quiet bookman and penman, indisposed for any company; and never seen to court the company of the ignorant and the vulgar, ever the resort of the fanatic: a man of few words, until compelled to talk, or talking for a purpose; cool in temperament; never rocked by passion or impulse: always, as far as humanity can be, in equilibrium, weighing all his thoughts and all his actions, perpetually bent on giving reasons for things; a man of strong inductive habits and powers, and consistent; a whole life of invariable rectitude and doctrines, and principles, ever above the hour; and ever from the period of his illumination, the same. — Is this the portrait of a Fanatic? . . .

"Can the reader be content to know nothing of this man? Can he be content any longer to know him only dimly and in shadow? Not that we may hope at all to comprehend him. He was a Titan, and must take his place among the very highest and widest minds of our world; his was truly a Norse intellect; he belonged to the wonderful race of Sea-Kings; he was one of the children of Odin, and we know that race — the writers and interpreters of the runes — the utterers of the rhythmic charm. Always over the Norse and Icelandic mind there had hovered the scenery of a wonderful spirit-land; that mind flames to this day over Europe, in action, and in contemplation. Who shall say to what extent we are indebted to that mind for the spirituality of our genius, and the sonorousness of our eloquence, the intrepidity of our action, and the boldness of our conception; these are the characteristics of the Scandinavian mind. Swedenborg, in the mightiest degree, inherited them all.

"Sometimes we have thought of his mind — of its awful solitude — its unbroken and terrible remoteness from ordinary minds. We stand in awe of him even yet. What subjects were those on which he daily conversed; what realms were those he daily visited? We are always interested in the history and portrait of a mind occupying an untrodden territory, making excursions into realms to which no traveller has penetrated — a land protected by its solemn silences from wing, or sail, or road. Lone old man! no wife, no child, no relative; no friend does he appear to have had; he stood solitary in mind and in life. Does biography record another instance of so lonely a man, so secluded from the world, so withdrawn from society? Yet never, surely, did we know one whose face in solitude so repels our pity, whose loneliness is so sacred. This anchorite went up into the high Himalayas of the soul. He lived to pen and utter the tones heard among those Delectable Mountains.

"It must ever be a mystery how, so constantly as he was travelling, he performed so much work; his works would stock a library, and keep for some years a most persevering and megatherian student at work. But he was ever moving from place to place; discipline and order must have characterized him in the highest degree. He travelled and he observed constantly, but all the while we feel that he had no part with man. He knew what others felt, but his feelings he ever conceals from us — rather shall we say, he does not feel, and has no feelings to record; hence in none of his writings have we any pathos. He transports himself from place to place on earth, from state to state in mind, from space to space in thoughts and things; doctrines, dogmas and facts, glide before us in his pages, cold and clear as the figures sweeping across the mirror." — *Swedenborg, a biography and an exposition, by* EDWIN PAXTON HOOD, *author of "The Age and its Architects;" "Andrew Marvell;" "John Milton;" "Literature of Labor,"* etc. pp. 157, 169–172.

22. *Thorild*, a celebrated Swedish poet and metaphysician, librarian and professor of the Swedish language and literature in the University of Greifswalde, says in the second part of his works, published in Sweden, under the head "Swedenborg," the following :—

"What are we to think of this truly extraordinary man? That he was a fool, say those little men whose good opinion never did good to any one. That he was an Arch-heretic, bawls Orthodoxy with loud and ferocious voice. What the philosopher sees in him, is a man of vast and consummate

learning, an honor and glory to his nation, who preserved the
veneration for his genius by the truly apostolical simplicity and
purity of his morals."

23. "There is not in history, there is not in any century, a
more remarkable man than Swedenborg, under the aspect of
the development of certain faculties of the soul; and in spite
of all that he has written, or that has been written about him,
there is no man that still offers to criticism a more worthy
study. According to that kind of history which the great
judge of the last century called the ' commonly received fable,'
Swedenborg is a *dreamer*, a *visionary*, a *weak* or *sickly* mind,
the mistaken dupe of his own illusions. Such is the universally
circulating picture and judgment concerning Swedenborg.
Now, the ' commonly received fable' has no doubt some
reasons for its existence, but it is not history.

"In the whole of the last century which produced so many
eminent men, there is not one that was more vigorously constituted as to body and mind than Swedenborg; and there is
not one who was a more industrious, more honest, more
learned, more ingenious and more fertile writer, and a more
lucid teacher. Not one in the whole of that century where
Rousseau proclaimed himself to be as virtuous as any other
man, was better than Swedenborg, nor more beloved, and
happier.

" I was going to say there were few richer in honors,
money and ideas. But this would not be a source of merit,
only a happy condition. In order to convince yourself that
such was the condition of Swedenborg, you need but read his
writings, and study his life, which manifest to the whole world
his virtues and scientific treasures."—M. MATTER, *Honorary
Counsellor of the University, formerly Inspector-General of the
Public Libraries, &c.,* in his work " *Emmanuel de Swedenborg,
sa Vie, ses Ecrits et sa Doctrine.* Paris: Didier & Cie. Libraire
Académique. 1863. pref. pp. vi., vii."

In another place he says, "Swedenborg might have become a member of all the academies of Europe if he had
sought for these honors; but he informs us himself that he

never took any steps in order to belong to any learned body. Essentially independent by fortune and character, loving work for its intrinsic attractions, and not appreciating distinctions which encroach however little upon our liberties, Swedenborg explored, worked and published by himself like an entire academy, and he assigned to himself scientific missions, as princes are wont to do, but he did not crave the distinctions which he thought would naturally follow as their consequences."—p. 32.

24. *From the " Medical Critic and Psychological Journal,"* for October, 1861, Art. VI.

" In the whole range of modern biography there is no life of greater interest to the medico-psychologist than that of Emanuel Swedenborg. His writings constitute a splendid monument of the extraordinary intellectual powers, the untiring assiduity, and the lofty religious fervor of the man. As a philosopher he will always occupy a conspicuous and honorable position in the history of modern philosophy, and as a theologian he gave birth to one of the most remarkable developments of Christianity in modern times."

25. " There is one genius, who has done much for this philosophy of life (*i. e.*, exploring the near, the low, the common), whose *literary value* has never been rightly estimated ;—I mean EMANUEL SWEDENBORG. The most imaginative of men, yet writing with the precision of a mathematician, he endeavored to ingraft a purely philosophical ethics on the popular Christianity of his time. Such an attempt, of course, must have difficulty which no genius could surmount. But he saw and showed the connection between nature and the affections of the soul. He pierced the emblematic or spiritual character of the visible, audible, tangible world. Especially did his shade-loving muse hover over and interpret the lower parts of nature ; he showed the mysterious bond that allies moral evil to the foul material forms, and has given in epical parables a theory of insanity, of beasts, of unclean and fearful

things." *—RALPH WALDO EMERSON, *in an Oration delivered before the Phi Beta Kappa Society, at Cambridge*, August 31, 1837.

In another place he says, " His (Swedenborg's) writings would be a sufficient library to a lonely and athletic student. Not every man can read them, but they will reward him who can. The grandeur of the topics makes the grandeur of the style. One of the missourians and mastodons of literature, he is not to be measured by whole colleges of ordinary scholars. No one man is perhaps able to judge of the merits of his works on so many subjects. It seems that he anticipated much science of the nineteenth century, anticipated in astronomy the discovery of the seventh planet; anticipated the views of modern astronomy in regard to the generation of earths by the sun; in magnetism some important experiments and conclusions of later students; in chemistry, the atomic theory, in anatomy the discoveries of Schlichting, Monro and Wilson; and first demonstrated the office of the lungs."

Again he says, " Swedenborg is a rich discoverer, and of things which most import us to know. His thought dwells in essential resemblances, like the resemblances of a house to the man who built it. He saw things in their law, in likeness of function, not of structure. There is an invariable method and order in his delivery of his truth, the habitual proceeding of the mind from inmost to outmost. What earnestness and weightiness,—his eye never roving, without one swell of vanity, or one look to self, in any common form of literary

---

* It did not strike us in our extensive studies of the works of Swedenborg, that his "shade-loving muse" in showing the connection between spiritual and natural forms dwelled by preference on the "foul material forms" which are "allied to moral evil"; on the contrary, it seemed to us that his muse especially delighted in the description of celestial forms; witness the whole of his wonderful epic "*The Worship and Love of God.*" The reason why, in his illustrations showing the connection between spiritual and natural forms, he was frequently compelled to draw upon "foul material forms," is, because the celestial forms which are allied to moral good, have become so fearfully few in our degenerate days, when the very face of nature bears witness of our sunken human nature.

pride! A theoretic or speculative man, but whom no practical man in the universe could afford to scorn. Plato is a gownsman: his garment, though of purple and almost sky-woven, is an academic robe, and hinders action with its voluminous folds. But this *mystic* is awful to Cæsar. Lycurgus himself would bow."

And again, "Swedenborg's 'Economy of the Animal Kingdom' is one of those books which, by the dignity of thinking, are an honor to the human race. . . . He is systematic and respective of the world in every sentence: all the means are orderly given; his faculties work with astronomical punctuality, and his admirable writing is pure from all pertness or egotism. . . . His varied and solid knowledge makes his style lustrous with points, and shooting spicula of thought; resembling one of those winter mornings when the air sparkles with crystals."—*Representative Men.*

26. "Swedenborg, by hereditary disposition, by early training and habit, was studious and laborious in an eminent degree. His mind was intensely active in the acquisition of knowledge on all subjects; no branch of science or knowledge escaped his attention, or surpassed his powers of investigation. Gifted with an ardent love of learning, carefully instructed and trained in the best of schools, and wisely encouraged and directed in the pursuit of knowledge, his understanding was gradually developed and expanded in directions which are but seldom found in combination in the same mind. . . . We find in him a quality of analysis, so searching and discriminative, as to be altogether microscopic in its character and application, united to a most wonderful power of generalization. By these faculties of his mind he was enabled to order and arrange all the particulars of scientific discovery and rational deduction, into the harmonious forms of general systems; and by a clear analytic and synthetic comparison of every whole with its parts and of the parts with the whole, as well as of the analogies existing between the various systems and their component members, to deduce the laws of order governing each, and so to communicate a rational idea of their several uses, and of their relation to the uni-

versal use of creation. By these means he accomplished
what was never done before, and what has never been done
equally well, if at all, since his day; he brought the sensual
scientific principle into harmony with the rational, and thus
opened science to the light of reason, or elevated it into its
true position, as the servant of a rational philosophy."—
REV. W. H. BENADE, *Report on the Nature of Swedenborg's
Illumination.*

27. *From the Corsair*, 1839, New York.

" Emanuel Swedenborg was, and the reader ought to know
it, one of the greatest and most respectable of men. He was
also more than this. He was deeply versed in every science
—a first-rate mechanician and mathematician—one of the
profoundest of physiologists—a great military engineer . . .
—a great astronomer—the ablest metallurgist of his time, and
the writer of vast works, which even at this day are of sterling
authority on mining and metals. Then he was a poet, and a
master of ancient and modern languages, and a metaphysician
who had gone through all the mazes of reflective philosophy,
and *done besides what metaphysicians seldom do, for he had
found his way out of the mazes, and got back to reality again.*
In short, as far as natural sciences go (and we include among
them the ' science of the mind '), it is much more difficult to
say what he was *not*, than what he *was*.

" He was fifty-five years in being, and doing the things we
have just recorded. Having thus laid an immense basis for
his mind in nature, and a knowledge of the actual, and yet
only a basis, he now, like a stately pyramid, rose into the ideal.
He pierced through the cloudy curtains of Space and Time.
Nature became to him but the mantle of living souls, giving
fixed images to the Reason, and distinctness of object to the
Will. The whole of his theological works, which have consigned him, for the present, to a neglect he anticipated and
had no care for, were now produced. The spiritual world
was the *object*, as well as the subject of his thought, and this
produced what may be called the Realism of his Psychology.
In his mind, Imagination and Sentiment, properly so-called,
had no place, but instead of Imagination there was Reason

producing itself in images; instead of Sentiment, affections forming themselves into Reasons. Hence, there is at once the greatest boldness, and the greatest method in his thoughts —one startling proposition developing itself after another, and each coming forth by the most fixed rules of genesis—a superficial formality, an internal freedom."

This article was reprinted from the "*London True Sun.*"

28. "Of Swedenborg himself, there should be but one opinion. He was a man of prodigious genius. . . . As a philosopher, he was distinguished for perceiving identity or sameness in things,—for his insight into the 'fine secrets that little explains large, and large little;' his doctrine of scale or degrees; his belief in the symbolical meaning of the universe; and that a dread, necessary, noiseless morality pervades it all, from the minutest to the largest objects. He was in a certain sense a seer, but of those broad principles which constitute the trunk and branches of the tree of the world."—GEORGE GILFILLAN, *Christianity and our Era: A Book for the Times.* Edinburgh, 1857.

29. *From the National Quarterly Review for March*, 1865.

"It is well known that the earlier period of Swedenborg's life, when men are most liable to be led astray by their imaginations, was devoted to chemical, mathematical, and philosophical researches, which must have effectually precluded all vagaries; nor did his illumination commence until he had established a literary reputation so irreproachable that his assertions were accepted as truth. If we regard him as an impostor, his whole life is a living refutation of the accusation. That a man so unobtrusive, so regardless of honor and wealth, should have imposed upon the credulity of friendship falsehoods which could in no way subserve his interest, would be a phenomenon without parallel in the history of the world. If we question his sanity, we are met by the assurance that in all cases the insane are found incapable of prolonged, connected mental effort, so that the books Swedenborg wrote, the languages he learned, the correspondence he has left, all bear conclusive evidence that his mental powers were unimpaired.

In whatever aspect we regard this man, he is still a mystery."

After giving an account of Swedenborg, and his minor philosophical works, the writer proceeds :—

"All these testimonials of Swedenborg's mental wealth seem to have dropped from his overburdened pen, rather as a relief to his own intellectual plethora, than from those ambitious aspirations that are supposed to inspire most authors. He is a wise man who can render himself necessary to his superiors by being useful to his equals. Swedenborg seldom, if ever, solicited patronage, nor does he appear to have given much thought to his literary productions after having prepared them, to the best of his ability, for the benefit of his fellow-men. Fortunately, they fell at the feet of an appreciating public, creating for him an *eclat*, despite his modesty, making him noble against his democratic will. Various and brilliant as these labors had been, they were but the lesser pyrotechnics with which he attracted the attention, not only of Sweden, but of all Europe."

Speaking of his " *Opera Philosophica et Mineralogica,*" he says :—

" In this work, sparkling throughout with mental brilliants, Swedenborg has vindicated his claim to an intellectual peerage, and is supposed to have originated many discoveries in philosophy, which, owing to his works being at one period much neglected, have not been attributed to him. In it he endeavors to unlock the mysteries of the causes and origin of the phenomena of the universe, asserting that in all her operations nature is governed by one general law, and is always self-consistent ; while experience, the power of arrangement, and the ability to reason are sufficient to enable us to solve her most intricate problems."

Of the " *Economy of the Animal Kingdom,*" he says :—

" Whether or not we endorse the conclusions which his subtle reasonings led him to embrace, we cannot but admire the unflinching temerity of mind and purpose with which he plunges into the labyrinth of symbols, and endeavors to wrest from heaven the secrets of the soul."

30. *From the Family Herald*, London

"We cannot refuse to acknowledge the immeasurable talent which he (Swedenborg) has displayed in his most voluminous writings, which form a little world of themselves, sufficient to occupy the whole life of any ordinary man, merely to discover their contents and analyze their doctrines.

"His works seem to be boring their way even into Catholic countries. In a little work called *Le Livre des Larmes*, or *The Book of Tears*, lately published by the *Abbé Constant de Bancour*, we find the following sentence: 'We may venture to say that the problem is already solved, and that the whole truth is found in the writings of the admirable Swedenborg.'"

31. *From the Southern Quarterly Review*, October, 1846.

"Time is beginning to pass a just judgment on the character of that extraordinary man, Emanuel Swedenborg,—certainly one of the most gifted geniuses that ever appeared on the face of the earth. Seventy-four years have elapsed since his death. This period has constituted the mere sunrise of his fame—the dawn of a meridian splendor that is yet to bless the nations. By his far-seeing contemporaries he was considered, and was pronounced, and justly too, the greatest man of his country and age, whether regard were had to the herculean powers of mind with which Providence had endowed him, his laborious researches into the mysteries of the universe, his profound knowledge of human nature, acquired in travels as extensive as those of the ancient philosophers, the light which he shed over every known department of science by his fearless investigations and wonderful discoveries, or finally, the exceeding beauty of a life sanctified by the sincerest piety, and glowing with the charms of the most enlarged and fascinating philanthropy. No author, since the discovery of the art of printing —nay, none since the invention of letters, has ever written so many books—or so many good ones—books that will survive the wreck of an ephemeral literature and a transient theology, and will exercise a benign and ennobling influence on the successive generations of men, whatever language they may speak, and wherever and whenever they may appear, to take their place and act their part on the great theatre of life.

"Who ever thought so profoundly on great and noble themes as Swedenborg? What patriot was ever more just, generous, considerate and active? What merely finite human being was ever so highly favored by the Almighty? Illustrious sage! A TRUE SAINT! if there ever was a saint, and yet one who never desired to be canonized. An apostle of truth, but one whose message, unfit for the market-place, was never heard in louder tones than in those of a deep and solemn conviction—a co-worker together with the Creator in the achievement of the grandest designs of Providence, but who regarded the title of His servant, if justly acquired, the highest glory to which man can aspire. The fame of Bacon and Newton and Locke—of Milton and Shakespeare and Scott, pales and grows dim before the brighter glory that clusters around the name and acts of this renowned individual! They acquired distinction for the splendor of their success in particular departments of inquiry, and in certain spheres of intellectual labor, but it was reserved for the more fortunate and celebrated Swede to master, not one science, but the whole circle of the arts and sciences, and to understand and reveal the great connecting links that subsist between mind and matter, time and eternity, man and his Maker, in a far clearer manner, than any of the most gifted and inspired of his predecessors.

"The world may be challenged in vain to produce, in the history of any single individual, such a combination of gigantic and well-balanced powers of mind, with such vast and magnificent attainments of all sorts. If Tully was thought to have bestowed high and immortal praise on the great Plato for saying that he brought down philosophy from the skies to dwell among men amid cool and shady retreats, where, in fact, it has been sullied and profaned by human passions, how much higher, and how much more immortal praise belongs to Swedenborg, who, with the spirit of an angel, has carried philosophy up to the skies, the birth-place and home of the just, where it glitters all over with the beautiful and brilliant rays that emanate from the Sun of Righteousness! Proceeding from the outer and earthly, he has penetrated to the inner and heavenly worlds proper to man, has revealed their mysteries, and promulgated the laws of the great Legislator which govern them. The whole universe, in its general aspects, is the object of his meditations and study, and, not omitting particulars, he finds as profound and beautiful significance, and sees as speaking a manifestation of the power and love of the great Creator in the pebble on the sea-shore, or the leaf that waves in the breeze, as in a star of the first magnitude that decks the firmament. He did not look upon the world around him with the eyes and feelings of ordinary men. With religious veneration, and in the spirit of a true philosophy, he at all times connected the finite with the infinite, and saw in everything that exists in the animal, the vegetable and the mineral kingdoms of nature, as well as in that kingdom which is above nature,—the spiritual,—some image or shadow of a great and Divine Providence."

32. " Swedenborg, as we shall presently show, makes great demands on our faith, but none on our charity. In the great and glorious roll of worthies who have ennobled humanity, there is no one that recurs to our memory just now who can stand a criticism with less fear of the ordeal than he can. Newton is a giant in science, but an old woman in theology; and if report speaks truly, not free from a moral weakness and timidity. Bacon, the prince of philosophers, has his fingers tainted with corruption, which always makes us sad when we think of it. And what shall we say of others—of the fierce language of Milton and Luther, or the dark and damning deed of Calvin, to say nothing of the failings of Byron, Coleridge, Dryden, or Cranmer. We excuse these men on account of the age in which they lived, the circum-stances by which they were surrounded, the force of human passion, and the weakness of our common humanity. Even prophets and apostles make these appeals to our sense of justice, or our feeling of compassion. But you may lay all this aside when you come to Swedenborg. Measure him as a man of science with Newton, and you will find him his equal in point of intellectual greatness. With Bacon and Plato he

is great, amongst the greatest of the philosophers. With Boerhaave and Haller, he is in the first rank of the physiologists. With the theological writers and Bible commentators, from Origen to Adam Clarke, and who has equalled him? All this is easily conceived and said, but who shall picture the innocence and purity of his life, the sublimity of his moral nature, the simplicity of soul which, whilst believing himself to be the chosen messenger of Heaven and the companion of angels, left the company of the great and learned, sat quietly to think and write in his study, or walked into Cold Bath Square to chat with the children. The resigning of one-half of his pension, and retiring from the brilliant and fascinating society of Court, is one of the finest instances of contented greatness that the world has ever seen, and can only be paralleled in Shakespeare's going home to Stratford-upon-Avon with his well-earned modest competence."—JOHN MILL, M.D., *in a lecture "On the Claims of Swedenborg," delivered in London*, 1857.

33. *From the "Idler,"* for June, 1856 : London.

"Whatever may be our opinion of his doctrines, we cannot avoid revering, if not loving the man : so simple, yet wise ; so humble, yet gifted ; so intensely devoted to the service of God, and so sincerely anxious to aid in the salvation of men. The remarkable industry of his life, the wonderful variety of his knowledge, the acuteness of his intellect, the grandeur of his imagination, and the strange passage of his soul through so many varying moods of thought, make him truly a wonder among men. How wide the sweep of his mind, how powerful his grasp over scientific thought, how brilliant his speculations in those theologic domains which he has rendered so peculiarly his own!"

34. *From Fraser's Magazine,* February, 1857.

"Heaven, or at least as much as our hearts can contain of it, is revealed to us in the visions of childhood and of early love. . . . Men of genius seem to be those who have been happy enough to retain more than others have retained of this 'original' virtue and intuition, and who have preserved in their lowest ebbs of spiritual life, and in their highest crises of material enjoyment and activity, an inviolated faith in that heaven which ' lies about us in our infancy,' and of which the commonly very faint recollection constitutes a chief mean whereby we are enabled to apprehend, and raise to the force of a motive, an idea of the heaven beyond the grave. Swedenborg, far beyond all modern men, seems to us to have preserved in his heart and spirit the wisdom of childhood ; the wisdom which even those who have denied and despised it in themselves, delight to recognize and to re-appropriate, as far as possible, when they hear it boldly spoken by the man of genius."

35. " Swedenborg was not so much a scientific man, as a man thoroughly master of the sciences. In Anatomy and Physiology he deserves the appellation of a Raphael or a Stoddart. Everything he knew ministered to his sublime ART. It might be said of him that he had been carried out, like Ezekiel, in the spirit of the Lord, and set down in the midst of the valley of dry bones, and that he had been commanded to prophesy and say unto them,—' Behold, I will cause breath to enter into you, and ye shall live !' He seems to have instinctively felt, what a French author remarks,— that the Church, which at first contained all the elements of social life, had gradually become unpeopled — that every century had seen a multitude leave the sanctuary under some particular banner ; and that every schism was summed up in that greatest and hitherto most irreconcilable of all—the schism and defection of science. For he now began to observe that those who never accepted anything but what they could really understand, were all gone astray, and were hourly sinking deeper in the terrible negation of spiritual things."— E. RICH, *a Sketch of Swedenborg and his Writings.* Americ. edit. p. 49.

36. *From the Veterinary Record,* April, 1845.

" It may be observed that Swedenborg's ' Animal Kingdom,' although differing *toto cœlo* from the ' Bridgewater Treatises,' is an endeavor to show ' the Power, Wisdom, and Goodness of God' as displayed in the organic creation. To work out this end Swedenborg has investigated, on entirely new principles, the formation, functions and uses of the various parts of the human body ; deeming, that if the *order* of all these could be rightly seen, the mind would be able to go beyond that common deduction which declares God to exist, and to be good, wise and powerful, in the same sense in which these attributes are attributable to man ; and to have different and higher views of goodness, wisdom, and power themselves. In fine, his work is not an attempt to lead men out of atheism, but to lift them above theism into *revealed religion.* In this it differs essentially from every other treatise of apparently similar pretensions."

On the same subject, says the editor of the *Monthly Magazine* :—

' " Revelation and philosophy, according to Swedenborg, could never be contrarious. Man is capable of perceiving what things are revealed and what are created—the rational is at one with the divine. Indeed, the end why reason is given to man is, ' that he may perceive that God is, and know that he ought to be worshipped.' "

37. " It is futile to assert that philosophy is not connected with theology ; since the contrary is demonstrated by Swedenborg as fairly as any law of matter is demonstrated by Newton. For Swedenborg took facts representing integral nature, and investigated them, and the order and mechanism of structure, and the pervading use or function, was found to be such as in every case to furnish truths relating to the moral or social existence of man. This was the issue of a scientific process, from which imagination was rigorously excluded. What inference is possible but that the inner parts of nature represent humanity ; such representation being the constitutive law of things ? It was not Swedenborg that made the answerableness in the two co-ordinates ; he merely discovered what existed already.* Bacon's hypothesis that final causes

---

* " Swedenborg appears to have been himself astonished at this result. In treating of the kidneys ('Animal Kingdom,' Part I. n.

have no place in the doctrine of nature, was overthrown by this result; for the mechanism of those causes was explained, and the connection between spirit and nature stood intuitively demonstrated therein. Neither did the doctrine of final causes turn out to be barren, as Bacon imagined; for the end of creation being no longer a bodiless figment, but consisting of the noblest organic creatures, it furnished the most powerful of analytic organs for arming the mental sight, and

---

293,) he has the following, which exhibits somewhat of the *naivete* of one who has come upon a truth unexpectedly :—

'293. As the blood is continually making its circle of life, that is to say, in a constant revolution of birth and death; as it dies in old age, and is regenerated or born anew; and as the veins solicitously gather together the whole of its corporeal part, and the lymphatics, of its spirituous part; and successively bring it back, reflect it with new chyle, and restore it to the pure and youthful blood; and as the kidneys constantly purge it of impurities, and restore its pure parts to the blood;—so likewise Man, who lives at once in body and spirit while he lives in the blood, must undergo the same fortunes generally, and in the progress of his regeneration must daily do the like. Such a perpetual symbolical representation is there of spiritual life in corporeal life; as likewise a perpetual typical representation of the soul in the body (u). In this consists *the searching of the heart and reins*, which is a thing purely Divine.

'(u) In our Doctrine of Representations and Correspondences, we shall treat of both these symbolical and typical representations, and the astonishing things which occur, I will not say in the living body only, but throughout nature, and which correspond so entirely to supreme and spiritual things, that *one would swear that the physical world was purely symbolical of the spiritual world:* insomuch that, if we choose to express any natural truth in physical and definite vocal terms, and to convert these terms only into the corresponding spiritual terms, we shall by this means elicit a spiritual truth or theological dogma, in place of the physical truth or precept; although no mortal would have predicted that anything of the kind could possibly arise by bare literal transposition; inasmuch as the one precept, considered separately from the other, appears to have absolutely no relation to it. I intend hereafter to communicate a number of such correspondences, together with a vocabulary containing the terms of spiritual things, as well as of the physical things for which they are to be substituted. This symbolism pervades the living body; and I have chosen simply to indicate it here, for the purpose of pointing out the spiritual meaning of *searching the reins*.'"

enabling it to discover the more in the less, and the great in the small: in short it authorized man to look upon nature from definite principles, and thus to become the image and vicegerent of God in the scientific sphere. Those who had a rule of impossibility were again shown to be at fault here, as indeed they have been from the beginning. They said that science was passionless and inflexible; that it had nothing to do with philosophy or theology; that it observed sequences, and made answerable formulas, or had a method, but not a soul; that it excluded all but material explanations and ideas. But Swedenborg appealed to the same facts as they, and with a different result. He found nature warm with the same spirit as humanity, and that her sternest laws are plastic when use requires: that hence illiberal logic is not meant to comprehend her. Also that nature is no other than philosophy and theology embodied in mechanics: or more reverently speaking, she is the mechanism or means of which truth and good are the end. Moreover, that the series of effects involves a corresponding series of causes, and this, a corresponding series of ends:* and that body or actuality is as much the predicate of one series as of the other. And further, that material explanations and ideas, when genuine, are readily convertible into spiritual truths: their convertibility being the

---

* "260. In the animal kingdom, the series, chain, progression and circle of causes, involve a corresponding series, chain, progression and circle of uses; for the principle of the cause, which is eminently a living principle in this kingdom, regards' nothing but perpetual ends. The effects which the cause produces from this principle, are the effects of an end, consequently of a use. Hence there is a similar progression of uses, as of effects; a similar progression of effects, as of causes; and a similar progression of causes, as of ends; the series of ends being in the soul itself. Such is the nature by which the living body is governed. This nature does not proceed one hairbreadth, that is, does not design the minutest fibre, or the smallest vessel, still less the entire fabric of an organ, without stamping upon it her series of ends, and respecting a use; and, indeed, in the primary use, respecting a mediate use; in the mediate, an ulterior use; and never in anything does she respect an ultimate use, without at the same time respecting in it the primary use. This is what we mean by the circle of use." ("Animal Kingdom," Vol. I. pp. 377, 378.)

test of their correctness and universal import. All this, we repeat, is so attained by Swedenborg, that science and induction are proper terms by which to characterize it; wherefore henceforth *the connection between science, philosophy and theology, is itself a scientific fact.*"—J. J. GARTH WILKINSON, *Member of the Royal College of Surgeons of London,* in his "Introduction" to Swedenborg's "Economy of the Animal Kingdom," 1846. pp. lxxvi.–lxxviii.

38. "Swedenborg arose at a time when some manifestation of God was needed by the world—an age of corrupt morals and stagnant faith—an age when the life had exhaled from the churches, and the dry bones rattled, and the ghastly eye-sockets glared unmeaningly upon the mysteries of Time. He came prefigured by no portent, heralded by no convulsions. He did not dash into the theological atmosphere like a blazing comet, attracting all eyes by the strangeness of its advent and the lustre of its fire. He rose like a star, moved steadily in his appointed orbit, and melted off into the light of heaven. From his earliest youth he did diligently and conscientiously that which was set before him. He perfected himself in all human science, and acquainted himself with all the terrestrial developments of Deity. His writings are a library in themselves, and display the most careful method and the most indomitable energy. He was eminently conservative; he quarrelled with no church; he set himself in opposition with no organized body. He did not stand apart in all the loneliness of prophetic fury, and denounce vengeance on degenerate man. He was too catholic to found a sect; he spoke the truth intrusted to him, and left it to permeate the lives and opinions of succeeding ages. His charity was broad as the ocean which rolls its waves on every shore, wide as the firmament which foldeth all the orbs of heaven within its ample bosom. The most magnificent scholar of his age, he was at the same time the humblest Christian. Favored by kings, intimate with nobles and statesmen, and the learned of every land, he was without one particle of vanity, and labored as assiduously and devotedly as the humblest parish priest. And as he was never exalted above measure, so he was never crushed by the terrors and the glories—dark visions, such as Dante never dreamed

4

—celestial pictures, more magnificent than ever visited the immortal Milton.

"Through the trackless paths of time, and the tremendous solitudes of eternity, he pursued his way with a courage that never quailed, and a wing that never tired. His brain never reeled as the nations of the damned rose, rank on rank, in all the ghastly splendor of unfading fire; his eye never blenched as the long line of sapphire palaces flashed back upon his vision the unutterable glories of Deity. He was, of all men I have met with, the calmest, wisest, deepest. He was a profound scholar, a true Christian, a loyal subject, a magnificent poet, an unrivalled philosopher, and a little child. He has dissolved the darkness that brooded over the Book of Life, and from the tangled web-work of sectarian speculation he has given us again the Word of God. Swept by his fingers, the cathedral organ of the universe, so long silent, has again sent forth a symphony, the reverberations of which are ringing yet in floating notes, and dying falls along the hills of time. He has touched with his magician's wand the dark waters of death, and they sparkle with the scintillations of immortality. He has flung a bridge across the baseless, boundless chasm which separated the present from the to-come, and brought us to an innumerable company of angels, to the church of the first-born, to the spirits of the just made perfect, and to our Redeemer, Father, God. He has elevated woman to her true position, and set once and forever the 'perfect music unto noble words.' He has built up the desecrated temple of marriage, relit heaven's fire upon its sacred shrine, and round about the porch engraved the sign and seal of heaven.

"Wider than Wesley, deeper than Whitfield, truer than Luther, he is the last great captain of the church militant; and as the army with their blood-flecked banners and their dinted armor defile across the bridge of death, and range themselves, rank on rank, for the grand review by the Lord of Hosts;—among the foremost, with peace within his eye, and on his brow the morning-star, shall stand the calm, the cloudless, the unconquerable spirit of EMANUEL SWEDENBORG."—J. W. FLETCHER, *in his Lecture on* "*Swedenborg*," pp. 16, 17.

39. "No wonder that Swedenborg's ethical wisdom should give him influence as a teacher. To the withered traditional church yielding dry catechisms, he let in nature again, and the worshipper, escaping from the vesting of verbs and texts, is surprised to find himself a party to the whole of his religion. His religion thinks for him, and is of universal application. He turns it on every side; it fits every part of life, interprets and dignifies every circumstance. Instead of a religion which visited him diplomatically three or four times,—when he was born, when he married, when he felt sick, and when he died, and for the rest never interfered with him,—here was a teaching which accompanied him all day, accompanied him even into sleep and dreams; into his thinking, and showed him through what a long ancestry his thoughts descend; into society, and showed by what affinities he was girt to his equals and his counterparts; into natural objects, and showed their origin and meaning, what are friendly and what are hurtful; and opened the future world, by indicating the continuity of the same laws. His disciples allege that their intellect is invigorated by the study of his books. There is no such problem for criticism as his theological writings, their merits are so commanding."—RALPH WALDO EMERSON.

40. *From Fraser's Magazine*, February, 1847.

"We are so continually surrounded and so profoundly affected by the appeals of material nature to the senses, that the best Christian may have good cause to thank the writer who succeeds in endowing spiritual facts with fresh interest and novelty of demonstration; and if ever there was a teacher signally gifted with this faculty, it was Swedenborg. As a preacher, moreover, of universally-admitted Christian doctrines of the most obviously practical import, he stands alone and super-eminent in his way. The inseparable union of charity and faith in the heart of the true believer is dwelt upon and demonstrated with a force and reiteration the profit of which those only who have read a good deal of Swedenborg can justly estimate. The connection of spiritual death with sin persevered in, against the remonstrances of the conscience, is propounded with an amount of quiet conviction, and proved with a peculiar force, which can scarcely fail to startle into thoughtfulness those for whom the accustomed forms of religious teaching have ceased, through repetition and neglect, to exercise any influence. In morality, no writer has ever more effectually impressed upon his readers the *juste milieu* between asceticism and self-indulgence, between the barren unworldliness, and ' other worldliness,' of the anchorite, and the earthly-mindedness of the worldling ; and indeed between each pole of the many pairs of vicious extremes adopted respectively by the unrighteous and the righteous overmuch. That noble and only true moderation which comes of the simultaneous and harmonious activity and inter-recognition of all right motives and impulses, was a very conspicuous merit of Swedenborg's life, and it is not less manifest in his teachings, which are excellent remedies for that morbid conscience, almost worse than no conscience at all, which afflicts its possessor with innumerable pangs, while its protest is silent or weak where it ought to be clamorous and irresistible."

SWEDENBORG'S CHARACTER.

41. " READER, might it not seem a wonder, if a person of so extraordinary and apostolical a character should better escape the imputation of madness than the prophets of old? O fie upon those uncharitable prejudices which have led so many, in all ages, to credit and propagate slanderous reports of the best of men, even whilst they have been employed in the heavenly work of turning many from darkness to light, and from the power of Satan unto God. Were an angel from heaven to come and dwell incarnate amongst us, may we not suppose that his conversation, discoveries, and conduct of life would, in many things, be so contrary to the errors and prejudices, the ways and fashions of this world, that many would say, with one consent, that he is beside himself; and where any one of our brethren, through the Divine favor, attains to any high degree of angelical illumination and communications, may he not expect the like treatment? I forget the name of the philosopher whose precepts and lectures were so repugnant to the dissolute manners of the Athenians : they sent to Hippocrates, to come and cure him of his madness; to which message that great physician returned this answer: that it was not the philosopher, but the Athenians that were mad."— *Dr. Hartley, Rector of Winwick, Northamptonshire: Preface to the First English Translation of Swedenborg's " Heaven and Hell."*

42. *From the Eulogy on Emanuel Swedenborg, pronounced in the name of the Royal Academy of Sciences of Stockholm, by* M. SAMUEL SANDEL, *Counsellor of the Royal Board of Mines, and member of said Academy, October 7, 1772.*

" Swedenborg's merit and excellent qualities shine with brilliancy, even where we are endeavoring to discover in him the weakness inseparable from human nature. I do not come here to defend errors or unintelligible principles: but I will venture to assert—and I reckon, gentlemen, on meeting your approbation in the assertion—that where others would have discovered a deficiency of intelligence and a confusion of ideas, Swedenborg has displayed an astonishing assemblage of knowledge; which he has arranged, according to his system, in such order, that the elements themselves would have striven in vain to turn him out of his course. If his desire of knowledge went too far, it at least evinces in him an ardent desire to obtain information himself, and to convey it to others: for you never find in him any mark of pride or conceit, of rashness, or of intention to deceive. If, nevertheless, he is not to be numbered among the doctors of the church, he at least holds an honorable rank among sublime moralists, and deserves to be instanced as a pattern of virtue and of respect for his Creator.

"He was the sincere friend of mankind; and in his examination of the character of others, he was particularly desirous to discover in them this virtue, which he regarded as an infallible proof of the presence of many more. He was cheerful and agreeable in society. By way of relaxation from his important labors, he sought and frequented the company of persons of information, by whom he was always well received. He knew how to check opportunely, and with great address, that species of wit which would indulge itself at the expense of serious things. As a public functionary, he was upright and just: while he discharged his duties with great exactness, he neglected nothing but his own advancement. Having been called, without solicitation on his part, to a distinguished post, he never sought any further promotion. When his private occupations began to encroach upon the time required for the functions of his office, he resigned it, and remained content with the title which he had borne while exercising it for one-and-thirty years.

"He was a worthy member of this Royal Academy; and though before his admission into it he had been engaged with subjects different from those which it cultivates, he was unwilling to be an unuseful associate. He enriched our

Memoirs with an article *on Inlaid Work in Marble, for Tables, and for other Ornaments.*

"As a member of the Equestrian Order of the House of Nobles, he took his seat in several of the Diets of the Realm; in which his conduct was such as to secure him both from the reproaches of his own conscience and from those of others. He lived under the reigns of many of our sovereigns, and enjoyed the particular favor and kindness of them all; an advantage which virtue and science will ever enjoy under an enlightened government.

"Swedenborg (and this I mention without making a merit of it) was never married. This was not, however, owing to any indifference towards the sex: for he esteemed the company of a fine and intelligent woman as one of the most agreeable of pleasures; but his profound studies rendered expedient for him the quiet of a single life. It may be truly said that he was solitary, but never sad.

"He always enjoyed most excellent health, having scarcely ever experienced the slightest indisposition.* Content within himself and with his situation, his life was, in all respects, one of the happiest that ever fell to the lot of man, till the very moment of its close. During his last residence in London, on the 24th of December, last year, he had an attack of apoplexy; and nature demanding her rights, he died on the 29th of March, in the present year [1772], in the eighty-fifth year of his age; satisfied with his sojourn on earth, and delighted with the prospect of his heavenly metamorphosis.

"May this Royal Academy retain as long, a great number of such distinguished and useful members!"

43. The following testimony respecting Swedenborg is from COUNT A. J. VON HOPKEN. This nobleman was one of the

---

* "How inconsistent is this with the story which has been invented and propagated in this country, that he was once attacked with a most violent fever, attended with delirium, from the effects of which he never recovered! In Sweden, where his personal history must have been best known, nothing, it seems, of the kind was ever heard of."— *Editors of "Documents concerning E. Swedenborg."* New York. 1847.

institutors of the Swedish Royal Academy of Sciences, which, being a man of eminent learning, he served for a considerable period in the capacity of Secretary. He afterwards was, for many years, Prime Minister of the kingdom; which station, in addition to his post as one of the sixteen Senators, with whom, prior to the revolution in 1772, the royal power in fact was vested, the King being merely the president of that body, made him the second person in the kingdom. He says:—

"I have not only known him [Swedenborg] these two-and-forty years, but also, some time since, daily frequented his company. A man, who like me has lived long in the world, and even in an extensive career of life, must have had numerous opportunities of knowing men as to their virtues or vices, their weakness or strength; and in consequence thereof, I do not recollect to have known any man of more uniformly virtuous character than Swedenborg; always contented, never fretful or morose, although throughout his life his soul was occupied with sublime thoughts and speculations. He was a true philosopher, and lived like one; he labored diligently, and lived frugally without sordidness; he travelled continually, and his travels cost him no more than if he had lived at home. He was gifted with a most happy genius, and a fitness for every science, which made him shine in all those which he embraced. He was, without contradiction, the most learned man in my country; in his youth he was a great poet. I have in my possession some remnants of his Latin poetry, which Ovid would not have been ashamed to own. His Latin in his middle age was in an easy, elegant, and ornamental style; in his latter years it was equally clear, but less elegant after he had turned his thoughts to spiritual subjects. He was well acquainted with the Hebrew and Greek; an able and profound mathematician; a happy mechanician, of which he gave proof in Norway, where, by an easy and simple method, he transported the largest galleys over the high mountains and rocks to a gulf where the Danish fleet was stationed. He was likewise a natural philosopher, yet on the Cartesian principles. He detested metaphysics as founded on fallacious ideas, because they transcend our sphere, by means of which theology has been drawn from its simplicity and become artificial and corrupted. He was perfectly conversant with mineralogy, having for a long time been Assessor in the Mineral College, on which science he also published a valuable and classical work, both as to theory and practice, printed at Leipzic, in 1734: if he had remained in his office, his merits and talents would have entitled him to the highest dignity; but he preferred ease of mind, and sought happiness in study. In Holland he began to apply himself to anatomy, in which he made singular discoveries, which are preserved somewhere in the *Acta Literaria*. I imagine this science, and his meditations on the effects of the soul upon our curiously constructed body, did, by degrees, lead him from the material to the spiritual. He possessed a sound judgment upon all occasions; he saw everything clearly, and expressed himself well on every subject. The most solid memorials, and the best penned, at the Diet of 1761, on matters of finance, were presented by him. In one of these he refuted a large work in quarto on the same subject, quoted all the corresponding passages of it, and all this in less than one sheet. . . . ."— *Letter to General Tuxen.*

44. Carl Robsham, *Director of the Bank of Sweden*, and the confidential friend of Swedenborg, has written a very interesting memoir of his life, which has been translated into English from the Swedish, and from which we make the following extract:—

"As Swedenborg, in his youth, had no thought of the employment of his coming life, it may be easily believed, that he was not only a learned man and a gentleman, after the manner of the times, but a man so distinguished for wisdom as to be celebrated throughout Europe, and also possessed of a propriety of manners that rendered him everywhere an honored and acceptable companion. Thus he continued to old age, serene, cheerful and agreeable, with a countenance always illuminated by the light of his uncommon genius. How he was looked upon in foreign lands I do not know; but in Stockholm, even those who could not read his writings, were always pleased to meet him in company, and paid respectful attention to whatever he said.

" Those who are capable of understanding the writings of Swedenborg, judge of his character in an entirely different manner from those who cannot; and it is remarkable that few ever read his works without becoming convinced of their truths, although many, from fear of the Jews, or perhaps for some more honorable reasons, were unwilling openly to allow their belief.

" Many persons have wondered that he never was in want of money for his frequent journeys, and other expenses ; but when it is considered, that he lived very moderately on his journeys, and that his books on philosophy and mineralogy, as well as his theological writings, never remained long on the bookseller's hands, but always met a ready sale, and that he inherited from his father, Bishop Swedenborg, a considerable sum, it will be easily understood how he was able to accomplish all his designs."

In another place he says,—" It is in the writings of the studious and contemplative that we must read their lives, and learn what they were ; and if we look at Swedenborg in this view, we are astonished at the greatness of his labors, the extent of his knowledge, the purity and consistency of his doctrines, the order and perspicuity of his discussions, all which bespeak a mind vastly above the common sort, indefatigable in its exertions, profound in its researches, illuminated and clear in its perceptions, pious, sober, and solid in its principles."

45. REV. ARVID FERELIUS, *the Swedish clergyman* who visited Swedenborg before his death, and performed the funeral service at his interment, in the Swedish Church in London, in March, 1772, says concerning him :—

" Many may suppose that Assessor Swedenborg was a very singular and eccentric person ; this was by no means the case. On the contrary, he was very agreeable and complaisant in company ; he entered into conversation on every subject, and accomodated himself to the ideas of the company ; and he never spoke on his own writings and doctrines but when he was asked some questions concerning them, when he always spoke as freely as he had written. If, however, he observed that any person desired to ask impertinent questions, or to ridicule him, he immediately gave such an answer, that the impertinent questioner must be silent, without becoming any the wiser."—*Letter to Prof. Tratgard, in Greifswalde.*

46. REV. N. COLLIN, *Rector of the Swedish Church in Philadelphia*, who was personally acquainted with Swedenborg, published in the *Philadelphia Gazette*, of August 5th, 8th and 10th, an account of his illustrious countryman ; from this we extract the following :—

" In the year 1765 I went to reside at Stockholm, and continued partly in that city, and partly in its vicinity, for nearly three years. During that time, Swedenborg was a great object of public attention in this metropolis, and his extraordinary character was a frequent topic of discussion. He resided at his house in the southern suburbs, which was in a pleasant situation, neat and convenient, with a spacious garden and other appendages. There he received company. Not seldom he also appeared in public, and mixed in private societies ; therefore sufficient opportunities were given to make observation on him. I collected much information from several respectable persons, who had conversed with him ; which was the more easy, as I lived the whole time, as private tutor, in the family of Dr. Celsius, a gentleman of distinguished talents, who afterwards became Bishop of Scania ; he, and many of the eminent persons that frequented his house, knew Swedenborg well."

In a letter addressed by Mr. Collin to the Rev. John Hargrove, of Baltimore, March 16, 1801, he makes the following statement :—

" Swedenborg was universally esteemed for his various erudition in mathematics, mineralogy, etc., and for his probity, benevolence and general virtue. Being very old when I saw him, he was thin and pale, but still retained traces of beauty, and had something very pleasing in his physiognomy, and a dignity in his tall and erect stature."

47. *The Author of a Dissertation on the Royal Society of*

Sciences at Upsal, published in 1789, mentions Swedenborg as one of its first and best members, thus : —

"His letters to the Society while abroad witness that few can travel so usefully. An indefatigable curiosity directed to various important objects is conspicuous in all. Mathematics, astronomy, and mechanics seem to have been his favorite sciences, and he had already made great progress in these. Everywhere he became acquainted with the most renowned mathematicians and astronomers, as Flamstead, De la Hire, Varignon, &c. His pursuit of knowledge was also united with a constant zeal to benefit his country. No sooner was he informed of some useful discovery, than he was solicitous to render it beneficial to Sweden, by purchase, or sending home models. When a good book was published, he not only gave immediate notice of it, but contrived to procure it for the library of the university." — *See Rev. N. Collin's account of Swedenborg.*

48. THE REV. DR. THOMAS HARTLEY, *Rector of Winwick, in Northamptonshire, England,* of whom Mr. Springer, the Swedish consul at London says, that he was " a man of profound learning, and a true servant of God, and the most intimate friend of Swedenborg," makes the following remarks in reference to a letter received by him from Swedenborg: —

"As the credibility of Swedenborg's extraordinary dispensation, in respect to his commerce with the invisible world, would receive additions from his private good character, I was accordingly led to call upon him by letter to publish some particulars of himself, for the satisfaction of the public; which he answered, giving me some account of himself and family; and the accuracy of his relation was confirmed to me by some that well knew him in his own country, and of the honors with which he was dignified there as a member of the Diet of the Equestrian Order of Nobles, and of the high esteem in which he was held by the royal family in Sweden, as also by the most pious and excellent men of that kingdom.

"Swedenborg was a man of uncommon humility, and so far from affecting to be the head of a sect, that his voluminous writings in divinity continued almost to the end of his life to be anonymous publications; and I have some reason to think that it was owing to my remonstrance to him on this subject, that he was induced to prefix his name to his last work."

Dr. Hartley translated into English Swedenborg's treatise "On the Nature of Influx," and prefixed a long preface to the work, in which he says: "I have conversed with him at different times, and in company with a gentleman of a learned profession, and of extensive intellectual abilities [Dr. Messiter] : . . . and both of us consider this our acquaintance with the author and his writings among the greatest blessings of our lives. The extensive learning displayed in his writings, evinces him to be the scholar and the philosopher; and his polite behavior and address bespeak him the gentleman. He affects no honor, but declines it ; pursues no worldly interest, but spends his substance in travelling and printing, in order to communicate instruction and benefit to mankind : and he is so far from the ambition of heading a sect, that wherever he resides in his travels he is a mere solitary, and almost inaccessible, though in his own country of a free and open behavior. He has nothing of the precisian in his manner, nothing of melancholy in his temper, and nothing in the least bordering on the enthusiast in his conversation and writings."

49. DR. MESSITER, *an eminent physician in London*, was an intimate friend of Swedenborg, and the "gentleman of a learned profession and of extensive intellectual abilities," mentioned by Dr. Hartley in the extract above. In 1769, he presented, by desire of Swedenborg, some of his works to the Professors of Divinity at Edinburgh, Glasgow and Aberdeen, for the universities in those places. In his letter to Dr. Hamilton of Edinburgh, Dr. M. says,—

"As I had the honor of being frequently admitted to the author's company when he was in London, and conversed with him on various points of learning, I will venture to affirm that there are no parts of mathematical, philosophical, or medical knowledge, nay, I believe I might justly say, of human literature, to which he is in the least a stranger; yet so totally insensible is he of his own merit, that I am confident he does not know that he has any ; and, as he himself somewhere says of the angels, he always turns his head away on the slightest encomium."

Dr. Hamilton, in his answer, candidly says, —

"I have seen enough to convince me that the honorable author is a very learned and pious man — qualities that shall ever command my respect."

So in his letter to Dr. Gerard at Aberdeen, Dr. Messiter, speaking of Swedenborg's works, says, —

"They are the productions of a man whose good qualities resulting from his natural and acquired abilities, I can with much truth, from my frequent converse with him, assert, are a high ornament to human nature. Credulity, prejudice, or partiality, seem to have no share in his composition or character ; nor is he in the least influenced by any avaricious or interested views. A proof of this last assertion was offered me, by his refusing an offer of any money he might have occasion for while in England, which was made him on a supposal that his want of connections in a place where he was a stranger might prove an obstacle to his divine pursuits."

50. *Testimony of Professor von Görres, Relative to Swedenborg's Scientific and Philosophical Character.*

Görres was Professor at the University of Munich. He was a man of influence in his sphere, and held in great esteem by a wide circle of admirers. During the progress of the Latin and German edition of Swedenborg's works, Professor Görres was induced to look into his writings, and to lay the results of his examination before the public.

"Amongst the signs of the present time," says the Professor, " must, without doubt, be numbered the new edition of Swedenborg's works, and the movement which, in certain places, is caused by the doctrines he unfolds. Most persons who have only read that portion of his writings to which they have had access, might feel disposed to consider them as the results of a mind involved in an inextricable maze, or bordering even on infatuation ; some also may be disposed to consider them as the results of wilful deception. Others, milder in their judgment, explain, as *Herder* did, the enigmatical appearance on the ground of a powerfully creative imagination, which, actuated by strong impulses, becomes at length habitual, generates in science, as in poetry, wonderful images of a spiritualizing enchantment, which sports in the weakened memory of age with the lively visions of youth, and which the incautious senses assume for the actual and real perceptions of intellect; and in this manner *objective* truth is unconsciously falsified by the *subjective*, self-derived productions of the mind.

"The case of Swedenborg, however, is not so easily settled as this two-fold mode of explanation supposes. Swedenborg *was not a man to be carried away by an unbridled imagination, still less did he ever manifest, during his whole life, the slightest symptom of mental aberration.* His natural disposition was *tranquil, equal, thoughtful, meditative;* as is the case with most of his Swedish countrymen, the powers of his understanding were preponderating, and he had carefully nourished and cultivated them, devoted, during the greatest part of his life, to unremitted studies. It is therefore not to be supposed that he in this gross manner, with wakeful eyes, deceived himself, and that what in one moment he himself thought, in another regarded as chimerical. On the other hand, *he was in life and disposition so blameless, that no man dare ever intimate any suspicion of concerted deception;* and " — we call the attention of our readers especially to the following passage — " POSTERITY HAVE NO RIGHT TO CALL INTO QUESTION THE UNSUSPECTED TESTIMONY OF THOSE WHO LIVED IN THE SAME AGE AS SWEDENBORG, AND WHO KNEW HIM WELL; IF THIS MODE OF JUDGMENT BE PERMITTED, ALL HISTORICAL EVIDENCE, EVEN THE HOLIEST AND MOST VENERABLE, MIGHT BE REDUCED TO NOTHING. . . . If it be permitted to say of a man, to whose *veracity, intelligence, science, irreproachable conduct, presence of mind, and fidelity to truth, his contemporaries bear testimony* — if it be permitted for posterity to say that such a man had either imprudently deceived himself and the world, or had knowingly dealt in mere falsehood and lies, there is an end to the verification of historical events."

In relation to Swedenborg's "Principia," the Professor says : —

"Indefatigable in meditating over the wonderful phenomena

in the created world; constantly occupied in exploring the laws in which the manifold variety of these phenomena is comprised, Swedenborg endeavored to penetrate the deepest depths of natural philosophy. He was guided in his researches by a *mind clear, acutely analytic, endowed with skill, and well disciplined by mathematics and logic.* He endeavored to raise the mind to that height from which the first created germ, acted upon by the creative spirit and power, might be contemplated, and from which the first principles of things might be seen growing from the impulsive force which God has implanted in their nature."

After giving an analysis of the work, he continues: —

"It may hence be seen that this is a well constructed system of dynamics, logically derived from the laws of magnetism; and that the manner in which he proceeds in the development of his principles is the algebraical. . . . The work, whatever may be still wanting to render it complete, will always be considered as a beautiful and bold production of the human mind — a production indicative of profound thought in all its parts, *and not unworthy of being placed on the side of Newton's mathematical Principia of Natural Philosophy.*

" Swedenborg had, indeed, not the brilliant genius of the Englishman, who, with a lucky cast of the die, always hit upon the right and the true; instead of which, however, he had a *deeply penetrating sagacity, and a great and clear understanding, endowed with an indefatigable power of thought,* which never ceased until he had sounded and explored his subject in all its depths. Swedenborg had not the skill in managing geometrical formulæ, which the founder of the doctrine of gravitation possessed in so high a degree ; but he kept himself entirely free from the ludicrous fear of deviation from old paths of philosophy, and he rather endeavored to direct the whole of his efforts to place metaphysics in the province of mathematics, and to make the former a visible object of perception. In conducting experiments, Swedenborg was *diligent, precise, attentive, trustworthy;* although he may be wanting in that elegance which makes Newton's work on optics a finished work of art or of scientific skill. And whilst a greater depth of speculation characterizes the work of the Swede, that of the

Briton is marked by a more widely-extended surface, and is more richly finished. Hence it is that the work of the former has been hitherto passed over in silence in the history of science, without making any great impression; whereas that of Newton, owing to the manifold practical results which have attended it, has formed an epoch in the history of human knowledge. The work of Swedenborg, however, contains, no doubt, *a rich treasure of enlarged and profound observations on nature.* Many of the ideas unfolded in that work . . . have, since Swedenborg's time, *been most wonderfully confirmed* through the investigations which Herschel has made into the structure of the heavens, and by the discovery of the polarization of light, and of the magnetic operations, performed by the galvanic battery. His spiral motion, which extends to every province in nature, into organic structures and their operations, and even into history, is an extremely appropriate expression by which numerous phenomena can be easily comprehended; and it might, in the hand of a person skilled in analysis, be made as fruitful in physics as the doctrine of gravitation has been for astronomy."

It seems a pity that the Professor had not an opportunity of also studying Swedenborg's works on the *Animal Kingdom* and its *Economy,* in which his philosophical principles are carried out in a most striking manner; we are certain that the author would have risen still higher in his estimation as a profound and original thinker. The Professor concludes his article on Swedenborg as follows : —

"It now remains that we give an impartial judgment on Swedenborg's character and his mental disposition, and on his moral physiognomy, in so far as it shines forth from the series in which his labors as an author were produced; and here we cannot but award him the most favorable testimony. Throughout the entire career of his learned researches and activity, we everywhere discover the pious and religious man, who, in all his sayings and doings, was intent upon good. In his inmost soul, he was entirely opposed to all those systems of materialism and naturalism which so wantonly prevailed in his time; and he built his own system on the foundation of an eternal Esse, and on its creating activities [from which, as from the only Origin and Cause, all things are created and preserved]. And throughout the entire course of his labors, he seizes every opportunity of pointing to this first great rational cause of all things, and, at the same time, he endeavors to show the absurdity of all opposite opinions. Nor did the sensualism of those of his contemporaries, which confines itself to the mere surface of things; nor did the more refined pantheistic abstraction of others, although penetrating more deeply below the surface, find any place in his system and works. On the contrary, his philosophy, as to all its principal and leading points, is founded on the eternal principles revealed in the Holy Writ. Throughout his works everything appears simple and uniform, especially as to the tone in which he writes, in which there is no effort at display in the imaginative powers, nothing overwrought, nothing fantastic, nothing that can in the remotest degree be construed into a morbid bias of a prevailing mental activity, nothing indicating an idiosyncrasy, or manifesting any peculiarity of a commencing mental derangement. Everything he undertakes is developed in a calm and measured manner, like the resolution and demonstration of a mathematical problem, and everywhere the operations of a mind composed and well ordered shine forth, with conviction as to the certainty of the results of its activity. In the cultivation of science, sincerity and simplicity of heart are necessary requirements to the attainment of durable success. We never observe that Swedenborg was subject to that pride by the influence of which so many great spirits have fallen; he always remained the same subdued and modest mind; and never, either by success, or by any consideration, lost his mental equilibrium.

"There nowhere appears in the writings of Swedenborg a self-destroying contradiction, nothing abrupt, disjointed, or unconnected, or arbitrary, or illogical, such as is accustomed to accompany the phenomena of dreams, or the effusions of an unregulated fancy; but everything that he writes is so connected and uninterrupted as to present a perfect whole. . ."

The editors of the "Documents, &c.," add the following remark: —

"No testimony can be more important, both as to impartiality, and as to the position the Professor occupies as a judge of mental productions." They likewise add that "the sentences in the above extracts marked with *italics*, are so marked in the German from which they have been translated."

51. Another celebrated German professor, and no less a person than Dr. v. Baur, the founder of the so-called "Tübingen School of Theology," said to some of his students who visited him at his house, that "*Swedenborg was the greatest mortal that ever lived.*" This statement was made to my father by my late uncle, Prof. Immanuel Tafel, of Tübingen, who likewise added that by the influence of Prof. v. Baur all the original editions of Swedenborg's works were bought for the University Library.

52. Dr. Immanuel Tafel, who was Professor of Philosophy and Librarian at the University of Tübingen, gives the following as the result of his investigations into the character and life of Emanuel Swedenborg : —

"From all these testimonies it appears that he was a man thoroughly at home in all departments of human science, and that he moved in them as in his own proper sphere. That he was by far the greatest scholar of his country ; that he was a most distinguished poet in his youth, an adept in the oriental and occidental languages, a thorough mathematician, a successful mechanician, a perfect metallurgist, an accomplished statesman, a profound philosopher, a sound theologian, and a man in whose character were combined noble and pure sentiments, with a spotless, industrious, virtuous and holy life, and who was adorned with all social virtues, so that he was venerated and beloved by all who knew him : a man, in fine, who in all his doings, seems to have been especially favored by Divine Providence." — *Preface to his Translation of Swedenborg's Works*, p. v.

53. Dr. Oettinger, *Prelate of Murrhard, in Würtemberg*, in his book entitled "The High Priesthood of Christ," published in 1772, says : —

"Swedenborg was from his youth innocent, pious and

exemplary, and by no means addicted to imaginary pursuits. Geometry, Algebra, and Mechanics had guarded him against everything like fantastic studies. Diotrephes barked loudly against John, the beloved disciple of Jesus; and why should we wonder that Swedenborg is so misrepresented and calumniated? Satan has his greatest delight, and his most delicious feast, when he can set theologians by the ears, and excite strife and animosity against them. But the Lord will bring to light that which has been concealed in darkness."

In another place he says, "Swedenborg is, in my estimation, the forerunner of a new era."

54. Prof. M. J. Schleiden, of the University of Jena, pays the following high tribute to the private character of Swedenborg : —

"If we are permitted in any man to judge of his innermost hidden worth, we are so in Swedenborg. From the time of his earliest youth to the hour of his death, in his 85th year, there is not one minute that accuses him. In his picture, whether drawn by his friends, by indifferent observers, or even by his theological opponents, (for enemies he had none,) there is not one feature which is not respectable, nay, lovable. Modest even to humility, simple and temperate to the highest degree in his dress and food, even at the time of his greatest opulence; without any desire for outward honors or pecuniary emoluments, and generally refusing even those which were offered to him without their being called for. Opposed to making proselytes, never taking the first steps towards collecting around himself a school, benevolent and philanthropical everywhere; of inviolable rectitude in his business and social relations, of incorruptible veracity and fearless frankness — such are the fundamental traits of a character, who never lent his hand to anything that had the slightest bearing to delusion and injustice." — " *Studien*," p. 191.

And yet Prof. Schleiden endeavored to prove that Swedenborg had been INSANE ! !

55. " The following is the opinion of COLERIDGE of the charge so often calumniously alleged against Swedenborg, that

he was mad. It is a manuscript note in Coleridge's copy of *De Cultu et Amore Dei*, on pages 4 to 6, in which Swedenborg briefly states his doctrine of Forms. 'This,' says Coleridge, ' would of itself serve to mark Swedenborg as a man of philosophic genius, radicative and evolvent. Much of what is most valuable in the philosophic works of Schelling, Schubert, and Eschermayer, is to be found anticipated in this supposed *Dementato*, or madman; O thrice happy should we be, if the learned and teachers of the present day were gifted with a similar madness,—a madness, indeed, celestial, and flowing from a divine mind!!' (S. T. Coleridge, Sept. 22, 1821, Highgate.) "— *Coleridge's Literary Remains*, Vol. iv. p. 424.

56. " Since Swedenborg's death all terms of ignominy and contempt have been heaped upon him; all sects have agreed to unite to despise him; few, few, few indeed have read him; but how far fewer have studied him. Alas! in most instances, we denounce the religion or the religious teacher taxing our energies, our thoughts, our affections too much. Religion is, according to some teachers, to be forever and forever a perpetually reiterated and reiterating Alphabet; not so to him who attempts to pass on to the Grammar of Religion, still more to him who dares to attempt to solve the deeper Problems of Religious History, who attempts to sound some of the heights, and depths, and lengths, and breadths of religious emotion and experience, of Religious Knowledge and Doctrine. A thousand times we have been compelled to ask, What, then, is no more religious experience possible? Will the Infinite Light reveal no new Relations — no new Illustrations?

" Swedenborg was a Mystic! My dear sir, what is a Mystic? We are all mystics when we engage in some operation our neighbor does not understand. 'Tis an ignorant word. What a shocking mystic is an expert chemist, perhaps more so an expert mathematician. Every art, every trade, every science is mystic to the uninitiated. We are all mystics; we have all our mystic world; we all see things temporal and eternal with our own individual eyes; we all have a world into which our friend and neighbor cannot enter, and we can all see clearly in that world, too, although it is a region of darkness to him.   Frequently, when you use the term mystic, you only express your own impoverished and wretched experiences.   Translated, it means, *I* never felt that — *I* never experienced that.   Especially all Christian experience is mystical.   A mystic is one who moves in an orbit larger than his neighbors, from the greater weight and power of his character.   In this sense, Swedenborg was a mystic. . . .

"Yet in another sense Swedenborg was no Mystic; for a mystic is too self-contained a man, usually; perhaps he communicates no light; he travels in his own orb, but he does not illuminate other minds: this is the difference between a Mystic and an Apostle.   The mystic solitarily absorbs all things within himself; the apostle receives to diffuse from himself. The sin of Idle self-contemplation which we have condemned is the charm of the mystic's life.   The apostle is never idle, and never muses within himself, but the fire burns, impelling to action and energy.   The mystic, therefore, from his intense egotism, leaves no light behind him, and has but few followers, perhaps none.   The apostle prepares a road for his successors; strews it with rich, and new, and obvious ideas; carves his name upon the rocks in the way, in many a noble achievement and high-wrought action; and erects at many a doubting turning, a faithful and truthful finger-post; in a word, the life of the mystic is in Speculation — the life of the apostle is in Use.   We shall number Swedenborg, not with the mystics, but with the apostles.   He broke up new ground; he disseminated new ideas; he has never been without a band of followers; all his studies and writings were directed to the useful; his energy was immense; his activity, mental and bodily, indomitable.   He was an apostle!

"One thing has been alleged against Swedenborg, indeed, to which it is very necessary that we now advert, namely, that he was Mad!   The charge of insanity is one very easily levelled against a character whose movements we do not clearly understand.   We know against whom the words were used: 'He hath a *devil*, and is mad, why hear ye him?'   And to an illustrious reasoner it was once said: 'Paul, Paul, thou art beside thyself; much learning hath made thee mad.'   Strange, that much learning should make a man mad ; might we not rather suppose that learning, of a true and valuable character, opened to the soul so many windows, and spread out before the understanding so many new prospects and fields of spiritual light, that to him the occupations and pursuits of the men and women wedded to the world appeared as comparatively insane ?

"But the question occurs, What is insanity ? And we may perhaps reply, without fear of contradiction, the morbid exercise of any faculty or power to the exclusion of other faculties. There are very few sane people living; for sanity is the due exercise of our whole manhood — body, mind, and spirit — the frame, the intellect, and the will or affections, — and it is obvious that this high sanity can only be in a state where sin, the great disjointer and deranger of humanity — sin, which is insanity, is excluded. But if we look at Swedenborg's career, we find all his life balanced and harmonized. If ever there lived a man who might claim to present to the world a completed being, he was the man. Can you convict him of Passion ? When you contradicted him, when you rejected his doctrines, when Filenius was traitorous, and Ekbom insolent, did you ever see the wrathful flame mantle on the old man's features ? Milton was one of the most perfect men, and we pay a higher homage to him than to almost any other man : but the anger of Milton sometimes sullies the glory of his pages. No ! those who have charged our writer with madness, have felt the difficulty of the position, and therefore it has been insisted by some writers, that he must have been possessed by a devil ; to this conclusion the Rev. Mr. Ettrick, M. A., of High Barns, near Sunderland, arrives, when he says : 'Swedenborg does not seem to have really labored under any natural derangement, or vulgar insanity. If madness of any kind can be rationally imputed to him, it can be no ordinary insanity or mere derangement of intellect from bodily or even mental disease.'" * — E. PAXTON HOOD, *Swedenborg: a Biography,* pp. 157–163.

---

* Paxton Hood (pp. 163–169) shows how this report of Swedenborg's alleged insanity first originated, and he lays it at the door of the celebrated John Wesley, who first published it in his *Arminian Maga-*

57.   " It has been said by some, and received implicitly, without further examination by others, that Swedenborg, after receiving his extraordinary commission, was mad, and became totally deprived of his rational senses ; but this insinuation is such a palpable contradiction to truth, and such an insult to common sense, being overruled by every page of our author's writings, as well as by every act of his life after that period, that we should have thought it altogether unworthy our notice, were we not aware that it operates powerfully with many, even at this day, to prejudice them against a character which otherwise they would revere, and against writings from which they would otherwise receive the most welcome instruction, whilst, in the meantime, they can give no reasonable account of their prejudice, nor trace its origin to any better source than the unjust calumny uttered of old against another respectable name : ' *Paul, thou art beside*

---

zine for August, 1783, p. 438, on the authority of a Mr. Brockmer, of London, and Mr. Mathesius, a Swedish clergyman. Mr. Brockmer, when interrogated afterwards by Mr. Hindmarsh, denied positively that he had ever made this statement to Mr. Wesley, and the Swedish clergyman Mathesius, who was known to be a *professed enemy* of Swedenborg, and with whom the whole plot seems to have originated, became insane himself a short time afterwards.

A similar case is recorded by Prof. Immanuel Tafel in his " Open Letter to Prof. Schleiden of Jena," who, as was noticed above, likewise publicly preferred this charge against Swedenborg. Prof. Tafel says :

" This charge of insanity, which you regard as a new discovery of your own, is in reality quite old ; it was made by others before, and among these by two academic professors who published it in their writings, but ended by becoming insane themselves. The first is said to have imagined himself to be a goose ; and the second, who (as I know from the very best of authorities), on passing through Tubingen, exhibited himself there to the professor of Zoology as a natural curiosity, viz. : as a walking statue with buttocks of steel, died quite recently in a lunatic asylum."— "*Offenes Sendschreiben*, &c.," p. 79.

The whole subject of Swedenborg's alleged insanity will be found abundantly discussed, and the slander exposed, in Rev. S. Noble's "*Appeal*," (Sect. v., pp. 249-282, Americ. edit.) where he proves that the true cause of the origin and propagation of this slander is this : " *that it is felt to be more easy, by raising the cry of insanity, to prevent mankind from examining his system, than, when examined, to prevent it from being embraced by the candid and well-disposed.*"

thyself; much learning doth make thee mad.'—Acts xxvi. 24."
Dr. Hurd, *History of the Rites and Ceremonies of all Nations*,
p. 705.

58. *From the New American Encyclopædia.*

"These works (the scientific and philosophical works of
Swedenborg) afford evidence of a remarkably well-balanced
mind, in which the beautiful and the practical, poetry and mathematics, were harmoniously blended together. His writings
always breathe a pure devotional spirit; and persons to whom
he was most intimately known, of high and low rank, bear
testimony to the excellence of his private character. The following *Rules of Life* were found noted down in several of his
manuscripts, evidently intended for private use, as they are
nowhere met with in his published works :— 1. Often to read
and meditate on the Word of God. 2. To submit everything
to the will of Divine Providence. 3. To observe in everything a propriety of behavior, and always to keep the conscience clear. 4. To discharge with fidelity the functions of
his employments and the duties of his office, and to render
himself in all things useful to society."

59. Professor Matter, in alluding to these "Rules of
Life," says :—

"In these rules of life of Swedenborg, we find that which
characterizes best his life: these studies of the sacred texts,
which led him to such a rare illumination; this constant
vigilance over his soul, which gave to him in reality, besides
a clear conscience, an extraordinary serenity of mind; this
constant application to what he calls the decorum of life,
which made his intercourse so agreeable to everybody; this
earnest devotion to his public duties, which inspired him with
a capacity of doing immense works for his country; and, I
add, which induced him to resign his commission, when he
believed himself invested with a new mission, which claimed
all his energies, and all his time."—*Vie de Swedenborg*, pp.
20–21.

60. Dr. Wilkinson sums up Swedenborg's character, as follows :—

" The upper parts of Swedenborg's character rose from the ground-work of excellent citizenship and social qualities. Naturally inoffensive and conservative, he was at one with the general polity, and never dreamt of innovations that should interfere with the State. Even his theology was referable, in his view, to an existing authority in the Bible, and in harmony with the earliest creeds of the church, so far as they went. He lent himself freely to his family ties, but never allowed them to interrupt his justice. As a friend he was staunch, and equally independent. The sentiment of duty ruled him without appeal in his public as in his private affairs: he had no acquaintances but society and his country when *their* interests were involved. In disseminating his religious ideas, he was open and above-board: placed his books within the reach of the Christian world, and there left them, to Providence and the readers. By no trick did he ever seek to force attention, and intrigue had no part in his character. Notwithstanding his attachment to his first admirers, he kept his own space around him, and was not impeded by any followers. Tender and amicable in nature, he was always distant enough to have that large arm's-length that so peculiar a workman required. Ambition he must have had in some sense, but so transpierced and smitten with zeal for his fellows, that we can only call it public love. The power of order and combination, is a main feature in his capacious intellect ; those who open him as a visionary, are struck with the masculine connection which he everywhere displays. His sensual nature was evidently an obedient though powerful vehicle to his mind. He was perfectly courageous in that kind that his mission needed ; firm, but unobtrusive, in all courts and companies, and ever bending whither his conscience prescribed. Religion was the mild element that governed the rest, converting them past their own natures by its lively flames, and he walked with the constant sentiment of God between him and his fellows, giving and receiving dignity among God's children. His life indeed is not heroic in the old fashion ; but take his account of it, and he has travelled far and perilled much : he has seen and been what would bleach the lips of heroes. Whether you receive his account or not, you must own that his structure was heroic, for how otherwise could he have outlived those tremendous 'fancies' of heaven and hell. But let that pass, and we still claim him as a hero in the new campaign of peace. The first Epic of the Study is the song that will celebrate him. There are many simple problems, but how few dare face them : it is more difficult to be courageous there than before batteries of cannon : it is more impossible to the most to lead the forlorn hopes of thought, discouraged since history began, to victory, than to mount the scaling-ladder in the imminent deadly breach. To do the one requires only command of body ; to perform the other needs courage over the brain itself ; fighting against organism and stupidity older and more terrifying than armies. Select your problem, and ask the world round who will besiege it until it cedes the truth, and you will soon find that of all the soldiers there is none who does not straightway show fatigue and sob impossible, which are cowardice under its literary name. In these ages there has been no man who stood up so manfully to his problems as Swedenborg, who wielded his own brains so like a spirit, or knew so experimentally that labor rises over death. Therefore we name him Leader of the world's free thought and free press ; the Captain of the heroes of the writing-desk."—*Life of Swedenborg*, pp. 245–247.

In his "*Introduction to the Economy of the Animal Kingdom,*" Dr. WILKINSON describes Swedenborg's character as manifested in his writings :—

"It would be an omission not to notice the *dogmatic character* of Swedenborg's writings generally. ' He speaks as one having authority, and not as the scribes.' What Bacon says is ' the true way,' ' he proposes things candidly, with more or less asseveration, as they stand in his own judgment.'* Yet, notwithstanding this boldness, no writer gives us a greater sense of modesty than Swedenborg. The absence of self from his pages,—the infinitely small consideration which

---

* "Advancement of Learning," prelim., p. lviii.

the *ego* there claims either morally or intellectually,—is the earnest of great humbleness ; and where this is felt, the calmest affirmations lose the character of self-complacency, and are justly taken as but the measure of the love of truth. Besides which, moral ideas, — and it is with these that Swedenborg deals even when it is least apparent,—by their own necessity require positive statement, and introduce even into their correlatives in physics a tone of certainty and dignified injunction : even nature, as the exponent of the Commandments, partakes of their absoluteness, and dictates her laws to mankind.

"The *temper of mind* apparent in these works is also remarkable. For Swedenborg, the philosopher, was read and commended by no one, and still he continued to travel onwards with a benignity unembittered by censure and undiminished by neglect. His practical labors were received with applause by his countrymen, and even procured him somewhat of a European reputation. But his affections were not committed to them. From youth upwards he conceived and began his peculiar philosophy, and here the favor of the learned ceased, at first declining into faint praise, which was soon exchanged for undisguised opposition. Influence over men's minds he had none ; and judging from the past, it seems that but for his theology, his philosophical works might have perished on the shelf where his immediate contemporaries placed them. But if he failed to impress the world, its apathy did not affect him. He knew the state in which it was sunk,* and only worked the harder when that knowledge was confirmed, by his views being treated with contempt or neglect. Amid the surrounding darkness he was cheerful and sunny in heart and mind, and his pages were brightened with his own happy temper. We are therefore sure of his veracity when he avows his carelessness of fame, and his power of waiting to be heard, though centuries should elapse before the public ear was disengaged. Not that he was supported by complacent vanity, the insane king of an imaginary kingdom, or with deep pride

---

* Compare the motto which Swedenborg adopted from Seneca, and which is contained in No. 4 of the present collection.

despised the opinions and overlooked the immortal concerns of others: but aware of the world's disabilities, which can only be removed by slow degrees, and not answerable for them, he was entitled, on the other hand, to all the delight that an open vision of truth imparts to whoever sincerely obeys and loves it. He knew that he was before his age, and had no quarrel with it, because of its misfortune; but committed all to Providence, contentedly performing his own allotment of arduous duties. Therefore he says at the close of the 'Principia,'—' In writing the present work, I have had no aim at the applause of the learned world, nor at the acquisition of a name or popularity. To me it is a matter of indifference whether I win a favorable opinion of every one or of no one, whether I gain much or no commendation; such things are not objects of regard to one whose mind is bent on truth and true philosophy; should I, therefore, gain the assent or approbation of others, I shall receive it only as a confirmation of my having pursued the truth. I have no wish to persuade any one to lay aside the principles of those illustrious and talented authors who adorn the world, and in place of their principles to adopt mine; for this reason it is that I have not made mention so much as of one of them, or even hinted at his name, lest I should injure his feelings, or seem to impugn his sentiments, or to derogate from the praise which others bestow upon him. If the principles I have advanced have more of truth in them than those which are advocated by others; if they are truly philosophical and accordant with the phenomena of nature, the assent of the public will follow in due time of its own accord; and in this case, should I fail to gain the assent of those whose minds, being prepossessed by other principles, can no longer exercise an impartial judgment, still I shall gain the assent of those who are able to distinguish the true from the untrue, if not in the present, at least in some future age. Truth is unique, and will speak for itself. Should any one undertake to impugn my sentiments, I have no wish to oppose him; but in case he should desire it, I shall be happy to explain my principles and reasons more at large. What need, however, is there of words? Let the thing speak for itself. If what I have said be true, why should I be eager to defend it ?—surely truth can defend itself.   If what I have said be false, it would be a degrading and silly task to defend it.   Why then should I make myself an enemy to any one, or place myself in opposition to any one?' *   And again he observes in the 'Economy,'—'Of what consequence is it to me that I should persuade any one to embrace my opinions? Let his own reason persuade him.   I do not undertake this work for the sake of honor or emolument; both of which I shun rather than seek, because they disquiet the mind, and because I am content with my lot: but for the sake of truth, which alone is immortal, and has its portion in the most perfect order of nature; hence in the series of the ends of the universe from the first to the last, or to the glory of God, which ends He promotes; thus I surely know Who it is that must reward me.' †   Of his sincerity in these declarations, as we before remarked, the repose which pervades his books, and the hearty pursuit of his subject at all times, bear incontestable witness.   'His life,' says Sandel, 'was one of the happiest that ever fell to the lot of man; ' ‡ and a prolonged observation of his writings enables us thoroughly to believe it. Because he esteemed opinion and fame at only their proper value, and truth as an object far more real, so when the need came, he gladly renounced his great possessions as a man of learning, and never once looking back, yielded himself to the service of the new cause to which his remaining life was to be devoted.   It is therefore not unaccountable, though certainly without parallel, that one who had solved the problems of centuries, and pushed the knowledge of causes into regions whose existence no other philosopher suspected, should at length abandon the field of science, without afterwards alluding so much as once to the mighty task he had surmounted.   This was in accordance with his mind even in his scientific days: the presence of truth was what pleased him; and he always joyfully exchanged his light for a greater and

---

* Part iii., Appendix.

† Part II., n. 218.

‡ "Eulogium on Swedenborg," pronounced by Sandel in the name of the Royal Academy of Sciences of Stockholm, October 7, 1772.

purer, even though cherished thoughts had to die daily, as the condition of passing into the higher illumination.

"Furthermore, there never was a man who belonged less than he to his own age or nation, notwithstanding he depended greatly upon the physical knowledge of his contemporaries, was widely read in philosophy also, and made free use of whatever he found in other writers that was true and to the purpose. But his genius was more than his materials; ' *materiem superabit opus*.' He wielded with ease the solid masses of learning, and they obeyed new motions and ran in systematic orbits. The naked rocks of science received a quickening climature, and greenness and life came upon them. The season was ripe, and the personal conditions fulfilled, and the willing earth yielded her increase as to the Jews of old. The acquired goodness of the individual became the spring of his genius; and hence he stood related to the world as the creation of God, and to man as his unrivalled creature, and went out from the soil that bore him, so that Scandinavia was his mother no longer. He became the example of a nobler energy than that which carried the Swedish kings over hostile Europe; an energy which sustained him to bear the lamp of humanizing science into the darkest places of the earth, where the phantoms of superstition terrify, and obscene atheism flits around on subtlest pinions. He showed a faith in the real God, and in the spiritual existence and interests of mankind, to which the profoundest homage of the North to her mythologic Odin, and her chiefs' and warriors' fastest belief in the promised Walhalla, are but weak, shadowy and unsubstantial. The triumphs he gained in the name of truth, and that his writings will gain in the coming ages, are fraught with importance which far eclipses the proudest victories of his martial countrymen. For it was his happy lot, not to fight temporal battles for Protestantism, or to be the prop of an old religion, whose very victories often precluded its communion with the Prince of Peace; but to be the means of averting destruction from the whole race of man, and of securing to all a hold on Christianity that can never fail; and in the course of this instrumentality, to walk undismayed in that other world which has been lost to knowledge for thousands of years, or preserved only in the unwritten parts of imagination, the misunderstood depth of ancient fable, or the narrations of the earlier poets.   Hence he is the first of the moderns to penetrate the secrets of nature, the first also to be admitted to the hidden things of the spiritual world: the two spheres of knowledge being realized at once ; wherefore henceforth he is our earnest, that since we are now on the right track, and the works of God are become our heritage, the progression in both may be practical and unending." — " *Introduction to the Economy of the Animal Kingdom,*" pp. lxxxvi–xc.

IV.

SWEDENBORG'S STYLE.

61.   "ACCUSTOMED as we are to the scientific style in current use, Swedenborg's works may seem imaginative from richness of illustrations; from the decoration clothing his ideas; from the unexpected beauty which often comes forth during a serious argument; and from the frequent recourse to analogies. For the usual mode of presenting knowledge is abstract, naked, passionless, and solitary.   But herein Swedenborg follows nature with greater reverence than the orthodox student.   For as in objects there is no dryness like what pervades the descriptions in books, so the latter are imaginative, by reason of the mean dress superinduced upon the subject; meanness of imagination being imagination still.   Only if the planet were an unvaried Sahara, could such descriptions be other than imaginative.   Nature, on the other hand, in the real world, is liberal and lovely, adorned as beseems the destined bride of humane philosophy.   Thus she is rich in collateral illustrations, because every series contains numerous elements that are suggestive of other series, and which serve for links with other series; all things being involved in all things, as Anaxagoras wisely intimated.   Nature is also clothed in ornament; and all things of good use tend to ornament; so that beauty is a portion of her works; and it comes out ever and anon, like a bright flower from a sober stem, when we least expect it: whence also surprise and wonder, as incitements to man, are distinct intentions in nature.   Moreover nature is a world of analogies; for every fact and substance is a distinct proportional between certain others, which it combines in a rational equation; so that nature resolves the discords of things by innumerable middle terms; and especially does she suggest

(69)

infinite analogies to the mind of man, because this is the greatest analogical term or proportion that can exist; the medium between soul and body, spirit and matter, the highest sphere and the lowest; reason or ratio being no other than the constant balance of the inward with the outward; or that which reconciles variety with unity, fact with theory, the world with heaven; or which sees one principle in many things, or in all things; and in all things a brotherhood, co-ordination or analogy by virtue of their common paternity in the one omnific beginning and end. On these grounds we suggest that any meanness in tone or manner of scientific works, amounts to unworthy treatment of nature, and is chargeable to the score of imagination, substituting its dreams for the face of creation, and preferring barrenness, so it be its own, to that various beauty which is the child of God."—J. J. GARTH WILKINSON, *in his Introduction to the "Economy of the Animal Kingdom,"* p. lxxiii.

62. *From a Swedish periodical entitled " Mimer."*

The following ably drawn sketch of Swedenborg, as *the Expounder of the Good, the True, and the Beautiful*, is written by PROF. ATTERBOM, *of Upsal*, one of the most celebrated poets of Sweden : —

" Three celebrated men in Sweden have distinguished themselves by writing sublimely and beautifully on the *beautiful;* Swedenborg, to whom LOVE was everything, as well as the relation established by love between the TRUE and the GOOD; *Thorild*, to whom NATURE was everything, as well as the relation established by nature between POWER and HARMONY; *Ehrensvård*, to whom ART was everything, as well as the relation established by art between GENIUS and the IDEAL. In the paper before us, the theosopher Swedenborg is considered chiefly as a thinker and writer on the *beautiful.* The *æsthetic* views of Ehrensvård and Thorild are easily accessible, partly from their own writings, and partly from extracts and expositions, which have lately appeared. But Swedenborg's views are not so easily accessible: the cause is in a twofold difficulty; *first*, because his æsthetic view of the world cannot be properly seen, before we have become acquainted with his views in general; and *secondly*, because he has not devoted a particular work or section to the subject. From a multitude of extensive works, written in Latin, we must bring together what he has said on this subject. His ideas on this topic are scattered in his treatises on his principal doctrines, especially concerning Life as being Love; on God and his unity, as being the original, prototypal, one only divine Man, from whom all finite created men derive that which constitutes them men; on the creation of all beings and substances, as receptacles of Life and Love, and on the destination of man, who, created with a *will* for the reception of the Divine wisdom, has a finite *esse* and *existere*, corresponding, when constituted in order, to the infinite *esse* and *existere* in God; on the Good and the True; on the Spheres, Degrees, and Correspondences of creation: on the relation between the different circles of life, descending by degrees from the highest to the lowest of created existences, and connected together in one universal harmonic whole by the laws of analogy and correspondence; but especially in that part of his writings in which he represents marriage as the emblem of the eternal union in God of Love and Wisdom, and likewise of the conjunction between himself and his church as grounded in that union established in the minds of men. In describing this delightful union, which is the ground and source of all virtue and happiness to the intelligent universe, Swedenborg says much respecting the angels, and the state of harmony and bliss in which they live. In treating of these subjects, he was led to exhibit loveliness and beauty in its objective form in the persons of angels, who were once men upon earth, but who, becoming regenerate, that is, filled as to their wills with the divine love, and as to their understandings with the divine wisdom, are in the enjoyment of that state in which all is harmony, perfection, and bliss, and which is properly called heaven; for all the affections and dispositions of the soul are imaged and reflected in their personal forms of loveliness and beauty. It is here where the *beautiful* in mind, in nature, and in art, has its origin, whence descending into the ultimate spheres and regions of creation, called the natural world, it gives rise to every thing beautiful and lovely we behold. Swedenborg thus traces the origin of science and art to the great first Cause, and to see the relation which they bear to the Divine Wisdom is the parent of all knowledge, science, and genuine philosophy. . . .

"The most beautiful, *as to style*, which Swedenborg ever wrote, is the '*Worship and Love of God*,' which is a kind of middle thing between a philosophic treatise and romance, on the origin of the earth, on the golden age of nature, and of man, on paradise, on the birth, youth, education, and love of Adam and Eve. This, of all Swedenborg's works, is that in which the Beautiful is most conspicuous. It is not only written in a brilliant and harmonious latinity, but with so much poetic life and inspiration, that if divided amongst a dozen poets, it would be sufficient to fix every one of them on the heaven of poesy as stars of the first magnitude. This, at least, is certain, that the more we consider his writings in relation to Philosophy and Aesthetics, the more we must admit, that amongst much dross,* there is considerable quantity of pure and solid gold. The holy and exalted state of mind in which he comprehended and contemplated the structure and order of the universe, and the pure and lofty, yet simple and intelligible manner in which he has treated his subjects and presented his views, are perfectly worthy of a divinely inspired seer. . . . In proportion as we learn properly to understand the writings of Swedenborg, we shall find them full of scientific worth, rich in materials of the beautiful for poetry, and highly honorable to his native country."

63. The following beautiful sketch of Swedenborg's "*Worship and Love of God*," from the pen of DR. WILKINSON, is a good specimen of his style, and substantiates the declaration of Mr. Emerson, who said that this author was among the foremost of English writers, now living. (See also *Fraser's Magazine*, February, 1857, on the same subject.)

---

* "From this it plainly appears that the author of this paper is no receiver of the Theological works of Emanuel Swedenborg, otherwise he would not speak of *dross;* we must consequently consider his judgment as so much the more impartial."—(Editor of the "Documents.")

" Nothing can be more vernal than the earlier portion of this work; the reader is guided deeper and deeper into a delicious embowerment, and treads the carpets of a golden age. Every clod and leaf, grove, stream, and a multitude of rejoicing inhabitants, all the dews, atmospheres, and skyey influences, the very stars of the firmament, busily minister with a latent love, and each with a native tact and understanding, to the coming heir of the world, the son of earth, the mind in a human form, who can look from the paradise of earth to the paradise of heaven, and venerate and adore the Creator, returning to God immortal thanks for himself and all things. At last, in the central grove, in the most temperate region of the earth, where the woven boscage broke the heat of day, and so ' induced a new spring under the general one'; and where the gushing streamlets veined the area, and lifted by the sun in kindliest vapors, hung upon the leaves, and descended in continual dews,—in this intimate temple of the general garden, lo, the tree of life, and the arboreal womb of the nascent human race. Truly a bold Genesis; but the steps that lead to it, though beautiful as sylvan alleys, are also of logical pavement, and the appreciating reader, for the time at any rate, is carried well pleased along in the flow and series of the strong-linked narrative. . . . It is in the philosophical narrative that Swedenborg has shown truly surprising powers which we may challenge literature to surpass: so far as this extends, the work is a great and rushing inspiration."
—*Life of Swedenborg,* pp. 64–65, American edit.

64. We shall now hear E. PAXTON HOOD descanting upon the same theme :—

" In this work Swedenborg throws away the crucible, the mathematical instrument, and the dissecting knife, and sings, . so to speak, a lofty hymn in honor of the creation. This work is the most exalted in its style of all Swedenborg's works; the imagination and the fancy flame and blaze over its pages, and, indeed, it gives forth in poetry what the ' *Principia*' and the ' *Animal Kingdom*' have given in prose. . . . In reading it we walk along as through a vast tropical forest. We feel the warm, warm sun of the young world even through the thick massive foliage; the leaves quiver and rustle with a wonderful and Eolian music. And what gorgeousness in the spicy and gummy trees,—the ground too, how soft and mossy; we see around us the flashing of innumerable pinions of birds, bright, swift and glancing in their plumage. We cannot read the first chapters without feeling that we are transported to the rich and vernal solitudes of Young Time,

> ' When the radiant morn of creation broke,
> And the earth in the smile of God awoke;
> And the empty realms of darkness and death
> Were moved thro' the depths by His mighty breath.'

" And we like the idea of the Perpetual Paradise, and would not wish the argument for the swift flight of the infant world around the sun destroyed.

" A forest world! a forest of beauty! But a forest of truths too. The aphorisms hang upon the pages of the book like the luscious ripe fruit upon the trees. Truly among the works of Swedenborg it occupies a very inconsiderable place; for its province is rather imagination than logic,—rather the poetry of Truth than truth itself; but it is a rich pomegranate, golden without, blood-red beauty within. It is a book of seeds, of seminal principles and figures,—the languages gush along in lines of light and fire. And how alive it is—how the world is peopled by the poet—how the mind itself is peopled by distinct beings and inhabitants and actors; and the book is balanced in all its parts by the weight of the strong judgment which every imaginative intellect possesses."— *Swedenborg : a Biography*, &c., pp. 88, 94–95.

65. Concerning the style of Swedenborg in his scientific works generally, Dr. WILKINSON has the following :—

" We find increased life in Swedenborg's style as we proceed with his works. *The Principia* is clear, felicitous, though somewhat repetitious, and occasionally breaks forth into a beautiful but formal eloquence. The ancient mythology lends frequent figures to the scientific process, and the author's treatment would seem to imply the belief that in the generation of the gods, there was imbedded a hint of the origin of the world. Occasionally subjects of unpromising look are invested with sublime proportions, as when he likens the mathematical or natural point to a 'two-faced Janus, which looks on either side towards either universe, both into infinite and into finite immensity.' The manner of the *Outlines of the Infinite* is not dissimilar to that of *The Principia*, only less elaborate, and somewhat more round and liberal. The style of *The Economy*, however, displays the full courtliness of a master, — free, confident, confiding; self-complacent, but always aspiring; at home in his thoughts, though voyaging through untravelled natures; then most swift in motion onwards when most at rest in some great attainment; not visibly subject to second thoughts, or to the devil's palsy of self-approbation; flying over great sheets of reason with easy stretches of power; contradicting his predecessors point-blank, without the possibility of offending their honored *manes:* in these and other respects the style of *The Economy* occupies new ground of excellence. The latter portion of the work, particularly 'On the Human Soul,' is a sustained expression of the loftiest order, and in this respect won the commendations of Coleridge, who was no bad judge of style." (See our extract, n. 66.) "The *Animal Kingdom*, however, is riper, rounder, and more free than even the last-mentioned work; more intimately methodical, and at the same time better constructed. The treatises on the organs, themselves correspondently organic, are like stately songs of science dying into poetry; it is surprising how so didactic a mind carved out the freedom and beauty of these epic chapters. It is the same with *The Worship and Love of God*, the ornament in which is rich and flamboyant, but upborne on the colonnades of a living forest of doctrines. We observe then, upon the whole, this peculiarity, that Swedenborg's address became more intense and ornamental from the beginning to the end of these works; a somewhat rare phenomenon in literature, for the imagination commonly burns out in proportion as what is termed sober reason advances, whereas with this author his imagination was kindled at the torch of reason, and never flamed forth freely until the soberness of his maturity had set

it on fire from the wonderful love that couches in all things."
—*Life of Swedenborg*, pp. 65–66, Americ. edit.

66. " It is well known, that Coleridge read the philosophical works of Swedenborg with much pleasure and admiration.
His notes on many passages in the *Œconomia Regni Animalis*,
and in the *De Cultu et Amore Dei*, evidently indicate and
prove this to have been the fact. We will here adduce a few
of his notes which he appears to have penned as he was reading through the *Œconomia Regni Animalis*. On the nn. 208
to 214 inclusive, he observes,—' I remember nothing in Lord
Bacon superior, few passages equal, either in depth of thought,
or in richness, dignity, and felicity of diction, or in the
weightiness of the truths contained in these articles.'—(S. T.
Coleridge, May 27, 1827.)

" On 251, he observes, that it is ' Excellent ; so indeed are
all the preceding in the matter meant to be conveyed ; but
this paragraph is not only conceived with the mind of a
master, but it is *expressed* adequately, and with scientific precision.' "—*Literary Remains of Coleridge*, Vol. IV., p. 424.

V.

SWEDENBORG'S SCIENCE.

67. *From Sandel's Eulogy on Swedenborg.*

" The scientific works of Swedenborg are so many incontestible proofs of a universal erudition, which attached itself in preference to objects which require deep reflection and profound knowledge. None can reproach him with having wished to shine in borrowed plumes, passing off as his own the labors of others, dressed out in a new form and decorated with some new turns of expression. It must be acknowledged, on the contrary, that without ever taking up the ideas of others, he always follows his own, and often makes remarks and applications which are not to be found in any preceding author. Nor was he at all of the same class as the generality of universal geniuses, who, for the most part, are content with merely skimming over the surface of things. He applied the whole force of his mind to penetrate into the most hidden things, to connect together the scattered links of the great chain of universal being, and to trace up everything, in an order agreeable to its nature, to the great First Cause. Neither did he proceed in the manner of certain Natural Philosophers and Mathematicians, who, dazzled by the light which they have been in search of, and have found, would, were it possible, eclipse and extinguish, to the eyes of the world, the Only True and Great Light. He, in the course of his meditations on the universe, and on creation, continually found new occasions for rising in love and adoration towards the Author of Nature. . . . .

" I think I shall not be mistaken if I assert that Swedenborg, from the time when he first began to think for himself, was animated by a secret fire, and ardent desire to attain to the discovery of the most abstract things. . . . . .

"He contemplated the great edifice of the universe in general. He afterwards examined such of its parts as come within the limits of our knowledge. He saw that the whole is arranged in a uniform order, and governed by certain laws. He took particular notice, in this immense machine, of every thing that can be explained on mathematical principles. He doubted not that the Supreme Creator had arranged the whole, even to the most complete mutual agreement: and this agreement, as a mathematical philosopher, he endeavored to develop, by drawing conclusions from the smallest parts to the greatest, from that which is visible before our eyes, to that which is scarcely discoverable, even by the aid of optical glasses. He thus formed to himself a system founded upon a certain species of mechanism, and supported by reasoning—a system, the arrangement of which is so solid, and the composition so serious, that it claims and merits all the attention of the learned: as for others, they may do better not to meddle with it. According to this system, he explains all that the most certain facts and the soundest reasoning can offer to our meditations."

68. Concerning the repute in which Swedenborg's scientific works are held at present among the learned, we extract the following from the "*Southern Quarterly Review*," vol. x. pp. 314–15 : —

"These works are in the very highest repute among learned men, and are daily increasing in reputation, of which the new translations, and costly editions, recently issued from the London press, afford evidence. It is now beginning to be discovered and acknowledged how much even the present enlightened age is indebted to the herculean labors and rare discoveries of this transcendent genius — a concession which would have been sooner made, had it not been that his greatest works were composed and published in a dead or foreign tongue, unfamiliar to the generality of readers ; besides that, his claims as an illuminated expounder of Divine Revelation have thrown a temporary cloud over his literary reputation, which is now being dissipated by the force of truth ; and we may add, that the great body of scholars of the present century have been too much occupied with modern works of value, to pay that attention to the labors of their illustrious predecessors, which their merits challenge at their hands. A period of literary repose of long continuance, and freedom from the distraction of wars and political convulsions, has, however, latterly furnished them with leisure for more thorough investigations, and enabled them to be more just to the claims of illustrious persons who have passed off the stage."

69. *From the Christian Examiner, July,* 1843.

" We shall now endeavor to take a brief review of Swedenborg's scientific progress, with particular reference to method, principles, and doctrines. His proper career may be dated from the publication of the ' Prodromus Principiorum ' (Principles of Chemistry). In this work he attempted to account for chemical combination, by a theory of the forms and forces of the particles of bodies ; and to resolve chemistry into natural geometry, that it might have the benefit of first principles, and the rank of a fixed science. Of these forms he gave many delineations. . . . .

" The rules which he proposed for investigating the constitution of the magnetic, luminous, and atmospheric elements, come next under our notice. 1. That we take for granted that nature acts by the simplest means, and that the particles of elements are of the simplest and least artificial forms. 2. That the beginning of nature is the same as the beginning of geometry ; that natural particles arise from mathematical points, precisely as lines, forms, and the whole of geometry ; and this because everything in nature is geometric ; and *vice versâ.* 3. That all the above elements are capable of simultaneous motion, in one and the same place ; and that each moves naturally without hindrance from the others. 4. That ascertained facts be the substratum of theory, and that no step be taken without their guidance.

" From these rules we pass to their application, in the outset, to which Swedenborg boldly averred that the records of science, accumulated as they had been for thousands of years, were sufficient for an examination of things on principles, and *a priori ;* that a knowledge of natural philosophy does not presuppose the knowledge of innumerable phenomena, but only of principal facts which proceed directly, and not of those which result obliquely and remotely, from the world's mechanism and powers; and that the latter species of facts confuse and disturb, rather than inform the mind. Also, that the restless desire from age to age for more facts, is characteristic of those who are unable to reason from principles to causes, and that no abundance would ever be sufficient for such persons." We shall pass over the reviewer's statement of the doctrine of the elemental world as proposed in the " Principia."

" In approaching the human body, Swedenborg again insisted on the necessity for principles and generalization, without which, he said, ' facts themselves would grow obsolete and perish ;' adding that ' unless we were much mistaken, the destinies of the world were leading to this issue.' A knowledge of the soul became the professed object of his inquiry, and he entered the circus with a resolve to examine thoroughly the world, or microcosm, which the soul inhabits, in the assurance that she should be sought for nowhere but in her own kingdom. In this search he repudiated synthesis, and resolved to approach the soul by the analytic way, adding, that he believed himself to be the first investigator who had ever commenced with this intention ; a surmise in which he is probably correct. We shall here content ourselves with a brief illustration of one of these doctrines which, with the most intense study, he elaborated for his guidance ; we mean the ' doctrine of series and degrees.' Each organ, he observed, commences from certain unities or least parts which are peculiar to it, and derives its form from their gradual composition, and its general function from the sum of their particular functions. The mass is therefore the representative of its minute components, and its structure and functions indicate theirs. The vesicles, or smallest parts peculiar to the lungs, are so many least lungs ; the biliary radicles of the liver, so many least livers ; the cellules of the spleen, so many least spleens ; the tubuli of the kidneys, so many least kidneys ; and the same function is predicable of these leasts, as of their entire respective organs, but with any modification which experience may declare to be proper to the minuter structures. This new method of analysis, in which the greatest things were presumed to indicate the least, with just such reservation as our experience of the least necessitates, was designed to throw light on the intimate structure and occult offices of single organs,—the same way it identified the higher with the lower groups of organs,—the cranial with the thoracic, and both with the abdominal viscera. Whatever is manifested in the body is transferable to the brain, as the source of all functions and structures. If the abdominal organs supply the blood with a terrestrial nourishment, the thoracic supply it with an aerial, and the brain with an ethereal food. If the first mentioned organs, by the urinary and intestinal passages, eliminate excrements and impurities, so the lungs by the trachea, and the brain through the sinuses, reject a subtler defilement. If the heart and blood-vessels are channels of a corporeal circulation, the brain and nerves, or spirit-vessels, are channels of a transcendent or spirituous circulation. If the contractility of the arteries and of muscular structures depends on the nervous system, it is because that system is itself eminently contractile, and impels forward its contents in the most perfect manner. If the lungs have a respiration rising and falling, and the heart a contraction and expansion, so the brain has an animatory movement, which embraces both the motions of the lower series. Thus every function is first to be traced to its essential form in the bosom of its own organ, and thence, through an ascending scale to the brain, ‘which is eminently muscle, and eminently gland; in a word, which is eminently the microcosm, when the body is regarded as a microcosm.’”

70. The reviewer closes with the following words of the “ *Penny Cyclopedia* ”: “ On the whole, we may admit these works to be a grand consolidation of human knowledge; an attempt to combine and reorganize the opinions of all the schools of medicine since the days of Hippocrates. The doctrines of the fluidists, of the mechanical and chemical physicians, and of the vitalists, and solidists, as well as the methods of the dogmatics and empirics, and even the miscellaneous novelties of the present day, have each a proportion and a place in the catholic system of Swedenborg. His works, however, are a dead letter to the medical profession, or known

only to its erudite members through the ignorant misstatements of Haller."

71. *From the Monthly Magazine,* 1841.

" In his anti-theological career, the course of Swedenborg was a scientific one ; and it has in it the unparalleled wonder of a man devoting himself undeviatingly for twenty-five years, to natural facts, and yet always having in view, and as an end, the highest objects. No writer ever kept more closely to the matter in hand of his several treatises (and these embrace nearly the circle of human knowledge), with a purpose which altogether transcended each present effort. There is, in fact, no discursiveness, no anticipation of the next step in the process, but a steady and legitimate evolution. This gives to his works the character of a great series, and makes them at any rate powerfully persuasive ; at the same time that the real end he had in view, the knowledge of spiritual things, forces him to the ultimate, to the very highest, physical deductions in each particular case. Nothing can be more opposed than this to the spirit of modern science, dwelling, as it ever does, in proximate inductions, and treating its own first principles as absurd and visionary. We read, the other day, of a medical author who declared that *he would sooner learn a new way of making a poultice, than enter on a physiological theory ;* a dictum which is a very correct exponent of the present reach of the scientific spirit — but Swedenborg had other ideas of science.

" Swedenborg's aim in his work on the *Principles of Chemistry,* was to arrive at the ultimate law of chemical combinations, which he saw intuitively could be no other than a definite form and correspondent force in the atoms of combining bodies. This form, he asserts, is pointed at (*indigitari*) by every property of material masses ; that, for instance, all the chemical effects of a quantity of acid on a quantity of metal, are but the aggregate of myriads of mechanical and geometrical relations between the ultimate particles of these two substances ; and that it is the business of the scientific man, in the gross result, to read the special cause,—in the relations and qualities of the whole,—to discern the casual form and force of the atom. If his method, in this work, be induction, the process, at any rate, is not given. He has delineated, as it would seem, intuitively, the shapes of the particles of numbers of substances, testing his positions *a posteriori* by known facts of the union of bodies, which bear him out, it must be confessed, in a wonderful manner. His general doctrine seems to be, that solids have been originally generated in the interstices of fluids, and have, therefore, the shapes of those interstices; the fracture and combination of these shapes, giving rise to all the varieties of inert substances. There is the clearest anticipation by Swedenborg, in this work, of the whole *doctrine* of the atomic theory; nay, he has even laid down, geometrically, the composite nature of water, and stated the chemical equivalents of its components at the admitted values of 8 and 1, always calling water 9. By the result of this inquiry, he seeks to marry the merely experimental sciences to the fixed, and to elevate them on the wings of geometry. Let us admit, that even every deduction which has been elicited by him be false, this spirit is a valuable one to work in.

" But Swedenborg, following his chief doctrine, that the greatest things instruct us of the least, — the largest visible of the smallest invisible, next proceeds to a theory of the formation of the universe. We cannot trust ourselves to launch into the ocean of his '*Principia*,' but must be content with a brief, and not very satisfactory or intelligible analysis of it, in the German '*Real-Encyclopedia*;' (vol. 10. Leipz. 1839,) which, however, so far as we know, is the only one before the public.

This analysis, as being wholly inadequate, we shall here omit.

" We find Swedenborg, after having gauged the height and depth of physics; after having carried the physical facts of his day, to the last possible deductions, turning his attention to the human microcosm. He mastered the whole of the anatomical materials necessary for his purposes; and now proceeded to construct a grand system of physiology. Here we see the same unity and precision, as in in his previous works, and the same serial character and relation in his proceedings; his physical man is an exactly fitted inhabitant of his finite universe; organ is adapted to object, and object to organ; and the world within and the world without are in kindly and indispensable relation. In his *Œconomia Regni Animalis* he gives his analysis of the blood-globule—a mechanical and geometrical analysis — building upon it, as a basis, the structures and functions of all the sanguineous organs. Beginning from a knowledge of the blood, he holds in his hand the end and principle of all the fabrics which generate that fluid; seeing their uses from an almost prophetic point of vision. Here he also commences to treat of the MOTIONS of the human body; a subject of which, indeed, he may be considered the discoverer. He demonstrates that the brain has a respiratory motion, a rising and falling, synchronous with the inspirations and expirations of the lungs, by means of which falling, the nervous fluid, (*fluidum spirituosum,*) is propelled all over the system, while the expansion of the brain draws the same fluid from the blood (of which it is the life) through the capillaries of the carotids, into the cortical substances (*corcula cerebri*), and so back into the nervous circulation. ' *Set the brain in motion,*' says he significantly, ' *and you will see the uses of all its parts.*' This motion generates the motions of the lungs, which react upon those of the brain, and serve as a subsidiary and external attractive cause of the circulation of the nervous fluid, of which the motions of the brain serve as the internal cause. Nor is respiration confined to the lungs, but by their means, as well as by the brain, is introduced into all the viscera; the whole being in a state of alternate swell and subsidence; which constitutes their life and activity, and excites them perpetually into the performance of their functions. Thus, with Swedenborg, definite structure has definite function; and definite function is none other than definite motion—' *Qualis determinatio substantiarum, talis accidentium et motuum, qui substantias, sicut stratos ponticulos percurrunt.* (As is the determination of substances, so is that of the accidents and the motions which run through the substances, like little paved bridges.) Every fibre has its own fluxion.

" In fact the human body, in its inmost recesses, in those manifold functions, which are ordinarily called *vital*, is but the realization of a transcendental geometry. All its operations take place in obedience to high mathematical laws, which rule in its stupendous forms. If the circle and triangle have certain properties, on which the powers of mechanical instruments in these forms are dependent, so the spirals and everlasting vortices of the brain, the vessels, the intestines, have also inalienable properties of their own, in which the corporeal organization lives, moves, and has its being. This leads us to say a few words of Swedenborg's DOCTRINE OF FORMS : — a doctrine of the principles by which Nature ascends from the mineral to the body of man." . . . .

This doctrine we prefer to state in Swedenborg's own words, as contained in " *The Worship and Love of God*," 2d Americ. edit. pp. 17, and 18 :

" 'The lowest form, or the form proper to earthly substances, is that which is determined by mere angular, and at the same time by plane subjects, whatsoever be their figure, provided they flow together into a certain form; this, therefore, is to be called an ANGULAR FORM, the proper object of our geometry. From this form we are enabled to contemplate the next superior form, or the form perpetually angular, which is the same as the CIRCULAR or SPHERICAL FORM ; for this latter is more perfect than the other in this respect, that its circumference is, as it were, a perpetual plane, or infinite angle, because totally void of planes and angles; on which account also it is the measure of all angular forms, for we measure angles and planes by sections and sines of a circle; from these considerations we see, that into this latter form something infinite or perpetual has insinuated itself, which does not exist in the former, viz., the circular orb, whose end and beginning cannot be marked. In the circular or spherical form, again, we are enabled to contemplate a certain superior form, which may be called the perpetual circular, or simply the SPIRAL FORM; for to this form is added, still further, somewhat perpetual or infinite, which is not in the former, viz., that its diameters are not bounded or terminate in a certain circumference of a circle or superficies of a sphere, which serves it instead of a centre, and that its diameters are bent into a species of a certain curve, by which means this form is the measure of a circular form or forms, as the circular is the measure of the angular. In this spiral form we are enabled to view a still superior kind of form, which may be called the perpetually spiral or VORTICAL FORM, in which again somewhat perpetual or infinite is found which was not in the former : for the former had reference to a circle as to a kind of infinite centre, and from this, by its diameters, to a fixed centre as to its limit or boundary ; but the latter has reference to a spiral form as a centre, by lines perpetually circular ; this form manifests itself especially in magnetics, and is the measure of the spiral form for the reason above mentioned concerning inferior forms.   In this, lastly, may be viewed the highest form of nature, or the perpetually vortical form, which is the same with the CELESTIAL FORM, in which almost all boundaries are, as it were, erased, as so many imperfections, and still more perpetuities or infinities are put on ; wherefore this form is the measure of the vortical form, consequently the exemplar or idea of all inferior forms, from which the inferior descend and derive birth as from their beginning, or from the form of forms."

Thus far Swedenborg.   We continue in the words of the editor of the " Monthly Magazine : "

" This scale of forms, with the motions which ascend and descend through them, ' like so many little paved bridges,' everlastingly is the one grand law of nature ; all organization deriving its perfection from being constituted in the higher forms and motions ; all body, taking its properties from the lower.   Thus Swedenborg makes Geometry co-extensive, perhaps synonymous, with nature.   His physiology is indeed the Euclid of the human body, which he would persuade us is not an occult and alchemistic thing, but supremely mechanical, — a law and shape infinitely distinct and perfect.

" Another remarkable position is his DOCTRINE OF SERIES. All substances, including organized substances, are composed of least parts exactly similar to themselves in all their properties, with only the reservation, that the least things are much more perfect, and more potent in their sphere than the greatest. The activities of masses are but general and gross results, presenting an image and shadow of the interior activities of their compound unities.   These unities must not, however, be confounded with particles, supposed to be infinitely small, since

Swedenborg entirely neglects the idea of infinite divisibility, as being of no scientific value. On the contrary, they stand for those things which are least in any series, and enter the form of that series as its essential parts, and which are peculiar to that series, and would suit no other were they applied to it. To exemplify, the pulmonary vesicle is the unity of the lungs, from which the lungs commence, and where their activities reside essentially. If we analyze the vesicle, we come to capillaries and nerves, which cannot be said to be peculiar to the lungs, inasmuch as they form the ground-work of the entire body. The vesicle then is the *least* of the lungs, constituting, in fact, a least lung, which has in itself, and produces from itself, all the powers which those organs possess in the aggregate. In the same manner the liver is made up of least livers; the spleen of least spleens; the kidney of least kidneys; each part of least exemplars of itself. 'Nature is always most similar to itself.' From these least parts, there is a gradual progression and composition to the greatest—to the organs such as the anatomist beholds them. Thus, whatever the common eye sees in the common object, the understanding, guided by this doctrine, is entitled to predicate in transcendental perfection of those parts of our frame which are too minute to become objects at all. What a key is this to the natural invisible! The terminus of sight is the beginning of understanding! The doctrine of the unities of structures, it will be perceived, introduces the atomic theory in a certain high form into the living body; and the analytical results which Swedenborg has procured thereby, are, as we might indeed expect, amazing.

"But perhaps the most important, and certainly the most difficult to state of his scientific doctrines, is the DOCTRINE OF DEGREES. Substances and accidents not only ascend, each in its own series, from least to greatest, and again pass from greatest to least, but are generated out of certain prior forms and forces, which contain potentially all that proceeds from them. Now Swedenborg saw clearly that the boundary of each series, of each organ, presented a barrier which was perfectly impassable by ordinary means; for instance, that the connection between nerve and muscle was as insoluble a difficulty (perhaps the same difficulty) as the connection between nature and spirit. In order, therefore, to leap from one series to another, some new guidance was necessary; and this he found in the Doctrine of Degrees. The brain, says he, is ALL in a super-eminent sense—it is the essential gland—the essential muscle—the essential lungs—the essential heart. In this point of view, the body is the mere weaving and tissue of its brain; each organ is but a lapse from its supreme form. The brain presents all other structures in the highest degree; as the spirituous fluid which it circulates, presents all other fluids. The nervous fibre in the body is the brain again in a lower form, and the muscular fibre in a lower still; or *vice versa*, as we stated before, the brain is the essential muscle; acting or contracting spontaneously, as muscle acts by delegation from the activity of the brain. In this manner the understanding is to trace the influx from superior into inferior forms and their connections—but not by the mere analysis of the inferior *per se*—inasmuch as, in the very generation of the latter, the higher has put off the properties by which we would recognize its presence. In fine, this doctrine would seem to import, that in touching the lower, we touch another *form* of the higher, (in which, however, that higher has been rendered latent,) and that thus, to the understanding, the *nexus* between, or rather, perhaps, the identity of the two stands revealed. Of course the Doctrine of Degrees being rendered necessary by the imperfection of the eye, does not contemplate making the ultimate connection between a posterior organ and its causal nerve, a fact visible for the senses. These degrees, by which Nature ascends and descends, are of two kinds, the one *continuous*, comprising the mere difference of larger and smaller, grosser and finer; the other *distinct*, (or, in the technical language of Swedenborg, *discrete*,) comprehending the differences between prior and posterior, universal and less universal, essential and formal.

"We have now hastily traversed some of Swedenborg's principles; but we should be likely to mislead, did we not say a few words respecting his power of reading *facts* and treating details. With too many speculatists, all particular facts lose their individuality under the glare of some eclipsing theory.

This was not the case with Swedenborg. On he went, in patient analysis, through structure after structure, and organ upon organ, treating their smallest points with all the reverence of the mere anatomist. He chiefly took his data from the best authors of his time, superadding, however, actual dissections and occasional experiments of his own. Time has proved that he had a happy faculty of selecting only the sterling materials from these authorities; and accordingly his deductions have been in no degree perilled, but rather confirmed by the boasted 'march of science.' It may be further observed, that Swedenborg's highest abstractions are ever allied to practical facts; that his doctrines occur as continual inferences from his details, and are not presented in a strictly consecutive order.

"Here Swedenborg ceases for us a professedly scientific man, his next phases exhibiting him in the transition from natural things to spiritual. This we see in his ' *The Worship and Love of God*,' which contains only the essence and elixir of his physical doctrines, sublimated into an analytic intellectual philosophy from which there was a direct highway to theology. The first part of it describes in gorgeous pomp of Latin, the creation of the planets from the Solar fire, and their procession in spiral gyrations from their parent, until they reached their present orbits. Then comes the birth of the first paradisal vegetable kingdom from the mineral kingdom, and, in like manner, and in succession, of the first animal from the first vegetable kingdom; and last of all, from the centre of the *Paradisus in Paradiso* ; the inmost of the vegetable kingdom, or *Arbor Vitæ*, the production of the ovum of the First Man. We shall not now touch on the mental half of this work, the ' *delitium et coronis*' of Swedenborg's science, but conclude a branch of our subject by extracting, as an average specimen of his Latinity at this time, a magnificent passage on the inspiration of life into the corporeal initiament of the First Begotten. . . ."

Then follows a lengthy extract in Latin from the last mentioned work of Swedenborg. This carefully written article is signed by the editor of the " Monthly Magazine," J. A. HERAUD.

72.   On account of the importance of Swedenborg's scientific doctrines for the proper understanding of his works, we insert here DR. WILKINSON's entire exposition of these doctrines from his " Introduction to the Animal Kingdom " :—

" It is impossible to understand either the Word or the works of God without doctrines, which in both cases require to be formed by ' one who is enlightened.' * The doctrines made use of by Swedenborg in the ' Animal Kingdom,' are the Doctrines of Forms, of Order and Degrees, of Series and Society, of Influx, of Correspondence and Representation, and of Modification.   These doctrines themselves are truths arrived at by analysis, proceeding on the basis of general experience; in short, they are so many formulas resulting from the evolution of the sciences.   They are perpetually illustrated and elucidated throughout the ' Animal Kingdom,' but never stated by Swedenborg in the form of pure science, perhaps because it would have been contrary to the analytic method to have so stated them, before the reader had been carried up through the legitimate stages, beginning from experience, or the lowest sphere.   Each effect is put through all these doctrines, in order that it may disclose the causes that enter it in succession, that it may refer itself to its roots and be raised to its powers, and be seen in connection, contiguity, continuity, and analogy with all other things in the same universe. † They may be compared to so many special organs, which analyze things apparently homogeneous into a number of distinct constituent principles, and distribute each for use as the whole requires. To deny any of these doctrines, or to give them up in the presence of facts that do not range upon them at first sight, is to nullify the human mind as the interpreter of nature.

" The Doctrine of Forms teaches that ' the forms of all things, like their essences and substances, ascend in order and by degrees from the lowest to the highest. The lowest form is the angular, or, as it is also called, the terrestrial and corporeal. The second and next higher form is the

---

* Arcana Cœlestia, n. 10589.

† By a universe, Swedenborg appears to mean any complete series as referable to its unities.

circular, which is also called the perpetual-angular, because the circumference of the circle involves neither angle nor rectilinear plane, being a perpetual angle and a perpetual plane; this form is at once the parent and measure of angular forms. The form above this is the spiral, which is the parent and measure of circular forms, as the circular, of angular forms. Its radii or diameters are not rectilinear, nor do they converge to a fixed centre like those of a circle; but they are variously circular, and have a spherical surface for a centre; wherefore the spiral is also called the perpetual circular. This form never exists or subsists without poles, an axis, foci, a greatest circle, and lesser circles, its diameters; and as it again assumes a perpetuity which is wanting in the circular form, namely, in respect of diameters and centres, so it breathes a natural spontaneousness in motion. There are still higher forms, as the perpetual-spiral, properly the vortical; the perpetual-vortical, properly the celestial; * and a highest, the perpetual-celestial, which is spiritual, and in which there is nothing but what is everlasting and infinite.' There is then a scale of forms, whereof the higher are relatively more universal, more perfect, and more potent than the lower. The lower again involve the higher and the highest, and are generated by them: so that where there is an angular body, there is a circular form and force intimately present as its ground; where there is a circle, it is the limit of an interior spiral; and so forth. For nature operates from the very principles of geometry and mechanics, and converts them all to actuality and use. The purer substances in creation gyrate through the higher forms; the less pure circulate through the lower, or are fixed in the lowest. All the essentials of the angular form are opposed to each other, whence the origin of gravitating and inert matter, intrinsically unfitted for motion. But the other forms, according to their eminence, are more and more accommodated to motion and variation.

---

* " Swedenborg here uses the term celestial, not in the sense which is peculiar to it in his theological writings, but more with the meaning attached to it in the phrase ' celestial globe,' as pertaining to the form of the universe."

" The Doctrine of Order teaches that those things which are superior in situation, are also superior in forces, in power, in dignity of office, and in use; and that a similar law determines the situation of the parts of things, and of the parts of parts. Corresponding to the highest or first of the series of subordination, is the central or innermost of the series of co-ordination.

" The Doctrine of Degrees teaches the distinct progressions through which nature passes when one thing is subordinated to, and co-ordinated with another. There are three discriminated degrees in all things, both natural and spiritual, corresponding to end, cause and effect. In the human body there is a sphere of ends, a sphere of causes, and a sphere of effects. The body itself, comprehending the viscera of the abdomen and chest, and the external sensoria of the head, is the sphere of effects; the brain, and the whole of its appendages, are the sphere of causes; the cortical substances of the brain are the sphere of ends or principles. These spheres are subordinated to each other in just series from the highest to the lowest. The highest degree or sphere is active, the lowest is passive or reactive. The above degrees, in their order, indicate the progression from universals and singulars to generals or compounds. But every organ again involves the same triplicity of spheres; it consists of least parts, which are congregated into larger, and these into largest. All perfections ascend and descend according to degrees, and all attributes, functions, forces, modes, in a word, all accidents, follow their substances, and are similarly discriminated. Each degree is enveloped with its common covering, and communicates with those below it thereby. There is no continuous progression from a lower degree to a higher, and in transcending that unity, we leap out of one series into another, in which all the predicates of force, form, perfection, &c., are changed and exalted. The Doctrine of Degrees enables us to obtain a distinct idea of the general principles of creation, and to observe the unity of plan that reigns throughout any given organic subject; and by showing that all things are distinct representations of end, cause, and effect, it empowers the mind to refer variety to unity, as the effect to the cause, and the cause to the end, and to recognize the whole constitution of each series as homogeneous with its principles.

"Series is the form under which the co-ordination and subordination of things, according to order and degrees, ultimately present themselves. The whole body is a series, which may be looked at either generally, from above to below, as comprising the head, the chest, and the abdomen; or universally, from within to without, as divisible into the three spheres already alluded to. All the organs of each region are a series; each organ in itself is a series; and every part in each organ likewise. In short, every thing is a series and in a series. There are both successive and simultaneous series, but the latter always arise from the former. Essences, attributes, accidents, and qualities, follow their substances in their series. Every series has its own first substance, which is more or less universal according as the series is more or less general. This first substance is its simple, unity, or least form, governing in the entire series, and by its gradual composition forming the whole. Each series has its limits, and ranges only from its minimum to its maximun. Whatever transcends those limits at either end, becomes part of another series. The compounds of all series represent their simples, and show their form, nature, and mode of action. The Doctrine of Series and Society teaches that contiguity and continuity of structure are indicative of relationship of function, and that what goes on in one part of a series, goes on also, with a determinable variety, in all the other parts: wherefore each organ is to be judged of, and analyzed, by all the others that are above and around it. In this manner, the whole series is the means of showing the function of each part of itself, and indeed of analyzing that function into a series similar to that of the whole; for the least in every series must represent an idea of its universe. Under the operation of this law, the point becomes a world analogous to the great world, but infinitely more perfect, potent, and universal.

"Such is a very brief illustration of the Doctrines of Order and Degrees, Series and Society, from which it will be evident how closely connected these doctrines are, and that they can hardly be stated without our seeming to repeat of one what has already been predicated of the others. Degrees appear to involve the distinct progressions of creation from above to below or from within to without: order, to appertain to the law of succession observed in degrees, whereby rank and height are given to excellence, priority, universality, and perfection; series, to involve the complex of the whole and the parts when created and co-existing; and society, to be the law of contiguity and relationship existing between different series, and between the parts of any single series. Perhaps it would not be far wrong to state in generals, that order and degrees involve the creating and successive; series and society, the created and simultaneous. But as we have said before, Swedenborg never stated these doctrines as promised in the ' Animal Kingdom,' but contented himself with using them as analytic instruments in the exploration of the body.

" The Doctrine of Influx involves the manner in which the lower substances, forms and forces of the body subsist, as they at first existed, from the higher and the highest; and in which the body itself subsists from the soul, as it at first existed; and the natural world from the spiritual. But there is not only an influx from within, but also from without; and by virtue of both, the body, which otherwise would be a mere power, is raised into an active force. *

" The Doctrine of Correspondence and Representation teaches that the natural sphere is the counterpart of the spiritual, and presents it in a mirror; consequently that the forms and processes of the body are images of the forms and activities of the soul, and, when seen in the right order, bring them forth and declare them. It shows that nature is the type of which the spiritual world is the ante-type, and therefore is the first school for instruction in the realities of that which is living and eternal.

" The Doctrine of Modification teaches the laws of variation and change of state in the several auras or atmospheres of the world, and in their spiritual correspondents. †

---

* " See ' Animal Kingdom,' n. 573, note o."
† " See ibid., n. 359, note c."

" What was stated of the Doctrines of Order, Degrees, Series and Society, as mutually supposing, or as it were interpenetrating each other, may be repeated generally of the whole of these doctrines, and this, because they are all but so many varied aspects of the one principle of divine truth or order. Like nature itself they are a series, each link of which involves all the others."

73. We shall now follow Swedenborg more in detail in his scientific career, with Dr. WILKINSON as our guide. He first " gathers up his character and properties " in his youth and early manhood, from 1688 to 1720, in the following words : —

" Swedenborg germinated, as nearly all children do, in theology ; rose thence into poetry and literature, speedily alternating them with mathematics ; out of these proceeded mechanical and physical studies having a reference to practice. His early manhood was devoted to active employment, and spent partly under the eye and command of the most severe of Swedish kings (Charles XII). Even at this time a widely comtemplative element glimmers from the treatises that he then produced. His ardent pursuit of geology, then a comparatively new science, was already converting itself into cosmogonical speculations. We are not indeed aware that any great brilliancy was displayed in his works up to this date, but rather great industry, fertile plans, a belief in the penetrability of problems usually given up by the learned, a gradual and experimental faculty, and an absence of precocity. In regard to general truths, he showed the evidence of a slowly-apprehending, persevering, and at last thoroughly comprehending mind. If we may use the metaphor, the masonry of his intellect was large, slow, and abiding, but by no means showy ; from the parts hitherto constructed, we could hardly prophesy whether the superstructure would be a viaduct, or a temple ; a work of bare utility, or a palace for sovereignty and state.

" On the moral side, we infer strong but controllable passions, not interfering with the balance of his mind, or the deepness of his leisure. His filial affection is brilliant, though we have no record of the extent of his obligations to his mother, whose

death took place in 1720, to his father's ' great grief and loss. '
His energy and fidelity in his business commended him to
those above him, and he was probably more indebted to intrinsic qualities for his position, than to his family connections,
or to clever courtiership on his own part.   His religious beliefs
at this time nowhere appear ; but, from indications in his
books and letters, it is certain that his mind was not inactive
upon the greatest of subjects, and that he was a plain believer
in revelation, though not without his own conjectures about its
meaning and import.   Such was Swedenborg in the spring
and flower of his long manhood." — *Life of Swedenborg, pp.
20, 21.*

In 1721 Swedenborg published " *Some Specimens of a Work
on the Principles of Chemistry, with other Treatises,*" and in 1722
" *Miscellaneous Observations connected with the Physical Sciences.*"   Dr. Wilkinson continues : —

" In the works we have just enumerated, Swedenborg began
his travels into future ages ; he manifested the tokens of a
light distinct from contemporary genius, and, with a very
decided intrepidity, attempted to scale the proximate heights of
nature.   The fortress of mineral truth was the first which he
approached, and with the most guarded preparation.   His
method was furnished by geometry and mechanics ; the laws
of the pure sciences were to be the interpreters of the facts of
chemistry and physics.   'The beginning of nature,' says he,
' is identical with the beginning of geometry ; the origin of
natural particles is due to mathematical points, just as the
origin of lines, forms, and the whole of geometry ; because
every thing in nature is geometrical, every thing in geometry
natural.'   As the phenomena of the heavens have at length
suggested an astronomy founded on mechanical laws, and involving definite forms and movements, so it was Swedenborg's
design to elicit from the phenomena of chemistry, the shapes,
motions and other conditions of the atoms or unities of bodies,
and thus to introduce clearness into our conception of chemical
combinations and decompositions.   Unlike the chemists of our
day, he made no doubt that chemistry, in its inmost bosom,
was amenable to the rules of mechanics, and that there was
nothing necessarily mysterious in it — nothing occult — nothing

but a peculiar portion of the ubiquitous clock-work of space
and time. His theory was this — that roundness is the form
adapted to motion ; that the particles of fluids, and specifically
of water, are round, hollow spherules, with a subtle matter,
identical with ether or caloric, in their interiors and interstices ; that the crust, or crustal portion, of each particle is itself
formed of lesser particles, and these again of lesser, and so
forth ; water, being in this way the sixth dimension, or the
result of the sixth grouping of the particles ; that the interstices of the fluids furnish the original moulds of the solids, and
the rows of crustal particles forced off one by one by various
agencies, furnish the matter of the same ; that after solid
particles are thus cast in their appropriate moulds, their fracture, aggregation, the filling in of their pores and interstices by
lesser particles, and a number of other and accidental conditions, provide the units of the multiform substances of which
the mineral kingdom is composed. According to this theory,
then there is but one substance in the world, namely, the first ;
the difference of things is difference of form ; there are no
positive, but only relative atoms ; no metaphysical, but only
real elements ; moreover, the heights of chemical doctrine can
be scaled by rational induction alone, planted on the basis of
analysis, synthesis and observation."

In another place he says : " There seems no reason why
the intellect should not at length reach such a position, though
how far Swedenborg has attained it, geniuses kindred to his
own, if the old method of thought be permanent, can perhaps
alone decide. We ought, however, to note that rigidly mechanical as our author's theory appears, it has at its core, in
what he calls ' the subtle matter,' a latent dynamical principle
which shapes and guides the mechanical one, and upon which
Swedenborg largely draws ; although it must be confessed that
in his theory of fire, he boldly pushes mechanics even into
that fluid restlessness, and harnesses the very horses of the
sun to the car of his ambitious geometry. Was he right, or
was he not, in supposing that knowledge of nature is only co-
extensive with mechanical ideas, and that though these do not
give motion, or life, yet where they are absent, being itself
falls through into nothingness ? We apprehend that the history

of science will tell us, upon whatever ascertained truth we fix, that that truth has a mechanical precision or basis, and that though it may have vital contents besides, yet these are only true in themselves so far as they also are similarly founded and embodied. The faith in this principle, as it is successively produced, appears in fact to be in the mind the essential outline of the new sciences; and the man who has the faith first, enters the field thereby, and is the first to reap the knowledge.

" Before dismissing the *Miscellaneous Observations*, we will remark upon the pleasant mixture of practice and theory which prevails in the work, and upon the extraordinary activity of the author's senses. Well does Sandel say, that it was not only mines he went to examine, but that ' of all that could fix the attention of a traveller there was nothing that escaped him.' His observations are told in an easy style, which win the reader's confidence, and one wishes that one had shared with his fellow-traveller, Dr. John Hessel, the way-side conversation of so instructive and amusing a pilgrimage.

" ' The Consistory of the University and the Academy of Sciences of Upsal,' as Sandel says, ' did themselves the honor of being the first to acknowledge the merit of their illustrious countryman, and to show him marks of their esteem. In 1724 the Consistory had invited him to accept the professorship of pure mathematics, vacant by the death of Nil Celsius; because, as they expressed themselves, his acceptance of the office would be for the advantage of the students and to the ornament of the University. But he declined the honor. The Academy of Sciences admitted him into the number of its members in 1729.'

" *Apropos* of pure mathematics," Dr. Wilkinson remarks here, " he makes some amusing remarks in a letter to his brother-in-law : ' I wonder at Messieurs the mathematicians,' says he, ' having lost all heart and spirit to realize that fine design of yours for an astronomical observatory. It is the fatality of mathematicians to remain chiefly in theory. I have often thought it would be a capital thing if to each ten mathematicians one good practical man were added, to lead the rest to market ; he would be of more use and mark than all the ten.' One can understand why a professorship of pure mathematics was not the chosen vocation of Swedenborg.

"During this time his books were reviewed with commendation in the *Acta Eruditorum*, published at Leipsic, the great literary and scientific organ of the times ; his contributions to art and science being thankfully acknowledged, although his theories brought the reviewers to a *non-plus*, and made them exclaim, with a postponement of which we also must avail ourselves — *let others* decide."

Dr. Wilkinson continues : —

"We are now about to enter upon another era of Swedenborg's life, when his tentative youth and manhood were past, and he came into possession of a region all his own, and presided there with an almost despotic strength of affirmation ; at which we must not wonder, for whether owing to the fault or discernment of his contemporaries, he inhabited his intellectual estate unquestioned, unlimited, uncontradicted and alone. No longer an issuer of pamphlets, or an ordinary petitioner of the arts and sciences, he had for years lain fallow of small attempts, and had accumulated the resources of his untiring industry and observation, in a work with which his great career may be said to have commenced. We allude to his *Principia*. . . . This was the first *folio* volume of three, collectively bearing the title of *Philosophical and Mineral Works*, which were completed and published at Dresden and Leipsic in the middle of 1734. . . .

"It is a strange general title which he chose — *Philosophical and Mineral Works*, but there is a meaning in this uncommon blending. Philosophy is nothing, just in proportion as it is not married with all things ; and in the *ascending* scale of its alliances, it first solicits the hand of the mineral universe, before arriving at the higher degrees. Such, at all events, was Swedenborg's method, which his title justly conveyed ; and he afterwards rose to the union of the philosophical and organic, and finally to the marriage of the philosophical and the human. It is there alone that philosophy realizes its first love, and subjugating the earthly bond, freshens itself age after age in contact with that better nature which contains the eternal.

"We must, however, sunder the philosophical and the

mineral, and look separately at each, for the author kept them perfectly free and distinct, though not disunited. And first for the treatises on mining. These were Swedenborg's offering to his business and position ; the earnest of his desire to leave the metallurgic world better than he found it. The second folio volume (p. 396) is on iron; the third (p. 516) on copper and brass. Facts speak well for their practical value. The chapters on the conversion of iron into steel were reprinted at Strasburg in 1737; and the treatise on iron was translated into French by Bouchu, and published at Paris in 1762 in the magnificent *Description des Arts et Métiers.* . . . Each volume has a threefold division; the first part on smelting, the second on assaying, the third on the chemical processes and experiments about the metals. Each volume is ushered in by a characteristic preface. In that of iron, the author avows his desire to collect and publish the mining and metallurgic secrets of different countries, and indignantly denounces those who keep them from the public for the purpose of private gain. He also shows his partiality for metallurgy as being a thoroughly practical science, ‘ all whose details are squared with works ’; yet desires ‘ that it may enter into friendly relations with chemistry, and the two join hands, and tend unitedly to one and the same goal.’ He further states, that it had been his intention to give ‘ a theoretical treatise on the metals,’ but that an integral survey of chemistry and the elemental world was necessary to such an inquiry : which again shows the practical tendency to unity, to regard his subjects in their planetary dimension, which was with him a constant method, and governed all particular investigations. In the preface on copper, we have a gorgeous description of his native mine at Falun, and a statement of the author's views of the causes and advantages of the deluge — not, however, the Noahtic, but a cosmogonic deluge ; of how it brought the treasures of the earth to the surface, and by opening the womb of the general mother, contributed to the multiplication of causes and occasions, and to the variety of telluric substances.

“ That a mind of such potent theoretical tendency should have had strength to undergo the dry labor of these compilations — that one who breathed his native air in a profound region of causes, should come for so long an abiding in the lower places of the earth, to record facts, processes and machineries, as a self-imposed task in fulfilment of his station as Assessor of Mines — this is one remarkable feature of a case where so much is remarkable, and shows how manly was his will in whatever sphere he exerted himself. The books of such a man are properly WORKS, not to be confounded for a moment with the many-colored idleness of a large class who are denominated ' thinkers.'

"The *Principia* next claims our attention, and calls forcibly to mind the truth of a remark by Mr. Emerson, that it would require ' a colony of men' to do justice to the works of Swedenborg. From the barest descriptions of iron and copper works, such as the Vulcanian workmen might themselves appreciate, we arrive by a step at the pinnacle of one of those mountains where a Newton and a Humboldt might be useful fellow-watchers of the most delicate laws on the one hand, of the panorama of a subjacent universe on the other. We pay the work no ill compliment, and have the authority of the translalor of *The Principia* with us, when we state our belief that it still belongs to the future. The following is a short account of the book from Mr. Clissold's preface : —

' The object of the *Principia* is to trace out a true *system of the world*, and in so doing the author has distributed his subject into three Parts. The First Part treats of the origin and laws of motion, and is mostly devoted to the consideration of its first principles; which are investigated philosophically, then geometrically, their existence being traced from a first natural point down to the formation of a solar vortex, and afterwards from the solar vortex to the successive constitution of the elements and of the three kingdoms of nature. From the first element to the last compound it is the author's object to show that effort or conatus to motion tends to *a spiral figure;* and that there is an actual motion of particles constituting a solar chaos, which is spiral and consequently vortical.

' In the Second Part the author applies this theory of vortical motion to the phenomena of magnetism, by which on the one hand he endeavors to test the truth of his principles, and on the other by application of the principles to explain the phenomena of magnetism; the motion of the magnetical effluvia being, as in the former case, considered to be vortical.

'In the Third Part the author applies the same principles of motion to Cosmogony, including the origination of the planetary bodies from the sun, and their vortical revolutions until they arrived at their present orbit; likewise to the constitution and the laws of the three kingdoms of nature, the animal, vegetable and mineral; so that the entire *Principia* aims to establish a true theory of vortices, founded upon a true system of corpuscular philosophy.'

"In this work, then, the author applies an active geometry to the mundane system, carrying the conception of a spiral movement down the stairway of natural being, and showing the productions and evolution of the motion in its various spheres; thereby accounting, on a single principle, for the properties of atoms, as of universes; and piercing the generative process of worlds by the same law that beholds their actual state. . . .

"In spite of the signal piety displayed throughout the *Principia*, the work was prohibited by the Papal authority in 1739, because, as Mr. Clissold thinks, it was held to contravene the position that God created all things out of nothing; and also because of the difficulty of reconciling such a process of creation as Swedenborg conceives with the literal interpretation of the first chapter of Genesis. Respecting the first reason, Mr. Clissold keenly remarks, that 'no definition is more common than that *truth is that which* is; hence, in a corresponding sense, untruth, error or falsehood is that which is *not*, and consequently that which is the genuine nonentity — or, *nothing*. Upon this ground, to say that God created all things out of *nothing*, is to attribute the origin of all things to error, and hence to evil.' "

At Dresden and Leipsic, in the same year, (1734,) with the volumes we have just described, he published, also, *Outlines of a Philosophical Argument on the Infinite, and the Final Cause of Creation; and on the Intercourse between the Soul and the Body.* Dr. Wilkinson says of this work, which he translated into English, "This work may be regarded, as in a measure, a supplement to the *Principia*, following a similar method with that treatise ; for the author here also proceeds from the common conceptions of the finite and infinite, and of the soul and the body, to construct a system of relations, which he afterwards applies to the facts of Revelation, and thus again imbeds the abstract world of truth in the real."

In another place (" Popular Sketch of Swedenborg's Philosophical Works," p. 13) he says, "This inviting book displays a noble liberty of thinking, and claims the right to philosophize on the deepest subjects ; and itself plants positive conceptions in some of the dimmest regions of inquiry ; discarding metaphysics as a mere simulation of method and knowledge, and leaning on the sciences as a needful step between common sense and universal philosophy. We may, however, also record that, like every one of Swedenborg's works, it insists or implies that the human mind has no innate ideas, but that man begins from total ignorance, and has everything to learn ; and that all knowledge may properly be questioned which is not capable of being carried on by stages and series, from less to more, and involving greater multiplicity of details, as well as increased unity of principle. Thus, those intuitions which are supposed to arrive at once at completeness, may safely be thrown into the retort of the sciences, to be re-distilled into other and more tractable forms. For progress is a law at once most general and most particular."

The publication of the preceding works gave Swedenborg a European reputation, and his correspondence was eagerly sought by Christian Wolff, and others of the learned. In 1734, Dec. 17, the Imperial Academy of Sciences, of Petersburg, appointed him a corresponding member. In 1740–41 he published, in 4to, at Amsterdam, his *Economy of the Animal Kingdom*,—" a large work," as Dr. Wilkinson says, " in which our courageous miner sank a shaft into the deep veins of the organic sciences." Probably on his return to his own country he became a Fellow, by invitation of the Royal Academy of Sciences of Stockholm, then first incorporated by a charter from the Crown, though founded as a private association by Linnæus and a few friends in 1739.

Before introducing us to the "*Economy*," Dr. Wilkinson

says, "We must now spend a few moments in tracing Swedenborg's advent to the Animal Kingdom, under which title he exclusively signified the human body.

"At the outset of his studies he lets us know in an early letter, that he had come to a ' determination to penetrate from the very cradle to the maturity of nature '—from the atoms of chemistry to the atoms of astronomy—from the smallest groups to the largest—from the molecular to the universal ; and his determination, which hitherto impelled him along the varied line of physics, now took wings, and combining with a higher nature, carried him into the realms of organization. He had touched upon this region many times in the course of his physical preamble, but gently and modestly, and as it were with pausing footsteps. In the *Miscellaneous Observations* he had admired the facile circulation of the blood in the capillaries. In a manuscript of about the same date he entered at considerable length into a doctrine of the membranes, and followed to a certain extent the same track as Hartley afterwards, in his famous scheme of vibrations. In the *Principia* he had laid down the law, that the human frame is an organism respondent to the vibrations and powers of all the mundane elements ; that there is a membrane and fluid within the body, beating time and keeping tune with airs and auras in the universe ; that man and nature are co-ordinate in the anatomical sphere ; that the body is one vast instinct acting according to the circumstances of the external world. In the *Outlines* this correspondence is re-asserted in a masterly style, and moreover the human body is opened somewhat, as a machine whose utter wisdom harmonizes with God alone, and leads right minds to God ; but in all these works the author's deductions are close to facts, comparatively timid, and limited to the service in each instance of the particular argument in hand. Yet it is easy to see from all, that he was laboriously wending his way from the first to the temple of the body, at whose altar he expected to find the soul, as the priest of the Most High God.

"It is evident that his studies for compassing this object, were of no common intensity. He made himself intimately acquainted with the works of the best anatomists of his own and preceding ages, and transcribed from their pages the descriptions suited to his purpose, forming what was in fact a manuscript encyclopædia for his own use. He made a note-book also of the technical terms of the sciences; and labored to be before his age in the *conveniences* of a scholar, as he was assuredly before it in the wants of his mind. We do not know to what extent he was a practical anatomist; he informs us that he had made use of the dissecting-room; and it is said he attended the instructions of Boerhaave, (died in 1737,) at the same time as the elder Monro; the authority for which is, however, only traditional. Be this as it may, it is plain that Swedenborg derived his knowledge of the body chiefly from plates and books, though assuredly he was one who lost no opportunity of pursuing his subject in the best way. We therefore conclude that he gained what experience he could by dissection, but relied in the main on the facts supplied by the accredited authorities, as hopeless to exceed these in accuracy, also as being more impartial over the data supplied by others, and, moreover, as feeling his own vocation to lie rather in the interpretation, than in the collection of phenomena.

"From 1741 to 1744, Swedenborg appears to have devoted himself entirely to the study of the human frame; indeed, when we consider the quantity of works and manuscripts which he has left on the subject, it is difficult to suppose otherwise than that his principal attention was directed to it from the time of the publication of his Philosophical and Mineral works,—a period of eleven years to 1744.* In 1744–45 he

---

* Considerable light is thrown on this question by the following passage taken from an untranslated portion of the "Animal Kingdom," (Vol. IV. p. 83,) where Swedenborg treats concerning the sense of hearing and the sight. He says: —

"1. *The sensations can never be explored without examining at the same time the atmospheres; for the one is most intimately connected with the other.*" After mentioning the different atmospheres and their modifications, he says: "*These things have been discussed in my Philosophical Principles, where the forms of the particles of each atmosphere are treated of and described.* 1. These things were written for our present purpose. 2. Now comes the application; I pass over all descriptions, for they are contained there."

Swedenborg's cosmological and physiological investigations were

published his *Animal Kingdom* in 4to, Parts I. and II., at the Hague, Part III. in London. . . . We shall now give a brief general account of his contributions to philosophical anatomy, including under our remarks the whole of his treatises in this department.

" *The Economy of the Animal Kingdom* treats of the blood and the organs which contain it, of the coincidence between the movements of the brain and lungs, and of the human soul; *The Animal Kingdom*, of the organs of the abdomen, of those of the chest, and of the skin. The descriptions of the best anatomists are admirably selected as a basis of facts for each chapter, and prefixed thereto, after which follows the author's induction or theory, and next a comment upon it, illustrated by the previous facts. The method obviously is, to state and study the facts first; thus to elicit from them a vintage of first principles; and then to keep and refine this wine of truths within the vessels of the facts, amplifying it wherever possible to the unfilled capacity of the latter. It is difficult to conceive a more excellent method for philosophical anatomy, or one which keeps the stages of truth-making more distinct, or more profitable to each other. There is one vessel which is all facts; there is a second which is all principles;

---

thus carried on simultaneously; for the sole purpose for which his Principia were written, was, according to his own declaration, that he might gain an insight into the mechanism of the eye. His anatomical and physiological studies were thus commenced at a much earlier period than even Dr. Wilkinson had supposed; and while Swedenborg, on the one hand, was investigating by a geometrical method the different atmospheres, finites, actives and elementaries which are discussed in his Principia, he examined, on the other, very carefully whether the results at which he arrived by his macrocosmical investigations, squared with those which he obtained by his microcosmical examinations. The peculiar excellence of this method is manifest; for Swedenborg, by its means, had a practical test of the truth of his deductions. When his macrocosmical and microcosmical results harmonized, there was a strong presumptive proof of their truth, but when they did not harmonize, it was impossible for them to be true. This method, therefore, furnishes another very powerful argument in favor of the truth of Swedenborg's theories.

there is a third in which the two come together, and the principles suggest new experiments, and the facts enlarged principles. The method is a little image of the grand circulation of the sciences, from facts or confused general truths, through universal truths, to particular or clear general truths. There is not one of such truths but becomes a fact before the method has done with it. . . .

" Swedenborg did not attempt to enter the body either abruptly or without assistance, but only after gathering up all his mind, and marshalling his forces, from the first generalizations, in which every childhood is fruitful, down to the last, which his maturity supplied. He advanced, in fact, under all the discipline and with all the machinery and strategy of his age and of his own genius, and with the name of the God of Battles and the Prince of Peace distinctly emblazoned on his tranquil banners. There is something really hushing and imposing in the measured tread of his legions, in the formal music which drills the very air where his staff of general truths is in the field, and in the absence of passion in so firm a host advancing to such important conquests.

" ' I intend to examine,' says he, ' physically and philosophically, the whole anatomy of the body; of all its viscera, abdominal and thoracic; of the genital members of both sexes ; and of the organs of the five senses. Likewise,

' The anatomy of all the parts of the cerebrum, cerebellum, medulla oblongata, and spinal marrow.

' Afterwards, the cortical substance of the two brains, and their medullary fibre; also the nervous fibre of the body, and the muscular fibre, and the causes of the forces and motion of the whole organism : diseases, moreover, those of the head particularly, or which proceed by defluxion from the brain.

' I purpose afterwards to give an introduction to Rational Psychology, consisting of certain new doctrines, through the assistance of which we may be conducted from the material organism of the body, to a knowledge of the soul which is immaterial; these are the Doctrine of Forms; the Doctrine of Order and Degrees; also, the Degrees of Series and Society; and Doctrine of Influx; the Doctrine of Corres-

pondence and Representation; lastly, the Doctrine of Modification.

'From these doctrines I come to the rational psychology
itself, which will comprise the subject of action, of external
and internal sense, of imagination and memory, also of the
affections of the animus; of the intellect, that is to say, of
thought and the will; and of the affections of the rational
mind; also of instinct.

'Lastly of the soul, and of its state in the body, its intercourse, affection and immortality; and of its state when the
body dies. The work to conclude with a Concordance of
Systems.

'From this summary or plan, the reader may see that the
end I propose to myself in the work, is a knowledge of the
soul; since this knowledge will constitute the crown of my
studies. This, then, my labors intend, and thither they aim.
. . . In order, therefore, to follow up the investigation,
and to solve the difficulty, I have chosen to approach by the
analytic way; and I think I am the first who has taken this
course professedly.

'To accomplish this grand end I enter the circus, designing
to consider and examine thoroughly the whole world or
microcosm which the soul inhabits; for I think it is vain to
seek her anywhere but in her own kingdom. . . .

'When my task is accomplished, I am then admitted by
common consent to the soul, who, sitting like a queen in her
throne of state, the body, dispenses laws, and governs all
things by her good pleasure, but yet by order and by truth.
This will be the crown of my toils, when I shall have
completed my course in this most spacious arena. But in
olden time, before any racer could merit the crown, he was
commanded to run seven times round the goal, which also I
have determined here to do. . . .

'I am, therefore, resolved to allow myself no respite, until
I have run through the whole field to the very goal, or until
I have traversed the universal animal kingdom to the soul.
Thus I hope, that by bending my course inwards continually,
I shall open all the doors that lead to her, *and at length con-
template the soul itself: by the divine permission.*'

"One of his MS.* again places these designs in a clear light. ' I have gone through this anatomy,' says he, ' with the single end of investigating the soul. It will be a satisfaction to me if my labors be of any use to the anatomical and medical world, but a still greater satisfaction if I afford any light towards the investigation of the soul.' The whole course of the sciences, he observes, has aimed at this effect. ' The learned world has striven hither without any exception ; for what else has it attempted, than the ability to speak from general principles, and to act synthetically on the lower sphere ; such, however, is angelic perfection, such is heavenly science ; such also was the first natural science, and such ambition is, therefore, innate in ourselves ; thus we too strain towards the integrity of our first parent, who concluded from principles to all effects, and not only saw universal nature beneath him, but commanded its subject spheres. All science by this account is the way back to a divine magic and a spiritual seership. Hence,' he adds, ' our mighty interest in attaining to the principles of truth.' He concludes by avowing that ' he knows he shall have the reader's ear, if the latter be only persuaded that his end is God's glory and public good, and not his own gain and praise.'

" His object, then, was to open a new way through natural knowledge to religious faith, and to transfer to Christianity the title-deeds of the sciences."

To the Two Parts of the *Economy of the Animal Kingdom*, the contents of which have been noticed above, Dr. Wilkinson has added a third, left in manuscript by our Author. This part has not yet been translated into English, but we expect to embody a translation of it in a future American edition of the author's Complete Works. This part treats principally *De Fibra*—of the Human Fibre. "A title at which," Dr. Wilkinson says, " the physiologist may possibly smile, though the unlearned reader will know better ; for is it not given in common language, that there is *a lax fibre*, an

---

* "Published by Dr. Tafel as the Seventh Part of *The Animal Kingdom*."

irritable fibre, a firm fibre, and so forth, lying at the basis of particular temperaments and constitutions?" He then proceeds to give us an idea of the contents of the volume. " This Third Part of the *Economy,*" he says, " expounds the various manners in which the beams and timbers of the body are laid ; specifically the construction of the frame ; somewhat as the *Principia* unfolds the elementary construction of the universe. It also considers the different kinds of fibres ; the form of their fluxion, and the Doctrine of Forms generally; and lastly, in a most masterly style, nay, with a power of observation and analysis new in medicine, the Diseases of the Fibres. In the weightiness of its truths, in sustained order of exposition, in felicity of phrase, and in finish and completeness, it is not surpassed by any scientific work that the author published : moreover, it contains so much that is peculiar, as to form an indispensable addition to his other volumes."

Connected with the same period of Swedenborg's life as the *Economy,* is another volume of MSS., edited by Dr. Wilkinson, both in Latin and English, under the title of " *Posthumous Tracts,*" the Latin title being, " *Opuscula quaedam Argumenti Philosophici.*"—These tracts are for the most part condensed statements of the subjects and arguments of the larger works, to the study of which they furnish good introductions. Another manuscript which belongs to the same series with the *Economy,* and is mentioned in the Third Part of that work as the Part on Correspondences (n. 378), is the " *Hieroglyphic Key,*" which is likewise edited in the original language, and translated into English by Dr. Wilkinson. This tract is an attempt to eliminate a natural doctrine of correspondences, and to show its application by examples.

After taking a survey of all the works belonging to this phase of Swedenborg's philosophical and scientific life, Dr. Wilkinson speaks of the execution of the " Animal Kingdom " in the following terms :—

" This, the last produced, is the noblest of Swedenborg's works on the human frame. The first two Parts of this treatise appeared in the author's 55th, the Third Part in his 57th year. There is in it the clearness of the faultless logician ; the utmost severity of the inductive reasoner ; the order of the consummate philosophical architect; the beauty, freedom and universal cordiality of the mighty poet; the strength of the giant, the playfulness of a child. Never was the path of science so aspiring, or strewn with such lovely and legitimate flowers, as in these astonishing volumes. But praise is a needless tribute to their goodness: they point only to applications and works, and beseech us not to stand long in the stupefaction of amazement, but to gather up our energies and summon our understanding for whatever the arts and sciences have yet to contribute to the true advancement of our race. Those only follow their spirit, who are actively endeavoring to extend their principles in new fields, unexplored even by Swedenborg.

"These are among the great works which revolutionize our consciousness, and engender new wants, and a new mind, in the human soul. And yet it is surprising how little Swedenborg was controversial or directly critical: with the exception of his Fragment on Leibnitz, he scarcely wages formal battle with another writer. Neither scolding science for its servility, nor metaphysical philosophy for its artful obscurations, he supplies elevated truths on the stage of his own mind, and leaves them to gain their prevalence without a syllable of literary recommendation. Verily a safe and great, yea, and the only course, for these principles inhabit a region where they have no opponents; nay, where the old falsities are clean out of their senses, and, without being aware of the consequences of the admission, confess to nothing at all."—*Popular Sketch*, etc. Dr. Wilkinson continues in his *Life of Swedenborg* :—

" Swedenborg's observations and facts are as superior to the ordinary foundations, as his method is better than the procedures which are still in vogue. His power of remark is more physiognomical than in any previous writer with whom we are acquainted. Other collectors of facts rushed at once into dissection and violence, and broke through the speaking face of things in their impatience. He, on the other hand, proceeded cautiously and tenderly, and only cut the skin when he had exhausted its looks and expressions, conversing first with the face, then with other parts of the surface, and at last with the inner inexpressive parts, the poor dumb creatures, which were the sole company of the anatomists. He was the most grandly

superficial writer who had then arisen,—a rare qualification
in its good sense, and which gives the benefit of travel to the
sciences, enabling them to take liberal views of their materials;
a qualification, moreover, which is the preparative for depth,
for the whole surface alone leads us to the centre, and when
complete is itself an apparent sphere, the most perfect of scientific forms. Accordingly, when Swedenborg goes upwards
or inwards, he is guided· to the sun, or the core, by myriads
of rays from the translucent skin, and ubiquitous fingers invite
and beckon him into the depths. Such is nature's privilege
for those who beseech her permissions, and read the wishes of
her broader lineaments.

" In illustration of these remarks we have only space to
allude to one fact and doctrine made use of by our author in
the foregoing works, but that one is of the utmost value both
in his system and history ; we mean his doctrine of respiration. Let any reader think for a moment of what he experiences when he breathes, and attend to the act. He will find
that his whole frame heaves and subsides at the time ; face,
chest, stomach, and limbs are all actuated by his respiration.
His sense is, that not only his lungs but his entire body breathes.
Here is a large surface of fact ; the foundation-doctrine of any
doctrine of respiration. The most unlearned experience contains it as well as the most learned, and often much more
vividly, for learning sometimes hinders the breath ; the plethora
of science and philosophy confines the heaving to the chest
alone, and the learned puff and pant. Now mark what
Swedenborg elicited from this fact, because he accepted it as a
material for science. If the whole man breathes or heaves,
so also do the organs which he contains, for they are necessarily drawn outwards by the rising of the surface ; therefore
they all breathe. What do they breathe? Two elements are
omnipresent in them, the blood-vessels and the nerves, the one
giving them pabulum, the other life. They draw then into
themselves blood, and life or nervous spirit. Each does this
according to its own form ; each, therefore, has a free individuality like the whole man ; each takes its food, the blood, when
it chooses ; each wills into itself the life according to its desires.
The man is made up of manlike parts ; his freedom is an

aggregate of a host of atomic, organical freedoms. The heart does not cram them with its blood, but each, like the man himself, takes what it thinks right; the brain and nerves do not force upon them a heterogeneous life, but each kindles itself with appropriate life, according to what it already has, and what it wants to have. There is character and individuality in every molecule; and the mind is properly built upon faculties analogous to its own, conferred upon material organs. It handles nature by the willing correspondence of nature in this high machine, with its own essential attributes. The body is a mind and soul of flesh.

"But furthermore, thought commences and corresponds with respiration. The reader has before attended to the presence of the heaving over the body; now let him *feel his thoughts*, and he will see that they, too, heave with the mass. When he entertains a long thought, he draws a long breath; when he thinks quickly, his breath vibrates with rapid alternations; when the tempest of anger shakes his mind, his breath is tumultuous; when his soul is deep and tranquil, so his respiration; when success inflates him, his lungs are tumid as his conceits. Let him make a trial of the contrary: let him endeavor to think in long stretches at the same time that he breathes in fits, and he will find that it is impossible; that in this case the chopping lungs will needs mince his thoughts. Now the mind dwells in the brain, and it is the brain, therefore, which shares the varying fortunes of the breathing. It is strange that this correspondence between the states of the brain or mind and the lungs has not been admitted in science, for it holds in every case, in every moment. In truth it is so unfailing, and so near to the centre of sense, that this has made it difficult to regard it as an object; for if you only try to think upon the breathing, in consequence of the fixation of thought you stop the breath that very moment, and only re-commence it when the thought can no longer hold, that is to say, when the brain has need to expire. Now Swedenborg, with amazing observation and sagacity, has made a regular study of this ratio between the respiration and the thoughts and emotions; he shows in detail that the two correspond exactly, and moreover that their correspondence is one of the long-sought links between the soul and the body, whereby every thought is represented and carried out momentaneously in the expanse of the human frame, which it penetrates by vicegerent motions or states. Thus, if the mind is tranquil, the body is similarly tranquil, and the two are as one, that is to say, *united*; if the mind is perturbed, the body is likewise so in the most exact similitude; if the mind loves what is high, the body looks to it and aspires to reach it; and while the two work for each other, that is to say, so long as health sufficient lasts, there *must* be connection between them, or the all-knowing soul would not profit by its own tool, its very double in the world. It is difficult to give a more plain or excellent reason of the tie between the body and the soul, than that the latter finds the body absolutely to its mind; while, on the other hand, the living body clings to the soul, because it wants a friendly superior life to infuse and direct its life. . . . . .

" Of Swedenborg's contributions to science, we have recorded the above as among the most valuable, and as incalculable in its results both upon thought and practice. In stating, however, any one point as remarkable in such a genius, we are in danger of having it understood that his claims in this respect can be enumerated by any critic or biographer. On the contrary, we should have to write a volume were we to devote but a few lines to each detail of his excessive fruitfulness. Suffice it to say, that there is no inquirer into the human body, either for the purposes of medical or general intelligence, above all, there is no philosophical anatomist, who has done justice to himself, unless he has humbly read and studied—not turned over and conceitedly dismissed — the *Economy* and *Animal Kingdom* of Swedenborg. The works, of course, are *past* as records of anatomical facts, but in general facts that are bigger than anatomy, they have not been excelled, and none but a mean pride of science, or an inaptitude for high reasons, would deter the inquirer from the light he may here acquire, in spite of meeting a few obsolete notions, or a few hundreds of incomplete experiments.

" The reception of Swedenborg's natural philosophy by the world furnishes a negative event of some interest in his biography. So long as he confined himself to the practical sphere, his treatises met with a fair share of approval, both in his own country and throughout Europe ; but the moment his own genius appeared, it consigned him, as we said at the outset, to temporary oblivion—a goal at which he arrived after passing through some preliminary opprobrium. *The Transactions of the Learned*, ('*Acta Eruditorum*,') published at Leipsic, was not slow to discover his uncommon qualities, or to denounce them. In February, 1722, the reviewer said of his *Chemical Specimens*, 'The author has displayed great abilities and equal industry ; but how far he has followed truth in his theories, let others decide.' In 1735, in reviewing his *Outlines of the Infinite*, the same journal charged him with materialism. And in 1747, it gave a derisive notice of his *Animal Kingdom*, ending with the significant words : 'So much for Swedenborgian dreams.'

" In the same year as the third part of the *Animal Kingdom*, i. e., in 1745, Swedenborg published in London another work in two parts, *On the Worship and Love of God*. This work may be regarded as an attempted bridge from philosophy to theology ; an arch thrown over from the side of nature towards the unseen shore of the land of life. As it is to this extent a link, so it has some of the ambiguity which attaches to transitional things, and accordingly by those who judge it from either side, may be misunderstood. For my part I see in its exuberant lines no want of clear truth, but simply the joy and recreation of one goal attained ; the harvest home of a scientific cycle ; the euthanasia of a noble intellect peacefully sinking back into its own spiritual country ; the Pentecost thence of new tongues as of fire, in which every man is addressed in his own language wherein he was born,—the language not of words, but of things. For here has science become art, and is identified with nature in the very middle and thickest of her beauty. Here the forgotten lore of antiquity begins to be restored, and principles ratified into truths take body in a mythological narrative, the first creation of the kind since the dawn of the scientific ages. Here the doctrine of Correspondences commences to re-assert its sublime prerogative, of bearing to man the teeming spirit of heaven in the cups of nature. This, I think, accounts for the singularity of the work; for its standing in a manner by itself among the author's writings. For the rest, if it be still reckoned scientific or philosophical, we must nevertheless say, that it is an offering up of both science and philosophy upon the altar of religion. Of its merits in this respect there can, I imagine, be but one opinion. Whatever of admiration we have felt for Swedenborg's former efforts, only increases as we enter the interior of this august natural temple. A new wealth of principles, a radiant, even power such as peace alone can communicate, a discourse of order persuasively convincing, an affecting and substantial beauty more deep than poetry, a luxuriance of ornament instinct with the life of the subject; intellect, imagination, fancy, unitedly awake in a lovely vision of primeval times; wisdom, too, making all things human: such is an imperfect enumeration of the qualities which enter into this ripe fruit of the native genius of Swedenborg. Whether in fulness or loftiness, I know of nothing similar to it—of nothing second to it—in mere human literature."—*Popular Sketch*, etc.

" The first portion of the work, and for the scientific philosopher probably its finest portion, represents the origin and progression of this universe from the sun, and specifically the origin of our own planet, with the reign of the general spring, and the consequent development of the first mineral, vegetable and animal kingdoms, one from another in succession; for nature at the beginning was big with the principles of all things, and the earth was near to its parent sun, with as yet no atmosphere but the serene, supernal ether. Next we are led to the human body, wrought by the infinite in the ovum furnished by the Tree of Life, in the innermost focus of the spring, and the paradise of Paradise: creation rising thus in a glorious pile, centre above centre. Thereafter we have the infancy and growth of the mind of the first-born in the state of integrity and innocence; with its elevation into three new kingdoms. Then there is the birth of Eve, and the manner of it, and her education by ministering spirits, and her betrothal and marriage to Adam. And ' this,' as Swedenborg concludes, ' was the sixth scene on the world's stage.' And the seventh was yet to come."

On taking a general view of Swedenborg's scientific labors,

and comparing them with the plan which he had laid out for himself in the beginning, Dr. Wilkinson says : " Swedenborg has fulfilled, it is true, but a small portion of his plan, being led to something better than the direct reconstruction of the sciences ; but still it is satisfactory to know, that his manuscripts, when we can publish them, will give an outline of his views on all the subjects of which he intended to treat. Thus there is, as before noticed, a continuation of the *Chemical Specimens;* there is also a continuation of the *Animal Kingdom*, a treatise *On the Brain*, an important manuscript *On Generation*, [since published in Latin by Dr. Tafel, and translated into English by Dr. Wilkinson,] a treatise *On the Human Mind*, namely, the five senses, and the various faculties, both concrete and abstract, the human loves and passions, and whatever follows therefrom [since published in Latin by Dr. Tafel, as Vols. IV. and VII. of the *Animal Kingdom*, but not yet translated into English]."

A list of the unpublished manuscripts of Swedenborg, treating on scientific subjects, will be given in the last chapter of our volume.

74. Some pertinent remarks on Swedenborg's treatment of facts are contained in the " *New Church Advocate*," Vol. II., pp. 236, etc.

" In judging of the philosophical facts of Swedenborg, we must not rest in the fact that he was not acquainted with the researches of Faraday, or Davy, or Berzelius or Liebig ; but we must first ask ourselves what his purpose and direction was, then inquire whether the experimental knowledge of his time was sufficient for him in this respect ; and last of all we may endeavor to find out whether particular facts of recent discovery will supply corroborations of his principles.

" At first, indeed, . . . it is too likely that not much direct relation will be found to exist between Swedenborg's philosophy and the facts of the day. But in the mean time let us *hold* that philosophy with an unrelaxing grasp. We have this attestation of its truth—that it is worthy of God and worthy of man : . . . that there are no principles to oppose it, and no *general* facts : that in God's works ' the highest reason is always the truest,' and that the reason given in Swedenborg's writings is the highest yet declared : that the contemplation of it tends to make man wiser and better, and to make his ' veneration of the Deity co-extensive with his wisdom, and as constant as the operation of his senses.' *   In fact, there is something of the same reason to hold to the philosophy of Swedenborg, even although it appear to lie open to the small fire of science, as there is to hold to Christianity in opposition to the atheists and deists, even although the letter of Scripture involve a host of petty difficulties and seeming contrarieties which no critic has yet been able to solve. Let us not throw away a mighty good, which is sound to the heart's core, because we do not find in it some little detail or details, which science with her microscopic eyes has concluded to be essentials. These may come afterwards, if they are wanted; or on the other hand, we may attain to more comprehensive states, and find the largeness of things more honest and significative than the details : we may perchance find all we want in the broad streets of creation.

" What we desire to advance is this : that if a principle, whether natural, moral or spiritual, approve itself to all the faculties of the mind, *excepting the senses*, . . . then, in despite of the senses, or failing their corroboration, such principle must still be maintained ; and must bide its time, and by incessant rational efforts on our part, it must be used to convert the inverted senses, and their sphere to its side. The senses, therefore, may be made use of to confirm it ; but they are not to be allowed an active power in the case ; nor are they to raise up serpent heads against that which is proved to be good and true in a better region than theirs.

" What then is to become of *facts?* Are we prepared to revert to those times when experience, such as we now have

---

* We may add here as another reason the following statement of Prof. von Görres : " There nowhere appears in the writings of Swedenborg a self-destroying contradiction, nothing abrupt, disjointed, or unconnected, or arbitary, or illogical, . . . but everything that he writes is so connected and uninterrupted, as to present a perfect whole."

it, was not in being, and the observations of science were almost coincident with those of daily life; when the face of nature revealed nearly all that was known of her, and the interiors of things had been scarcely disturbed by the rudely analytic hand of man? This is clearly impossible. The world cannot undo what it has already done, nor forget what it knows. Yet if the truth must be told, facts have yet to obtain their real place, and to be estimated at their proper value. They have yet to be sorted into direct, and remote or oblique facts.* At present, science mingles all together in one confused heap. Let us dwell a little longer upon this division.

" First, however, we will venture to affirm, that there were multitudes of facts known in Swedenborg's day, and known moreover to Swedenborg himself, which did not find any direct place in the series of his reasonings. In this respect the present state of science does not differ, *in essence*, from the state of science in his time; but only in magnitude and multitude. There is no principle involved in the case as affecting modern science; but only the circumstance, that there are *many more* facts now which Swedenborg would not have thought it worth his while to use, than when he wrote his *Principia*. We indeed admit fully that there are also many which would have furnished him with ready corroborations; but on this it is not our intention to dwell in this review.

" To return to Facts, they occupy in the scientific world something like the same place which Property occupies in our Houses of Parliament : they are the only thing, or nearly the only thing, which is legislated for, ' protected,' and declared to have ' rights' in the human mind. They are in truth ' protected ' at the expense of our brains. . . . . Now we think the brains require the protection, at least in this case. ' Is not life more than meat, and the body than raiment ?'

" We shall now attempt to say a few things respecting the

---

* The learned writer of the above article will allow us to leave out for the present his allusion to a third kind of facts—"contrarious or inverse facts "—which only complicate the subject, and to call attention only to those two kinds of facts which Swedenborg himself specifies in the extract quoted from him below by the writer.

division among facts. It is stated by Swedenborg in the *Principia*, where he treats of the 'Means conducing to True Philosophy,' that 'in order to acquire a knowledge of natural principles,—in order to conceive the theory of nature,—there is no occasion for such an infinite variety of phenomena as some persons deem necessary: that we need only the more important, or such as bear directly and proximately upon the point; and that we do *not* need those that diverge obliquely and remotely from the series and powers of the world: that the latter as being remote and merely collateral, *may be safely laid aside* as not essential; and that they would rather tend to divert the mind from the object, than to lead it onward in the great high road of its investigation.' (Part i. chap. i. n. 1.) Now this at once shows the propriety of sifting facts into two classes; one class comprising those which are in the direct order of creation, . . . the other class consisting of those which are oblique, or divergent from the main line. . . .

" If this view be correct, what are we to think of the indiscriminate love of natural facts? Is it a love of truth, or does it proceed from a love of truth? Must we not regard it as the case of compound darkness of intellect,—of a state in which the blindness of obscurity is combined with the blindness of error? Must we not counsel our brethren and the world to begin in science the work of separation, preparatory to throwing aside much of the vast heap of facts which is now accumulated? We are well aware that this will be startling advice. The miser and his money-bags are not easily parted, even though it be plainly proved to him that he cannot use his possessions. The love of property and the love of use are distinct things. Within the last half-century the world has built new barns, and laid up goods therein for many years. It has said: ' Soul, take thine ease; facts are too multitudinous for any theory to comprehend them: happily in this way thou hast gotten rid of theory and spirituality; and thy sleep may now be undisturbed after ages of restlessness and discomfort.' But are we to follow this spirit? Are we to countenance the lazy work of carrying fresh sand and pebbles to the unbuilt mountain of them which exists already? Are we not, on the contrary, to be architects of a new building; to use what is available in the old and new materials ; and without reserve, and without a superstitious reverence for facts, firmly and resolutely to put aside whatever is unfit for our purpose ? Thus philosophy, under the auspices of religion, will raise her head, and elevate science by her side, and the human understanding will no longer be dragged like a slave at the chariot-wheels of circumstance.

"But we hear it whispered, that by assuming this discretional power over facts, we run the danger of generating new scholasticism ; that we go away from nature, and betake ourselves to chopping endless and fruitless logic; that history presents us with ' dark ages ' as a warning against this course ; and that if we follow it, we shall carry back knowledge into cells and cloisters, and institute a new race of Aquinases, and other most subtle doctors. To this we reply, that the useless aspect of the scholastics was *not* due to the circumstance of their using their intellects, and making their senses subservient ; it was mainly due to the mistiness of their intellects themselves, and to their having no true principles to guide them in the interpretation of nature, or the Word. They could not instruct the ignorant, or give light to the world at large, because they had no *organic ideas* in their own heads. Not that they had too many ideas, and too few facts, but that their ideas, having no power of assimilation, were unable to take shape and body in the ultimate world. Instead of being as souls that could realize themselves and present an image of creative order, they were like puffs of wind in the bag of Æolus, blowing indeed where they listed, but developing no good and no beauty such as the common heart or eye could recognize and love. Therefore they could neither concentrate nor diffuse knowledge, nor build their house upon that rock of ultimate truths which affords the mind a secure position amid the ceaseless contingency and change of things. But widely different from this was the case with Swedenborg; as it will also be with those who study his philosophical and scientific doctrines for the sake of use. To them, to use the words of Carlyle, ' this vague, shoreless universe will be a firm city—a dwelling which they know.'

"We hope we have now emboldened the reader to think,

that if natural facts are to have votes in matters affecting high truths and principles, yet that this does not necessarily apply to all facts, and consequently the suffrage is not universal in this sphere; that some facts are without present qualification, being dumb and insignificant; and that others are downright aliens and enemies, and must not vote, because they mean no good to the human mind.

"This is no uncomfortable or illiberal doctrine, but one imperatively necessary for self-preservation and sound progress. If we are always to be undermining our buildings in order to inspect the strength of their foundations, to what height can we carry them, or with what safety can we abide within their walls? The truth is, that when legitimately acquired general experience confirms a principle, it is as if a law had been passed after solemn debate in some great national assembly; no individual can thenceforth successfully question it, nor can it be repealed excepting by the same or similar power to that which called it into existence. So it is with the philosophical and scientific principles of Swedenborg. The learned world, by the efforts of ages, had presented him with a certain general experience; this he accepted, and still farther generalized and eliminated it; and when it was thus prepared, he was gifted to impregnate it with true principles of order, and so it grew into an organic human body. The body thus formed has indeed a power of assimilation; but the condition is, that the food shall submit to the body, and not the body to the food; and that whatever is useless, or becomes so, shall be put aside, or cast into the drought."

75. "*What is the Import of the Scientific System which Swedenborg has left?*"

To this question DR. WILKINSON gives the following answer:—

"We have seen that this system arose from a catholic experience and observation, and carried the particular sciences which it traversed, beyond the limit of class-cultivation. We have seen that the philosophic miner brought forth the human frame from the colleges of medicine, and conferred the right to know it upon all who study universal knowledge. We have also seen that he incorporated the formulas of the old philosophy, making them no longer abstractions, but the life or order of these sciences. We may now then state that Swedenborg's philosophy attains its summit in the marriage of the scholasticism and common sense, with the sciences, of his age; in the consummation of which marriage his especial genius was exerted and exhausted. In him the oldest and newest spirit met in one; reverence and innovation were evenly mingled; nothing ancient was superseded, though pressed into the current service of the century. He was one of the links that connect bygone ages with to-day, breathing for us among the lost truths of the past, and perpetuating them in unnoticed forms along the stream of the future. He lived, however, thoroughly in his own age, and was far before his contemporaries, only because others did not, or could not, use the entire powers of its sphere. We regard him therefore as an honest representative of the eighteenth century. He, in his line, gives us the best estimate of the all which any man could do in Europe at that period."

In another place he says :—

" Briefly to sum up the gain which we derive from these books of Swedenborg, we may say that *mathematically* and *physically* they are to human anatomy, what the modern astronomy is to the heavens; they rescue it from the condition of a mere *tableau,* in which there is no order, depth, or centre, and contemplate it as a solid microcosm, in which corporeal principles, causes and effects succeed each other in real order; wherein force and motion are implied and supplied for the active existence of the body. . . ." Again,—

" To sum up in two words the distinguishing feature of all these works, it may be said to consist in their WISDOM AND INTEGRALITY. By their *wisdom* I mean the attainment of principles in nature that may practically benefit the human mind, and the statement of which is with reference to this result. Their *integrality*, on the other hand, signifies that these principles have the willing support of all the sciences, and to use Lord Bacon's words, are no ' islands cut off from other lands, but continents which join them;' each principle being a common or general truth subsisting as such from the unanimous suffrage of nature. But permit me to illustrate this by an example. Although the human body is a substance by itself, yet it holds communication with the entire universe. For we stand with our feet upon the ground; we eat the fruits of the earth; we breathe its atmosphere; we live in its auras; we appropriate its existence and meaning with our senses and other faculties. Now as the body in this wise embraces in its own ends the universe, so the doctrine of the body must in the same manner comprise the doctrine of the universe. And therefore the integrality of these writings, on this head, is thus:—The doctrine of the brain is confirmed and extended by the doctrine of the auras, and of *all with which the brain is connected.* The doctrine of the lungs comprehends that of the atmosphere, &c.; the doctrine of the blood, that of the earth; and in general the entire theory of organization communes with the entire theories of psychology and physics, even as man subsists in the world, and receives and gives in the sphere of nature. Thus, as Swedenborg says, The discernment of universal connection and continuity amounts to the discovery of truth.

" With regard to the intellectual newness of these works, it lies perhaps in the just embodiment of the spiritual in the mechanical. These two spheres, or this world and the higher world, had been, till Swedenborg arose, disjoined, and hostile to each other : but happily he has commenced a reconciliation between them, and the mechanical is no longer low or dead, or the spiritual void and intangible. A great hope this for all time. For the mechanical in its various degrees up to the spiritual-formal, is the expression of all means and causes— of all intellect—of all definite knowledge—of all precise ways of action. An unmechanical state of finite existence would exclude the operancy of the Divine Wisdom and Righteousness ; an unmechanized faculty, an unclothed mind, in man— and metaphysics has been such a faculty—would look—and has looked—upon the creature as non-existent,—upon the Creator as a nonentity ; while as for action, it would have no body to execute it, no distinct mind to conceive it, no will but towards waste and dispersion. To such a faculty immortality would be a contradiction. How signal then is the Providence which has once again invested us with understanding, and pointed out in these writings the created amity between spirit and nature, the soul and the body, through the medium of forms ' accommodated at once to the beginning of motion and to the reception of life.' "

11*

VI.

IMPORTANCE OF SWEDENBORG'S PHYSIOLOG-
ICAL WORKS, ESPECIALLY FOR THE MEDICAL
PROFESSION.

76. From a "Brief Review of Swedenborg's 'Animal Kingdom,'" by a celebrated Professor of Anatomy at one of our Universities, in the *Phrenological Almanac*, or *Psychological Journal*, for 1844, Glasgow, we extract the following :—

"These works being strictly scientific, have of course nothing whatever to do with the peculiar theological views of the author; and we trust they will be received by the medical profession, to which they more particularly belong, with that favor to which their merits may justly lay claim. They may perhaps be viewed as the commencement of that revival of old medical authors, which the projected publications of the Sydenham Society will continue and complete. For in reality these works give us the opinions of some of the ancient anatomists, and for the most part in their own words—opinions founded on minute research and accurate observations, the old medical philosophers being very generally allowed to have been much better observers than the moderns. This plan, upon which Swedenborg formed his works on the natural sciences, is perhaps peculiar to himself. There is no doubt he was acquainted with anatomy practically, but he seems to have considered that the celebrated anatomists who had gone before him were better authorities than himself. Accordingly in the work before us the descriptions of the organs are taken *verbatim* from the works of Heister, Malpighi, Swammerdam, Boerhaave, Winslow, etc., etc., and from their descriptions he deduces opinions of his own, which, if not correct, are certainly ingenious, and indicate powers of mind, original, acute, and deeply imbued with abstract truths. The translator, in his preface, states that the ' merits of the work lie principally in its

(126)

principles and doctrines, and only secondary in its details. The facts made use of by Swedenborg were of course the facts of his own day—the facts of perhaps the most illustrious anatomists who ever lived—but still imperfect, as the facts of our day will be imperfect in the year 1943. Principles, however, are immortal, and the roll of centuries serves only to confirm and establish them. They have, moreover, a power of eliminating and throwing off spurious facts, when such facts have served a provisional end, and more real data are prepared to take their places. The principles of Swedenborg, the translator believes, have this increasing root in the world, and this power: he believes that they are more true now to the rational inquirer than they could possibly be to the men of Swedenborg's own day;—that wherever he adopted false facts, they furnished a worse basis for his system than the more solid materials of modern discovery.' "—(Preface, p. 8.)

The Professor then gives an extensive review of the contents of the volume, and continues :—

" Upon the whole, we have derived much pleasure, and not a little profit, from the perusal of this volume. We shall hail with satisfaction the appearance of the other volumes, when we shall be more at home in reading and commenting on the author's views of the mortal part of man : the brain and nervous system, with his moral and intellectual faculties. Meantime we beg to close this article by quoting a few sentences from the very able article ' Swedenborg,' in the *Penny Cyclopædia*, in which are summed up, in a very succinct manner, his peculiar views concerning the human body."—(This extract constitutes n. 70 of the present volume.)

77. *From the London Forceps, for November,* 1844.

" This (the ' Animal Kingdom ') is the most remarkable theory of the human body that has ever fallen into our hands ; and by Emanuel Swedenborg, too ! a man whom we had always been taught to regard as either a fool, a madman, or an impostor, or perhaps an undefinable compound of all three. Wonders, it seems, never *will* cease, and therefore it were better henceforth to look out for them, and accept them whenever they present themselves, and make them into ordinary things in that way.   For thereby we may be saved from making wonderful asses of ourselves and our craft, for enlightened posterity to laugh at.

"To return to our book, we can honestly assure our readers (which is more than would be safe to do in all cases), that we have carefully read through both volumes of it, bulky though they be, and have gained much philosophical insight from it into the chains of ends and causes that govern in the human organism.   What has the world been doing for the past century, to let this great system slumber on the shelf, and to run after a host of little bluebottles of hypotheses which were never framed to live for more than a short part of a single season?   It is clear that it yet 'knows nothing of its greatest men.'   The fact is, it has been making money, or trying to make it, and grubbing after worthless reputation, until it has lost its eyesight for the stars of heaven, and the sun that is shining above it.

"Emanuel Swedenborg's doctrine is altogether the widest thing of the kind which medical literature affords, and cast into an artistical shape of consummate beauty.   Under the rich drapery of ornament which diversifies his pages, there runs a framework of the truest reasoning.   The book is a perfect mine of principles, far exceeding in intellectual wealth, and surpassing in elevation, the finest efforts of Lord Bacon's genius.   It treats of the loftiest subjects without abstruseness, being all ultimately referable to the common sense of mankind.   Unlike the German transcendentalists, this gifted Swede fulfils both the requisites of the true philosopher; he is one ' to whom the lowest things ascend, and the highest descend, who is the equal and kindly brother of all.'   There is no trifling about him, but he sets forth his opinions, irrespective of controversy, with a plainness of affirmation which cannot be mistaken; and in such close and direct terms, that to give a full idea of his system in other words would require that we lesser men should write larger volumes than his own.

"The plan of the work is this: Swedenborg first gives extracts from the greatest anatomists of his own and former times, such as Malpighi, Leuwenhoek, Morgagni, Swammerdam, Heister, Winslow, etc., etc., so that these volumes contain a body of old anatomy (translated now into close English) such as cannot be met with in this shape elsewhere. He then gives his own unincumbered deductions from this 'experience,' under the heading 'analysis.' Each organ of the thorax and abdomen in this way has a two-fold chapter allotted to its consideration, which chapter is a complete little essay, or we may say, epic, upon the subject. The philosophical unity of the work is astonishing, and serves to unlock the abstrusest organs, such as the spleen, thymus gland, super-renal capsules, and other parts upon which Swedenborg has dilated with an analytic efficacy which the moderns have not even approached; and of which the ancients afforded scarcely an indication. Upon these more mysterious organs, we think his views most suggestive and valuable, and worthy of the whole attention of the better minds of the medical profession. Of the doctrine of series, since called by the less appropriate term, 'homology,' he has afforded the most singular illustrations, not confining himself to the law of series in the solids, but boldly pushing it into the domain of the fluids, and this with an energy of purpose, and a strength of conception and execution, such as is rarely shown by 'any nine men in these degenerate days.' We opened this book with surprise, a surprise grounded upon the name and fame of the author, and the daring affirmative stand which he takes *in limine;* we close it with a deep-laid wonder, and with an anxious wish that it may not appeal in vain to a profession which may gain so much, both morally, intellectually, and scientifically, from the priceless truths contained in its pages."

78. *From the London Medical Gazette, August* 5, 1842.

"To the EDITOR of the MEDICAL GAZETTE:

" SIR—In a late number of the Penny Cyclopædia of the Society for the Diffusion of Useful Knowledge, the claims of Swedenborg as a human physiologist are urged at length, and some account given of his peculiar doctrines. He is also mentioned with approbation in Fletcher's ' Physiology,' and in the ' Medical Repository' for 1829. Prevost and Dumas, in France, have lately taken the pains to give a critique on his chemical theories. In Germany, Wolfgang Menzel relates that Goethe was a student of his works, which is, *a priori*, rendered probable by the fact, that something very like Goethe's morphological theory pervades the system of Swedenborg. The ' Monthly Magazine ' for May and June, 1841, and the ' British Magazine ' for the current month, also contain some notices of Swedenborg as a writer on physical sciences." The writer encloses a translation of the chapter " on the Intestines " from the " Animal Kingdom," and requests an insertion of this chapter in the " Medical Gazette ; " the chapter appeared in the number of August 5, 1842.

79. *From a Letter of J. J. Garth Wilkinson, dated September 2, 1842.*

" You will be pleased to hear that the London Medical Gazette, of August 5, contains a translation of Swedenborg's chapter on the Intestines, from the ' Animal Kingdom.' The Gazette is a weekly publication, and one of the most respectable and widely circulated of the medical journals. Not much, perhaps, is to be expected from any one article of the kind appearing in such a vehicle ; for Swedenborg's physiological doctrines are so new, deep, and comprehensive, that when presented to even a candid mind, full of ordinary notions, and breathing the gross atmosphere of modern science, they will probably appear to be little more than a confused mass of assumptions. Such is my experience of their first effect on my own mind. Now, however, I am every day becoming more penetrated with the truth and consequent importance of these works. . . . They are the results of rigid physical induction. And it is both curious and satisfactory to observe, that medical authors have been for ages approximating, in the way of effects and details, to some of the principles elicited by Swedenborg. To instance one of these cases — the influence of the respiratory movements on, and their propagation to the viscera and to the whole body. The law, that the body in general and in particular, respires with the lungs — that the perpetuation of all the functions, and, in a word, of corporeal life, depends on the universality of this action, as a law—is peculiar to Swedenborg. And yet, for centuries, the fragments of this truth have flitted across the mental vision of physiologists. *Glisson* has declared it of the liver—*Blumenbach*, of the spleen — *Barry*, and many others, of the heart — *Bell*, of the neck — *Schlichting*, of the blood in the brain — *Portal*, of the circulation in the spinal cord: and I could easily add many other names and instances to this list. Another principle discovered by Swedenborg, is the permeability of membranes, and the circulation of fluids through them in determinate channels; some of the details of which are now grouped under the names 'Endosmosis' and 'Exosmosis,'—two phenomena which are thought discoveries of the present day. With regard to the lymphatic system, Swedenborg has thoroughly anticipated the beautiful theory of *Dr. Prout*, etc. And although it is as a discoverer of principles that Swedenborg is undoubtedly most valuable, yet his subordinate, theoretical details, are also far superior to those of other authors, because they refer themselves to a head, and derive from it a universalizing vital essence."

80. *From the Boston Medical and Surgical Journal,* 1846.

SECOND NOTICE OF THE " ANIMAL KINGDOM."

" Swedenborg has collected together the various facts brought to light by the anatomists of his time, and presents analyses of their labor. But before giving an opinion, he first exhibits the results of the researches of the highest class of minds of that day, in the particular department which he subjects to the fiery furnace of his own masterly powers of analysis. If others have been less gratified in reading Dr. Wilkinson's beautiful edition of the 'Animal Kingdom,' than ourselves, it must be that they have not discovered how much and in how many ways Swedenborg actually anticipated some of the modern book-manufacturers, who claim distinction on the score of suggestions or discoveries, that are as old as his Latin manuscripts. There is not so much attention given to the philosophical disquisitions of Swedenborg as they merit. Perhaps this is to be imputed to prejudice on account of his theological views, and the doctrines he promulgated respecting a new system of divine revelation.

"An opening prologue to the 'Animal Kingdom,' Vol. I., is a beautiful specimen of refined reasoning, and of itself would be no mean exhibition of intellectual strength. . . . To qualify himself to write on the structure and functions of the organs discussed in this volume, he studied all the authorities extant, which are quoted in full, and his own opinions and conclusions are annexed, at the close of each discourse. Accompanying the detailed quotations, there are notes and comments in such abundance, that we are postively amazed at the prodigious amount of Swedenborg's chirographical industry, independent of the mental exercise that must have preceded it. There are no such scholars in Europe now. Are there any in the world?

"Without fear of contradiction, we honestly say that Swedenborg, as a physiologist and natural philosopher, is either not known or appreciated by those who have access to his works, or a studied injustice still keeps him from being acknowledged, universally, one of the most extraordinary men that have appeared since the dawn of true science."

81. *From the " Veterinary Record,"* April, 1845.

"*Swedenborg's 'Animal Kingdom.'*—The publication of these volumes is, in more points than one, no uninteresting occurrence. In fact, they admit of at least a two-fold consideration. In the first place, the anatomical basis on which the views they contain are founded, is supplied directly from the works of the great anatomists of former times,—of those who were the fathers of the organic sciences, whose discoveries were our inheritance, and whose accumulated wealth, re-cast in the moulds of the present day, furnishes even yet the most passable and purest coin that we have in circulation in our schools of science. In the second place, they attempt a theory of organic nature, and specifically of the human body; and they aim to show the connection of the natural sciences with each other, and afterwards with the human mind, and with human society; in fine, with a philosophy of causes."

The reviewer, after noticing at some length the great anatomists of former times, referred to by Swedenborg, says,—

"But we have said enough, perhaps too much, concerning

these forgotten anatomists : something must be said of Swedenborg, or the chief character would be omitted from the drama ; and yet how to speak of him is a question, for Swedenborg is a mystery which in its whole extent a scientific journal is not the place to attempt to solve.

" The view which he takes of the body is, to a great extent, mechanical ; but then he predicates a mechanism of the fluids as well as of the solids. He applies everywhere the Doctrine of Series. Some glimpses of this important instrument for rational physiological knowledge have been seen by *Carus* and other writers ; and it has been applied by them to the bones. Thus they have aimed to show, that all the bones, including those of the cranium, are repetitions of the vertebræ ; in a word, that in the bones there is but one principle, and many modifications. Now, Swedenborg has carried this law through the soft parts as well as the bones, and through the fluids equally with the solids. With him ' every thing is a series, and in a series.' The whole of the viscera are a stupenduous series, in the higher parts of which (the brain, for instance,) every thing goes on that goes on in the lower. Thus the lower are so many legible illustrations of the higher ; the diffuse organs of the abdomen and chest are explanations of the concentrated cerebrum. We shall not dwell further on this law, but simply observe that Swedenborg so consistently applied it as to arrive by induction at the existence of an animatory motion in the brain, *synchronous* with the respiratory motion of the lungs ; a doctrine which has much to do with the whole of his physiology.

" His opinions upon the spleen, the thymus gland, and the supra-renal capsules, are, to say the least, extremely curious, and at any rate consistent with the rest of his theory : how far they may be admissible in modern science, or consistent with it, is another and a widely different question. This, however, we will say, that the amount of mere anatomical knowledge of these organs which has been added to the store since his time, is (notwithstanding Sir Ashley Cooper's splendidly printed quarto on the thymus) altogether insignificant ; so that Swedenborg may upon these points be almost as well tested by the knowledge of his own day as by that of ours.

" Swedenborg's ideas of respiration are, to our mind, altogether new, and, if true, of great importance as modifying our views of nearly the whole field of physiology. We shall therefore conclude this Review by citing the following notice of them from the 'Translator's Introductory Remarks,' begging our readers for a few brief moments to forget oxygen, hydrogen, and carbon, or, if that be impossible, to give those necessary elements only a secondary place in their conceptions."

A long extract from Mr. Wilkinson's Introductory Remarks, pp. xxiv.—xxvii., then follows; after which the reviewer concludes thus :—

" So far the translator. We have now done with the *Animal Kingdom;* and we honestly declare, that, be its merits great or none, or in whatever intermediate category it be placed, it stands alone amid scientific writings, and is a monument, at any rate, of the persistent daring and originality of Swedenborg's mind."

82.   *From Dr. Wilkinson's " Introductory Remarks" to the " Animal Kingdom," Vol. I. pp. xliii. etc.*

" Swedenborg's analysis is professedly supported upon the foundation of the old anatomists, who flourished in the Augustan age of the science. At his time nearly all the great and certain facts of anatomy were already known ; such for example as the circulation of the blood, and the existence of the lymphatics and the lacteals. Anatomy, too, had long been cultivated distinctly in the human subject, and was to a great extent purified of the errors that crept into it at first from dissecting the lower animals. Many of the old anatomists were men of a philosophic spirit, who proposed to themselves the problem of the universe, and solved it in their own way, or tried to solve it. They were the first observers of nature's speaking marvels in the organic sphere, and described them with feelings of delight, which showed that they were receptive of instruction from the great fountain of truth. They worked at once with the mind and senses in the field of observation. There was a certain superior manner and artistic form in their treatises. They believed instinctively in the doctrine of use. They expected nature to be wonderful, and supposed therefore that the human body involved much which it required the distinct exercise of the mind to discover. Hence their belief in the existence of the animal spirits ; a belief which they based upon common sense, or what amounts to the same thing, upon the general experience of effects ; at the same time that they recognized its object as beyond sensual experience, and not to be confirmed directly by sight.* They used the microscope to assist and fortify the eye, and not to substitute it, or dissipate its objective sphere. Even the greatest among them, who addicted himself to the bare study of structure and the making of illustrative preparations, expressed a noble hope that others would complete his labors, by making as distinct a study of uses.†

"But the picture is not without its darker side. Although they had strong instincts and vivid glimpses of truth, yet when they attempted to carry their perceptions out, they degenerated into mere hypotheses, and systems of hypotheses. They did not ascend high enough before they again descended, nor did they explore nature by an integral method ; and hence they had no means of pursuing analogies without destroying the everlasting distinctions of things. They stopped in that midway where scepticism easily overtook them, and where, when that enemy of the human intellect had once penetrated, there was no possibility of maintaining themselves, but the fall to the sensual sphere was inevitable. The reason of this was, that they had not conceived the laws of order, and therefore could not claim the support which nature gives to all her truths. Nay, it was so impossible that they should proceed further without the tincture of a universal method, that their minds came to a stand-still ; the truths already elicited were rendered unsatisfactory, and mere progress demanded their fall. They fell therefore, and a race which knows them not is dwelling now in tent and hut among their mighty ruins.

"At the very crisis of their fate, Swedenborg took the field, and at once declared, that unless matters were carried higher, experimental knowledge itself would perish, and the arts and

---

* Heister. † Ruysch.

sciences be carried to the tomb, adding that he was much mistaken if the world's destinies were not tending thitherwards.
The task that he undertook was, to build the heaps of experience into a palace in which the human mind might dwell, and
enjoy security from without, and spiritual prosperity from
within. He brought to that task requisites, both external and
internal, of an extraordinary kind. He was a naturalized
subject in all the kingdoms of human thought, and yet was born
at the same time to another order and better country. To the
various classes of schoolmen he appears never to have attached
himself, excepting for different purposes from theirs. He pursued mathematics for a distinctly extraneous end. As a student of physiology he belonged to no clique or school, and had
no class-prejudices to encounter. In theology he was almost
as free mentally, as though not a single commentator had
written, or system been formed, but as though his hands were
the first in which the Word of God was placed in its virgin
purity. Add to this that he by no means disregarded the
works of others, but was learned in all useful learning. He
had a sound practical education, and was employed daily in the
actual business of life for a series of years. He was thoroughly
acquainted with mechanics, chemistry, mathematics, astronomy, and the other sciences as known in his time, and had
elicited universal truths in the sphere of each. From the
beginning he perceived that there was an order in nature.
This enabled him to pursue his own studies with a view to
order. He ascended from the theory of earthy substances to
the theory of the atmospheres, and from both to the theory of
cosmogony, and came gradually to man as the crowning object
of nature. He brought the order of the macrocosm to illustrate the order of the microcosm. His dominant end, which
he never lost sight of for a moment, was spiritual and moral,
which preserved his mind alive in a long course of physical
studies, and empowered him to see life and substance in the
otherwise dead machinery of the creation. He was a man of
uncommon humbleness, and never once looked back, to gratify
self-complacency, upon past achievements, but travelled onwards and still onwards, ' without fatigue and without repose,'
to a home in the fruition of the infinite and eternal. Such

was the competitor who now entered the arena of what had, until this time, been exclusively medical science; truly a man of whom it is not too much to say, that he possessed the kindliest, broadest, highest, most theoretical and most practical genius that it has yet pleased God to bestow on the weary ages of civilization.

"Swedenborg perceived that the permanence of nature depends upon the excellence of its order, that all creation exists and subsists as one thing from God; that divine love is its end; divine wisdom, its cause; and divine order, in the theatre of use, the simultaneous or ultimate form of that wisdom and love. He also perceived, that the permanence of any human system, whether a philosophy or a society, depends upon the coincidence between its order and the order of creation; and that when this coincidence exists, the perceptions of reason have a fixed place and habitation on the earth, from which it will be impossible to dislodge them by anything short of a crumbling down of all the faculties, both rational and sensual; a result which, if the human heart be improving, the belief in a God forbids us to anticipate. But Swedenborg did not rest, as the philosophers do, in a mere algebraical perception of truth, or in recognizing a want without supplying it; but like a good and faithful servant he actually expounded a system of principles at one with nature herself, and which will attest their order and their real Author by standing for ages and ages.

"But his still, small voice commanded no attention, and what he predicted took place: the sciences *were* carried to the tomb, where they now are buried, with the mind their subject, in the small dust of modern experience. This brings us to say a few words of the physiology of the day.

"Facts are the grand quest of the present time, and these, particular facts: general facts are less recognized now than they were at the beginning of the last century; for short-sightedness has so increased upon us, that we must look close in order to see distinctly, and hence extended surfaces do not fall under our vision. The physiologist defers reasoning, until the accumulation of facts is sufficiently great, to suggest reasons out of its own bosom. This is a step beyond ordinary materialism. The individual materialist considers that matter must be organized into the form of a brain before it can think and will; but that compound materialist, the scientific world, expects dead matter to open its mouth and utter wisdom, without any such previous process. It thinks that at present there is not matter enough, or this result would ensue; little dreaming that there is a fault in itself, and that the larger the stores it possesses, the more impossible it will be to evolve their principles, or to marshal them under a theory. The common facts of the body having been pretty well explored, the physiologists go inwards, and gather further facts. Without waiting to ascertain the import of these, they submit them to the microscope, and again decompose them; and so on to the limits prescribed by nature to the optician, and by the optician to the scientific inquirer. But is the field of leasts more easy to discern than that of compounds; or if we cannot read nature's secret in her countenance, can we expect to divine it from her very brains? The truth is, that the modern state of physiology is a universal dispersion of even sensual knowledge; its pretended respect for facts is not real; otherwise it would inquire into their general significance before resolving them into further elements. It perpetually illustrates the principle that facts cannot be duly respected unless they are seen as agents of uses, and results of ends and causes; and that if they are not so regarded, they become mere playthings, to which novelty itself can lend scarcely a momentary charm.

" But as every end progresses through more means than one, so science is undergoing dispersion in another direction also. Not only are the generals of anatomy forgotten for its particulars, but the human frame itself is in a great measure deserted for comparative anatomy. The so-called human physiologist pursues his diffuse circle from animal to animal, from insect to insect, and from plant to plant. Man is confounded with the lower and lowest things, as if all the spheres of creation were in one plane of order. The consummation of this tendency is already more than indicated above the horizon, when the lowest range of existence will be the standard of all, and then the chaos of organic nature will become the legitimate . property of the chemists, to be by them resolved into gases and the dead materials of the earth.

" Another characteristic of the times is the almost total breach of continuity between the present and the past. The terminology of science is so much altered that it is impossible to read the older works with benefit, unless after a course of study something like that requisite for learning a dead language. In consequence, the mere anatomical value of the fathers of anatomy is not at all understood; their rich mines of observation are no longer worked, and their forgotten discoveries are now and then again discovered, with all the pains of a first attempt, by their ill-informed successors. Can anything be less human than this,—that the parents should transmit so little to the children, or rather that the children should be willing to receive so little from the parents? It exchanges the high destiny of man for the fate that attends the races of animals, in which each generation lives for itself alone, and again and again repeats the same limited series, without improvement or the possibility of evolution.

" In the midst of this humiliating condition, what loud sounds do we not hear of ' march of intellect' and ' progress of the species,'—so many discharges from the impotent artillery of self-conceit. This indeed is the last and worst sign of a decadent science. The poor sick sufferer is delirious, and possesses for a moment superhuman strength in his own exhaustion. . . .

" But it would be far from the present line of argument, to maintain that the moderns are performing no useful function in the ' progress of the species.' Such a proposition would be incompatible with what we know of the divine economy, in which human degeneracy itself is converted into a new point in the circle of uses. Nay, the moderns have their direct value; in the first place, they have enlarged the *catena* of observation in many departments. In the second, they have corrected innumerable minute errors in their predecessors, who were more intent upon their general than particular accuracy. And thirdly and chiefly, although in this respect no credit attaches to them, they have gone so low in their inquiries, that as it is even physically impossible to go lower, so by the law of the contact of extremes a revolution may now take place, and the ascending passage be commenced, as it were from the skin to the brain, or from the lowest sphere to the highest.

"It would be interesting to trace the successive stages by which the physiology of the ancients declines into that of the moderns, to review the grounds on which great doctrines were given up, and to test the sufficiency of the reasons which were adduced for the change. The state delineated in the well-known lines—

> 'I do not like thee, Doctor Fell,
> The reason why, I cannot tell;
> But this alone I know full well,
> I do not like thee, Doctor Fell.'

—this state was the moving cause of it. In short, it was a change in the human will, and not primarily in the understanding, which faculty appears to have been called upon subsequently, to confirm the new turn of the inclinations. Such at any rate we know to be the case with the doctrine of the animal spirits, which, as Glisson said, was in his time believed in ' by nearly all physicians, and by all philosophers.' It might have been supposed that the animal spirits were demonstrated out of existence by some beneficent genius who substituted something better in their place ; at least that they fell honorably in a well-fought field of argument. No such thing ; they fell by the treachery of the human heart loving the sensual sphere more than the intellectual. Is such mere waywardness as this a part of the ' progress of the species ?' The ancients believed in the existence of the animal spirits without pretending that they could become objects of sight. ' Tam subtile sit coucipiendum [fluidum hoc subtilissimum],' says Heister, '. . . ut instar lucis velocissime se diffundat ; quod profecto non oculis, sed ex effectibus et phaenomenis, . . . ope judicii sive mentis oculis cognoscendum. . . Ita aërem, animam, et multa non videmus, quae tamen ex effectibus, quemadmodum spiritus animales, esse et existere intelligimus.'*

---

*Comp. Anat., n. 301, not. a. "This subtlest fluid must be conceived of so subtle as to spread in the quickest manner like light ; it cannot indeed be discovered with the eyes ; but with the help of the understanding or the mind's eyes from its effects and phenomena. Thus we do not see the air, the soul and many other things, and yet we know from their effects, that they have being and exist, just as the animal spirits."

But the moderns reject whatever they do not see, and will credit the existence of nothing that absolutely outlies, and must in its conditions forever outlie, the senses. It is needless to say that a state like this is based upon neither reasons nor sensations, but is purely negative or sceptical, and must be referred to sheer will without any admixture of wisdom.

"We promised at the outset to speak of the relation in which Swedenborg's philosophy stands to the science of the day, but it will now be seen that there is no direct relation between the two, but a plenary repugnancy. For the one is order, the other is chaos: the one is concentration, the other is infinite division: the one enlarges its limits in that interior world where creation exists in all its spiritual amplitude, the other loses its limits, and its distinct life along with them, in the great vacuities of space and time: the one is a rod and staff giving the mind a practical support in the exploration of nature's fields, the other is a mist of hypotheses crawling along the ground, and making every step uncertain and perilous. . . .

"The reader may probably be led to inquire, how far the 'Animal Kingdom' embodies doctrines which were current at Swedenborg's day, and how far its deductions are peculiar to our author. To this it may be answered, that many doctrines to be met with in the Work are by no means peculiar to Swedenborg, but were the common intellectual property of his contemporaries and predecessors. We have seen that a host of writers held the doctrine of the animal spirits. It was also no uncommon belief that they were elaborated by the cortical substances of the brain, and circulated through the nerves. Vieussens held that there were distinct degrees of them. Brunn propounded the same doctrine as Swedenborg respecting the pituitary gland; and numerous instances to the same effect might readily be adduced from other writers. Perhaps the best means to be certified on this head, will be the perusal of Boerhaave's 'Institutiones Medicae,' — a work where the theories of many ages are condensed into an eclectic system. It appears as though Swedenborg freely availed himself of the treasures that were accumulated around him and before him, and was altogether destitute of that passion for originality

which has been the besetting sin of so many learned. He
distinctly states that he has relied upon his own experience to
but a small extent, and that he has deemed it wiser, for the
most part, to ' borrow ' from others.*   So also where he found
true doctrines and deductions,—these likewise he borrowed,
and this, with generously grateful acknowledgment. But what
he really brought to the task were those great principles of
order to which we have before alluded, and which touched
nothing that they did not universalize and adorn ; nay, which
built the materials of experience and the deductions of reason
into a glorious palace that truths could inhabit. It is as the
architect of this edifice that Swedenborg is to be viewed ; and
his merits are to be sought for not so much in its separate
stones, as in the grand harmonies and colossal proportions of
the whole.

" After this statement it is scarcely necessary to observe,
that Swedenborg is not to be resorted to as an authority for
anatomical facts.   It is said, indeed, that he has made various
discoveries in anatomy, and the canal named the ' foramen of
Monro ' is instanced among these.† Supposing that it were
so, it would be dishonoring Swedenborg to lay any stress upon
a circumstance so trivial. Whoever discovered this foramen
was most properly led to it by the lucky slip of a probe. But
other claims are made for our author by his injudicious friends.
It is said that he anticipated some of the most valuable novelties of more recent date, such as the phrenological doctrine of
the great Gall, and the newly practised art of animal magnetism. This is not quite fair : let every benefactor to mankind
have his own honorable wreath, nor let one leaf be stolen from
it to the already laureled brow of Swedenborg. True it is that
all these things, and many more, lie *in ovo* in the universal
principles made known through him, but they were not developed by him in that order which constitutes all their novelty,
and in fact their distinct existence. For in the first place it
is impossible for the human mind to anticipate facts ; these

* " Economy of the Animal Kingdon, part i., n. 18."
† " See ' Animal Kingdom,' n. 190, note (r)."

must always be learned by the senses ; and secondly, Swedenborg was too much a man of business to turn aside from the direct means to his end, or attempt to develop anything beyond those means. His philosophy is the high road from the natural world to the spiritual, and of course has innumerable lateral branches leading to the several fair regions of human knowledge : but through none of these by-ways had Swedenborg time to travel : nay, could he have done so, there is nothing to show that he would there have discovered what his successors have done. He had his mission, and they have theirs. His views are at harmony with all that is new and true, simply because they are universal, but in no fair sense do they anticipate, much less supersede, the scientific peculium of the present century. Swedenborg, therefore, is not to be regarded as an Aristotle governing the human mind, and indisposing it to the instruction designed to be gained from nature ; but as a propounder of principles the result of analysis, and of a method that is to excite us to a perpetual study in the field of effects, as a condition of the progress of science. . . .

" The professional reader of the ' Animal Kingdom ' will not fail to discover that the author has fallen into various anatomical errors of minor importance, and that there are occasionally marks of haste in his performance. This may be conceded without in any degree detracting from the character of the work. These errors do not involve matters of principle. The course which Swedenborg adopted, of founding his theory upon general experience, and of only resorting to particular facts as confirmations, so equilibrates and compensates all mis-statements of the kind, that they may be rejected from the result as unimportant. To dwell upon them as serious, and still more to make the merit of the theory hinge upon them, is worthy only of a ' minute philosopher,' who has some rule whereby to judge a truth, instead of the law of use. Such unhappily was the rule adopted by the reviewer of the ' Animal Kingdom ' in the ' Acta Eruditorum Lipsiensia ' (1747, pp. 507–514) : the book was despised by this critic because Swedenborg had committed an error in describing the muscles of the tongue, and because he had cited the plates of Bidloo and Verheyen, which Heister and Morgagni had then made it a fashion to disparage; and for other equally inconclusive reasons. All they amounted to, was, that Swedenborg had not accomplished the reviewer's end, however thoroughly he had performed his own.

"But fortunately such criticisms are never decisive; a single truth can outlive ten thousand of them. The 'Animal Kingdom' appeals to the world at this time, a hundred years since the publication of the original, as a new production, having all the claims of an unjudged book upon our regards. For during that hundred years not a single writer has appeared in the learned world, who has in the slightest degree comprehended its design, or mastered its principles and details. The reviewer to whom we have already alluded, judged it by a standard which was suited only to an anatomical manual and text-book. Haller bestowed a few words upon it in his invaluable 'Bibliotheca Anatomica,' but he knew nothing of Swedenborg's views; and his notice of the 'Economy of the Animal Kingdom,' contains errors too numerous not to invalidate his censure, had he bestowed it, which, however, he has not done directly. Sprengel, in his 'History of Medicine,' has offered a few lines upon the work, but these merely of a bibliographical import. The past, therefore, has found no fault in it, and it comes before the reader with an uninjured character, and demands as a good, true and useful book, to be taken into his service, and to receive a full trial at his hands. The modern physiologists having no theory of their own, have no reference to it, nor until they quit their present ground can they be allowed to have an opinion on the subject. Their censure would not be more relevant than would the opposition of a Red Indian to the problems of the mathematics.

"But it may fairly be asked, what are the prospects that the 'Animal Kingdom,' and the scientific works of Swedenborg generally, will be received at this day, when they refer to an order of facts almost forgotten, when they involve a scientific terminology which has become partially obsolete, and especially when it is considered that there never perhaps was an age so well satisfied with itself and its own achievements as the present one? Their prospects in the high places of science are not, indeed, encouraging: it would be vain to build up hopes in that quarter, or to address expostulations to it. A commission of any Royal Academy in Christendom would soon decide our claims in the negative. But fortunately there are abundant signs of a breaking up. The scientific world, and specifically the medical world, which is always the highest exponent of the state of science, is in a state of intestine revolution ; nay, what is saying much, it is nearly as full of dissension as the church itself. It would be exceedingly unpalatable to dwell upon its divisions, to specify the sects which have separated from the maternal body, and to show the irreconcilable nature of the differences that subsist between orthodox medicine and her refractory children. The future historian, standing upon the grave of once venerated institutions, may do this with impartiality, and not without a feeling of pity. Meanwhile it is our privilege to rejoice, that amid the decadence of science new ground is being broken, and new spirits raised up, to some of whom the new truth may be accommodated and delightful.

" We use the phrase ' new truth,' although the works which contain it have been buried in the dust for a whole century ; but in so doing we simply allude to the principles involved in these works. The confirmatory facts by which these principles were brought into relation with the science of Swedenborg's day, may doubtless from time to time be superseded by better attestations : particular facts are but the crutches of a true theory, and are not, strictly speaking, its basis ; for the basis itself is spiritual, since it is the order and tenor of effects that form it, and not the matter. The principles themselves are eternal truths,—the same yesterday, to-day, and forever.

" There are cycles in all things, and even now there are some indications of a revival of medical learning. The weakness of the present state of things is perceived by those who have no appreciation of its barrenness ; the temper of the public is an unmistakable demonstration to this effect. Hence many begin to revert to the past, and laying aside for a moment the vociferation of ' march of intellect' and ' progress of the species,' they are content to march and progress, like the crab, backwards, and to claim Hippocrates, and Galen, and Sydenham as their fathers. This is at any rate so far good, that it

13

shows how a forgotten range of facts and an antiquated terminology may be re-acquired as soon as there is a sufficient
motive : nay, it nourishes the hope, and that under the pressure from without, the large body of dependents, if not the
feudal lords of science, may come to even greater and more
unexpected results than these. Who shall say that they may
not ultimately see that it is their interest, as practitioners of
medicine, to deposit their cloak of mystification, to bring to
market something which is intelligible and useful to humanity,
to go wherever truth leads them, even though that truth be
' stranger than fiction,' and to come to our Swedenborg in his
double character, and acknowledge with humble thankfulness
that a greater than a Hippocrates is here—a man who has
married practice to theory, who has dissected the living body
without destroying it, and has so opened the sciences of anatomy and physiology, that they must sooner or later become
branches of *human* education, in which case the medical profession will have a solid basis in the social world, and be as a
golden crown of wisdom and practice resting securely upon
the correct knowledge and common sense of mankind.

" To all those who are in possession of truths which are not
recognized, or are rejected, by the systems of the day, the
writings of Swedenborg may be perfectly invaluable. Those
writings will prevent them from being dependent, in any department of reason, upon the old state of science. They will
furnish a high rallying point where a number of such distinct
truths may be combined, and derive that strength which is the
result of union, and especially of the union of truths. They
will put weapons of offence and defence in the hands of causes
which are now repressed almost into nothingness, and give
power to those who are strong in spirit, yet weak in body.
They will add force to faith, and sustain the earnest soul
through the day of small things, and meanwhile yield it a
peaceful delight, prophetic of a glorious future. To all such
persons these writings ought to be as glad tidings, and should
be received with hearty thankfulness, and a determination to
lose no time in converting them to use."

VII.

IMPORTANCE OF THE PHYSICAL AND MINER-ALOGICAL WORKS OF SWEDENBORG.

83. *From the Parlor Magazine, No. 15, August 9, 1851. Printed in the Crystal Palace, London.*

On the Metallurgy of Iron. By Swedenborg.

The editor commences the article with the observation, "Iron is, doubtless, of all metals the most important. We may almost estimate a nation's might by the quantity of iron it consumes. In fact, the whole industry, and, consequently, the whole wealth of a nation, depends upon iron." He then dwells upon its universality and innumerable uses, and adds, that "notwithstanding the importance of this product, the fabrication of iron was left for centuries to *chance*. It was committed to the hands of ignorant and uncultivated workmen," &c. "No mind of an elevated cast chose to stoop to the labors and investigations which were necessary to collect the details of manipulations so majestic as a whole, but apparently so mean and trivial when viewed apart. There was only existing one single work in which any information on the subject could be obtained, and this, too, incomplete. It was under these circumstances that there appeared upon the stage of metallurgic science—although, alas! for too brief a moment—a man whose memory has been immortalized by his visionary pursuits, whilst his solid attainments have been forgotten. We speak of Swedenborg. A child of Sweden—which seems to deserve pre-eminently the title of the land of iron—his thoughts naturally turned more especially towards that metal, but his original idea was to write a complete history of metallurgy in general." There now follows a description of the work, and the editor resumes—"Some judgment may be formed of the difficulties he had to encounter, from his preface, of which I

(147)

shall only translate a single passage, curious from the idea it conveys of the opinions and prejudices of that day on the matter of metallurgy :—

" ' I foresee,' said Swedenborg, ' that there will not be wanting those who will whisper in my ear that the modes of fusion, and the processes of extraction in divers countries, which have been discovered through the labor and experience of centuries, ought not to be thus lightly divulged, and rendered familiar to the world at large. There is not a single class of metal founders who do not possess certain secrets which they would deem it a crime to reveal. These they conceal, lest they should be imitated by their companions, over whom they triumph in a sort of fancied superiority. There are many others, in a higher walk of life, who resemble these in every respect, who also have no desire to know anything save for themselves, and who like to be considered the possessors and keepers of a secret. There is nothing in which people of this class take so much pleasure as in withholding from the public all useful information ; and if anything does happen to come to light which is likely to forward the cause of science, they look upon it askance, with an air of dissatisfaction, and murmur against the author of the discovery, as if he were a violator of a secret.

" ' I know that I cannot expect to be viewed in a kindly spirit by such as these, for this reason : that persons of this class would think themselves *less* wise, if their neighbors were *as much so* as themselves. But even allowing that they do possess some useful secrets, which they have purchased from those who look upon science merely as an article of traffic—is *this* a reason why such knowledge should be withheld from adding its contribution to the increasing light of the age ? All which it is worth while to know, ought to be published in the market-place : the rights of man demand that it should be so ; the laws of the republic of letters require it ; for, unless we each aid to the advancement of science and the progress of industry, until, flourishing more and more each year beneath our fostering care, they attain that perfection which has been desired by all ages, we can never hope to become wiser or happier by the lapse of time.

" 'The longer the earth is the scene of man's abode, the more widely the power of thought and of observation is extended amongst the human race : the greater the number of *minds* which multiply upon this earth, the more may we hope to see all the industrial sciences perfected, and to witness the growth of improvements in every department of labor, such as we have been favored with during the course of the last century, in the department of metallurgy alone.' "

Well may the editor exclaim—" These are, assuredly, noble words, and such as clearly mark Swedenborg's *presentiment* as to the future influence of metallurgy on the destiny of nations. We may seek in vain in all the authors who, before his time, treated of this science, for views thus liberal and profound. Although written more than a century ago, one might almost imagine these words to be an utterance of our day. It is the distinctive mark of most great minds thus to speak the language of posterity ; and therefore it is, that whilst in their *own* age they are too often reviled or misunderstood, *posterity* treasures up their sayings."

84. In Mr. G. F. Richardson's useful elementary work, " Geology for Beginners, etc.," we meet with the following *qualified* testimony to the genius of Swedenborg :—

" The celebrated Emanuel Swedenborg, (1720,) in the early part of his career, acquired considerable proficiency in the physical sciences. . . . His publication, entitled ' Opera Philosophica et Mineralogica,' in three volumes folio, with numerous engravings, was justly regarded as a most extraordinary performance. On its appearance, various learned bodies vied with each other in electing him a member of their respective societies : and the Academy of Sciences of Paris translated into the French language for their *Histoire des Arts et des Métiers*, his Treatise on Iron from this work, as affording the most valuable authority on the subject then extant. His scientific observations . . . contain some sound principles and instructive facts ; and the nebular theory of the solar system, the original fluidity of our planet, the various preparatory changes of the earth, as opposed to the prevailing idea of its instantaneous creation in its present matured con dition ; the succession of various tribes of animals ; these, with other assertions, the truth and accuracy of which has been demonstrated by modern science, are the lights which shine through *the misty maze of superstition and absurdity of which his productions so largely consist.* [?]   It may incidentally be noticed, that the writings of this extraordinary man evince that he was also acquainted with phrenology." p. 63.

85. In the translation of *Cramer's Elements of the Art of Assaying Metals, by* DR. CROMWELL MORTIMER, Secretary to the Royal Society, Swedenborg's Work on the Mineral Kingdom is mentioned by the translator in the following terms :—
" For the sake of such as understand Latin, we must not pass by that magnificent and laborious work of Emanuel Swedenborg, entitled ' Principia, etc.,' in the second and third tomes of which he has given the best account, not only of the method and newest improvements in metallic works in all places beyond the seas, but also those in England, and in our colonies in America, with draughts of the furnaces and instruments employed.   It is to be wished we had extracts of this work in English."

86. " The immense essay which fills the first volume of the ' *Opera Philosophica et Mineralogica,*' excited only a sort of stupid wonder ; but the practical utility of the two other volumes was at once recognized by the learned. ' We should never be able to finish,' says a good judge, Prof. Schleiden, ' if we should attempt to enumerate all the improvements which Swedenborg introduced in the working of the mines of his native country, and it would be impossible to say how great were his merits in promoting the industry and the arts of Sweden.' "—M. MATTER, *Vie de Swedenborg*, p. 40.

87. " The work of Swedenborg, which you were so kind as to put into my hands, is an extraordinary production of one of the most extraordinary men, certainly, that has ever lived. . . This much I can truly say, that the air of mysticism which is generally thought to pervade Baron Swedenborg's ethical and theological writings, has prevented philosophers from paying

that attention to his physical productions, of which I now see they are worthy. Many of the experiments and observations on magnetism, presented in this work, are believed to be of much more modern date, and are unjustly ascribed to much more recent writers."—PROFESSOR PATTERSON, *of the University of Pennsylvania, in a letter to* **Dr. Atlee.**

88. "In the 'Principia' Swedenborg may be regarded as taking his place by the side of Newton, Kepler, and Humboldt ; climbing to the high places and mountain peaks of nature, and overlooking the material universe ; that work belongs to the future still, but ever since it was written the mind of man has been marching up to it. Philosophers have neglected these writings, from the supposition that they were the productions of a mystic ; hence the ignorance of scholars, of the writings of this illustrious man, is amazing."—E. PAXTON HOOD, *Life of Swedenborg*, p. 77.

89. " When first we proposed to ourselves a thorough and systematic study of the *Principia*, we were little prepared to find that the fundamental facts and principles, forming the *nucleus* of each of the sciences of sidereal astronomy, cosmogony, terrestrial magnetism, and others, discovered and elaborated since his time, are to be found in this single work, fully, clearly, and explicitly stated. The cases to which we have referred * are some of the luminous points which glimmered with their first faint light through the darkness of the eighteenth century, for periods varying from a few years to a century before either conjectured or discovered. Indeed, apart from the higher psychological discoveries made known to the world through him, his scientific discoveries alone justify us in affirming, that at no prior period since the origin of society has the *sphere of ideas* been so suddenly and so wonderfully enlarged. The magnitude of the areas, and their distribution in space, first made known to man by his breaking through the

---

*These cases are contained in Part II. of the present volume.

enclosure of the heavens, and consequent discovery of the immensity of creation beyond or outside the visible starry firmament; also the cognition of great and mighty cosmical relations and forces, made known to man by his theoretical discovery of the fact, that there are no *fixed* stars,—that the whole starry heaven has a magnetic course along the milky way, whilst its general form, and also that of the infinitude of starry firmaments outside our own, depend on the developed perfection and general form of the magnetic axis or inward stream of magnetic force flowing through the interior of each firmament; these have furnished ideas of SPACE and FORCE, so mighty and enlarged, and withal so exhibiting sublimity, beauty, and beneficence, in the most extensive because unlimited scale, as to stand unrivalled by any other in the human mind which have as yet entered therein."—SAMUEL BESWICK, *the learned commentator of Swedenborg's ' Principia,'* in the *Intellectual Repository* of 1850, p. 212.

In another place he speaks of the " *Principia* " in the following manner : —

" The work in question is designated ' *Principia*,' because in it the author explains his views of the *first principles* of the universe. The question proposed for solution is, therefore, the following : —How has creation issued forth from the Creator ; and what is the order and character of the series ? This the *Principia* proposes to solve. It is one of primary importance, both in a philosophical and religious sense. The outbirth of creation is a question involving the ALL of Science and Philosophy. It has a range of application so universal, and so utterly beyond the sphere of human observation and experiment, whilst it appears to present a demand on human reason and credulity of so mighty and illimitable a character, involving processes and cycles of processes, that it would seem more a mark of insanity than of wisdom to attempt its solution. Many there are of the best and wisest of men whose highest aspirations in the regions of philosophy have been to discover this grand *principium* of all our philosophies. It is the undiscovered fountain of natural truth, by whose waters the Muses delight to dwell, and from whence stream forth continuously and in plenitude those showers of scientific truth which, in the history of man, have so copiously fallen on the successive scenes in his intellectual progress. As an attempted solution, Swedenborg has offered us his *Principia*. In this work, therefore, he proposes to explain the outbirth of Creation from the Infinite, and to trace the steps of each successive substance and attendant process of formation and development, from the first living force, through the elemental world, until he arrives at the solid and inert substances and matters of which the earths in the universe consist. And it is worthy of remark, that every subsequent discovery has done something, more or less, towards the confirmation of his views. Throughout the long course of his experience . . . . . he never once cast aside his *Principia*, or renounced the fundamental doctrines, formulæ, or first principles, by which he was guided in his youthful investigations. From the first he appears to have seen clearly, and to have marked out its broad outline, the path which subsequently led him, like Columbus, to a region of undiscovered truth, unsurpassed (world-wide as the extent of human knowledge now is) in richness, beauty, and fruitfulness. From the first he appears to have discovered those *new methods* by which he made his *new attempts* at a philosophical explanation of the universe ; and which constituted a *new guide*, by which he soared higher and penetrated far beyond the limits of previous investigation."—*Intellectual Repository*, 1850, pp. 250–51.

90. *From the "Journal Encyclopédique," Sept. 1, 1785, Vol. VI. Part 2.*

Remarks by the MARQUIS DE THOME, *on an assertion of the Commissioners appointed by the King of France for the examination of Animal Magnetism.*

" GENTLEMEN,—

" In the report of the commissioners appointed by the King for the examination of animal magnetism, these gentlemen have affirmed that there does not yet exist any theory of the magnet. This assertion has occasioned many remonstrances ; and I shall here make one, and, as I think, the most just of any, in favor of an illustrious man of learning, some years since deceased. Three folio volumes were printed at Dresden and Leipsic, in 1734, under the following title : *Emanuelis Swedenborgii Opera Philosophica et Mineralia.* The first of these volumes is entirely devoted to a sublime theory of the formation of the world, founded on that of the magnetic element ; the existence, form, and mechanism of which are demonstrated by the author from experience, geometry, and the most solid reasoning founded on these two bases. The subject of the other volumes, being foreign to that of this letter, I shall content myself with saying, that in the whole of the work, there is such an abundance of new truths, and of physical, mathematical, astronomical, mechanical, chemical, and mineralogical knowledge, as would be more than sufficient to establish the reputation of several different writers. Accordingly, he acquired so much fame by its publication, that the Academy of Stockholm hastened to invite him to become one of its members. This production of the Swedish philosopher has continued to maintain the same degree of esteem in all Europe, and the most celebrated men have not disdained to draw materials from it to assist them in their labors ; some, too, have had the weakness to dress themselves in the feathers of the peacock, without acknowledging where they obtained them. On reading the paragraph in the first volume, page 387, entitled *De Chao Universali Solis et Planetarum, deque separatione ejus in Planetas et Satellites ;* and that at page 438, *De progressione Telluris a sole ad Orbitam,* it will be seen how much the Count de Buffon was mistaken in saying, in his discourse on the formation of the planets, that nothing had ever been written on this subject ; and it will doubtlessly be regretted, that the French Pliny has not profited by the discoveries of the Stockholm Academician, who, whilst he equals him in point of style, is infinitely superior to him in everything else. A cursory perusal of the first volume, will also be sufficient to repress our astonishment at the experiments of M. Lavoisier, Swedenborg having already shown, that earth and water are not to be regarded as elements, nor elements as simple substances. I should forbear to add that M. Camus, who has performed such surprising things with the magnet before our eyes, admits that he has derived from this author almost all the knowledge that he has exhibited on this subject, and, in short, that without having studied him, our acquaintance with magnetism must be very imperfect;—I say, I should forbear to mention this if the commissioners appointed by his Majesty to examine animal magnetism had not affirmed, that there as yet exists no theory of the magnet. How can this assertion be reconciled with the authentic and positive fact I have now stated? The farther one is from imagining that such a declaration on the part of the academicians and physicians can be the result of haste, of ignorance, or of partiality, the more difficult the thing becomes. Are we not to believe, that, to acquit themselves worthily of their commission, and to justify as they ought the confidence with which the sovereign has honored them, they would neglect nothing that could contribute to make them perfect masters of the question of animal magnetism, and enable them to decide upon it, and that they would accordingly read and consider everything which has hitherto been published on the subject: at least everything that has proceeded from the pen of the most celebrated naturalists? The work which has occasioned this remonstrance, being without contradiction the most complete and profound of all, ought principally to have fixed their attention; and this being granted, the saying of the commissioners, that there does not yet exist any theory of the magnet,—that is, that nothing which has yet appeared is to be regarded as such,—is saying that the theory of Swedenborg is none at all; that a theory demonstrated by experiment, geometry, and reasoning, and in agreement with them all, is not a theory. Such, I believe, is the exact amount of the assertion of the commissioners, which, therefore, it remains for them to prove.

" I shall now proceed to enable the public to declare, whether the Swedish philosopher was not most intimately persuaded, that, in natural philosophy, every theory which is not supported by experience and geometry ought to be regarded as chimerical. In the first page of the first volume, he thus explains his views on this subject: ' *Qui finem vult*, &c. He who wishes to attain an end, must also wish to acquire the means. Now these are the means which more especially lead to knowledge truly philosophical; experience, geometry, and the faculty of reasoning.' In the following page he insists, in these terms: '*Magna quidem*, &c. Arduous is the attempt to explain philosophically the hitherto secret operations of elemental nature, far removed, and almost hidden from our view. I must endeavor to place, as it were, before the eyes, those phenomena which she herself is careful to conceal, and of which she seems most averse to the investigation. In such an ocean I should not venture to spread my sail, without having experience and geometry continually present to direct the hand and watch the helm. With these to assist and direct me, I may hope for a prosperous voyage over the trackless deep. These shall be my two stars to guide me in my course, and light me on my way; for of these do we stand most in need in the thick darkness which involves both elemental nature and the human mind.' At page 184 of the same volume, he says, again, '*Nisi principiorum*, &c. Unless our principles be geometrically and mechanically connected with experience, they are mere hallucinations and idle dreams.' Behold, further, how he establishes that even elemental nature is under the government of geometry, and always like herself in the little as well as the great; a principle which opens to the human mind an infinite career, and puts us in the route which it is necessary to take to arrive at all possible discoveries: '*Natura enim*, &c. Elementary nature (says he) is a motive power variously modified; a motive power variously modified, is a system of mechanism; a system of mechanism is geometry in action, for it must needs be geometrical: geometry is the attribute of a certain substance possessing figure and space: as, then, geometry is the attribute of a substance, and thus is inseparable from every substance, whether simple or compound, either in motion or rest, and from motion itself, it accompanies nature from its first origin and rudiments, from its least form to its greatest, through the whole world: and as geometry is the same in the greatest substance as in the least, hence nature, being a motive and modified power, being mechanical and geometrical, is exactly like herself in each extreme; that is, towards each infinite of smallness or greatness, &c.' p. 121. The question then is, whether Swedenborg has proceeded according to these principles ? This question all naturalists and geometricians are invited to determine : and when they have agreed on their determination, which will certainly be in conformity with what I have advanced, they will unanimously admit, if I am not mistaken, that the theory of the Swedish author is a true theory of the magnet, and of all magnetism ; that it proves incontestably the existence of the magnetic element ; that it proves further, that the particles of this element being spherical, the tendency of their motion, in consequence of this form, is either spiral or vortical, or circular ; that each of these motions requiring a centre, whenever these particles meet with a body, which, by the regularity of its pores, the configuration and the position of its parts, is adapted to their motion, they avail themselves of it, and form around it a magnetical vortex ; that, consequently, every body which has such pores, and such a configuration and position of its parts, may become the centre of such a vortex ; that if this body has an activity of its own, if its parts are flexible, and if its motion is similar to that of the particles, it will be so much the more disposed to admit them, &c., &c. ; whence it follows, that magnetical substances are such merely by virtue of the element whose existence Swedenborg has demonstrated, and thus that the magnetism of bodies depends, not on their substance, but on their form : —a truth which is hinted at by the learned Alstedius in his excellent Encyclopædia, printed at Lyons in 1649, in which, drawing a comparison between electricity and magnetism, he says, ‘ *Motiones electricæ a materia, magneticæ vero a forma pendent.*’

“ To ascertain the influence of the magnetic element on the question of animal magnetism, suppose we apply the result of the summary view that I have given of it to the three kingdoms of nature. It will be easy to convince ourselves, that of these, the mineral kingdom is the least favorable to this element, by reason of its inertness, of the irregularities of its pores, of its angular forms, and of the rigidity of its parts : hence, were it not for iron and the loadstone, magnetism would be almost entirely banished from this kingdom. Proceeding to the vegetable, we may easily perceive that its more regular pores, its rounder forms, its more flexible parts, the sphere of activity, which results from its organization, and from the circulation which takes place within it, offer much greater facilities to the operations of the magnetical fluid. Arriving at the animal kingdom, which is the quintessence of them all, as being more rich in volatile spirits, and approaching thereby more nearly to elemental nature, and which is gifted more eminently, according to the perfection of its organs, with the same advantages which we have just observed in the vegetable kingdom ;—we find that this kingdom, by the exalted life of some of its subjects, is clearly the most active centre that the magnetic element can lay hold of ; and as, besides, it presents it in the abundance of its fluids, in its circular vessels and veins, and in its spiral fibres, with nothing but analogous forms, of an extreme flexibility and capacity of motion, we cannot but conclude, that this is a kingdom which favors in the highest degree the admission of this element. To avoid exceeding the limits of your journal, I omit, gentlemen, an infinity of things which I might here mention in support of these truths ; amongst which I should include the respiration of animals, their hunger, their thirst, their loves, the functions of their absorbent and resorbent pores,—phenomena which, well analyzed, would be so many proofs of the existence of animal magnetism, and would evince that, in reality, animals are nothing but living magnets.

" Let me not, however, for what I have here said, be suspected of being a disciple of the too celebrated Dr. Mesmer. Believing with him in animal magnetism, the existence of which has long since been as evident to me as that of the sun, if I intended to make use of it, it would be in a manner totally different from his ; as I find in M. Mesmer's mode many things that are not only vicious in point of morals, but also very dangerous in a physical respect. For want of knowing what Swedenborg has said respecting forms, series, degrees, correspondences, and, above all, respecting the element of man and human spheres, this physician has abandoned himself to a blind practice, the effects of which, sometimes good, as often bad, and most frequently none at all, fully evince either the incapacity of the practitioner, or the inefficiency of his remedy. But to learn in what M. Mesmer is deficient, it will not suffice to have read the work which I have just been describing, but will also be necessary to be acquainted with most of those which follow it : for the indefatigable Swede continued to write upon the most difficult and abstract subjects, and, what is peculiar to himself, he always possessed the art of enabling all his readers to understand them, by the method, precision, and clearness with which he conducted the discussion.

" Since an opportunity here offers to speak of his works, permit me, gentlemen, to avail myself of it, to disabuse the public respecting the bad impressions which have been attempted to be imposed on it concerning this great man.   Prior to his *Opera Philosophica et Mineralia*, he had written on almost all the sciences.   Amongst others was his work on Algebra, entitled, *The Art of the Rules ;* a new method to find the longitude by land and by sea, by the aid of the moon ; another for the trial of new ships, &c., &c., &c. ; not to mention some literary productions which were the first essays of a youth which had been employed in learning the principal living languages of Europe, and all the dead ones.   He was so well versed in the latter, particularly in Latin, and the Oriental languages, that he was consulted by those who made the study of them their particular profession.   Posterior to the year 1734, we have of his, *The Animal Kingdom ; The Economy of this Kingdom ; An Essay on the Infinite, the Final Cause of Creation, and the Mechanism of the Operation of the Soul and Body ;* with a poem on *The Birth of the Globe and that of the First Man ;* works which are above all praise.   But what shall we say of his theosophical treatises, where the greatest secrets are revealed without emblem and allegory ; where the science of correspondences, which has been lost for near four thousand years, and of which the hieroglyphics of Egypt were but useless monuments and relics, is again restored ? I will say that a perusal can alone give any idea of them ; that the more the principles, equally new and fertile, which are accumulated in these works, are reflected on, the more they are applied to nature, to ourselves, to everything that can become an object of our thoughts and affections, the more clearly the truth will shine, the more we shall be compelled to pay homage to the superiority of enlightenment [lumières] which has given them birth, and to acknowledge in them the evidences of a wisdom more than human. . . . (Here follows our extract, n. 16.)

" This, gentlemen, is what I thought it my duty to make public for the benefit of society, from a regard of truth, and in gratitude to him to whom I am indebted for the major part of the little that I know ; though, before I met with his writings, I had sought for knowledge amongst all the writers, ancient and modern, who enjoyed any reputation for possessing it.

" I have the honor to be, &c.,

" Marquis De Thome."

" Paris, Aug. 4, 1785."

91. Balzac, in his " *Seraphita* " * gives the following interesting account of the occasion which called forth the preceding article of the Marquis de Thomé ; he says :

" The Marquis de Thomé, by calling the commission appointed by the King for the investigation of magnetism to account for some expressions which had escaped them, procured great honor to the name of Swedenborg in the controversy which had arisen in Paris in the year 1785, on the subject of animal magnetism, in which controversy almost all the scientific men of Europe took part. The commission, namely, had declared that up to the present time there existed no theory of the natural magnet, while the Marquis proved that such a theory had been propounded by Swedenborg as early as the year 1720. The Marquis at the same time showed the reason why the most celebrated scientific men suffered Swedenborg to remain in oblivion, to be this, that they wished secretly to adorn themselves with the feathers stolen from his hidden treasures ; wherein he especially alluded to Buffon's theory of cosmogony. In short, by many quotations taken from Swedenborg's encyclopædic works, he succeeded in establishing the complete proof, that this great seer was far in advance of

---

*In the edition published by Hallberger, in Stuttgart. 1836. p. 99.

the slow course of the human sciences. In order to convince yourself of this you need but read his philosophical and mineralogical dissertations. So he is the precursor of modern chemistry by announcing in a passage that all the products of organical nature are decomposable, and that water, air, fire, are by no means elemental substances. In another place, in a very few words, he enters into the deepest mysteries of magnetism, and thus deprives Mesmer of the honor of first discovery."

14*

VIII.

SWEDENBORG'S PHILOSOPHY.

92. *From the Critic*, 1847.

" SWEDENBORG was, specially in these modern times, the
man of intuition ; this to him was genius, or more than genius.
. . . . Along, however, with his boundless prodigality of
intuition, there were the keenest powers of observation, uncommon skill in seizing and grouping facts, and in penetrating
them with the significance of his own intellect. The difference
between the great poet and the great philosopher is, that the
poet absorbs the universe and its forms into himself, while the
philosopher puts himself forth into the universe and its forms.
The poet seeks to be identical with the infinite by appropriation, the philosopher by emanation ; and by the power of
appropriation in the one case, and by that of emanation in the
other, must the worth of every poet and of every philosopher
be measured. Swedenborg was therefore eminently a philosopher, since he had eminently the energy of giving the forms
of the universe to his own spirit. Much of modern philosophy
consists in a process as remote as possible from this,—in
stamping, namely, the impress of the beholder on the forms of
the universe that he contemplates, which is equivalent to the
substitution of a human form for a form divine ; and, consequently, philosophy such a process cannot, without flagrant
inaccuracy, be called, since the philosopher himself takes the
place of the sole object of philosophy. Hence a philosophy
of this kind ever inevitably ends where it began—in a barren
and monotonous repetition of a self-beholding, whose natural
result is a huge and hateful self-glorification. Yet those who
pursue philosophy after a fashion so unphilosophic, seem to
the multitude the only philosophers, since it is they alone that

(162)

appear to work revolutions in philosophy. To transform will always show to the undiscerning eye a mightier operation than to transfuse, since it is marked by far more external change. Descartes was the most memorable of the transforming philosophers. He burst, consequently, into immediate celebrity. His was no tiresome march to wide and fulgent glory. Descartes was a Frenchman ; and if we were to call French philosophy by one word more applicable than another, we should name it the transforming philosophy. We cannot say absolutely and without qualification that Swedenborg was the most memorable of the transfusing philosophers ; but if not the foremost of all, he stands in the first rank. Much, however, as this may recommend him to the earnest and the truly philosophic, it has been an immense obstacle to the diffusion of his fame and the extension of his influence. Because its scientific ideas have accomplished no striking transformations, we have either been unconscious of their presence or ignorant of their import."

93. The following pages on the nature of Swedenborg's Philosophy are quoted from Dr. J. J. GARTH WILKINSON'S Introductory Remarks to the English translation of Swedenborg's " Economy of the Animal Kingdom " :

" We may premise, that although we call these works of Swedenborg scientific (deriving the name from the basis they rest upon, and the limits they observe), yet they are properly philosophical also, since they rise through the particular sciences to that universal science which alone is philosophy. For as the physical doctrines of Swedenborg are the reconciliation, or at-one-ment of philosophy with science, so these works may be designated from either term ; let it only be borne in mind, that they are not philosophical in any sense in which philosophy is considered independent of physical science ; nor scientific, so far as science is not permitted to obtain light and life from real philosophy.

" The compound relation of the two fields of science and philosophy is a remarkable feature in these works ; and the more so, as Swedenborg is the only writer in whose hands the matter of the sciences, and the way of induction, legitimately engender philosophical ideas. Other writers have proposed the same result, but he alone has attained it. Notwithstanding which he avoids the error of deriving the higher knowledge from the lower, or making the senses govern the mind; for he uses the sciences but for steps to lead to the upper rooms of the intellect, and allows every faculty its distinct exercise, at the same time admitting all experience, to whatever faculty it may appeal. While he gives a scientific foundation for faith, it is by the energy of an enlightened, and, for the most part, a new faith disposing the sciences. He moves and works according to the matter supplied by general and universal experience, and revelation is as much this matter in one sphere as the phenomena of the mind in another, and nature in a third. The soundest ideas of method are illustrated in his writings; and, according to that shrewd saying of the reputed father of induction, that 'the art of discovery will increase with discoveries themselves,' Swedenborg has taught us, by a legible and grand example, the most perfect manner of eliminating the higher sciences. Yet he differs from Bacon in what he has done and proposed, and also in the proportion that subsists between his intentions and executions. For he has substantially connected the organic sciences with philosophy and morality; so that body and soul are no longer two, but are in their harmonies. A breadth, height and continuity of use, unsuspected by physiologists, are shown to pervade the mechanic frames of living beings; the new uses being demonstrated. The qualities of things are definitely shown, where the recognition of the things themselves was the last result of the former analysis. Many of the 'forms' or essential causes which Bacon sought by an operose calculus, came to Swedenborg with direct force as natural truths, and the consequence is, that in important principles his works are a hundred-fold more fruitful than those of the English philosopher. In wit and brilliancy of style the latter is indeed without a rival; his eminence in these respects is such as beseems the great critic of two thousand years; yet in their degree such qualities would have been out of place in the writings of Swedenborg, which deal, not with the opinions of man, but with the works of nature; and point to inward truths, and prepare the mind for their pursuit by simplicity of manner; whereas it is somewhat fascinated, not to say detained in the lower sphere, by the eccentric piquancy of the Baconian ornament. Neither has Swedenborg written with a primary regard to the economical or civil 'endowment of human life,' with new arts and inventions, but for the reformation of man and his mind, as the spring of all wholesome changes and successful operations. Accordingly he gives no bond to reconstruct society; nor professes to be able to drag the secrets of truth into day by an unerring or mechanical method; but having obtained a sufficiency of doctrinal instruments for present use, and mindful that active life is the best lot of man, and the finest means of improvement, he builds such an edifice as his materials and opportunities permit, and arrives at such an end as a good man may be satisfied with. The perfecting of instruments he knows must be successive, but that the use of them must not be postponed, and therefore he lays out his possessions to the best advantage, in the confidence that this is the true way to benefit posterity. Only a small part of his works is devoted to explaining his method, but its successful application is seen everywhere, and the results elicited show what it is, and how well it has been used. He is therefore small in pretension and great in performance; his works not being an organon for generating knowledge, but natural knowledge itself in its own organic form.

"The paramount success of Swedenborg with his simple apparatus, should tend to discourage exclusive attention to the means of knowledge; though indeed we may also gather the same lesson from the history of failures. It is certain that the organon of Aristotle,—the framework of syllogistic logic,—has distraught the intellect from the nature of things, rather than helped their comprehension; for it is a gymnasium, at the entrance to which we are required to know less by art than the mind itself knows at once by experience, by virtue of its own construction. The organon of Bacon is liable to the same reproof, although it is of seemingly opposite tendency; for it is as inefficient in physics as that of Aristotle in metaphysics, and is in fact but a new incumbrance to the mind. It is, however, but fair to allow, that Bacon did not assert its absolute necessity in all cases, but rather proposed it as a school in which prejudices and 'idols' of various kinds might be dispossessed of their authority, and the eyes be unsealed, and the mind prepared by a negative process for closing with nature.* Still in Swedenborg we have a brighter light on this subject, and we can fully assent to the fact, that 'the mind itself, in its own nature, is philosophical,'† and that when we can raise up materials into its sphere of operations, they receive all the formation, information and analysis which any method is presumed to impart. It would therefore appear that no organon is of use to supply the nature of the mind, but only to lift up matter to its ken, and there to proffer and leave it. To this office Swedenborg confines his organon, viz., the doctrine of series and degrees, and the mathematical philosophy of univer-. sals; the former being the orderly or natural means of raising experience to the intelligible sphere; the latter, the means of expressing, by new symbols, those analytic results in the higher spheres which are inexpressible by ordinary language. For

---

* "This passage is so illustrative of our present argument, that we give it entire. 'It is now time,' says Bacon, 'we should propose the art itself of interpreting nature; wherein, though we conceive that we have laid down highly useful and just precepts, yet we attribute no perfection, or absolute necessity, to this art of ours, as if nothing could be done without it. For it is our opinion, that if men were possessed of a just history of nature and experience, were thoroughly versed therein, and could command themselves but in two particulars; the one, in laying aside received opinions and notions; the other, in withholding the assent, for a season, from general conclusions, they might, by their proper and native force of mind, without any other art, fall upon our form of interpretation, for the whole is no more than a genuine and natural work of the mind, when the obstacles to it are removed, though, doubtless, all will be made readier for use, and receive great strength, by our precepts.

"'Nor do we say that nothing can be added to these precepts of ours; on the contrary, we who do not highly esteem the mind in its own faculty, but chiefly so far as it is furnished and joined with things, ought to lay it down, that the art of invention may grow up with inventions themselves.'"—("Novum Organum," part ii., sec. vii., § 130.)

† "On this subject see the 'Economy of the Animal Kingdom,' Part II., n. 277; 'Animal Kingdom,' n. 312 (b), n. 462 (c), n. 573 (o), 'Arcana Cœlestia,' n. 4658."

Swedenborg's instruments leave to man the whole play of his faculties, and indeed require their utmost exercise ; and merely feed them, through an appropriate channel, and in proper quality and quantity, with matter derived from the various degrees of the created universe. And he nowhere deems that the sciences can advance towards philosophy, independently of moral requisites in those who cultivate them ; for the mind of necessity operates on its materials, however brought to it, according to its own nature ; and if that nature be at variance with the moral ground-work of things, in short, with the ends of the universe, no organon can influence it towards the truths of creation, while its own prepossessions are on the side of error and evil.* And here is a new ' idol' affecting the growth of the sciences, and which Bacon but faintly allowed : for he excluded final causes from the scientific doctrine of nature,† and consistently enough, therefore, from the conditions of studying nature : and although he admitted that the understanding is drenched in the affections, yet by the tincture of the affections he meant little more than erroneous habits of thought, derived either from idiosyncrasies or circumstances ; in short, prejudices of various kinds.‡ On the contrary, we learn in the writings of Swedenborg, that doctrines cannot permanently elevate knowledge, unless they work with experience, are handled by genius, and are used with good inten-

---

* " See the ' Principia,' Part I., Chap. I., n. 4 ; ' Economy of the Animal Kingdom,' Part I., n. 20—22 ; ' Animal Kingdom,' n. 12, 13 ; n. 463."

† " ' The inquiry of final causes is a barren thing, or as a virgin consecrated to God.' " (Bacon, " Advancement of Learning," section vi.)

‡ " The light of the understanding is not dry or pure light, but drenched in the will and affections, and the intellect forms the sciences accordingly ; for what men desire should be true, they are most inclined to believe. The understanding, therefore, rejects things difficult, as being impatient of inquiry ; things just and solid, because they limit hope, and the deeper mysteries of nature, through superstition ; it rejects the light of experience, through pride and haughtiness, as disdaining the mind should be meanly and waverly employed ; it excludes paradoxes, for fear of the vulgar. And thus the affections tinge and infect the understanding, numberless ways, and sometimes imperceptibly." (Bacon, " Novum Organum," part i., sec. ii., § 12.)

tions. For they tend in no degree to produce equality between human minds, but rather to manifest, in their operation, delicacies of intellectual distinction between different men, and finer points of moral dissimilarity. The mind may be likened to a chemical substance, rich in affinities for other substances, and capable of innumerable reactions; doctrines being the vessels wherein those substances are brought to it for test or analysis; and the integral series of reactions is all the philosophy and science that the mind is capable of. If the central power and substance be weak, imperfect, or vicious, neither the vessels in which things are brought to it, nor those things themselves, can adjust the mischief; nor can the series of reactions be other than correspondent as well to the mind as to its defects.

"In one point of view, Swedenborg is the synthesis of Aristotle and Bacon. For Bacon desires, unassisted by philosophical doctrines, to scale the heights of nature, hoping that one correct induction piled upon another, will enable him at length to arrive at the apex of the pyramid; meanwhile he disallows the mind so greatly, that its intuitions are affronted, and its proper experience undervalued; so that though he indeed aims at principles, yet he has negatived the faculty which alone can receive and apprehend them. Aristotle, on the other hand, accepts the experience of the mind, and draws it out into logical explanations, but he has not determined it by matter, and he has therefore but a slight hold on nature, compared with what is at present necessary for marshalling the sciences. Swedenborg embraces the merits and avoids the imperfections of these writers, and he alone has propounded a science constituted of principles, which as it were spontaneously are physical in the physical universe and philosophical in the mind of man, and by which we may pass and repass from the one into the other, so as to contemplate the end of creation in connection with the means, and *vice versa*. The ascending method of Bacon, and the descending one of Aristotle, are in fact both realized by Swedenborg, and being connected to each other at either end, they form a legitimate and widening spiral, revolving from the senses to the mind, and from the mind to the senses.

"A knowledge of the human soul is the author's aim in the

present volumes. The same subject apparently is the goal of the 'Principia,' and still more plainly of the 'Prodromus on the Infinite.' Whether Swedenborg was conscious from an early period of this direction of his labors, is hard to determine; but it is certain that he rose from one study to another, in regular order, without proposing an ultimate end, until he proclaimed his resolution to investigate the soul. His theory of the mathematics and dynamics of chemistry, brought him in view of the elemental kingdom, the fluids of which are 'the formed forces of nature.' The exploration of this kingdom is a remarkable stage in his career, but it did not crown his desires; for he proceeded forthwith to that which is the determination of the whole elemental world and terrestrial kingdom, viz., to the organic animal kingdom, and to its first and last subject, the human body. Here again he bent his course continually inwards till he contemplated the primordial currents and stamina of natural life. The activity of the highest fluid of the microcosm he tells us is the soul for which he has been searching. The predicates of the soul, in the language of universals, agree with the predicates of the spirituous fluid, and the two are consequently identical, according to all sound reason. Still, however, in the 'Animal Kingdom' we find him embarking in a new voyage of discovery in the regions of the soul; thus furnishing an extraordinary example of ending and beginning; of progress, not by renunciation of principles, but by alteration of forms, till at last they will contain, and adequately express the truth. And so he admitted that he was too hasty in attempting a passage to the soul, after investigating but a few provinces of the empire of the body. For as the soul is the inmost order and law of the whole system, he must perforce scrutinize to the core each organ and the whole, before the soul can appear as the universal and the complement of that microcosm which she animates. Even in the 'Animal Kingdom' he has still not treated sufficiently of the brain and the body, to empower him to predicate anything positive of the soul; therefore he puts forth certain hypotheses, with a view to accommodation, until such time as the truth declares itself. In the treatise on 'The Worship and Love of God,' we have still further statements on the soul, and a recognition of the spiritual world as distinct from nature. And here his mingled physiological and psychological endeavors terminate. Thenceforth he discerned the soul, neither through the dark glass of science, nor through the mists of philosophy, nor through the curtains of nature, but in a manner more rare and homely; viz., by spiritual sight and experience, rightly apprehended by a prepared or spiritual mind.

" As Swedenborg pursued the sciences for so high an end, or for the attainment of moral and rational psychology, so in his hands they were means of a new order, and disclosed truths of corresponding elevation. Above all, the anatomy of the human body proved to be a mine of unexpected treasure."
—pp. x.–xvii.

94. *From " An Historical and Critical View of Speculative Philosophy of Europe in the Nineteenth Century," by J. D.* Morell, *Vol. I., second revised and enlarged edition, London.* pp. 315–323.

" To give anything approaching to an adequate view of the Swedenborgian philosophy, we feel to be a matter of great difficulty, and, indeed, in a brief compass, almost impossible. The difficulty of the case arises partly from the frequent obscurity [?] with which his thoughts are expressed, and partly from the differences of opinion upon many important points, which exist among his followers. Although according to his own testimony he was accustomed from a child to think much upon spiritual things, yet his earlier manhood seemed to be altogether engrossed in scientific pursuits. The results of these studies exist to the present day in the form of volumes and tracts, which travel over almost the whole surface of natural history and science, and in which, it is only just to say are found, more or less obscurely, many of the germs of recent and brilliant discoveries.

" It was in the ' Prodromus,' a brief treatise upon ' The Infinite and the Soul,' that the philosophical and theological thinking of Swedenborg began. I say philosophical and theological, because it was his firm conviction from the first, that revelation and philosophy were fundamentally identical, that all religion was to be made scientific, and all science to be made religious.

"The first question which suggests itself with reference to the Swedenborgian philosophy is this : What is the method it proposes, by which truth is to be attained ?   Some philosophers had attempted to deduce all truth from *a priori* principles ; others had attempted to ascend by an inductive process from the particular to the general.   What is the methodology that Swedenborg adopted ?   To answer this question accurately, we should premise, that he set out upon no fixed metaphysical principles whatever ; he went to work as a solitary and independent observer, to find truth ; and the method to be pursued formed itself as he proceeded.   As any unphilosophical [?] thinker naturally would do, he began his career by a wide observation of facts ; his system, therefore, was cradled in simple inductive processes ; it was analytic, or if we may use a word implying authority, it was Baconian.   Few perhaps who have only listened to vague rumors respecting this philosophy, would imagine that it commenced in a collection of facts far greater than those of which the father of experimental science himself had any conception.

"After passing successively through the regions of mechanics, with the corresponding properties of matter ; after traversing the province of chemistry, throwing light upon the action of imponderable agents, and suggesting the germ of the atomic theory, by pointing out the geometrical relations existing between the ultimate atoms, Swedenborg comes at length to the animal kingdom.   Here the course of his research begins to gain point and pregnancy.   The human body may be regarded as that in which all the operations of nature are concentrated and perfected.   Here, therefore, is a microcosm—a perfect representation of all being—an image of the whole creation ; here, consequently, a theatre, upon which philosophy may achieve its noblest conquests.   In this department, then, we begin to see more clearly some of the scientific formulas or methods which, evolved, as he tells us, by intense thought and patient observation, are potent to cast light upon the nature and uses of all things around us.   First of all there is the *doctrine of forms*.   Nature, he considered, is purely mechanical in all her movements; hence every higher region in which she appears, from the mineral to the man, is represented by movement in a particular form. All the movements of the mineral kingdom are angular, as seen in the crystal; the next form is circular, as seen in the bodily organization, in the circulation of the blood, etc.; the highest form is the spiral, the type of *spirit* itself. [There are other and higher forms enumerated, of which see in nos. 71, 72.—*Editor.*]

" In developing the physiology of the human body, another philosophical principle comes clearly into view, namely, the *doctrine of series.* Anxious to know the real structure of the various organs of the human frame, Swedenborg conceived that the doctrine of monads, and of ultimate atoms, would only bring him to a dark, unintelligible point, in which all form or organization ceased; and that the notion of the infinite divisibility of matter would lead to a nonentity, from which nothing could be drawn. Every organ, then, he conceived, must be made up of perfect atomistic organs, each of which expresses the thing itself far more completely than the whole; just as society is made up of individual men, and each man is the most perfect pattern of humanity. Everything in nature, therefore, consists of a series of perfectly organized atoms— the lungs, *e. g.*, innumerable microscopic lungs, the heart of numerous smallest hearts, and so forth with all the other organs.

" Having gone through the regions of philosophy, Swedenborg came to the confines of the province of Spirit itself. Often, he tells us, had he searched for some light upon the nature of the soul, but as often had been disappointed, until at length he got upon the right track, and entered the sacred chamber.* To gaze upon the soul by the senses was manifestly impossible; but was it not possible to reason up from the material to the immaterial, and from the facts of the one to see into the nature of the other? The validity of such a process was grounded upon the *doctrine of degrees*—a doctrine, he says, which is necessary ' to enable us to follow in the steps

---

* " See his 'Economy of the Animal Kingdom,' chap. iii., on the Soul."

of nature; since to attempt without it to approach and visit her in her sublime abode would be to attempt to climb heaven by the Tower of Babel; for the highest step must be approached by the intermediate.'* The doctrine of degrees, accordingly, is that which teaches us that there is a relation or parallelism between all things in nature, from the lowest sphere in which it exists, to the highest. Thus the brain contains potentially the whole body, and what is essentially true of the body, is true of it. Again, the animal spirits, which flow through the nerves, in a higher and more ethereal sphere, perfectly represent the more gross and obdurate human organization; so also the soul itself, in a still higher region, must be a perfect type, or rather co-ordinate archetype of the body. Accordingly, all nature by these degrees ascends from the lowest to the highest, and descends from the highest to the lowest; so that by the aid of this philosophical formula we can study the spiritual world by means of the knowledge we possess of the material.†

"Even in the spirit itself there are degrees. The lowest is that which is only cognizant of sensations; the next above this is the *animus*, whose office is to imagine and desire; thirdly, there is the mind, which understands and wills; and, lastly, there is the soul, whose office is to represent the universe, and have intuitions of ends.‡ Such is man, so far as the form of his being is concerned; but where is the life which is to animate him? The body is dead matter, but it is vivified by the soul—but whence the life of the soul? It is the love of God.§ God, according to Swedenborg, is perfect man. The essence and form of God are respectively perfect love and perfect wisdom; the former is represented in the human will, the latter in the human understanding.

"Having thus traced the philosophy of Swedenborg to its highest point, we may look back for a moment upon his whole method of procedure. Evidently it is the inductive and

---

* "Economy of Animal Kingdom, chap. iii., section 210."

† "This is an application of the doctrine of correspondences."

‡ "Economy of Animal Kingdom, chap. iii. sect. 6."

§ "Angelic Wisdom, Part I."

15*

synthetic method combined.   Commencing by observation, his mind seized upon certain high philosophical axioms, and from them reasoned downwards to the nature and uses of particular objects.   Perhaps it is the only attempt the world has seen (with the exception of the unsuccessful efforts of Comte) at rising upwards to purely philosophical ideas from positive and concrete facts.

" Having attained thus to the highest region of philosophy, Swedenborg enters the world of theological truth.   For gazing upon the spiritual world, he conceives we have purely spiritual senses, and a spiritual understanding.   To most men the spiritual world is closed ; because, absorbed in the lower or sensual life, they have no intuition of it.   To many, moreover, who do obtain spiritual intuitions, there exists not an enlightened spiritual understanding to interpret what the inward eye beholds.   Spiritual or theological truth only becomes clear when both these requisites unite ; where the purely moralized or unsensualized soul gazes upon the higher world, and where the spiritual understanding can comprehend what is seen. . . .

" Swedenborg was assuredly a great intellectual phenomenon.   Seldom, perhaps never, have so many systems concentrated in a single mind.   He began a simple observer—a Baconian analyst ; from that he raised himself to the region of the rational and ideal truth, and ended a mystic [?]—the favored channel of a new dispensation to mankind.   In him sensationalism, idealism, mysticism, were united—the only phase through which he never passed was that of scepticism. . . ."

95.   The following shows the interesting position that Prof. Matter assigns to Swedenborg in philosophy :—

" Swedenborg is the supernatural in the presence of the criticism of the eighteenth century.   The supernatural, however, is not only the highest question which is most agitated amongst us, who are the children of the eighteenth century in a much higher degree than we imagine ourselves to be, but it also always has been, and will forever be the most absorbing question that can engage the human intellect, before which all other questions grow pale and are put in the shade.   And if Swedenborg is the supernatural in the presence of criticism, he is also the greatest reconciliation that has ever been attempted between the natural and the supernatural, between the rational and the marvellous.

"Now this noble attempt, which has been in the order of the day ever since man has been, will be so forever, at least as long as God and human reason will be. For the question of the supernatural concerns not only the existence of the spiritual world, but also the relations existing between the two worlds. And now suppose that man, according to Swedenborg's idea, is at the same time the most beautiful problem and the most eloquent solution of these relations? In this case human intelligence would be perfectly in the right in having always preferred, and in continuing to prefer above anything else to cope with this problem.

"The criticism of the last century considered itself stronger than the supernatural; and in its hours of blind confidence it has not hesitated to throw the whole question overboard. It was regarded as one of those superannuated conceptions which henceforth were to be submitted to pure reason and common sense. And how shall I say? By a kind of irony of destiny, or by a dispensation of Providence at this very time of mortal strife, in the face of this criticism, the supernatural suddenly presented itself in its boldest and most ambitious forms; for it never has and it never will assume more startling forms than it has assumed in the life and doctrines of Swedenborg. A scholar of the first order, a creative mineralogist in the art of smelting metals and of exploring nature, has become as it were the supernatural incarnate; at all events, he is the expression of the supernatural in its highest power."—*Vie de Swedenborg*, Preface, pp. iii.–v.

96. Swedenborg's importance in Psychology has been very ably advocated in the following extract from a little work, entitled: "*Wisdom, Intelligence and Science, the True Characteristics of Emanuel Swedenborg*," by "MEDICUS CANTABRIGIENSIS":—*

---

* The late DR. SPURGIN, formerly President of the Royal College of Physicians in London.

"It should be remembered that Swedenborg himself took the lead in this department of knowledge (*i. e.*, psychology); for so long ago as the year 1740 he published his INTRODUCTION TO A RATIONAL PSYCHOLOGY,—a work which will amply repay repeated perusal, and which, in fact, so profound are its views, will require it. We would venture to recommend this work to all who take an interest in psychological subjects; more especially to all who write upon them. We have studied it with much interest and advantage, and not with the cursory glances that distinguish modern reviewers. Forty years of reflection, of comparison, and of observation, should, perhaps, enable us to assert for the work the preeminence which it merits. This estimate of it is, moreover, strengthened by the suggestions which we find at the outset of it. 'Whether,' says the author, 'there be truth in what I have advanced, and in what remains to be advanced, may be easily ascertained from the four following considerations: *First*, If the truth spontaneously manifests itself, and, as it were, establishes a belief in its presence, without requiring any support from far-fetched arguments: For we often, by a common notion, and, as it were, by rational instinct, comprehend a thing to be true, which afterwards, by a multiplicity of reasonings drawn from a confused perception of particulars unarranged and unconnected with others more remote from our notice, is brought into obscurity, called in question, and at last denied. *Secondly*, If all experience, both particular and general, spontaneously favor it. *Thirdly*, If the rules and maxims of rational philosophy do the same. *Lastly*, If the proposed view makes the different hypotheses which have been advanced on the subject coincide, supplying us with the proper condition or common principle, which brings them into order and connection; so that, contemplated in this manner, they are agreeable to the truth.'—*Economy of the Animal Kingdom*, Part I., n. 579.

"This *Introduction to a Rational Psychology* is based upon the doctrine of series and degrees, which teaches the mode observed by nature in the subordination and coördination of things; and the principal natural sciences are embraced within it, because we everywhere find in nature the laws of order. This doctrine is most strikingly and perfectly exemplified in the animal kingdom by every animal, the constituent parts of which are so subordinated and coördinated that they exist simultaneously in subordination and coördination, and from causes produce correspondent actions; for in every single action, will and thought, whether instinctive or human, are discernible as its producing cause.

" At the conclusion of this incomparable *Introduction*, which is but preparatory to a clearer understanding of the cerebral functions and movements, with regard both to their influence upon the body, and to the bodily diseases which affect them in turn, Swedenborg addresses his readers in these very striking terms :—' I have now completed the first part of my Transactions on the Economy of the Animal Kingdom. But I am not sure whether I have followed up the truth everywhere. I place no reliance upon myself, but leave it to the candor of my readers to weigh carefully what I have advanced so far. If I have been betrayed into a mistake, the following parts, in proportion as they are based upon true science, will correct it. But what is truth? Will it be the work of ages either to discover it, or to recognize it when it is discovered? Is it with truth now as it was with the illustrious Harvey when he discovered the' circulation of the blood? The fashion, however, of a judging of a work by the felicity of the writer's language, rather than by its truth, cannot be eternal. The former proceeding is easy and common in polite circles, so called, but the latter presents a difficulty to be surmounted only by great mental industry. Still, as was remarked by *Seneca*, '*Tenue est mendacium; perlucet, si diligenter inspexeris.*' (' Falsehood is flimsy ; on careful inspection it shines through.' —Epist. lxxix.)

" Having treated specifically, first of the cerebral motion, and afterwards of the cortical substance of the brain,—regarding this substance as the principal efficient cause of all the operations, both of the brain and the body, and as the first and last term of all,—he proceeds to the great subject of Psychology itself, viz., the human soul.

" The third chapter of the second part of Swedenborg's *Economy of the Animal Kingdom*, which treats of the human soul, is, we do not hesitate to say, a production unparalleled for excellence in the whole compass of human philosophy. Neither Galileo nor Harvey, in their demonstrations of truth, struggled a whit more manfully than did Swedenborg against the false impression of appearances. The two former contended against the fallacies which impress the outer senses of humanity; the latter contended against those which deceive the rational perceptions also of our being. Appearances, indeed, would confirm the notion that the rational perceptions spring from the outer senses; but Swedenborg demonstrates most scientifically that appearances, when taken for realities, subjugate every mental faculty, whether sensual, rational or spiritual; and he himself initiated the charge against his own age, governed as it was by appearances, that 'the senses are subjugated by false impressions.' The present age has retorted the charge upon him, while it adheres to the fallacious appearances which he exposed and even anticipated, as likely to frustrate his mission."—pp. 11–14.

97. Swedenborg, at one period of his philosophical career, held partly materialistic ideas of the soul, though they were never coupled with atheism. This phase of his mental development we will find discussed in the following extracts :—

From the " New Church Quarterly Review," Vol. I. p. 290.

" Swedenborg's Outlines or Prodromus of the Infinite."

" . . . Altogether, the perusal of this chapter on the 'Infinite' has afforded us another evidence of the exceeding truthfulness of Swedenborg's mind. Starting from the lowest point of philosophical naturalism, he has steadily and honestly pursued his way; tracking maze after maze and subtilty after subtilty, he presents us at each turn in the path with the exact truth of his position; and, as a last result, faithful to the dreary course he has been induced to follow, conducts us to the cold and darksome altar upon which is inscribed, ' To the Unknown God.' It seems as if Swedenborg had been permitted to tread this cheerless wilderness in order that he might see by actual experience the folly and utter futility of all such lifeless speculations. At all events, if we are disposed to profit by the lesson, it may be one of life-long import to ourselves. How forcibly are we reminded of the warning in reference to this very matter, which he gives in the last and crowning work of his wondrous career. Speaking of the danger and folly of all reasonings concerning the infinite, founded upon the fallacies of the senses, he says : ' I myself was once convinced of this by experience ; I was thinking what God had been doing from eternity, what before the establishment of the world, whether he was deliberating about the Creation, and was laying out the plan according to which this would have to be effected ; whether in a pure vacuum a deliberative thought could exist, and other equally incongruous things. But lest I might be brought into delirious states, I was elevated by the Lord into the sphere and the light, in which the interior angels are ; and after the idea of space and time, in which my thought had been detained before, had there been removed a little, it was granted to me to understand that the eternity of God is not an eternity of time, and that, because there was no time before the world, it was altogether useless to entertain any such speculations about God.' " ("*True Christian Religion*," n. 31.)

98. On this same subject DR. IMMANUEL TAFEL, Professor of Philosophy and Librarian at the University of Tübingen, author of a " Fundamental Philosophy," a " History and Criticism of Scepticism and Irrationalism," etc., and editor of many of the posthumous works of Swedenborg, speaks in a communication to the editor of the " *New Church Quarterly*," as follows :—

"The philosophy of Swedenborg's time was either idealism, or dualism, or materialism, and his own former philosophy was, as we know, a kind of materialism, but the most innocent that ever existed, and therefore capable of being turned into spiritualism. There were three classes of materialists : 1. The *Atomists*, who supposed that the soul was a compound of a peculiar kind of atoms, lifeless in themselves, such as Leucippus, Epicurus, etc.,—against whom it could be said, that the compound cannot contain what is not in its constituent parts, because *ex nihilo nihil fit;* wherefore Bayle said in his Dictionary (article 'Leucippus,' note c), that the difficulties

in the system of Leucippus would have been removed, if
he had attributed to his atoms a living soul, as, according to
Plutarch, had already been done by Democritus, who, however, could not sufficiently explain how matter can think, or
how it can be alone considered as substance ; wherefore, 2.
the *Harmonists* said that the soul is a mere word, and that it
consists in the harmony or organization of the body ; to these
belonged some of those against whom Plato wrote in his
' Phaedo' (and Aristotle in his '*De Anima,*' i. iv.), at a later
time Aristoxenus and Dicaearchus—who in other respects
were Aristotelians—and in our times, the author of the
'Système de la Nature,' 1770, and La Mettrie, of the Academy of Berlin. . . .   According to him, the soul is a part
of the brain ; wherefore King Frederic the Great, in his
' *Eloge de la Mettrie*' (Oeuvres de Frédéric, ii., tom. 3, p.
169), said, ' It appears that the disease, knowing with whom
it had to do, in order to destroy more surely, was artful
enough to attack the brain first. He took a raging fever,
accompanied with violent delirium ; and died Nov. 11, 1751,
when 43 years of age.   The experience La Mettrie had
quoted, proved only the dependence of the thinking power
upon its present instruments, but by no means that body and
soul are only one material substance, as had been shown
afterward by Eli Luzac in his work : *L'homme plus, que
Machine*, Londres, 1748.   He could, moreover, refute him
with the same arguments that Plato had already urged. . .
This hypothesis had been previously refuted by the reasonings
of Gassendi, who proved that no part of matter can act on
itself.   There was, therefore, a strong necessity of separating
the soul from the body, and of supposing, at least, that the
soul is a purer matter ; and nearly all philosophers before
Descartes, although they said that the soul was an immaterial
substance, thought, nevertheless, that it consisted of a subtler
matter, which was, however, endowed with intrinsic life, and
was so simple that it could not perish with the body.   This
third species of materialism was that of *Swedenborg*, in his
' Prodromus de Infinito,' where he nevertheless said :—

" ' Actives regarded separately from their membrane or
envelope cannot be conceived as occupying place or determinate

situation; or as forming a contiguity or expanse; of which, therefore, in themselves they are devoid; nor do they at all imply the relations of upward and downward, or of resistance, but only pure agency; thus nothing elemental, nor passive, though notwithstanding they involve pure mechanics.' — (p. 145.)

" But now we could object to him that in his ' Prodromus ' all finite substances are extended in space, and subject to mechanical and geometrical laws, and therefore still matter, which is incompatible with the thinking power and even with sensation; or as Eli Luzac says, ' Subtility being only relative, it is no more absurd to conceive, or rather to suppose gross matter endowed with these attributes, than subtile matter (p. 6). . . . It is proved by incontestible experience that matter is inert; that is to say, that it is of such a nature, that once in repose, it requires a determinate force from without to put it into action; and once in motion, it requires a like external force to change the direction of its motion, or reduce it to repose. Let us see, if this faculty of thought can co-exist with this attribute of matter. The exercise of thought cannot be conceived of without action or passion; but the idea of matter in perfect repose, namely, in such a state that it does not suffer either pressure or any other operation of any substance whatever; —in other words, the idea of matter considered only in so far as it exists, excludes all idea of action and passion. This amounts to saying, that to receive ideas, to compare them, to reproduce them, to form a judgment, and to prefer one condition to another, in a word, to think, supposes either passion, or a substance in activity, and cannot be the attribute of matter in repose, etc.' (p, 9,) [i. e. of matter according to a true idea of its nature]. He proves, also, by ' the idea of movement, by that of relations, by that of activity, and by the idea which we have of extent, that matter cannot possess the attribute of thought.'—(pp. 10–12.)

" Similar reasons must have determined Swedenborg to change his materialism into spiritualism, and to state that only the spiritual is substantial, and as such not subject to geometrical and mechanical laws: wherefore he said in his ' Diary ' (in the year 1748) :—

" ' Everything organical in man, everything corporeal in him, as well as in the animal and likewise the vegetable kingdoms, is formed for use, and according to use ; so that use is, as it were, the forming principle. Wherefore, whoever from use investigates organical things, can then see the connection of things, but not who from the parts investigates the use.'—(n. 2510.)

" ' It was given to me to see in a spiritual idea, which is the same as the angelic idea, that there cannot be anything material in use, when yet use forms everything material : for everything in general and in particular is for use and according to use ; and as there is nothing material in use, by which yet all things, as it were, are formed, it became evident to me from the spiritual idea, that use is Divine, because it forms, and that it is absurd to think of its being natural ; for the natural cannot be distinguished from the material : just as heat, moisture, dew, rain, because natural, are at the same time material.'—(n. 2512.)

" Still in his ' Prodromus,' as I have already stated, the soul is a part of nature. . . . So much the more interesting, however, is his metamorphosis. Among the most effective reasons by which this was brought about, there was no doubt his own spiritual experience. Thus we find also in antiquity, that the first philosopher who taught that the spirit is separate from, or independent of matter, viz., Anaxagoras, was the immediate disciple of Hermotimus, who, according to fourteen witnesses of the ancients, was in a state similar to that of Swedenborg."

99. The Editor of the " New Church Quarterly," (Vol. I., pp. 8, etc.,) alluding to the change by which Swedenborg from a materialist became a spiritualist, examines the subject more at large ; he says :—

" The change to which Dr. Tafel alludes in one part of the preceding letter, as having led Swedenborg away from the mere exegesis of material or mechanical laws, is in many parts of his writings referred to by the author himself. IIis metamorphosis is plainly spoken of, for example, in ' Arcana Cœlestia,' (n. 3985,) where he informs us, that during his transit from the lower sphere of thought a heavenly light appeared to him, which accelerated his progress and led him upward, so that he could look down upon worldly and corporeal ideas as no longer belonging to himself. So true is one of his later aphorisms, '*Imago evanescit cum ipsa effigies apparet.*'

"In the 'Economy of the Animal Kingdom,' Vol. III., when proceeding to treat on 'how forms are successively exalted into such as are more perfect,' he cautions the reader that 'he is speaking only of natural things, not of those which are above nature, as the spiritual and the divine, concerning which neither quality, nor mode, nor any other accident, except by the way of supereminence, can be predicated.' This caution is the more remarkable, perhaps, when connected with his own efforts in some of the subsequent pages to arrive at a conception of the spiritual through an evolution of forms. 'Angelic beings and our own souls,' he observes, 'cannot properly be called spiritual [consequently supra-natural] forms, but rather more perfect celestial [*i. e.* inmost natural, from *cœlum,* the sidereal heaven of the natural world] forms, created and accommodated to the reception and influx of the spiritual form.' This is altogether so singular that we cannot pass on without taking an accurate observation of Swedenborg's position when he penned it.

"He had but just completed his description of the 'perpetual vortical,' or the form 'which is properly called celestial,' and which he had designated as 'the highest of all natural forms.' It is the form which alone rules in the expanse of the sidereal infinitude: its centre is neither a point, nor a circle, nor a spiral, but a vortical gyre; it is the 'very beginning' of all the active forces of nature: 'most constant of all forms to its integral state:' 'void of figure, of extense, of magnitude, of weight, and of lightness, therefore not material.' Its real existence, nevertheless, was not to be held in the slightest shade of doubt, for without it the vortical, and other lower forms, the fluxion of the simple fibre in the animal kingdom, and other pure essences could not exist. . . .

"The Author, when he arrived at this point, appears to have been sensible that he was theorizing beyond experience, in imitation of the great master of gentile philosophy —

Aristotle ; and he therefore boldly pleads, in the way of excuse, the necessity he was under of trusting to a rational induction. The gist of his argument is sufficiently simple, namely—although but a few of the phenomena of this aura emerge into the sphere of our senses, yet its existence is not to be doubted ; for without it there could be nothing to enter by influx into the really demonstrable forms, and without such influx even these could not subsist. This supreme aura, however, though beyond the reach of experimental philosophy, could be grappled by geometrical analysis, or abstraction of forms, and this capability, considered in connection with the argument for the necessity of such a form, completed the evidence in its favor, and brought it within the bounds of nature, or finite things. Whether we are to identify this conception with the last analysis of matter, or consider it as evidence of something superior to material laws, can hardly remain a question when it is known that the author puts it forward as the proper exponent of the ' *ens simplex* ' of Wolff, the ' *monad* ' of Leibnitz, and the ' *materia prima* ' of more ancient philosophers.

" This celestial form, then, was the last which the author could approach even by a process of mathematical abstraction, and seeing that it was just within the bounds of nature, and therefore subject to the highest laws of fluxion, or to the most subtle touches of time and space (by which natural things are distinguished from spiritual), it was almost compulsory on him, either to attribute this form to the soul, or to call the soul spiritual : by the former it was made a part of nature, by the latter alternative (according to the philosophical definition of the word ' spiritual ') it was deprived of figure and extense ; to avoid one horn of this dilemma, our author describes angels and human souls, not as celestial or highest natural forms, but as ' more perfect forms of this kind ' ; and yet, that he might escape the other, not as spiritual forms, but forms adapted to receive the spiritual—*ad receptionem et influxum formæ spiritualis creatæ et accomodatæ.* It is worth notice that the schoolmen who preceded Swedenborg had, in their way, arrived at a like result.

" ' Whatever,' they reasoned, ' actuates matter, puts it into shape, and causes its existence or development, is substance ;

but form does all this, therefore form is substance.' This is almost the counterpart of Swedenborg's idea of the relation between the perpetual vortical and spiritual forms, but, unfortunately, it was not only put forth as a mere syllogism itself, but it was preceded and followed by mere syllogisms, the substratum of facts peculiar to Swedenborg's unique method being wholly wanting. In consequence of this lack of impletion the poor reasoners were sadly posed, by questions which may appear easy of determination to those who possess this double advantage of Swedenborg's philosophical insight and spiritual intercourse. What is meant, it was asked, by actuating matter? By giving it existence and figure? And what form can you demonstrate but what is the adjunct of matter itself? In this way what the Thomists or Scotists, as men, built up in day-time, they pulled down, like mischievous gnomes and fairies, in the night.

"It was because he saw the utter futilily of these proceedings that our author resolved to commence a new era, by eliminating his metaphysical doctrines from the analysis of material things; and thus he really gained a position from which it was impossible he could be driven. Having inferred an 'incomprehensible' and 'inexpressible' form and force, from the insufficiency of his purest substance to account for the phenomena of life, and having acquainted himself with all the accidents and modes of nature, he was also gradually preparing to speak ' *ex auditis et visis* ' (from things heard and seen), and could never be surprised into a surrender of his argument; he was invincible on the very ground which the metaphysicians had been compelled to abandon.

"As evidence, however, that, after all, his spiritual experience was corrective of his position, we quote the following interesting passage from the 'Spiritual Diary.'—It exhibits most clearly what relation the 'celestial form,' or aura, of the philosophy, bears to the human mind; the same thing being spoken of in this passage as the 'purest ethereal sphere':—

"'There are four natural spheres which arise from the sun; the atmosphere which causes hearing is known. A purer atmosphere, separate from the aerial, is that which produces sight, or causes things to be seen, by the reflections of light from all objects : how far this atmosphere penetrates into the natural mind, and whether it presents material ideas, as they are called, or phantasies and imaginations, cannot be clearly stated, but it appears probable, from various considerations. This, then, will be the first atmosphere, which reigns in the natural mind. Another atmosphere, which is a still purer ether, is that which produces the magnetic forces, which reign not only about the magnet in particular, but also around the whole globe ; but to what extent, it is not necessary to describe ; it produces there the situation of the entire terra-queous globe, according to the poles of the world, and also many things which are known respecting the elevations and inclinations of the magnet. This sphere, in the natural mind, appears to produce reasonings, in which, however, a spiritual principle must needs be present, that they may live, as like-wise in the sight, and in every other sense, in order that they may perceive. The purest ethereal sphere is that universal sphere in the universe which exists around the ratiocinations of the same mind. Hence it is that this mind is called the natural mind, and its interior operations, when perverse, are called ratiocinations, but when according to order, they are simply called reason, and are a species of thoughts, by virtue of the spiritual influx into them. These spheres arise from the sun, and may be called solar, and are consequently natu-ral. With respect to the interior mind, however, there is nothing in it that is natural, but what is spiritual, and in the inmost mind is what is heavenly or celestial. These principles are produced by God Messiah alone, and are living, and are to be called spiritual and heavenly spheres.'—S. D. 222.

" This passage disposes of the notion that our souls are '*formæ cœlestes perfectiores*,' (more perfect celestial forms,) in a most satisfactory manner ; what they really are, however, it does not show, or intimate even by analogy. . . . .

" Correspondence is the *lex magna* which mediates between natural and spiritual things ; for one mechanical form is only within another within certain limits, passing beyond which we enter the region of ideas, which such forms had only repre-sented in a certain image. The more we multiply the sides or angles of a polygon, for example, the nearer we approach a circle, but we can only arrive at the idea of a perfect circle by the total dissolution of the angles contained in the polygon; in like manner, also, the circle must be utterly dissolved, in order that the spiral may succeed, and so on to the highest natural form; when, at length, the most occult laws of geometry with every vestige of space and time must pass away, in order that we may comprehend the existence and form of pure spiritual substance. Swedenborg has himself spoken directly on this subject in the ' *Spiritual Diary* ' :—

" '. . . . I was afterwards led by the Lord so as to have some perception of forms, the idea of which exceeds immeasurably those drawn from geometry; for the lowest human forms, those of the intestines, for instance, exceed the forms of all geometric notions to such a degree, that they cannot be perceived by them at all; and if the intestinal spirals and the forms described by them, and still more the forms of their operations are such, that the most subtle of them cannot be conceived at all by the geometricians and their calculus of infinites, because they transcend indefinitely their calculus of infinites, how then can the forms of the more subtile organs be perceived by them from their geometrical formulæ, and how the vital forms, or those accommodated for the reception of life, which transcend the organic forms indefinitely, and also the sight. . . . ?'—n. 3482.

" '. . . . The limits of geometry are such that it does not even reach to the detection of the operations connected with the evacuation of the excrements, and still less to the form of the intestines, which are far above the geometrical calculus of the infinites.'—n. 3483.

" 'Lest, therefore, I should be held in these lowest and most finite things, a notion was given to me from the Lord of forms which transcend geometrical forms; for geometry ends in the circle, and the curves which have reference to the circle; all of which are terrestrial, and do not reach to the lowest atmosphere, not even to water. By removing from these lowest or terrestrial form imperfections, such as those which cause gravity, rest, cold, etc., it was granted to me to see in a most general manner forms which are not thus impeded ; and because some of these imperfections still remained, forms were perceived which were less limited, and again such as were still freer, until finally forms were presented in which not even a centre could be conceived of in any point whatsoever, so that they consisted of mere centres; afterwards all circles and peripheries, every point of which thus far had reference to centres, and *vice versa*, and together with them the whole of the lowest form was removed, in which form those boundaries are contained which constitute the limits of space and time, and I at last beheld myself transferred to forms which are almost without any boundaries, and thus without spaces and times. Nevertheless all these forms are still finite, because an idea may still be conceived of them, by withdrawing from them to a certain extent such things as are more finited; yet they still remain finite, and all these forms are still within the limits of nature, and are without life. Wherefore as long as the mind keeps itself or is kept within these forms it is still without life, but the things which are within or above them are alive from the Lord, and yet they are organical, because like the forms in nature they have no life in themselves. From all these considerations I now perceive, while I am writing concerning forms, that no one is ever enabled by abstraction to have any conception of the forms which are contained within the natural forms; I confess at last, that within the most subtle forms of nature there are spiritual forms, which can never become perceptible.'—n. 3484.

" But if such was the language of Swedenborg when taking a retrospective glance at his own masterly efforts, it will be interesting to compare it with his prospective views as a philosopher :—

" ' The doctrine of series and degrees, however, only teaches the distinction and relation between things superior and inferior, or prior and posterior; it is unable to express by any adequate terms of its own, those things that transcend the sphere of familiar things. If, therefore, we would ascend to a higher altitude, we must use terms which are still more abstract, universal, and eminent, lest we confound with the corporeal senses things of which we ought not only to have distinct perceptions, but which, in reality, are distinct. Hence it is necessary to have recourse to MATHEMATICAL PHILOSOPHY OF UNIVERSALS, which shall be enabled not only to signify higher ideas by letters proceeding in simple order, but also to reduce them to a certain philosophical calculus, in its form and in some of its rules not unlike the analysis of the infinites; for in higher ideas, much more in the highest, things occur too ineffable to be represented by common ideas. But, in truth, what an herculean task must it be to build up a system of this kind! What a stupendous exercise of intellectual powers does it require! For it demands the vigilance of the entire animal mind, and the assistance also of the superior mind or soul, to which science is proper and natural, and which represents nothing to itself by the signs used in speech, takes nothing from the common catalogue of words, but by means of the primitive and universal doctrine we have mentioned,—connate both with itself and with the objects of nature,—abstracts out of all things their nature and essence; and prepares and evolves each in the mutest silence. To this universal science, therefore, all other sciences and arts are subject; and it advances through their innermost mysteries as it proceeds from its own principles to causes, and from causes to effects, by its own, that is, by the natural order. This will be very manifest, if we contemplate the body of the soul, the viscera of the body, the sensory and motory organs, and the other parts which are framed for dependence upon, and connection and harmony with, each other; in fine, are fitted to the modes of universal nature; and this, so nicely, skilfully, and wonderfully, that there is nothing latent in the innermost and abstrusest principles of nature, science or art, but the soul has the knowledge and power of evoking to its aid, according as its purposes require.'—*Economy of the Animal Kingdom*, Part II., n. 211.

" Locke, as Swedenborg afterwards mentions, hinted at the necessity there was to elicit this ' science of sciences,' and our author himself has more definitively alluded to it, in his ' Introduction to Rational Physiology,' where he speaks of the ascent from the sphere of particular and common expressions, to that of universal and general ones, and quotes the celebrated Wolff as an authority for including such a mathematical philosophy among the desiderata of learning. That it had become the one ruling idea in his own mind is again evident from the epilogue to the second part of the 'Animal Kingdom,' where he reverts to it as the means for promoting a connection or concentration of all the sciences into one; so that the soul might descend through all the mysteries of geometry, mechanics, physics, chemistry, optics, acoustics, pneumatics, logic, psychology, etc., as through its familiar haunts, into the very work-rooms of the social fabric. It was not, however, as a mere synthesis of the sciences, that Swedenborg had entertained this bold conception, but as a means of unlocking the most profound secrets of our being, and of bringing the contest between truths and assumptions to a glorious consummation; and because, in short, he felt it impossible to carry his analysis of the operations of nature to any ulterior conclusions without it.

"While, however, it was certainly his intention to elicit the formulæ of this universal science, and present the world with a complete apparatus for the computation and deduction of truths, it is just as certain that he left his 'herculean labor' unfinished. We infer, therefore, that on his actual intromission into the sphere which he had approached with so much labor, he discovered that the highest flights of his genius were, after all, on a level with mere observation; that a course of experience awaited him, and those who might become his followers, which not only supplied the place of his highest physical deductions, but carried them infinitely further; that henceforth the necessity of inventing characters and methods, as a means of arriving at psychological truths, must be over-ruled by the sensuous discernment of psychological phenomena; that in this way it had been the good pleasure of the Lord to lead him away from those metaphysical subtleties into which he must otherwise have plunged himself, and which (in their logical form) he had himself condemned in the schools, and, finally, that this very experience would furnish the rules of a true metaphysical doctrine for the future church.

"This view is strongly confirmed by what our author has said in respect to the introductory rules of his proposed science of universals, in his '*Economy of the Animal Kingdom*,' Part I., n. 648 :—

"*If we would explore the efficient, rational, and principal causes of the operations and effects existing in the animal body, it will be necessary first to inquire what things, in a superior degree, correspond to those which are in an inferior degree, and by what name they are to be called.* In other words, what things in one and the same series mutually succeed each other, are dependent on and have respect to each other by degrees; for so separate from each other do they appear, that without the most internal and analytic rational intuition, it seems impossible that the things of a superior degree should be recognized and acknowledged as the superior forms of things inferior; for the sensory of the inferior forms, they are incomprehensible, and appear as in continuity with them (n. 623–626). In other words, unless the things of the inferior degree were distinct from those of the superior, they could not be compared with a substance which subsists by itself (n. 589), but would be the same things with the superior ones, taken in the aggregate, or collectively (n. 629–630). In order then to ascertain and to know what that is in a superior degree which corresponds to its proper inferior, rules must be discovered to guide us in pointing it out, which we are enabled to do under any of the following circumstances :—

"1. In case in the several things, which are beneath any given one, and not only in the one proximately beneath, but in all which follow, it be found to be the common and universally reigning principle. 2. In case it be so distinct from the superior that it subsists by itself; or is able not only to subsist together with the other, but separately by itself without it. 3. In case it be unknown whether it be its superior correspondent, except by way of analogy and eminence; and we are ignorant of its quality except by reflection, or by the knowledge of inferior things, as in a minor. 4. Hence in case it has to be marked by an entirely different name. 5. In case there be a connection between the two, otherwise the superior and inferior entity of that series would have no dependence on each other, or mutual relation. ' By reflection and abstraction alone,' says Wolff, ' universal notions are not made complete and determinate. For reflection is wholly occupied in the successive direction of the attention to general principles;

nor is anything obtained by abstraction, except that those general principles are seen to be different from the objects of perception in which they exist.   .   .   .   Thus it does not hence appear, whether those general principles contain more or fewer particulars·· than are sufficient to   .   .   .   distinguish the things of that genus or species from those of another.   .   .   . Therefore it is unknown, whether they are complete and determinate.'   (Psychologia Rationalis, § 401.)   'The making the discovery, therefore, *is a work demanding both a knowledge of facts and skill in judging of them:* for if we rely either on reason without facts, or on facts without reason, our endeavor to find what we seek will be to no purpose.'

"'The observance of these rules in a course of investigation would doubtlessly have led to a strong presumption in favor of the separate existence of the soul; but when its separate existence is actually seen, *that experience* and not these rules becomes the foundation of the metaphysical structure; and the physical inductions themselves, as we shall immediately see, put on a significance very different to that which has connected them with the rules which they suggested.

" All the physiological truths elicited by Swedenborg group themselves around two centres—the animation of the brains, and the conjoint relation of the heart and lungs to the system. The distribution of spiritual life by the will and understanding, of which the two brains are the organs, and to which the heart and lungs in the second sphere of the body respectively correspond; while the grand product of the lungs to the whole system, or the motion, which we cannot say they generate, but, which they administer to all the viscera, etc., imports also by analogy the free determination enjoyed by man's spirit, which enables him to act from his own will or intention; this analogy establishes the heart and lungs in a certain relation to the will and understanding, so that in the word of Swedenborg, ' from the correspondence of the heart with the will, and of the understanding with the lungs, may be known all things that can be known of the will and understanding, or of love and wisdom, consequently all that can be known of man's soul.' (Divine Love and Wisdom, 394.)   Coming as a part of the author's spiritual philosophy, these few words throw a light of startling brilliancy over a wide field of investigation ; but transplant them to the list of his philosophical inductions—separate them from the experience of 1745 and subsequent years, they become a veritable *apocalypsis* on which reason might exhaust its resources in vain. It is perfectly mysterious to compare the will to the heart, if we suppose the same laws of form and motion to govern both, . . . and the comparison between the lungs and the understanding is equally recondite ; yet if the true idea of spiritual existence is to be arrived at by a course of mathematical abstraction, we see no way of avoiding the mystery. We may even deceive ourselves by harping on the terms analogy and correspondence (for nature is full of analogies) if we do not discriminate between what is spiritual and what is natural in the terms.* The circulation of the animal spirit, for example, is in a certain analogy to the circulation of the blood, and if an abstract geometry can be supposed to present the form of the one, it can also, by further abstraction, represent the other ; but then both terms of the analogy belong to the natural sphere, and this is the reason why we cannot, by a still further abstraction of mathematical or mechanical laws, obtain the representation of the spirit. Swedenborg himself recognized this principle when he abandoned the terms '*perpetual vortical*,' or '*celestial*,' '*perpetual celestial*,' or '*spiritual*,' and '*perpetual spiritual*,' as exponents of the living forces within nature, in which sense he uses them in the 'Economy of the Animal Kingdom,' vol. iii.

"The kind of experience from which the correspondence of the human organization was elicited by the author, is, we believe, unparalleled. We have just instanced the heart and lungs as examples of the manner in which physiological terms are convertible into the nomenclature of psychology. . . . This kind of evidence concerning spiritual things might be added to a thousandfold from what the author has written on these subjects, but we have quoted sufficient to establish our position that spiritual things are wholly different in kind from

---

* "To this effect indeed are the observations and rules of the author in the last quotation, which may be regarded as an effort to accomplish that by a scientific method, which the mere opening of his spiritual sight has adapted even to the simplest apprehension."

material things; and as the author himself has guarded us against identifying them as a part of that mathematical unity in which it was his noble aim to comprise all the sciences.

"All spiritual activity, in short, is the activity of affection and thought; and if 'geometry with its whole array of infinites' cannot grasp at all, even 'the forms of the intestines,' how can we imagine that the heavenly forms of love and intelligence are to be thus mechanically represented? The simple truth is, that the influx of spiritual activity into our natural organization causes that organization to work mechanically; and so far as we may be able to represent its motions by geometrical lines, or by any mathematical calculus, so far, and no farther, will the laws of geometry represent spiritual things as they are in themselves."

This extract shows the limit of natural philosophy, and where spiritual philosophy commences. In case any of our readers wish to become acquainted with Swedenborg's spiritual philosophy after his illumination, we recommend to them a study of his work on "Divine Love and Wisdom," which has been adverted to above.

100. The following summary of Swedenborg's position in philosophy and theology is given by PROF. IMMANUEL TAFEL, in his "*History and Criticism of Scepticism*," pp. 442–446.

"Emanuel Swedenborg placed faith above reason and experience, but he combined these three spheres again into one, and showed that divine things, provided they are true, may be comprehended as well as natural things, and that what cannot be thought of in connection with other things, can also not be believed. If we wish to be just, we must admit that it was Swedenborg who first removed philosophically the great difficulties contained in the doctrine of freedom, and that the problem of the world in general was first solved by him in a satisfactory manner. Wherefore Fichte also, as it seems, toward the last drew from him, and only recently another philosopher who had twice risen against Hegel, declared in a journal of Northern Germany, that 'in order to have a just opinion of Swedenborg, we must first learn a great deal from him.'"

IX.

SWEDENBORG'S THEOLOGY.

WE have observed Swedenborg's progress through the sciences and philosophy, and have seen how, beginning at the lowest depths of nature, he gradually worked his way up to the very confines of the spiritual world. Here we must leave him; for the limits of our volume do not permit us to follow him in his theological career. Our readers will have to content themselves with a few extracts that we have already given in a previous chapter (nos. 38–40); but in order to show them that Swedenborg in his theological writings has preserved the same characteristics which distinguished him in his scientific career, and that the eccentricity and obscurity which are frequently attributed to these writings, are in fact our own, which we impute to them, we shall present to the thoughtful consideration of our readers the following true occurrence, which is related in the same little work from which we have quoted our extract, n. 96. *Medicus Cantabrigiensis* continues :—

"Not many weeks since a brother Fellow of the Royal College of Physicians observed to us, that he believed that Swedenborg was a great philosopher; but that when his religious career began, his unsoundness of mind set in. This observation harmonizes with the notions too generally prevalent amongst the better educated portion of society at the present day. Many moreover of the less educated are not aware that Swedenborg has any claim whatever to the character of a philosopher. They regard him as a mere fanatic, or even as a positive lunatic, without lucid intervals; whilst theologians in general consider that his system of theology—his ' UNIVERSAL THEOLOGY,' as he terms it—is the offspring of mental delusion.

"Now, since theologians are especially interested in this branch of the question, we would meet their view of Swedenborg's mental condition, by the narration of a simple but interesting fact, which occurred within the sphere of our own acquaintance. The fact is connected with a clergyman, a member of the University of Oxford, who, meeting with a volume in the library of the Royal Institution, entitled 'THE TRUE CHRISTIAN RELIGION, containing THE UNIVERSAL THEOLOGY of the NEW CHURCH,' etc., was desirous of ascertaining the nature of its contents. He was somewhat disconcerted at finding that Swedenborg was the author of the volume, but nevertheless took it home for perusal. He read a few pages without making anything of them, and his interest in the work ceased. The book was left amongst others on a table, where it attracted the notice of his man-servant, who used to read it, leaving it open from time to time. At length his master, returning one day from his round of clerical duty, and having his curiosity excited at so repeatedly finding the book open, asked the man whether he was reading it. 'Yes, sir,' he replied. 'Do you understand it?' 'Every word of it, sir; it is beautiful!' The answer induced my friend to try the volume again. He did so, and the happy result was, that he became one of the most intelligent and active defenders of the system of theology which Swedenborg was the instrument of propounding to mankind.

"Our friend's mind was pre-occupied with ideas and thoughts that rendered Swedenborg's teaching unintelligible to him. The servant's mind, being free from all such bias, was able to discern a meaning which was at once simple and intelligible, where the master thought all was obscure or discordant. But the master, with true moral courage and humility of soul, took up the book again, and soon found that the native simplicity of his servant's mind formed no obstacle whatever to the right reception of truth, and its enlightening influence upon a comparatively untrained intellect.

"Our clerical friend, after an honest and impartial examination of Swedenborg's writings, found them throughout distinguished for wisdom, intelligence and science, and in every respect worthy of most cordial and universal adoption. And after the lapse of many years, he, like ourselves, finds increased and increasing reasons to recommend them heartily to the perusal of every sincere lover of truth, especially the minister of the Church of Christ. It would indeed be difficult for psychologists and theologians of the present day to explain the facts, that an unlettered servant was able to discern that which the accomplished scholar at first failed to find in the theology of Swedenborg; and that the same accomplished scholar, as he read and examined for himself, found his prejudices against Swedenborg vanish, and his mind become more enlightened by the teaching of this great and good man, than by all the learning that the University of Oxford could bestow. But let it not be supposed that this is a solitary instance of the triumph of that truth which Swedenborg proclaims. It is one amongst hundreds of the same kind, and can only be ascribed to the greatest of all psychical blessings — the possession of an ' honest and good heart' in the search of truth."

The following extract from " Remarks on the Assertions of the Author of the ' Memoirs of Jacobinism' respecting the character of Eman. Swedenborg and the tendency of his writings," (Philadelphia, 1800,) shows the estimate which an eminent statesman placed upon Swedenborg's Theology in its effect upon civil life.

" His Excellency the Senator Count Hopken, when he was Prime Minister of Sweden, one day observed to his Majesty, King Gustavus, that if the Swedes should hereafter establish any colony, the doctrine which Swedenborg has published ought to be taught in it, because that agreeable to the principles he lays down, the colonists would truly possess the love of God and charity as the end of all their actions: that they would be active, industrious, and intrepid in dangers, being verily persuaded that what we call death is no more than a passage from this life to one that is more happy, thus that in reality death is only a continuation of life."

17*

X.

THE PUBLISHED AND UNPUBLISHED SCIENTIFIC AND PHILOSOPHICAL WORKS OF SWEDENBORG.

We divide Swedenborg's literary career into three periods. The first preparatory or chaotic period in which, as he expresses it, he " alternated his mathematical works with poetry," and where he " desired all possible novelties, ay, a novelty for every day in the year, provided the world be pleased with them," commenced in the year 1709, when he was twenty-one years old, and reaches to the year 1720, when he gathered up his manifold energies, and on the one hand " made up his mind to seek his fortune in his business, which is all such things as concern the advancement of mining," and on the other prepared for those solid scientific and philosophical works which belong to his second period. This period commenced in the year 1720, and extended to the year 1745. In this year his illumination began, in which his theological works were written—this third period lasted to the hour of his death in 1772. So that Swedenborg's literary career extended over sixty-three years, from 1709 to 1772!

First Period, *from* 1709 *to* 1720.

1. L. Annæi Senecæ et Pub. Syri Mimi forsan et aliorum Selectæ Sententiæ. Quas notis illustratas edidit Emanuel Swedberg [Swedenborg]. At fidem rarissimæ editionis principis anni 1709 denuo publici juris fecit et fragmenta nuper reperta adjecit *Dr. J. F. E. Tafel.* Tubingæ, 1841.—The first edition was published at Upsala, in 1709.

Select Sentences of L. Annæus Seneca, and Pub. Syrus Mimus, and a few others, edited with notes by Emanuel Swedberg [Swedenborg].

(198)

2. Ludus Heliconius sive Carmina Miscellanea, quæ variis in locis cecinit EMAN. SWEDBERG [SWEDENBORG]. Edit. iii, emendata et locupletata recensuit *Dr. J. F. Eman. Tafel.* Tubingæ. 1841.—The first edition was published at Skara in 1710.

Heliconian Sports or Miscellaneous Poems written in various places by Eman. Swedberg.

3. Camena Borea cum Heroum et Heroidum factis ludens: sive Fabellæ Ovidianis similes cum variis nominibus scriptæ ab EMAN. SWEDBERG [SWEDENBORG]. Ad fidem editionis principis anno 1715. Gryphiswaldiæ excusæ denuo edidit *Dr. Jo. Fr. Im. Tafel.* Tubingæ, 1845.

Northern Muse, sporting with the deeds of heroes and heroines: or Fables in the style of Ovid, with different titles, written by Eman. Swedberg.

4. Daedalus Hyperboreus, sive nova Experimenta Mathematica et Physica. Upsaliæ, 1716, 1717, 1718. 4to.

This work, consisting of new experiments in mathematics and physics, by Swedenborg and several of his scientific friends, was published in six parts, all of which are in Swedish, but the fifth part has a Latin version also.

5. Foersock, att finna Oestra och Westra Laengden igen, igenom Mânan. Upsala, 1718, 8vo., pp. 38.

Attempts to find the longitude of places by lunar observations.

This is the original Swedish edition of the work subsequently published in Latin at Amsterdam in 1721, of which a second edition was printed about the year 1766, as we learn from a letter of Swedenborg to Dr. Menander, Archbishop of Sweden.

6. Regel-Konsten författted i Tijo Bökker, etc. Upsala, 1718, 8vo., pp. 135.

Algebra, or the art of rules, comprised in ten books, etc.

This work is reviewed at considerable length in the *Acta Literaria Sueciæ*, (vol. i. p. 126,) and is mentioned with great honor—not only because the author was the first Swede who wrote on the higher branches of the subject, but for the excellence of the treatise itself, the clearness of the language, and the examples showing the application and uses of the rules.

Each book is divided into three parts. The following is a brief outline of the contents of this work :—

Book I. contains the definitions and explanations of the terms employed, and the simpler arithmetical processes.

Book II. The mechanical powers, the lever, pulley, inclined plane, etc., with a variety of problems.

Book III. The laws of proportions and ratios ; also with numerous problems.

Book IV. Geometrical theorems, stereometry, and specific gravity.

Book V. The properties of the Parabola and Hyperbola.

Book VI. The properties of the Parabola more fully considered, with numerous other problems.

Book VII. On the theory of Projectiles and Artillery, with many problems.

Books VIII., IX., X. On adfected Roots, and on the integral and differential Calculus.

7. Om Wattnens Hoegd, och foerra Werldens starka Ebb och Flod, Bewis utur Swerige. Stockholm, 1719, 8vo., pp. 40.

Arguments derived from appearances in Sweden in favor of the depth of the water and greater tides of the sea in the ancient world.

8. De Monetarum Mensurarumque Ordinatione Decimali.

On the Decimal System of Moneys and Measures, to facilitate calculation and abolish fractions. This work was published in Swedish with the following title, " Forslåg till vårt Mynts och Måls Indelning." Upsala, 1719, 4to. In the Catalogue of the Upsala Library, another edition of this work in octavo, 1795, is mentioned.

9. Om Jordenes och Planeternas Gång och Stånd. Skara, 1719, 8vo.

On the Motion and Position of the Earth and Planets.

10. Om Vennerns fallende och stigande.

On the rise and fall of Lake Wenner, with an accurate sketch of the cataracts of the river Gotha Elf.

This is a manuscript dissertation of Swedenborg's, founded on various observations transmitted to him in letters by scientific persons. It is mentioned in the *Acta Literaria Succiœ* (p. 3), but the notice does not say whether it was ever printed, nor is the size of the dissertation stated. Reference is made, however, to page 79, and the review would lead us to suppose that the original treatise was a very interesting work.

11. On Docks, Sluices and Saltworks. 1719.

This work is recorded by Dr. Wilkinson as having been written by Swedenborg in Swedish; we could not find any reference to it in any other author, nor does it seem to have been noticed in the *Acta Literaria*.

12. Fabula de Amore et Metamorphosi Uranies in Virum et in famulum Apollinis; ad illustrissimum et excellentissimum R. S. Senatorem, comitem Mauritium Wellink. Naupotami, 1722. 4to. carmine elegiaco.

This poem is noticed in the ' Acta Literaria,' vol. i. p. 589.*

To the unpublished works of Swedenborg of this period belongs the collection of

13. *Original Letters and Papers by* EMANUEL SWEDENBORG, discovered at the Gymnasium of Linköping in Sweden.

This collection contains the following articles :—

1. Petenda Societatis Literariæ.
2. Project for a new Society of Sciences at Upsala.
3. Plan and description of a Flying Machine.
4. On the Causes of Things.
5. On the Improvement of Trade and Manufactures.
6. On the Establishment of Saltpetre Works in Sweden.
7. On the Nature of Fire and Colors.
8. A new Method of Sailing against the Wind.
9. Machinery for carrying Vessels against the Stream.
10. A ' Dragmaschin.'
11. Memorandums on some minor trials and experiments.
12. On different sorts of Soils and Muds.
13. Project and Calculation for a Pile-driving Machine.
14. Proportiones Aërometricæ, and new Stereometric Rules.
15. Description of a Crane.
16. New ways of discovering Mines and Treasures.

---

* To the account of Swedenborg's works, Nos. 5 to 12, we are indebted to Dr. Ch. Edw. Strutt in his translation of Swedenborg's work on Chemistry.—EDIT.

17. New method of finding Longitudes by Lunar Observations.

18. On Mechanical Inventions.

19. An Anthropological Treatise.

20. On the Sulphureous quality of the Atmosphere.

The letters addressed to *Benzelius*, the brother-in-law of Swedenborg, are written on the following subjects :—

21. Respecting his appointment as Assessor of the Board of Mines.

22. On a peculiar Air-pump to be worked by Water.

23. On Mechanical Inventions, 1715.

24. Containing information respecting Charles XII., 1715.

25. On calculating Interest by means of a Triangle, 1716.

26. On the regulation of Salaries in a Mathematical Society, 1716.

27. On his Invention of a method of finding the Longitude, 1716.

28. On the construction of a Canal between Gottenburg and Lake Hjelmar, 1717.

29. On the same Canal, and on Salt-works, 1717.

30. Containing a project for an Observatory at Upsal, 1717.

31. On Salt and Salt Sources, 1718.

32. On a Water Communication between Kattegat and Norkopping, 1718.

33. On the King's Campaign in Norway, 1718 (4 letters).

34. On Astronomical Hypotheses, 1719 (2 letters).

35. On the Decimal System of Money and Measures, 1719.

36. On the Lymphatics, 1720.

37. On the establishment of a Lottery, 1720.

38. On his (Swedenborg's) Anatomy, 1720.

39. On his determination with respect to Fire and Metals to penetrate " A primis incunabilis usque ad maturitatem," 1720.

40. Containing Literary Notices and communications, 1722–24 (6 letters).

" These letters," says Dr. Wilkinson, " have been purchased some time since by the ' *Swedenborg Association*' [now merged in the ' *Swedenborg Printing Society* '] at considerable cost. They are in Swedish, but a translation of most of them has been prepared by Mr. Charles Edward Strutt, and the whole will shortly be in English. There is, however, no prospect that at present the Association can publish these highly interesting documents, at least unless its funds are very differently supported from what they are at present."

This has been written in 1847, almost twenty years ago, and these letters have not yet made their appearance before the public. As they were written between Swedenborg's 27th and 34th years, of which period of his life very little is known to us at present, it seems very important that they should be no longer withheld from us. We call the earnest attention of all the friends of Swedenborg to these letters, and hope that the funds may soon be forthcoming to secure their publication.

Second Period, *from* 1720 *to* 1745.

14. Prodromus Principiorum Rerum Naturalium, sive Novorum Tentaminum, Chemiam et Physicam Experimentalem Geometrice explicandi. Amstelodami, 1721.

Specimens of a Work on the Principles of Natural Philosophy, comprising New Attempts to explain the Phenomena of Chemistry and Physics by Geometry.

This volume forms part of a work still existing in manuscript in Sweden, but which has not yet been published. It does not appear to have gone through a second edition, but fresh title pages were used, as some copies bear the date of 1721, others of 1727, whilst others are published at Hilburghausen, in 1754.

The following are the contents of the volume :—

On the first Generation of Salts, &c., in the Primeval Ocean, with a few Remarks on the Depth of that Ocean.

Principles of Natural Philosophy.

Part VIII. On the different Positions of Round Particles.

Part IX. The Theory of Water; briefly showing the Geometrical Properties and Internal Mechanism of its Particles.

Part XI. The Theory of Common Salt, containing Geometrical and Experimental Demonstrations of the Internal Mechanism of its Particles.

Part XII. The Theory of Acid, containing Geometrical and

Experimental Demonstrations of the Particle of the Acid of Salt; and showing the Mechanism of its Figure.

Part XIII. The Theory of Nitre; containing Geometrical and Experimental Demonstrations of its Particles, and showing the Mechanism of their Shape and Position.

Part XIV. The Theory of Oil and of Volatile Urinous Salt; stating the Experiments on these Substances, and briefly explaining the Geometry of the Particles.

Appendix, containing some General Rules concerning Transparency, and White, Red, and Yellow Colors, taken from Swedenborg's Theory of Light and Rays.

Part XXV. The Theory of Lead: containing a Geometrical and Experimental Demonstration of its Particles or Internal Mechanism.

Experiments on Silver, and Mercury.

15. Nova Observata et Inventa circa Ferrum et Ignem, praecipue circa Naturam Ignis Elementarem. Amstelodami, 1721.

New Observations and Discoveries respecting Iron and Fire, and particularly respecting the Elemental Nature of Fire: together with a New Construction of Stoves.

Mr. Strutt remarks concerning this treatise: "It is a short disquisition on Iron and Fire, with observations and theoretical suggestions, based on actual data obtained at a large iron foundry. It contains many curious remarks, particularly on the laws observed by fire in penetrating hard substances.

"The information derived from the iron foundry as to the nature and properties of fire, is reduced to practice in the paper on the construction of stoves. In these new stoves, the object has been to obtain a pleasant and equable temperature, with a constant supply of fresh warm air, at the least possible expense of fuel."

This stove, invented by Swedenborg, is generally known in our country under the name of "air-tight stove." It was patented in Washington, although the principle of this stove was discovered and made known by Swedenborg more than a hundred years ago. (See the "Intellectual Repository," for February, 1842, where Swedenborg's claim is minutely examined, and a detailed description of the stove is given.)

16. Modus Construendi Receptacula Navalia; Amstelodami 1721, or A Mode of Constructing Dry Docks for Shipping.

Nova Constructio Aggeris Aquatici; or, A New Mode of
Constructing Dykes to exclude Inundations of the Sea or of
Rivers.

Modus Mechanice Explorandi Virtutes Navigiorum ; or, A
Mode of ascertaining, by Mechanical Means, the Qualities of
Vessels.

These three little treatises, together with the Latin translation of n. 5. " Methodus Nova Inveniendi Longitudinem
Locorum, Terra Marique, Ope Lunæ"; or, A New Method of
finding the Longitude of Places, on Land and at Sea, by Lunar
Observations, were published together in a small pamphlet,
in Amsterdam, at the same time with nos. 14 and 15. These
three works, (our nos. 14, 15 and 16,) have been translated into
English by Mr. Charles Edward Strutt, and were published
by the ' *Swedenborg Association* ' in one volume in 1847, under
the title,—*Some Specimens of a Work on the Principles of
Chemistry, with other Treatises.* (pp. 241.)

Concerning the work n. 16, Mr. Strutt says, in the ' Introduction ' to his translation : " The new method of constructing
docks, in seas where there are no tides, gives us an interesting
account of a difficult undertaking, and is a good specimen of
Swedenborg's abilities as an engineer. Unfortunately, the
plates which illustrated the description do not exist in any of
the copies of the work which the translator has been able to
procure ; but the whole process is so clearly set forth, that the
reader will have no difficulty in understanding it, notwithstanding the absence of the illustrations. The plates belonging to
the plan for making dams are also lost ; but it is hoped that a
copy containing them may yet be met with. The volume concludes with a few suggestions for ascertaining the sailing and
other qualities of vessels, by experiments on a small scale,
with a view to their application to ship-building."

17. Miscellanea Observata circa Res Naturales ; praesertim
Mineralia, Ignem et Montium Strata.

Miscellaneous Observations on Natural Things, particularly
on Minerals, Fire, and the Strata of Mountains.

This work was published at Leipsic in 1722, in three parts,

18

to which a Fourth Part, published in the same year at Schiff-beck, near Hamburg, was subsequently added. An English translation of this work, by Mr. Ch. E. Strutt, was published by the 'Swedenborg Association' in London, in 1847, under the title,—"*Miscellaneous Observations connected with the Physical Sciences.*" (pp. 149.) In the same volume they likewise published a translation of the papers in n. 18.

Contents of Part I.

On the different kinds of Mountains in Sweden, with a disquisition on their origin.

On the Petrified Plants found at Liege.

On the Strata of Shells at Aix-la-Chapelle.

On the harder Strata, consisting of the common Granite, and their origin.

On inclined Strata, and the causes of their inclination.

On the causes of the varieties in Strata.

Observations, and points to be observed, concerning Strata, their separation, arrangement, and differences.

On Stony Marl, or Margenstein.

On the Circular Crusts found in certain stones, and on Mountain Nuclei.

On the Primeval Matter of Earth, with reasons for conjecturing that it was Water.

On the Subsidence of the Seas towards the North.

Observations and Experiments on the origin, temperature, and saline components of Hot Springs.

Part II.

On Vitrification, and the change of Particles into Glass.

On the softening of hard Bodies, and on the origin of Actites, Belemnites, &c.

On the entrance of Liquids, as, for example, Water and Fire, into hard Bodies.

Observations on Cooling, as on the escape of Fire from Bodies.

On the improvement of Stoves in Sweden.

A new construction of Fireplace.

On Wind or Draught Furnaces.

The Causes of Smoke in Rooms.

A New Construction of Air-pump, worked by Mercury.

On the Salt Works on Parts of the Swedish Coast.

A Method of ascertaining, by means of a Triangle, the Individual Weights of mixed Metals, from the Weight of the Mass previously ascertained in Water and in Air.

The Glass of Archimedes; an Instrument for ascertaining the Proportions of mixed Metals mechanically, without any Calculations.

Reasons showing the Impossibility of transmuting Metals, especially into Gold.

The Blood circulates through the Capillaries more easily than through the Trunks of the Arteries.

Part III.

On a New Germination of pure Water when converted into Ice.

A Hypothesis of the Figure and Different Magnitude of Elementary Particles.

On the Great Power and Intense Motion of the Smaller Bullular Particles especially.

Hypothesis of the Undulation and Vibration of Bullular Particles.

Hypothesis of the Figure of the Particles of Fire and Air.

On the Interfluent Subtle Matter between the Particles of Water.

The Mechanism of Bullular Particles.

On the Centripetency of heavy Bodies in Elements consisting of Bullular Particles.

The Notion of a Central Fire.

The Phenomena of Phosphorescence of the Ignis Fatuus, explained according to the Bullular Hypothesis.

On the Increments and degrees of Heat in Bodies, according to the Bullular Hypothesis.

Part IV.

On a new Sexagenary Calculus, invented by Charles XII., of glorious memory, late King of Sweden.

Reasons to show that Mineral Effluvia, or Particles, penetrate into their Matrices, and impregnate them with Metal, by means of Water as a Vehicle.

On Stalactites, and Crystallizations of Stone; with remarks upon the resemblance of these formations to Congealed Water.

On the Petrifying Fluid or Juice; with remarks to prove that it is not indentical with the water that produces the Stalactite.

On the formation of Quartz and Spar, with reasons showing the probability of their past diluvian origin.

General observations on Furnaces for smelting Iron, with suggestions for improving them.

" In all these papers," says Mr. Strutt, " the acute observation and practical sagacity of the author are conspicuous; and if a few of his deductions may be considered as somewhat questionable, others have since been corroborated by modern researches. . . The papers on the Elementary and Bullular Hypothesis are evidently the first ideas of the theories afterwards so ably developed in the ' *Principia.*' The ' *Principles of Chemistry*' likewise throw considerable light on several of the subjects treated of in these pages; and in their turn, they also derive support from the theories and experiments in these *Miscellaneous Observations.* So true it is, that the same idea of thought runs through the whole of the author's philosophical writings, susceptible of amplification and expansion; so that as our facts increase, they may each be arranged in their proper place and order; of which, indeed, several recent discoveries in the higher departments of science are remarkable illustrations."

18. Papers by Swedenborg, from the " *Acta Literaria Succiæ.*"

1. Letter to Jacob a Melle, on the Primeval Ocean, extracted from the " Acta, etc.," vol. i., 1721, pp. 192–196.

2. New Rules for maintaining Heat in Rooms.—" Acta, etc.," vol. i., 1721, pp. 282–285.

3. An Elucidation of a Law of Hydrostatics, demonstrating the Power of the deepest Waters of the Deluge, and their Action on the Rocks and other Substances at the bottom of their bed.—" Acta, etc.," vol. i., 1721, pp. 353—356.

Two of these papers (Nos. 1, and 2,) were translated into

English in the *Acta Germanica*, vol. i.; London, 1742. All three papers are added as an Appendix to Mr. Strutt's translation of the "*Miscellaneous Observata*."

19. Opera Philosophica et Mineralia. Tres Tomi. Dresdæ et Lipsiæ, 1734, folio (vol. i., pp. 425, vol. ii., pp. 385, vol. iii., pp. 534).
Philosophical and Mineral Works.
Vol. I. Principia Rerum Naturalium, sive, Novorum Tentaminum, Phænomena Mundi Elementaris Philosophice Explicandi; or, The Principia; or, the First Principles of Natural Things, being New Attempts toward a Philosophical Explanation of the Elementary World.
This volume has been translated into English by the Rev. Augustus Clissold, M. A., and was published by the "*Swedenborg Association*," in London, in two volumes, (1845 and 1846,) vol. i., pp. 380, vol. ii., pp. 383.
Vol. II. Regnum Subterraneum sive Minerale, de Ferro; or, the Subterranean or Mineral Kingdom, consisting of a Treatise on Iron.
This work was translated into French by Bouchu, and published at Paris, in 1762, in the magnificent *Description des Arts et Métiers*, issued by the Royal Academy of Sciences; "because," as they said, "this work was found to be the best on this subject." The chapter on the conversion of iron into steel had been previously translated into French, and published in Strasburg (1734).
Vol. III. Regnum Subterraneum sive Minerale, de Cupro et Orichalco; or, The Subterranean, or Mineral Kingdom, on Copper and Brass.

20. Prodromus Philosophiæ Ratiocinantis de Infinito, et Causa Finali Creationis: deque Mechanismo Operationis Animæ et Corporis. Dresdae et Lipsiæ, 1734.
Outlines of a Philosophical Argument on the Infinite, and the final Cause of Creation; and on the Intercourse between the Soul and the Body, pp. 149.
This work had been translated into English as early as 1795, when it was published at Manchester. "This transla-

tion," says Dr. Wilkinson, "was by no means a successful rendering of this difficult work." The Doctor's own translation was published by the Swedenborg Association, in 1847 (pp. 149); a reprint of this translation has also been published in Boston.

21. Dissertationes duæ de Fibra et Succo Nervoso, 8vo. Romæ, 1740.

Two Dissertations on the Nervous Fibre and the Nervous Fluid, Rome, in 1740.

Dr. Wilkinson says, respecting this work : " It is recorded in one list of his works, and we have obtained collateral evidence of the fact, that he published this work at Rome in 1740 ; yet it is hardly probable that he returned to Rome in that year, and accordingly his authorship of such a publication is doubtful. Nevertheless it is easiest to account for the assertion by supposing its truth ; and certainly the title of the work bears a Swedenborgian aspect." *Swedenborg, a Biography*, American edition, p. 39.

In a foot-note to this, Doctor Wilkinson adds the following : " Sprengel, in his *History of Medicine*, (the French translation by Jourdan, vol. iv., p. 326,) mentions a work which he supposes to be Swedenborg's, viz. : *Dilucidationes de Origine Animæ et Malo Hereditario*, 8vo. Stockholm, 1740. As we have not been able to meet with these *Thoughts on the Origin of the Soul and Hereditary Evil*, we cannot say what intrinsic evidence they may present of his authorship. It is likely that he returned to Stockholm this year."

22. Œconomia Regni Animalis in Transactiones Divisa : Anatomice, Physice et Philosophice, perlustrata. (Trans. I. II.) 4to. Londini et Amstelodami, 1740, 1741.

The Economy of the Animal Kingdom, considered Anatomically, Physically, and Philosophically.

Part I.

INTRODUCTION.

Chap. I. The Composition and Genuine Essence of the Blood.

Chap. II. The Arteries and Veins, their Tunics, and the Circulation of the Blood.

Chap. III. On the Formation of the Chick in the Egg, and on the Arteries, Veins, and Rudiments of the Heart.

Chap. IV. On the Circulation of the Blood in the Fœtus; and on the Foramen Ovale and Ductus Arteriosus belonging to the Heart in Embryos and Infants.

Chap. V. The Heart of the Turtle.

Chap. VI. The peculiar Arteries and Veins of the Heart, and the Coronary Vessels.

Chap. VII. The Motion of the Adult Heart.

Chap. VIII. Introduction to Rational Psychology.

Part II.

Chap. I. On the Motion of the Brain; showing that its Animation is coincident with the Respiration of the Lungs.

Chap. II. The Cortical Substance of the Brain specifically.

Chap. III. The Human Soul.

This work has been translated into English by the Rev. Augustus Clissold, M. A., and was published by the " Swedenborg Association," in 1845 and '46, in two volumes. Vol. i., pp. 574; vol. ii., pp. 357.

23. Regnum Animale Anatomice, Physice et Philosophice perlustratum (Parts i. ii. iii.). 4to. Hagae Comitum et Londini, 1744, 1745.

The Animal Kingdom, considered Anatomically, Physically, and Philosophically.

Part I. The Viscera of the Abdomen, or the Organs of the Inferior Region.

Part II. The Viscera of the Thorax, or the Organs of the Superior Region.

Part III. The Skin, the Senses of Touch and Taste, and Organic Forms generally.

This work has been translated into English by Dr. Wilkinson, and was published in London in 1843 and '44, in two volumes. Vol. i., pp. 526; vol. ii., pp. 593.

24. De Cultu et Amore Dei, Londini, 1745.
On the Worship and Love of God.

Part. I. On the Origin of the Earth, on the State of Paradise in the Vegetable and Animal Kingdoms, and on the Birth, Infancy, and Love of Adam, or the First-born Man.

Part II. On the Marriage of the First-born, and on the Soul, the Intellectual Mind, the state of Integrity, and the Image of God.

The first edition of the English translation, made by Mr. Clowes, was printed at Manchester, in 1816; the second at London, in 1828. An American edition has lately been published in Boston, (1864,) pp. 240.

This is the last of Swedenborg's Scientific and Philosophical Works, which he published himself; the following works he left in manuscript, and they have been published since his death.

25. Opuscula quædam Argumenti Philosophici, Ex autographo in Bibliotheca Regiæ Academiæ Holmiensis asservato, nunc primum edidit Jac. Jo. Garth Wilkinson, Reg. Coll. Chirurg. Lond. Memb.   One vol. 8vo.

The same was translated into English, with the following title :—

Posthumous Tracts. Translated from the Latin, by James John Garth Wilkinson, one vol., pp. 149. London, 1847.

Contents of the Volume.

The Way to a Knowledge of the Soul.
Faith and Good Works.
The Red Blood.
The Animal Spirit.
Sensation, or the Passion of the Body.
The Origin and Propagation of the Soul.
Action.
Fragment on the Soul.

26. Clavis Hieroglyphica Arcanorum Naturalium et Spiritualium, per viam Repræsentationum et Correspondentiarum. Opus posthumum Eman. Swedenborgii, 4to.

A translation of this work appeared under the following title :—

A Hieroglyphic Key to Natural and Spiritual Mysteries by way of Representations and Correspondences. Translated from the Latin, by J. J. Garth Wilkinson. London, 1847.

27. Œconomia Regni Animalis in Transactiones Divisa, Quarum hæc Tertia de Fibra, de Tunica Arachnoidea, et de Morbis Fibrarum agit: anatomice, physice, et philosophice perlustrata. Ex chirographo in Bibliotheca Regiæ Academiæ Holmiensi asservato, nunc primum edidit J. J. Garth Wilkinson. Londini, 184-.

A translation of this work had been announced by the Swedenborg Association, under the following title :—

The Brain and the Fibres, considered Anatomically, Physically, and Philosophically; including a Treatise on the Diseases of the Nervous System. Being Part III. of the Economy of the Animal Kingdom.

This translation has never been published.

28. Regnum Animale Anatomice, Physice, et Philosophice perlustratum cujus Pars Quarta de Carotidibus, De Sensu Olfactus, Auditus et Visus, de Sensatione et Affectione in genere, ac de Intellectu et ejus Operatione agit. Ex chirographo in Bibliotheca Regiæ Academiæ Holmiensis asservato, nunc primum edidit Dr. J. F. E. Tafel, Philosophiæ Professor et Regiæ Bibliothecæ Universitatis Tubingensis præfectus. Tubingæ, 1848.

This work has not yet been translated into English. It is called by Dr. Tafel Part IV. of the " Animal Kingdom," and treats of the following subjects :—

1. The Carotids, or the Arteries carrying the Blood to the Head.

2. The Senses of Smelling, Hearing and Sight.

3. Concerning Sensation and Affection in general.

4. The Intellect and its Operation.

29. Regnum Animale Anatomice, Physice et Philosophice perlustratum cujus supplementum sive Partis Sextæ sectio

prima de Periosteo et de Mammis, et sectio secunda de Gene-
ratione, de partibus Genitalibus utriusque Sexus, et de For-
matione Fœtus in Utero agit. E Chirographo in Bibliotheca
Regiæ Academiæ Holmiensis asservato, nunc primum edidit
Dr. J. F. E. Tafel, &c. Tubingæ, 1849.

The first section of this part (the sixth) of the Animal
Kingdom treats of the Periosteum and the Breasts ; the second
section of Generation, the Genital Organs of both Sexes, and
the Formation of the Fœtus in the Womb. This work has
been translated into English, and published under the following title : *The Generative Organs*, considered anatomically,
physically, and philosophically. A Posthumous Work of
Emanuel Swedenborg, translated from the Latin, by J. J.
Garth Wilkinson. London, 1852.

30. Regnum Animale Anatomice, Physice, et Philosophice
perlustratum, cujus Pars Septima de Anima agit. E Chirographo nunc primum edidit Dr. J. F. E. Tafel. Tubingæ,
1849.

This Seventh Part of the Animal Kingdom, which treats
of the Soul, is a great summing up of the whole work, and is
its worthy conclusion. It has never been translated into
English.

31. Itinerarium ex operibus Eman. Swedenborgii pos-
thumis. Partes i., ii. Nunc primum edidit Dr. J. F. E.
Tafel.

This work contains Swedenborg's Journal, written during
some of his travels. Part I. describes those undertaken in
1733 ; Part II. those in 1736 and 1738. Part I. was originally written in Latin, Part II. in Swedish ; it was translated
into Latin by Dr. A. Kahl, of the University of Lund, in
Sweden. Neither of these parts have yet been translated
into English.

The following important scientific works of Swedenborg are
still preserved in manuscript in the Library of the Royal
Academy of Sciences in Stockholm. It is hoped that the
publication of our present volume, which proclaims by a

hundred voices the importance of the scientific works of Swedenborg, may induce some of his admirers to defray the expenses of their publication. To think that we allow these works to lie idly in manuscript, in an out-of-the-way library, where scarcely a person ever goes to consult them—these works, for which the Science of the Future will be willing to give everything that has been done for it since Swedenborg's time—instead of sending them out on their noble mission of revolutionizing science, and enabling it to rise out of its low sensual state into rational light! Surely we are derelict in our administration of a most sacred trust, if we allow these works any longer to remain mouldering in the dust.

32. The Principles of Natural Philosophy, 4to., pp. 569.

This is the treatise of which the Author published some *Specimens*. (See our No. 14.) It is indispensable to complete his mechanical Theory of Chemistry and Physics.

33. A Treatise on Common Salt, 4to., pp. 343.

This is an important Treatise, particularly considering the remarkable position that the Theory of Salt occupies in the Author's views of nature.

34. A Treatise on the Brain.

This is an unpublished part of the "Animal Kingdom," and in fact its most important part, on the same grounds that the brain is the most important organ in the human body. Its very size bespeaks its importance; for Dr. Swedbom, the Librarian of the Royal Academy of Sciences in Stockholm, writes that it fills 1482 pages in 4to., "carefully written out, and not difficult to read." "Pages 1 to 73," he writes, "are wanting;" but Dr. Wilkinson suggests the probability that they have been already printed in the "Economy of the Animal Kingdom," where there is a chapter "On the Cortical Substance of the Brain."

This treatise is a real desideratum by modern physiology, which affords but little aid to an understanding of the theory of the brain, and especially of the cerebellum.

35. A treatise on the Ear and Hearing (containing 29 pages), and one on the Eye and the Sense of Sight, (pp. 40.)

These two treatises are contained in the same manuscript volume, from which No. 28 had been published; but by an order of the Swedenborg Association, Dr. Tafel did not print these two volumes. (See his preface to said volume, p. vii.)

36. Ontology.

Dr. Swedbom says concerning this work: "From the commencement of this Dissertation, certain subjects are considered in general, and are afterwards treated severally under various heads. These heads are as follows: I. Form, Formal Cause; II. Figure; III. Organ, Structure; IV. State, Changes of State; V. Substance; VI. Matter, Materiality; VII. Extense, Extension, Continuum, Continuity; VIII. Body, Corporeals (the other heads are not numbered);—Essence, Essentials;—Attribute; Predicate;—Subject;—Affection; Contingencies;—Modes;—Modification. As for the manner of treatment, the opinions of Wolff, Baron, and others, are for the most part stated first, and the author's own opinion then given, or at least intimated."

This work is the only one in which Swedenborg discusses abstractions like the rest of the philosophers. It would be very interesting to know how his eminently real mind treats these questions. This treatise, Dr. Tafel was likewise instructed by the Swedenborg Association to omit, in his publication of the rest of the volume (our n. 29): see his preface, p. vi.

37. Excerpta ex Platone, Aristotele, Augustino, Grotio, Leibnitio, Wolfio, Malebranche, Cartesio, Spinoza, Scriptura Sacra, and others; with an Index on the matters.

This volume would be mostly interesting on account of the light which it throws on Swedenborg's philosophical studies.

THIRD PERIOD, *from 1745 to 1772.*

The works belonging to this period are all theological in their nature, and their discussion does not properly belong in the present volume. For the information of our readers, we would, however, state that Swedenborg himself published fourteen different theological works, which in the English translation, as published in London, fill twenty-two volumes. Since his death, twelve posthumous works have been published in thirty-two volumes; to which three or four additional works will accede that have not yet been published. So that it appears that Swedenborg wrote quite as many theological as scientific works, and is thus the most voluminous of writers.*

---

* Those of our readers who wish to make themselves acquainted with Swedenborg's Theological System, we refer to the List of Books appended to the present volume.

PART II.

EMANUEL SWEDENBORG AS A MAN OF
SCIENCE.

INTRODUCTION.

WE wish it to be distinctly understood by our readers, that we do not regard the "confirmations" contained in the following pages as, by any means, an exhaustive treatise on Swedenborg's scientific theories, in the light of Modern Science. We have simply collected and digested into a whole the materials we have found scattered in the various publications, composing the "Swedenborg Literature" of the last eighty years. To these we have added a confirmation of Swedenborg's "Theory of Leasts," (Chap. I., n. 2,) and also of his theory of the "Influence of Thought upon Respiration." (Chap. II., n. 6.) It will be observed that fully two-thirds of the following pages consist of articles written by Samuel Beswick, Esq. He is, in fact, the only scholar who has ever systematically analyzed any of Swedenborg's scientific works, and compared its results with those of Modern Science. In his articles on the "Principia," he has done justice to Swedenborg, and credit to himself; and we sincerely trust that their republication in this form, may lead to the preparation of more of the same sort, in accordance with his promise made in the "Intellectual Repository" for 1850, p. 462, and in the "New Church Repository" for 1856, p. 239. At the same time, we may be allowed to express the hope, that their author will pardon the liberty we have taken in re-arranging and condensing some of these articles, under the conviction that their usefulness would thereby be enhanced, and that the attention of the learned would be more readily drawn to them, in recognition of their real merit.

19* (221)

May the following collection be regarded as a first tribute of Modern Science to the genius of Swedenborg: and may the work here begun not be suffered to rest where we leave it, but be taken up and carried forward by unprejudiced and ardent scholars, who, not wedded past redemption to present systems and methods of science, shall not fail to reap great and abundant harvests of knowledge, in the field where so much light has already been sown. To such we would especially recommend, as most grateful subjects of study and investigation, Swedenborg's Theory of Optics and Colors, and his Mechanical Theory of Chemistry.

I.

SWEDENBORG'S THEORIES OF FORM.

1. The Doctrine of the Spiral Form

(a.)—*From a Letter of Dr. Wilkinson, January, 1843.*

"Before I leave altogether the subject of Swedenborg's scientific works, I will mention his striking foresight of one law of nature which is now only beginning to be discerned in its importance by the scientific world. I allude to *his doctrine of the spiral form*, and of its universality in the organic and elemental kingdoms. This doctrine is largely treated of in the 'Regnum Animale;' in the chapter of which, On the Stomach, he says, 'A similar form occurs in the intestines or the ultimates of the body; in the brains, or the beginnings of the body; and throughout in the intermediates. This form must be called the perpetual-circular, or properly, the spiral form: it is the essential form of motion, or of the fluxion of organic substances in the animal world.' Here then the doctrine is enunciated as a law. Now what says our age of facts in confirmation or disapproval? Let us hear Mr. Grainger, the professor of Anatomy and Physiology at St. Thomas's Hospital; and one of the most distinguished teachers in this metropolis. In a late lecture ' *On Microscopic Researches in Anatomy,*' he says :

" ' By selecting some of the more simple or cellular plants, the botanist is enabled, with the assistance of the microscope, to demonstrate that tendency to the *spiral* disposition of the component parts, which so strongly pervades the vegetable kingdom. If, for example, we examine the different species of confervæ, it will be seen that the organic corpuscles are deposited in spirals. The membranous tube which precedes

(223)

the vascular tissue of the higher plants, becomes charged with innumerable granules, which, after a short time, begin to adhere to the inner surface of the tube, assuming a spiral direction or form, and thus lay the foundation for the vascular tissue. In the circulation of the chara, something of the same kind is noticeable ; the little globules which indicate the currents going on in each cell of this plant, follow in the larger cells, a definite spiral direction, so that the globules describe curved currents. In these instances we have an opportunity of perceiving, in its simplest but most evident manifestation, that spiral form which is so eminently displayed in the whole vegetable kingdom.' Now for the animal kingdom.

" ' The allusion to the spiral arrangement in the vegetable kingdom will tend to show the great importance of that disposition in one of the grand divisions of the Organic Creation. There are many facts familiar to botanists which will throw light on some views presently to be noticed, respecting the presumed existence in the animal kingdom of a similar principle of arrangement. It is known, for example, that by carefully tracing the spiral tissue of the plant through the several stages of its first development, and of its subsequent transformations, it can be demonstrated that various and sometimes even apparently most anomalous forms, such as annular vessels, dotted ducts, and reticulated cells, are produced simply by modifications of the fundamental or typical spiral fibre.

" ' Now the animal kingdom presents, as it would seem, an exactly parallel transformation, in the structure of the breathing tubes or tracheæ. In the class insecta, it is familiarly known that the tracheæ, instead of being composed as in man and the other vertebrate animals, of interrupted and imperfectly closed rings, consist of a continued spiral and round filament. It has, however, been noticed by Burmeister, that in such larger tubes the spiral becomes interrupted, and forms, as in the apparently similar case of the annular ducts of plants, perfectly closed rings. But the exquisitely beautiful structure seen in the bilobed tongues of the musca vomitoria, or common horse-fly, affords a more palpable demonstration of this transformation of a continual spiral : for you will distinctly perceive that whilst the larger tubes of this remarkable organ are formed like the ordinary tracheæ of insects, that is to say, of a continuous filament, the smaller tubes proceeding from it are composed of imperfect rings, of a horse-shoe form, and presenting in their divaricated extremities a peculiar porcate appearance. When to these facts we add, that in one of the herbivorous cetacea, namely, the dugmy or fabled mermaid, the trachea is composed, as in insects, of the coils of a continuous cartilage, there can remain little doubt that the interrupted and imperfect rings of the windpipe of the vertebrata generally, are in reality developed on the principle of a spiral.

" ' A celebrated microscopical observer, M. Mandl, contends that a spiral arrangement is also observed in the cutaneous appendages of animals, as in the barbes and barbules of feathers, in the scales of fishes, and in the growth of hair.

" ' Having thus cursorily noticed that there are evidences of a spiral arrangement in the animal kingdom, I may state that Dr. Barry conceives that this disposition is more or less displayed in the various fibrous organs of the body, and consequently in the muscular fibre.

" ' According to Dr. Barry, whose views on this subject are familiar to many present, the ultimate muscular fibre is composed of a double spiral filament, which, for the sake of illustration, might be compared to the two strands of a twisted rope, to which objects, indeed, the fibre, when seen under the microscope, often bears a striking resemblance. In examining different specimens, single spirals are occasionally seen, presenting, in some instances, an appearance exactly like the turns of a corkscrew; but the fully formed fibrilla seems, according to the account and drawings published, to be composed of two spirals. The formation of the spiral fibre of muscles and other organs is first developed, according to Dr. Barry, in the red particles of the blood, of which process he has given a minute account. The plates in the Philosophical Transactions represent a coil of disc-like bodies, variously disposed within the elliptical corpuscles of reptiles, and the circular particles of the mammalia. And here I may mention, that it is an important part of Dr. Barry's general theory respecting the high importance of the cytoblasts of nucleated cells, that the coils just mentioned are produced by the division and multiplication of the nucleus of the red particle.

" ' Such are the accounts of the two other most recent observers of the muscular fibre. It would, of course, be presumptuous indeed to attempt to decide the question ; I will, therefore, merely mention one or two circumstances which may now throw some light on this subject. That there is a peculiar spiral connected with the muscular tissue, is now admitted by the best observers. Dr. Barry figured in one of his plates, a spiral fibre wound around a fasciculus ; in some months previous to the announcement of Dr. Barry's researches, Dr. Leeson had discovered and demonstrated to some gentleman connected with the hospital, a spiral of the same character, that is to say, which is wound around a primitive fasciculus. This seems, as far as I can judge, from several examinations, to correspond in position to the delicate transparent sheath of the primitive fasciculus so beautifully demonstrated by Mr. Bowman, and called by him the sarcolemma. A few evenings since I was present, when Dr. Leeson showed his spiral to Mr. Bowman and Mr. Busk, when the former gentleman, with characteristic candor, admitted it was a structure he had never seen before. But you will observe, gentlemen, that this part of which I am now speaking does not touch the main question—the nature, namely, of the ultimate *fibre;* for the spiral demonstrated by Dr. Leeson surrounds the primitive *fasciculus.* At the time mentioned, however, Dr. Leeson had satisfied himself that the ultimate fibre itself consists of a spiral.

" ' It is proper to notice, that in the year 1838, Mr. Mandl must have seen something of the same kind ; for he states, though this part of his account is incorrect, that the well-known transverse striæ seen on the muscular fasciculi are merely the coils of a band of cellular tissue, *spirally* disposed around the ultimate filaments.' "

(b.)—*From the Intellectual Repository, January, 1848, London.*

" To the Editor of the Intellectual Repository :

" *Sir,*—In his Preface to the Principia. Swedenborg says : ' We affirm, moreover, that in every finite there are three motions, namely, a progressive motion of the parts, an axillary, and a local motion, provided there be no obstacle.' And, ' We affirm again, that all these motions proceed from one fountain head, or from one and the same source, namely, from a SPIRAL motion of the parts,' &c. . . . ' This motion is most highly mechanical, and most highly natural.' Again it is stated,—' Nature is similar to herself, and cannot be different in the largest elementary volume from what she is in the smallest ; in the macrocosm from what she is in the microcosm.'

" Now from these ' *Principia*' it follows, that all the planetary bodies, including, of course, the earth on which we dwell, must be considered as ' finites ' on the greatest scale ; and as each of these bodies appears to be in the condition of having ' no obstacle ' to prevent the manifestation of their inherent motions, we ought to find them exhibiting each of the three motions above named. That they do all exhibit two of these motions, namely, an axillary and a local or orbital motion, is now universally admitted ;. but until a comparatively recent period, no other regular and defined motion seems to have been suspected. That the solid crust of the earth is liable to elevation and depressions, is among the ascertained facts of geology, but I am not aware that any law or rule has been shown for these changes. It was therefore with no small interest that I read in a paper on ' Creation,' in the last number of *The Westminster Review,* a statement which goes to prove, from actual observation, that the ' parts ' of the earth have that ' progressive motion,' which, according to the philosophy of Swedenborg, they ought to possess, and from the very cause which he assigns for it ; namely, a *spiral* motion of the axis ; and that your readers may participate in the interest which attaches to the subject, I transcribe for their perusal an extract :—

" 'There is,' says the writer, 'one problem of the earth's motion, connected with what is called the precession of the equinoxes, of which only an imperfect and unsatisfactory solution has hitherto been given, and which has a most important bearing upon the geological phenomena to which we are now alluding.' (That is, to the remains of tropical productions in arctic climes, &c.) 'By the precession of the equinoxes is understood an annual change of the place, or precise spot, at which the sun in the ecliptic crosses the plane of the equator, producing, twice in the year, equal days and equal nights all over the world. The two points of intersection of the spring and autumnal equinox recede from east to west, at the rate of fifty and a quarter seconds annually, or one degree in seventy-one and a half years; and travel round the entire circumference of the earth in 25,869 years, the period which was termed by the ancients ' a Platonic year.' Its physical cause is ' the attraction of the sun and moon upon the protuberant parts of the earth's equator combined with the diurnal rotation.' *

" 'The effects of this attraction have been described by astronomers as producing both the precession of the equinoxes and a slight oscillation of the axis of the earth, called its *nutation*, by which, twice in the year, the plane of the equator inclines towards the ecliptic, and returns as often to its former position.

" ' It is now held by some, that this motion of the earth's axis is not oscillatory, but SPIRAL : *involving a gradual change in the relative position of the different parts of the earth in reference to the equatorial and polar regions*, although the mass itself retains the same general inclination ;—as in a spinning ball, which has always an upper and a lower side, although the *same* side is not always the upper or the lower. This change, we are told, is so minute, as to be scarcely perceptible in a hundred years; but amounts, in the course of the precessional round of the Platonic year, to a difference in the latitude of all places, of about three and a half degrees.

" 'For the mathematical data upon which this hypothesis is

---

* "Encyclopædia Brittanica," vol. xviii., page 506.

founded—first submitted to the Astronomical Society by Captain Bergh—we must refer the reader to the Tables of M. de la Lande, the observations of Dr. Maskelyne, in 1788, and Vince's Astronomy. The fact of any changes in the axis of the earth, excepting that of a semi-annual oscillatory movement, has been stoutly denied, and the question will admit of much discussion ; but the evidence in favor of the New Theory has made sufficient impression on our minds to induce us to call attention to the subject, and, assuming its correctness, we would briefly note the conclusions to which it leads.'

" Then follow various speculations on the power of this motion to occasion the geological phenomena adverted to within brackets above. And it is also stated, in foot notes, that scarcely any astronomer of eminence can agree with his predecessors as to the exact latitudes of the long-established public observatories ; and that all reasons but the right one have been adduced to account for these discrepancies: namely, that the *sites have really changed their position;* and it is further affirmed, that ancient churches, and other buildings, erected due east and west, are now found to deviate from that position.

" The length of time necessary to elapse before this progressive motion can be shown, by repeated observation, to be the result of an order as fixed and determined as that which is the basis of Kepler's Laws, or the Newtonian System of Gravitation, renders it probable that many years may roll away before the Swedenborgian hypothesis is fully admitted. Nevertheless, we may have sufficient faith in the stability of Eternal principles to anticipate it as a ' fact accomplished,' and that the giant genius of Swedenborg, which enabled him to generalize a century in advance of his age, will eventually be both acknowledged and appreciated."

2. The Doctrine of Leasts.

This doctrine is taught by Swedenborg in the following passages :—

" It is one of the rules in the doctrine of degrees, that a particle of any volume or homogeneous mass constitutes its least volume or its least mass, or that this particle is a small volume or small mass in its smallest term or boundary, or is a unit of the volume or homogeneous mass in which it is. This particle or unit, how often soever it may be repeated, in whatever numbers it may be congregated, however it may be increased in multitude; or on the other hand, to whatever fractions its aggregate may be reduced, however it may be diminished in number, or decreased in multitude, yet never makes any transition into an inferior or superior degree. Thus water, oil, spirits, whether we assume a part of it, a small drop, a streamlet, a lake, or an ocean, does not cease to be water, or oil, or spirits. . . . Common salt, nitre, alum, stone, metal of any given species, whether it be a portion, a mass, a mountain, does not cease to be salt, stone, or metal, belonging to that species. . . . The same rule holds in regard to all other things, the division of which continues, without any change of nature, even to their component units, or the constituent elements of that degree."—*Econom. of A. K.*, Part I., n. 156.

" No series can be complete or effective without involving at least a trine ; that is, a first, a middle, and a last. These three must be so ordered, that the first term disposes the second, and disposes the ultimate both mediately and immediately." Again, " Nothing can be bounded, completed, or perfect, that is not a trine. Sometimes even a quadrine is necessary, or a still more multiple series or sequence, exactly according to the ratio between the first and last term, that is, to their distance from each other. Meanwhile, whatever be the relation, there must be at least a trine, to procure harmony. Otherwise no termination or conclusion is possible. . . . So in every science and art: the binary is ever the imperfect; hence some third thing is always involved either tacitly or openly."—*Animal Kingdom*, Part I., n. 229.

" In a series of three degrees there are three distinct units, or three distinct quantities of units ; or, should any one prefer another mode of expressing it, in a series of three degrees, there are three substances or simple forces to be considered as units ; one of which is more simple than another, yet having a mutual relation to each other; thus the other things com-

posed of them, are as numbers composed of such units,
each of which is homogeneous to its own unit (n. 156).
Thus in the animal kingdom there are three successive
fluids to be considered as quantities, viz., the red blood, the
intermediate blood, and the spirituous fluid, each of which
has reference to its own unit as the most simple particle
of its own degree (n. 115, 156). . . . It is the same
also in the vegetable and mineral kingdoms, thus in every
species of metal, mineral, earth, stone, salt, water, oil, and
spirit, in every degree of composition of which there are particles, which are the units of their quantities. . . . . .
Consequently, as this is the case with substances, so it is the
case with their essences, attributes, accidents, and qualities
(n. 619–627). . . . "—*Economy of A. K.*, Part I., n. 629.

" Every series of things simultaneous, or, in other words,
every aggregate of things co-ordinate, admits of being *divided*
till you arrive at its unit ; beyond which you cannot proceed
further, and yet leave a unit, or a part of that degree ; for if
this unit be resolved, there no longer remains a unit of its
own degree, but of a superior degree. For a unit itself is a
series of several other units, because it is itself in the series
of the universe ; nor can anything be conceived as not being
in a series, except the first substance of all (n. 586). Consequently, a superior unit, and the proximately inferior unit
of the same series, are to each other in a triplicate ratio ;
that is, the one bears the same ratio to the other as the root to
its cube : the case is the same with the rest. Thus they are
not homogeneous to each other ; neither are the units of different series, [though they be of the same degree,] unless they
are contained under the same genus. For to the production
of all the variety that exists in the universe, it is requisite
that there be a distinct series, viz., one within another, one in
juxtaposition with another, and one for the sake of another ;
yet all are wonderfully connected with each other, and all have
reference to the first series of the universe. Units thus considered are either of a determinate or certain quantity or
quality, as in all terrestrial things ; or of one that is undetermined or varying, as in the auras of the world, amongst the parts
of which therefore there is a harmonious variety (n. 604–606),

parts which, nevertheless, in respect to their own ratios, are determinate."—*Id.* n. 630.

"The least or prior forms are the models and the ideas of the larger or posterior forms; each of them comprehends in it all those things that follow in order, and that carry the end to the ultimate effect."—*Anim. Kingd.*, Part I., n. 44.

"Prior substances, viewed in themselves, and in their own nature, are more perfect than such as are posterior viewed in themselves and their nature (n. 176). They are more perfect, for instance, in regard to form, essence, attributes, accidents and qualities; consequently they are more distinct, similar, unanimous, constant, and fluid; they are in the fuller enjoyment of their elastic force; they are also more beautiful, and more disposed to agreement; hence also it follows, that they are less limited, more free, in greater potency, more sensible, more rational, more durable (n. 100–102, 115, 238, 259)."—*Econ. of Anim. Kingd.*, Part I, n. 615.

"Everything is still more perfect in the superior degree, so perfect indeed as to be considered as it were the analogue, the eminent, and unassignable correspondent, of the similar qualities, powers, faculties, and modes of the inferior degrees."— Id. n. 176.

By this doctrine the following points are established :—

1. Every substance of the animal, vegetable and mineral kingdom may be divided into its least parts without losing any of its qualities and attributes.

2. In every substance of the animal, vegetable and mineral kingdom there is a series of three degrees. When the division has been carried down to the component units of the lowest degree, by a still further diminution the parts of the second degree are laid open, and so on until the component units of this degree are reached, when by a continued reduction the particles of the inmost degree are finally set free.

3. The greater the reduction of a substance into its constituent particles, the more distinct are its effects, and the greater its power.

The first of these points has been proved in a remarkable manner by the discoveries made by the Messrs. Kirchhoff and Bunsen with the "spectroscope." By this instrument it has been discovered that every elemental substance, especially the alkaline, presents a peculiar image in the flame in which it is burned. These images are minutely described by the spectroscopists; and by their means they can discover elemental substances in immeasurably smaller quantities than by the most delicate chemical tests; thus proving that these alkaline substances preserve their identity and their individual qualities, as far as human ingenuity has been able to trace them.

The other two points of this doctrine have been proved in an equally convincing manner by the medical system, called "Homœopathy." The practitioners of this system have discovered that substances, which in their crude form exercise a scarcely perceptible influence upon the human system, when administered in a triturated or diluted form produce the most marked effects. They have also found that, when the human system (by disease) is rendered peculiarly sensitive, or predisposed to receive impressions from certain substances in nature, it is affected by medicines in the very highest state of mechanical attenuation. Another result of their experience is, that chronic diseases which are deeply seated in the system frequently yield only to medicines in the highest possible attenuated form; because in this form " they are more perfect in regard to form, essence, attributes, accidents, and qualities," and are " less limited, more free, in greater potency, more sensible, more rational, more lasting."

20*

II.

SWEDENBORG'S PHYSIOLOGICAL THEORIES AND ANATOMICAL DISCOVERIES.

1. *Introductory Remarks.*

THE number of rational discoveries made by Swedenborg in Physiology is in excess of those arrived at by him in any other science; but the difficulty of confirming them by the results of modern science, is greatly enhanced by the fact that the Physiology of the present 'day has no theories worthy of the name. Physiologists appear to regard the human body as little more than a compound of detached parts, and not as an organized whole. The only real effort towards a rational consolidation of these parts is found in Prof. Hyrtl's celebrated work on Anatomy,* where he elucidates the different *regions* of the human body. These *regions* Swedenborg has arranged into one grand, rational, organic whole.

" There are certain organs in the body which have always been looked upon as the *opprobria* of physiologists, who indeed appear to fail wherever nature does not speak by an ultimate fact ; that is to say, wherever there is a clear field for the understanding as apart from and above the senses. The absence of an excretory duct is sufficient to consign an organ in perpetuity to the limbo of doubt. Surmise, indeed, respecting its functions is still allowed, but proof is considered impossible. We might as well pretend to know the nature of the world of spirits as to know the function of the spleen. We should be as rank visionaries in the one case as in the other, since we should be placing an implicit dependence upon reason, in a matter where the bodily senses give no direct information.

---

* Handbuch der Topographischen Anatomie, von Joseph Hyrtl.

Swedenborg did pretend to know both; and ill he fared in consequence with the scientific world, and with the first reviewer of his 'Animal Kingdom' in the 'Acta Eruditorum Lipsiensia.' They said he was a 'happy fellow,' and laughed outright. Without stopping to do more than direct the reader's particular attention to his doctrine of the spleen, the suprarenal capsules, and the thymus gland, as being satisfactory and irrefragable, it may be wondered why the physiologists should single out those organs as especial subjects whereon to make confession of ignorance. There is modesty in their confession, but it ought in justice to have embraced more. These organs are closely connected to others, and ignorance respecting them involves ignorance respecting the others also. Connection of structures in the body is also connection of functions, forces, modes, and accidents. If the function of the spleen be unknown, so precisely to the same extent are the functions of the pancreas, the stomach, the omentum, and the liver; if the functions of the succenturiate kidneys be unknown, so are the functions of the diaphragm, the kidneys, the peritonæum, and indeed of the whole body; for the body is a continuous tissue, woven without a break in nature's loom. To be ignorant of a part, is to be ignorant of something that pervades the whole. The disease that affects the spleen affects the whole, for the spleen is in all things, and all things are in the spleen. To recur to the liver; what is the amount of knowledge respecting its functions? Precisely this, that the hepatic duct proceeds from it, and carries bile into the duodenum. The bile and the duct are the sum and substance of the modern physiology of the liver; it is *prorsus in occulto* why either bile or duct should exist. The truth then is, that there is as much known about the liver as about the spleen, and no more; in the one case it is known that there is an excretory duct, in the other that there is none. Alas! the scientific mind is steeped in the senses, and is the drudge of their limited sphere."—"*Introduction to the Animal Kingdom.*"

We shall now subjoin a few extracts, showing that the little progress made in rational physiology since Swedenborg's time, has all been anticipated by him.

2. The Vitality of the Blood.

From the Daily Tribune, New York, 1847.

" In the number of Silliman's Journal for January, 1847, pp. 108–9, under the head of ' Researches on the Blood,' we have an account of some interesting experiments performed by the distinguished French philosopher, M. Dumas, by which the vitality of the blood globules is demonstrated.   After some account of his experiments and their results, the Report says : ' In attempting to overcome this difficulty, M. Dumas discovered the remarkable property of the blood globules, that as long as they were in contact with the air or aërated water, —in short, as long as they were in the arterial condition,—the saline solution containing them passed colorless through the filter, and left them upon it ; on the contrary, as soon as the globules have assumed the violet tint of venous blood, the liquid passes colored.'   Toward the close of the report, the following conclusion is drawn from the experiments of Dumas, and considered fully demonstrated by them :—' *Thus the globules of the blood seem to possess vitality*, as they can resist the solvent action of sulphate of soda as long *as their life continues*, but yield to this action readily when they have fallen into asphyxia from privation of air.'

" Now, it is to be observed, that the doctrine respecting the vitality of the blood, which Dumas has now demonstrated experimentally, has not been the generally received one among men of science, though some have regarded it as a highly probable theory.   But in one of Swedenborg's Philosophical Tracts, which has recently been published, and the translation of which has just reached this country, we find a short treatise on ' The Red Blood,' in which the author distinctly asserts that the blood is a living substance.   The following is the heading of one chapter on this subject :—

" ' The globule of the red blood contains within it the purer blood and the animal spirit, and the latter the purest essence of the body, that is to say, the Soul ; whereby the blood is a *spirituous and animated humor*.'—And the heading of another chapter is,—' There is a common and *obscure* life in the red blood !' ' "

Our most eminent surgeons are beginning also to admit this truth. Mr. LISTON, Professor at the London University, in the last edition of his work on Surgery, writes thus: "Some have denied the existence of *vitality* in the blood; and to some minds it may perhaps be difficult to conceive how a fluid could be possessed of this principle. But no one can either doubt or deny that the blood in its distribution, in its manner of receiving increase, in the secretions furnished by it, and in its various morbid changes, is governed by laws and principles which cannot be explained by those of chemistry and mechanics, but must belong to some other power. No one can plausibly object to the laws by which the blood is governed being referred to the power of *life*, and to their being called *vital principles*."—(Elements of Surgery, edit. 1840.)

BICHAT says that "the chemist who analyzes the fluids has at best but their *caput mortuum* as it were, as the anatomist possesses only the skeleton of the solids he dissects." And again, "I doubt much if fluids purely inert could circulate in living vessels. Life is indispensable both to the vessel and its contents."—(General Anatomy.)

Alterations in the vital properties of the *blood* are now considered by many as the principal cause of disease.

DR. ALISON, Professor of Medicine in the University of Edinburgh, says, in a "*Dissertation on the State of Medical Science from the Termination of the Eighteenth Century to the present time*," "the most important inference that has been drawn from recent labors is certainly this, that the important phenomena of disease mostly depend on alterations in the *strictly vital properties* of the fluids, especially the blood."—(*Cyclop. of Practical Medicine*, Vol. I.)

Swedenborg says on this subject, "For this reason it is, that the universal body is sick when the blood is sick, and *vice versa;* and that in the greater number of diseases, it is sufficient to find a medicine for the blood alone, to restore the body to health."—(Tract on "The Red Blood," chap. iii.)

3. THE MOTION OF THE BRAIN.

In a work entitled "*Institutiones Physiologiæ*," 1787, (s. 201,) Blumenbach, treating of the brain, says: "That after birth it undergoes a constant and gentle motion, correspondent with respiration; so that when the lungs shrink in expiration, the brain rises a little, but when the chest expands it again subsides." In a note he adds, that John Daniel SCHLICHTING (Comment. Litter., Nov. 1744, p. 409) first accurately described this phenomenon. But the discovery seems due to Swedenborg, as he fully described it in the " Economy of the Animal Kingdom," 1740, Part I. n. 280, 283, 367–369, 551; Part II. 35–37, which was published before Schlichting wrote.

4. THE MOVING POWERS EMPLOYED IN THE CIRCULATION OF THE BLOOD.

In another part of the same "Institutiones Physiologiæ," when speaking of the causes of the motion of the blood, Blumenbach has the following remark: " When the blood is expelled from the contracted cavities, a vacuum takes place, into which, according to the common laws of *derivation*, the neighboring blood must rush, being prevented, by means of the valves, from regurgitating." In the notes, this discovery is attributed to Dr. Wilson, the author of *An Inquiry into the Moving Powers employed in the Circulation of the Blood.* (See also Dr. Young's Croonian Lecture in the Phil. Trans. for 1809.) But it appears that the same principle was known long before to Swedenborg, and is applied by him to account for the motion of the blood. In the " Economy of the Animal Kingdom," in the section on the circulation of blood in the fœtus, and on the *foramen ovale*, (Part I., n. 349,) he says: " Let us now revert to the mode by which the cerebrum attracts the blood, or, according to the theorem, subtracts that quantity which the ratio of its state requires. If now these arteries, veins and sinuses are dilated by reason of the animation of the cerebrum, it follows, that there must necessarily flow into them thus expanded, a portion of fresh blood, and that indeed by continuity from the carotid artery, and its tortuous duct in the cavernous receptacles, and into this by continuity from the antecedent expanded and circumflexed cavities of the same artery; consequently from the external (or common) carotid, and thence from the aorta and the heart; nearly similar to a bladder or syphon full of water, one end of which is immersed in the fluid; if its sides be dilated, or its surface stretched out, and more especially if its length be shortened, an entirely fresh portion of the fluid flows into the space thus emptied by the enlargement; and this experience can be demonstrated to ocular satisfaction. Now this is the beneficial result of a natural equation, by which nature, in order to avoid a vacuum, in which state she would perish, or be annihilated, is in the constant tendency towards an equilibrium, according to laws purely physical. This mode of action of the brains, and their arterial impletion, may justly be called physical attraction; not that it is attraction in the proper signification of the term, but that it is a filling of the vessels from a dilation or shortening of the coats, or a species of suction such as exists in pumps and syringes. A like mode of physical attraction obtains in every part of the body; as in the muscles, which having forcibly expelled their blood, instantly require a re-impletion of their vessels." In another part, n. 458, he says: "There exists a great similitude between the vessels of the heart, and the vessels of the brains, so much so, that the latter cannot be more appropriately compared with any other. 4. The vessels of the cerebrum perform their diastole, when the cerebrum is in its constriction and *vice versa;* so also the vessels of the heart. 5. In the vessels of the cerebrum there is a species of physical attraction or suction, such as that of water in a syringe; and this, too, is the case with the vessels of the heart, for in these, by being expanded and at the same time shortened, the blood necessarily flows, and that into the space thus enlarged." Swedenborg says also, "that it is the constant endeavor to establish a general equilibrium throughout the body, which determines its various fluids to every part, whether viscus or member, and which being produced by exhaustion, the effect is such a determination of the blood, or other fluid, as the peculiar state of the parts requires."

5. Endosmosis and Exosmosis.

Dr. Wilkinson says in a letter quoted in our first part (n. 79): "Another principle discovered by Swedenborg, is the permeability of membranes, and the circulation of fluids through them in determinate channels; some of the details of which are now grouped under the names 'Endosmosis' and 'Exosmosis'—two phenomena which are thought discoveries of the present day. With regard to the lymphatic system, Swedenborg has thoroughly anticipated the beautiful theory of *Dr. Prout,* etc."

6. Swedenborg's Theory of Respiration.

Dr. Wilkinson says in the same letter: "It is both curious and satisfactory to observe, that medical authors have been for ages approximating, in the way of effects and details, to some of the principles elicited by Swedenborg. To instance one of these causes—the influence of the respiratory movements on, and their propagation to the viscera and the whole body. The law, that the body in general and in particular respires with the lungs—that the perpetuation of all the functions, and, in a word, of corporeal life, depends on the universality of this action, as a law—is peculiar to Swedenborg. And yet, for centuries the fragments of this truth have flitted across the mental vision of physiologists. *Glisson* has declared it of the liver; *Blumenbach,* of the spleen; *Barry,* and many others, of the heart; *Bell,* of the neck; *Schlichting,* of the blood in the brain; *Portal,* of the circulation in the spinal cord,—and I could easily add many other names and instances to this list."

On the influence of the thoughts and the affections, and thus of the brain, which is their organ, upon respiration, Swedenborg says the following :—

"The general state of animation cannot be seen better reflected than in the general state of the pulmonic respiration. For as often as the brain is intent, and thinking deeply, or is occupied with anxious cares, the lungs draw their breath tacitly and slowly, and the breast either rises to a fixed level, and fears by any deep breath to disturb the quiet of the brain, or else compresses itself, and admits only a small amount of air. When the brain is exhilarated and joyous, the lungs expand and unfold. When the brain collapses with fear, the lungs do the same. When the brain is disturbed by anger, the lungs are the same. And so it is in the case of all other

affections, in which similar states are observed to be superinduced upon both, and this, sometimes, without any sensible
change in the vibration of the heart and arteries of the body."
—*Economy of the Animal Kingdom*, Part II., n. 10.

Again, " Whenever the human brain is pondering reasons,
and directing the rational mind to them, it desires to be at
rest, and to draw breath quietly, as is usual with intense
thinkers."—*Id.*, Part II., n. 42.

See, also, what Dr. Wilkinson says on this subject, in n. 73
of our first part.

The effect of the state of the mind and of thought upon
respiration has since been very minutely described by KEMPE-
LEN, in his " *Le Mécanisme de la parole*," Vienne, 1791, where
he says :—

" § 32. We know that all violent movements and efforts of
the human body cause variations in the respiration ; they retard
and accelerate it, and sometimes suspend it entirely for some
time. Even the very slightest movements occasion such
changes. It is sufficient, for instance, in order to disturb a
regular periodical respiration, simply to turn your eyes upon
another object, or to lay your hand upon something else.

" § 33. The changes which our soul undergoes also influence the respiration. A shock, fear, anger, pity, joy, love, all
this makes an impression upon our lungs, as well as upon our
heart. But not only the violent emotions and passions of the
soul exercise such an effect ; the least trifles produce a similar,
corresponding change. When the mind fixes its attention
upon the smallest object, as upon a grain of sand, the respiration sometimes stops altogether, in order not to cause the least
movement of the body which might affect the application of
our senses. . . . We might even divine, by paying attention only to the respiration of a person, without his saying a
word, the state of his mind, whether he is tranquil or restless,
contented or irritated. We often notice in persons who are
enjoying a most perfect repose of the soul, a sudden change,
and we are thus enabled to tell the moment where one idea is
succeeded by another. This may be noticed not only when
the new idea is sad or disagreeable, but even when it is of an
absolutely indifferent kind."

7. The Foramen of Monro.

From the Monthly Review, 1844.

" The first person who publicly claimed the discovery of this passage or communication between the right and left, or two lateral ventricles of the cerebrum, was Dr. Monro, the second, of Edinburgh. For a long time many anatomists denied its existence ; and a story is told, we think of one of the Bells, who, when demonstrating the cerebrum to his pupils, used to push the blowpipe through the parietes of the ventricles, and exclaim, ' This is the foramen of Monro ! ' However, it was at last conceded that there *was* a foramen, but that it was known before Monro's time. Yet we do not remember to whom the honor of the discovery was generally attributed, but certainly *not* to Swedenborg. This great man, however, was not always to be denied the credit which was due him, for a writer in the *Intellectual Repository* for 1824, p. 170, took up the cudgels, and proved Swedenborg's title to the discovery, though up to this date we do not remember any treatise on the brain, in which the author even alludes to Swedenborg. Monro's first intimation in public of his discovery, was on the 13th of December, 1764, when he read a paper to the *Phil. Soc.* of Edinburgh on the subject ; but in his work, entitled ' *Observations on the Structure and Functions of the Nervous System,*' he says, that he demonstrated the foramen to his pupils as early as the year 1753. Monro allows that a communication was known to exist between these two ventricles and the third, long prior to his time ; but he shows that it was never demonstrated or delineated in the manner he had done, nor in any way that could convey any precise idea concerning it—' much less was implied the existence of the foramen.' The channel of communication, which was admitted by the anatomists, seemed to be referred to the posterior, or back part of the lateral ventricles ; whilst the foramen Monro described, is situated at the anterior or front part of the ventricle. Now, says the writer in the *Repository*, in the ' Regnum Animale of Swedenborg,' p. 207, the following striking observation occurs :

'Foramina communicantia in cerebro vocantur anus et vulva præter meatum seu emissarium lymphæ quibus, ventriculi laterales inter se, et cum tertio, communicant,'—which may be thus translated: 'The communicating foramina in the cerebrum are called anus and vulva, beside the passage or emissary canal of the lymph; by these the lateral ventricles communicate with each other, and with the third ventricle.' This work was printed in 1744, or nine years prior to the earliest notice by Dr. Monro, of the foramen in question!"

We are not inclined to lay much stress on discoveries such as these that may be attributed to Swedenborg; for it is not in the discovery of facts that his great genius shines, but in that of principles.

III.

SWEDENBORG'S CHEMICAL THEORIES.

1. SCIENCE OF CRYSTALLOGRAPHY.

(a.)—*From " The New Jerusalem Magazine," for Nov.* 1830.

" THE science of *Crystallography* is of recent origin, and has lately attracted the notice of some very able men. Nearly all simple substances, and many of the compounds found in nature, have regular forms. These are of almost every variety of shape, but each substance *has its own;* and this original figure, as it may be called, often serves to distinguish substances which it would be difficult otherwise to discriminate. The basis of the science is an analysis of the various figures, so that they may be reduced to a very few simple forms, which, by addition one to the other, may make all the existing varieties. This subject is mentioned in a work on ' Chemical Philosophy,' recently published in Paris, consisting of a course of lectures delivered in the college of France by M. Dumas, a gentleman of much and deserved celebrity. There is a notice of this work in the forty-fifth number of the *Foreign Quarterly Review*, published in London. M. Dumas distinctly ascribes to Swedenborg the origin of the modern science of crystallography. He says, ' It is then to him we are indebted for the first idea of making cubes, tetrahedrons, pyramids, and the different crystalline forms, by grouping the spheres ; and it is an idea which has since been renewed by several distinguished men, Wollaston in particular.' "

(b.)—*From the Intellectual Repository, No.* 160, 1853.

" In a lecture on ' Atoms, and the Molecular arrangement and properties of bodies,' recently delivered at the Royal Insti-

(244)

tution in Manchester, by the eminently scientific lecturer on Chemistry, Prof. F. C. Calvert, it was asserted by the lecturer that ' *Swedenborg* was the first to discover that atoms were spheres, and that with them cubes, octohedrons, etc., could be formed.' But *Dalton* added another most important fact; it was that every atom was surrounded by an atmosphere of heat, which he held was necessary to prevent all matter becoming solid through the force of molecular attraction." *

2. The Relation of Water to the Salts, Acids and Bases.

The following account, showing a remarkable confirmation of Swedenborg's "Principles of Chemistry" by modern science, is taken from a review of this work which appeared in the " *New Church Quarterly Review,*" vol. i., pp. 37, 271, etc. :—

We first transcribe from the reviewer the following statement of Swedenborg's idea of the composition of water : " As the series of actives ends in fire, so the series of finites ends in the pure material finite or water; the particles of which are in reality inert, being rendered fluent by an extremely low degree of heat, occasioned by the circulation of the ether, which is interfluent among them. The expansion of the ether and the evolution of heat we have already noticed as co-ordinate effects ; it follows, therefore, that the more the ether is expanded, the more fluent is the body of water, because its particles are kept so much farther apart ; and, on the other hand, the more the ether is compressed, the more concrete is the water, its particles approaching nearer to each other until they become aggregated even into a solid mass. In this way, water hardens into ice."—p. 37.

The reviewer continues on page 271 : " 'The atom of water is described as a round, hard, hollow body, formed by an arrangement of particles, or ' crustals,' which have a similar

---

* From the next article it will appear that Swedenborg was well acquainted with this "other most important fact."

nature to itself, but are of less magnitude. A subtle matter is described as interfluent among the atoms or large particles, not only according with their relative situation, but in some measure producing it, and the situation itself is quadrilateral, so that if a volume of water be represented by a number of balls, the first layer would form a square, and every successive layer would be placed perpendicularly over the one subjacent, the centres of all the globules intersecting right lines. This position is demonstrably the most natural to motion, for if we suppose one layer to be moved diagonally over another, so that the convex parts of the upper might fall into the interstitial concavities of the lower series, the whole volume would be locked into a solid, and, on the other hand, in the given quadrilateral position, the contact of the atoms is only in one point. This position also has the further advantage of supposing a pressure equal in all directions, according to the well-known hydraulic law, which Swedenborg illustrates, and in fact identifies, with the local motion of the particles. It supposes likewise a thoroughfare, admitting in all directions of the free ingress and egress of their interfluent element, and thus of the increase or diminution of its relative quantity, which again supposes a variation of distance between the particles, according to circumstances. These conditions being given, let it be granted that the crustals of the water particles are held in their configuration by the interfluent ether, and we have the leading principles which connect the author's theory of water with his mechanical theory of chemistry. We obtain at the same time also a view of the earth's surface from the vanishing point of geology, where it passes into another science (cosmogony) by the last resolution of its strata and rocks; or, conversely where that other science passes into geology by the generation of the primary solids, and scatters over the wide plain of chemistry its more brilliant scintillations.

"The first solid, then, was produced in the depths of the primeval ocean by two causes,—the want of a certain depth of the interfluent ether, and the superincumbent pressure of the waters; the effect of which was the disintegration of the particles, and their gravitation into the interstitial spaces subjacent to them. In these spaces the particles were moulded into angular or terrestrial forms, consisting, first, of a *stoma*, which may be described as a cube with all its sides cupped out; and secondly, of arms and branches like hollowed triangles, attached to each of its corners. In a word, this primitive solid being moulded between the globules, and exactly filling their spaces, is in the perfect image of its matrix.

"The solid thus formed is, by the hypothesis, a *perfect salt*, and from this, as the first earthy atom—from the mutations to which it is subject, and its continually changing relation to the particles of water—are derived other saline and acid substances, metals and configurations innumerable. On the present occasion we overlook the whole of the deducible series, and confine ourselves to the foundation of the theory, premising that the facts to which we may allude, having any reference to the present state of chemistry, are derived from the last edition of TURNER's standard work,* and consequently represent the results of the most recent investigations.

"Three important generic designations, namely, *salts*, *acids*, and *alkalies*, have undergone a considerable extension of their meaning consequent on the progress of modern discovery. Until a very recent period, an acid was defined as ' an oxidized body which has a sour taste, reddens litmus paper, and neutralizes alkalies;' but it was at length discovered, first, that oxygen is not essential to acidity; next, that the test of litmus is not always valid; and, lastly, that there were acids which could not totally overcome the reaction of potassa.† '*Facts of this kind have induced chemists to consider as acids all those compounds which unite with potassa or ammonia, and give rise to bodies similar in their constitution and general character to the salts which the sulphuric, or some admitted acid forms with those alkalies.*' Similar is the extension given to the meaning of the term *alkali*, it being now agreed to place among the alkaline

---

* Elements of Chemistry, etc. By the late Edward Turner, M. D. Edited by Baron Liebig and Dr. Gregory, 1847.

† " We are risking the appearance of a discrepancy (which, however, does not really exist) between this paragraph and the next but one, by passing lightly over these facts, but we quote them for the *results* to which they have led."

bases '*all those bodies which unite definitively with admitted acids, such as the sulphuric and nitric, and form with them compounds analogous in constitution to the salts which admitted alkalies form with the acids.*' The notion of salt, again, has undergone extension on a similar principle, it having been found, first, that oxygen was not inseparable from the character of alkalinity; and next, that hydracids would unite with the alkaline bases, and produce salts. This progress has been followed of late by the discovery of an analogy between the double sulphurets and oxygen salts by the Baron Berzelius, and other advances which must end in the introduction of entirely new views on this class of bodies. '*The researches of Graham on the phosphates, those of Liebig on the constitution of the organic acids and their salts, and the experiments of Dumas, Clark, Frémy, Thaulow, Péligot, and many others, have gradually converged to the point of recalling to the recollection of chemists certain profound views first suggested by Davy in regard to chloric and iodic acids and their salts, and afterwards applied (apparently without previous knowledge of what Davy had done) by Dulong to the salts of oxalic acid. These views have the inestimable advantage of uniting all acids into one series, and all salts into another ; nay, these two series may even be considered as one.*' What, then, will be said of a theory formed more than a century ago, and about half a century before even the existence of oxygen, hydrogen and nitrogen was known, being yet exactly adapted to a state of the science so advanced that the editors of Turner's work confess the chemical world to be unprepared for the change which it (we mean their own new classification) must necessarily introduce?

"We are sincerely desirous of avoiding any exaggeration on the score of Swedenborg's claims, but what are the facts of this remarkable case of anticipation? Swedenborg begins his chemical manipulation with the particle of salt described above, and requires our assent to one of the simplest causes of change which it is possible to conceive, namely the separation, by a slight cause of disturbance, of the branches of the salt from its stoma, when the latter becomes an *alkaline base*, and the former constitute *acids*. It follows as one of the simplest consequences, from this theory, that the reunion of the acute particles which form the acid with the basic atom forming the alkali, must reproduce the original salt. Now what can be more singular than the fact that the definitions of these three substances have, a few years past, been drawing closer and closer to Swedenborg's theory, and what amounts to a very close approximation, indeed, is considered as a thing that must be ?

"But, again, the constituent particles of a perfect salt, in Swedenborg's theory, are the constituent particles of water, and these in modern chemistry are hydrogen and oxygen in the proportion of 1 to 8 ; the equivalent of water, therefore, by our own analysis is 9, and *it is the same in Swedenborg's theoretical calculation.* But if his notion of the formation of a salt by the disintegration of water be a true one, and if acids and alkalies be formed, according to his theory, by the disintegration of salts, our analysis ought to prove that all these substances contain what we know to be the constituents of water, namely, oxygen and hydrogen. Now what say the editors of Turner's work in extenuation of the new views to which we have alluded, as the result of discoveries by Berzelius and others ? '*In regard to acids,*' they remark, '*the first point to be noticed is, that all so called oxygen acids, in the free or what may be called the active state, contain hydrogen. . . .* Sulphuric acid and phosphoric acid, no doubt, may be obtained anhydrous ; but it is worthy of special notice, that in this state *they do not possess the properties of these acids,* and only acquire them on the addition of water.' The demonstration, therefore, that hydrogen as well as oxygen is in intimate association with the acids, lies at the basis of the new classification. It is equally remarkable, that the strongest arguments in favor of the proposed theory are derived from an examination of the salts ; for it is found that a salt is formed when the acids are neutralized by a metallic oxyde, or by ammonia, etc., and in this case a separation of water occurs, not to mention the conversion of sulphur-salts into oxy-salts—a most significant circumstance in relation to Swedenborg's theory.

"The whole circle of modern chemists, we presume, are prepared to shake hands with us on the fact that *crystallization* is governed by mechanical laws; since herein the occult geometry of nature gives its lines and surfaces to the broad daylight. The same laws, however, which explain the several phenomena of affinity and combination, become in our author's theory the exponents of crystallization. The saline particle itself is of course a crystal, but by the combination of such particles with atoms of water, the production of larger crystals, in their well-known solid forms, is explained. 'When,' Swedenborg observes, 'owing to a deficiency of water, there are no longer six aqueous particles to surround a saline particle, that combination of the salt and water called crystallization begins.' The neatness of this conception can hardly be exhibited without a reference to the illustrative figures and calculations in the work before us; it consists, however, in the fact, that the water and the salt are supposed to be both together fluid so long as there are a sufficient number of water-particles to fill up the concavities of the salt, and give it a certain roundness by the protrusion of their convex surfaces beyond the points; and that this fluidity ceases when, instead of being surrounded by water, the salt incloses or surrounds *it*, so that the angular parts are protuberant, and commence the formation of visible lines and surfaces by their conjunction in indefinite numbers. By locking their arms together, two particles of salt inclose one atom of water so effectually, that there is no way of escape except by disintegration; while the atoms which are received within the outer concavities may of course glide away with comparative ease. Now there is a singular coincidence in Turner's " Elements."

" ' The water of crystallization is retained by a very feeble affinity, as is proved by the phenomena of efflorescence, and by the facility with which such water is separated from the saline matter by a moderate heat, or by exposure to the vacuum of an air-pump at common temperatures. It is frequently observed, however, that a portion of the water is retained with such obstinacy that it cannot be expelled by a temperature short of that at which the salt is totally decomposed. This water, as in the case of the hydrated acids, is considered to act the part of a base, and is hence commonly called basic water. But from the observations of Graham, it would appear that the water thus retained does not always act the part of a base, but is in a peculiar state of combination, characteristically different both from basic water and water of crystallization. (Pr. Tr. Ed. xii. 297.) In his original paper he distinguished it as saline water; but in a recent report, read to the meeting of the British Association in Liverpool, he has called it constitutional water. It is readily distinguished from water of crystallization, by being retained by a stronger affinity, and by being essential to the existence of the salt of which it constitutes a part. From basic water it differs by not being removed from its combinations even by the most powerful alkalines, whereas it is readily removed, and its place in the compound assumed by certain anhydrous salts : it is also expelled from an acid more readily than basic water. From an example, the character of water in these different states of combination will be readily understood. The crystals of the common phosphate of soda are composed of 1 eq. of phosphoric acid, 2 eq. of soda, and 25 eq. of water. On exposing them to a temperature of 210°, 24 eq. of the water are readily expelled; but the 25th eq. is retained with such power, that a red heat is necessary to effect its complete separation. By the loss of the 24 eq. of water, the crystalline form and texture of the salt is entirely destroyed, but the residual amorphous mass has all the properties of the common phosphate ; whereas by the loss of the 25th, an entirely different salt, the pyrophosphate of soda is produced. It will hence appear, that the 24 eq. of water which were lost at 212° were only essential to the existence of the crystal, while the loss of the 25th eq. effected that of the salt.' "

3. SWEDENBORG'S THEORY OF THE ACTIVES, FINITES, AND ELEMENTS OF CREATION.

In order to enable our readers to obtain a rational insight into the following articles, treating on the chemical elements of the common atmosphere and water, it becomes necessary for us to present them with a succinct statement of Swedenborg's theory of the above substances and forces in nature. We shall do so in Mr. Beswick's words, whom we have already introduced to our readers as the able commentator of Swedenborg's "*Principia*." The materials of the following articles are all drawn from his elaborate series of papers on the "*Principia*," which appeared in the years 1849–50, in the "Intellectual Repository," in England, and during the years 1855–56, in the "New Church Repository," in New York, where this gentleman at present resides.

THEORY OF CREATION.

(a.)—*The Simple, or Natural Point.*

" In the *Principia*, Swedenborg has placed the primal generative force, issuing immediately from the Infinite, in a conatus towards spiral motion, which, from its being circular in all its dimensions, he regards as one perpetual *ens* possessed of the highest perfection and the mightiest capabilities, because being at once most highly mechanical and most highly geometrical. This primary movement, connecting the finite with the Infinite, he called the SIMPLE, or first natural point. It means, in fact, the disposition of the *Infinite Himself* to produce creation—the potential or initial act of intending. This concentration to a certain *determinate* end, though the end or limit comprises an infinitude of particulars, and an endless duration of things, is nevertheless regarded as the first limit or determination of the infinite capabilities of the Divine Nature. As yet there is no creation ; consequently nothing mechanical nor geometrical, for these imply finitude and boundary. Of this SIMPLE, he says, ' it is pure and total motion,' Part I., chap. ii., No. 12 ; and that, ' it belongs *to* the Infinite, and exists *in* the Infinite ;' and in the next number (13) he defines it to be ' an internal state or effort (*conatus*) to motion ; hence he says :—

" ' Thus it will be like effort or *conatus* itself ; for in conatus not only is motion everywhere present, but with it also its force, direction, and celerity. This *conatus*, or effort towards motion, may be called its internal state,' n. B. .   .   .   .

" The SIMPLE, therefore, as we have stated, means the conatus or first internal effort of the Infinite to commence the work of creation. This work, evidently, includes all that the Divine being could desire, will, and design; and hence its realization, though its continued working includes eternity, is regarded as the limit of his endeavor. All the efforts of an Infinite Providence may be summed up in one single object, and to this everything has ever tended and ever will tend. And because this SIMPLE, or internal effort of the Infinite, had only one object in view as the end of its action, or the end of Creation—because of this, Swedenborg has represented it as having only one limit, or one tendency. Of course this one tendency is applicable to the Infinite as a being wherein there are infinite things. As Swedenborg observes, (Divine Love and Wisdom,) 'an Infinite without infinite things in himself, is not infinite, but as to the bare name,' n. 17, Part I. So likewise in the *Principia*, he considers these infinite things in the Infinite have each this limit or unity of tendency; hence there will be an infinitude of these SIMPLES, points, tendencies, or efforts; all having the same end in view. Herein lies the final cause of the infinite diversity in Creation."

(b.)—THE FIRST FINITE.

" As yet there is nothing but the Infinite, in which there are infinite things, having a unity of purpose and a similar tendency to action. The next step would discover them in harmonious and enduring activity,—omnipotent within their limits · and having the utmost uniformity of fluxion. It is evident that the form of fluxion will be the most powerful and potent in being,—it must be omnipotent, because it moves and wields the whole aggregate of being. This form of fluxion, Swedenborg affirms, is the spiral, because being circular in all its dimensions, it is one perpetual *ens*, possessing the highest mechanical power, and the most perfect geometrical figure; and hence having the greatest perfection and the mightiest capabilities. Inasmuch as each of the infinite things in God is at once both omnipotent and omnipresent in the spiral figure thus formed, we can have no difficulty in seeing that the figure formed by each is the first actual subject of Creatiou; it is the first creation of *space* and figure; before it there were no changes; and therefore no time, and no degrees of celerity by which its instants are measured. But inasmuch as it is God, or each of the infinitude of things in God, which are thus active, it is clear an infinitude of spiral spaces or figures will be created, forming a sphere of living activity. . . . . Here, therefore, is the beginning of creation. These existences are bounded both as to *time* of birth and *outline* of figure. They are therefore finites; but inasmuch as they are the first existences, they are aptly designated the FIRST FINITES. The Infinite has now surrounded Himself with an halo of living glory, forming an atmosphere of living substances, in which he is enshrouded, and in which he is, or the infinite things of Himself are, both omnipotent and omnipresent. These finites are also called first substances or substantials; because this latter term is applied in the *Principia* only to created subjects."

(c.)—The First Active and Second Finite.

"In Swedenborg's theory, the first finite expresses the transmitted force from the SIMPLE or conatus of the Infinite, in a substantial form. The finite, therefore, expresses the limit or outline of its operations, and the consequent figure formed thereby. We say a substantial form, because being omnipresent, that is, instantly or ever present in every point of the space thus formed, a substantial figure would result; as in the case of a little ball which is whirled round by a string. On this account, the first finites are actually spiral figures or substances. The transmitted force of the simple, however, keeps them, when formed, in constant activity in a spiral direction. The common understanding of the reader will easily conceive that when these spiral figures, in constant activity, come in contact, they will spontaneously fit in each other's spires, and form a mass of spirals, beautifully arranged, from which an aggregate will be formed. He will also perceive that, in consequence of each spiral figure pressing on each other in the same direction, in order to turn round in their respective places, but cannot, the whole mass will be moved in the same direction, and will thus spontaneously give to itself an axillary motion. The *figure* thus formed will be a new substance; being, in fact, a new compound, which has formed itself entirely of first finites, or spiral substances. This new compound is called a SECOND FINITE. On the other hand, should these spiral substances of the first finite not be in contact, they will then be projected, and run off into a spire, into which they will be impelled by the transmitted and irresistible force within them. They will, therefore, have a local fluxion in the form of a spire, where, from their velocity, they will be omnipresent in every point thereof. These are called actives of the first finite."

In order to represent the true nature of an active, Mr. B. introduces Swedenborg's diagram, representing a little ball, which, by being whirled round a centre by means of a string, produces the resemblance of a circle. The point where the ball is present is perpetually substantial and material. If the velocity be so great that its progressive gradations and moments are imperceptible, it follows that in every point of the circle the ball is, as it were, present and perceptible. A resemblance to a substance may therefore be produced by motion.—*Principia*, Part I., chap. v., n. 8.

"The only difference, therefore, between an active and finite is simply this: A finite has no local motion, it has only an axillary; whilst an active is a finite *in* local motion. That local motion may either be spiral or circular, according as the figure itself is spiral or circular."

(d.)—THE FIRST ELEMENT OUT OF WHICH SUNS AND STARS ARE FORMED.

"We have now two kinds of particles, both of which have been formed from the first finites or substances. The one is an aggregate of substantial spires called first finites, entirely passive as to local motion; the others are of the same class of first finites, unaggregated, free, and in an active state of spiral fluxion. Hence we should naturally expect the actives, more or less in number, to whirl and collect around themselves the inactive masses of first finites. The internal space will then consist of actives, and the external surface purely of bundles or aggregations of first finites, which aggregations are called second finites. Such an arrangement of two kinds of particles is called an ELEMENT; and as this is the first created arrangement, the substances so formed are called the first elements. Swedenborg affirms that of such substances the suns and stars are made."—(See Part I., chap. x., n. 3, 4.)*

(e.)—OTHER KINDS OF ACTIVES, FINITES, AND ELEMENTS.

"Other kinds of actives, etc., are formed by a continued application of the above processes,—by the aggregation of finites to make a new finite; or by the local fluxion of a finite to make an active, or the formation of new elements by the combination of actives with finites, in such a manner as to allow the latter to surround the former; the internal space always being filled by actives. In this manner are the vortical, magnetic, ethereal, and other elements successively formed. . . . It appears, therefore, that this philosopher views creation as a substantial outbirth from the Creator—a graduated manifestation of his Infinite activity in the production of spaces and forms of uses; the gradation being marked in the scale of creation by the various *finites* or limits. The first gradation is marked by the first finite, or first substance; the second by the second finite, or second substance; and so on to the most inert substances in nature, in which the Infinite activity has ceased to manifest itself in the form of an independent local fluxion of each substance,—nothing but gravitation now remains. Centripetation, or gravitation, in its ordinary acceptation, very beautifully expresses the entire loss of that Infinite activity to which we have referred, which always confers the power of individual exertion and independency of local fluxion, or the power to occupy additional space

---

* According to these passages, the solar space seems to consist of the actives of the first and second finites, and the elementary particles appear to take their rise around this large active space, (see chapt. x., n. 5,) and thence to spread through the system.

as a field of action. Gravitation, as ordinarily used, is a term inapplicable to the vortical, magnetic, ethereal, and other elements capable of self-action, or of taking upon themselves a local fluxion. It is a term applicable only to substances *at rest*, and hence they gravitate or form into dead inert masses, incapable of self-fluxion. Creation, therefore, is conceived to be a graduated outbirth of substantial forms or spaces from the Infinite himself; which forms have been determined by the living energy and activity having been united with a definite tendency whilst in the Infinite, but which has been modified through each successive gradation. This activity, running throughout Creation, is in the hands of the infinite, who, having infinite resources and capabilities in his Infinite Love, Wisdom, and Power, will to eternity improve its *tendency*; and thus endless diversity and increasing perfectibility of Creation itself await the unborn generations of the family of man. Herein lies the ground of our belief, that no philosophical theory yet propounded is so grounded in fact, philosophy, reason, and common sense, as that of Swedenborg's *Principia*. It enables us to enter rationally and scientifically into the mysteries of that great truth,—the progressive improvement of Creation, as a whole, to eternity."—*Intellectual Repository*, 1850, pp. 252–59.

4. The Compound Nature of Atmospheric Air.

" The actual discovery of that twofold nature of atmospheric air, as consisting of oxygen and nitrogen, was reserved for Priestly in 1772–4, Scheele in 1774–5, Lavoisier and Trudaine in 1775, Cavendish in 1784–5, and for Dumas and Boussingault in our own time; the latter of whom have presented the world with a demonstration of its compound nature by a most refined analysis of its constituents. Cavendish appears to have the merit of first discovering the exact proportion of the constituents of air in the popular sense of oxygen being one-fifth." We give Mr. Beswick's argument.

Swedenborg, as early as 1722, was well acquainted with the compound nature of air, and knew the gases of which it is composed. Oxygen, in his phraseology, was "the fifth finite," and nitrogen " the first and second elementaries." By simply exchanging his terms for those which are now in use, the fact of his " fifth finite " being identical with oxygen, and the " first and second elementaries " with nitrogen, must become evident to every one that has any knowledge of the properties of these gases. In the following quotations from his works we shall accordingly effect this change, but in all other respects preserve the language of the translator.

" Air consists superficially of oxygen, and within it are enclosed particles of nitrogen," Principia, Part III., chap. vii.

" Oxygen has entered into the surface of the aërial particle, and nitrogen into the internal space."—*Id.*

In Part III., chap. v., n. 19, he gives representations of air-particles, showing the relative arrangement of the oxygen and nitrogen particles under different pressures; and thereby accounting for the elasticity of the air.

In the following passages oxygen, *i. e.*, " fifth finites," are shown to be supporters of fire :

" Oxygen (*i. e.* ' fifth finites') creates the common culinary or atmospherical fire."   Part III., chap. viii., n. 2.

" Let us consider more especially the active state of oxygen, which is the cause and origin of our common atmospherical fire."—*Id.*, n. 4.

" Oxygen constitutes the surface of a particle of air, and supplies fire with its element."—*Id.*, Part III., chap. vi.

" Fire is no other than oxygen itself set at liberty."—*Id.*, chap. viii., n. 4.

In the " *Miscellaneous Observations*," (Part III., article— " Hypothesis of the Figure of the Particles of Fire and Air,") Swedenborg speaks of oxygen as igneous matter, or fire. Hence he says,—

" The particles of air are bullular, with exceedingly minute particles of fire [*i. e.*, ' fifth finites,' or oxygen] *on* their surfaces."

" Fire forms the crust of the air-particles."

" The air affords matter for supporting fire."

" If the crust of the particle of air consists of igneous matter [*i. e.*, oxygen], it follows, that there is more fire when the supply of air is large, provided it be fresh."

As oxygen sustains flame, so nitrogen extinguishes it. "This," Mr. Beswick says, "is the great characteristic of nitrogen: it is neither combustible nor a supporter of combustion; for if a burning body be immersed in a jar containing it, the fire is instantly extinguished. It is therefore antagonistic to, and an extinguisher of, fire. And Swedenborg has not only marked out this substance as one of the constituents of atmospheric air having a greater volume than oxygen, but he has beautifully described this essential characteristic; and what is far more valuable, because being a desideratum to the chemical and scientific world, he has propounded a philosophical exposition of its cause. 'Fire,' he says, 'is no other than the "fifth finite" (*i. e.*, oxygen,) itself set at liberty, or flowing in a space where it can run freely.'—Principia, Part III., chap. viii., n. 4.

"Should we present a substance like the 'elementaries' forming nitrogen, which have a chemical affinity for these 'finites' by convoluting them around themselves into new surfaces or particles, the result would be an instantaneous fixation and cessation of activity. So says Swedenborg:—

"'The "fifth finites" cannot actuate themselves in a volume of the "elements" without immediately being converted into new aërial particles.'"—*Id.*, n. 1.

"In the language of the day, this simply means that the particles of oxygen cannot support fire, or be the active agent of combustion in a volume of the elementary particles of nitrogen, without immediately being converted into atmospheric air. And the reason is thus stated:—

"'Inasmuch as "elementaries" are present to impede them, and to convolute them into new surfaces.'—*Id.*, n. 1.

"According to this theory oxygen, or the 'fifth finite,' in an active state, produces heat and fire, whilst nitrogen, or the 'elementary' substance forming the interior of a particle of air, is directly antagonistic to, and destructive of, fire, and ever tending to convolute or form around itself the substance or element by which heat or fire is supported.

"It is a matter of deep regret, and of deep humiliation to his admirers, that this theory of Swedenborg has not had an elaborate and an able exposition. All our knowledge tends to make these apparently loose and inapplicable *Principia* matters of every-day proof, and of dry familiar detail in the elemental school and laboratory. He who can understand this theory will soon appreciate its value, because it furnishes some of the best solutions to many of the otherwise inexplicable problems of nature. It explains, upon the simplest principles in dynamics, why oxygen alone is breathed, and why it is the chief physical agent in the important operation of breathing or respiration of animals; the main reason being on account of its dynamic virtue, of becoming active and forming heat, and thereby actuating to everything in connection therewith throughout the system. Nitrogen, on the contrary, if admitted in considerable quantity, would put an end to this excursive or actuating tendency in oxygen, by withdrawing it around and fixing it to itself, thereby depriving it of its dynamic virtue; action in such a case must cease, and death result. This singular relationship of the two constituents of atmospheric air was most beautifully expressed and extensively illustrated by Swedenborg in his *Principia*, about half a century before these facts were known. It also presents a solution to an important mystery in the economy of the vegetable world. It explains why vegetables, when actuated by the sun during day, give out oxygen; whilst during the night oxygen is absorbed on account of its dynamic virtue, and to promote a circulation of the fluids.

" Swedenborg likewise declared that the element least in quantity, or that which occupies only the surface of the air-particles, is a constituent of both air and water; for, so long back as the year 1721, he published the following announcement, that—

" ' The particles of water belong to the sixth kind of hard particles . . . that on its surface there are crustals of the " fifth kind " [*i. e.* oxygen].'

" The above is given in his *Principles of Chemistry* (Part IX. n. 1). To the same effect is his chapter ' On Water ' in the *Principia,* published thirteen years subsequently. In both works the ' fifth finites,' or oxygen, is represented as forming the surface, and a considerable portion of a water particle. . . .

" In Swedenborg's works we find, not only the acknowledged theory that one of the elements of the air is the grand supporter of atmospheric combustion; but also the highly important theory, that this same constituent of air enters largely, by decomposition, into actual combination with solids of every description, and is again released by decomposition of the solids, and again enters into the formation of particles of air. Hence he says:—

" ' There are many evidences to show that the oxygen (*i. e.* " fifth finites ") enters into the texture of terrestrial bodies, such as animal, vegetable, oily, and sulphurous substances.'— *Principia*, Part III., chap. viii., n. 8.

" We may arrive at the same conclusion *a priori;* since the particles of oxygen (*i. e.* ' fifth finites ') are of such a nature that the hard parts of vegetables may be compounded of them.—*Id.*

" But this chemical combination requires the dissolution of the air particle, so as to release the oxygen and nitrogen. Hence—

" ' The air undergoes a process of dissolution when entering into the compages of the parts of vegetables: if these compages be dissolved, the air (oxygen and nitrogen formerly separated) returns again to its former state . . . and the earth restores that which it had borrowed.'—*Id.*

" In the *Principles of Chemistry*, Swedenborg shows that these ' fifth finites,' or oxygen particles, enter more largely into the composition of the earth's solids and fluids, into water and the whole mineral kingdom, than any other substance; and that they have been mainly derived from the atmosphere by decomposition. Now, what are the known facts of the case? Let the following suffice for a confirmation:—

" ' Of almost every form and kind of matter which surrounds us, oxygen forms an ingredient. Its compounds are more numerous and diversified than those of any other substance with which we are acquainted.

" ' It forms a part of every earth we tread upon, and of every vegetable we see around us; and when combined with another gaseous body, hydrogen, it forms water; an important and essential form of food to all the animal and vegetable creation.'—*Encyclopædia Metropolitana*, Heat and Chemistry, p. 647.

"'Oxygen constitutes a fifth part of our atmosphere, eight-ninths of the weight of water, and a large proportion of every kind of rock in the crust of the earth.'—*Vestiges*, p. 19.

"Yet the idea that an element of air had entered so extensively into combination with almost every substance by decomposition, is due to none other than Swedenborg. It is true, the Stahlian or phlogistic theory existed; but it never conjectured the possibility of decomposing atmospheric air; for its fundamental teaching involved the supposition that air is a simple and undecomposible substance. The highly important fact of its decomposition, and the extensive union of one of its elements with terrestrial substances, is now, and probably will ever be regarded, as one of the greatest and most useful discoveries in chemical science; for certainly no other discovery has given such an impetus, or enlarged the boundaries of experimental chemistry, or will exercise so important an influence in the future history of science, as that of the decomposition of atmospheric air. And hence we doubt not but that it will call forth from future generations their admiration of this neglected and despised philosopher, as the first *herald* to publish the Physical Principia of Nature."

The object which we have in view in pressing the importance of the scientific works of Swedenborg upon the notice of the learned, is not so much to induce them to examine his claims as the first expounder of theories that have since been adopted by science, and of which she has conferred the honor of first authorship upon others of her votaries, as to aid in the general advancement of science. For there is so much vitality in the scientific principles of Swedenborg, and they have such a lofty rational foundation, that it will take science many ages to reach *unaided* that point from which he has viewed the universe in its largest and smallest dimensions. Let science, therefore, take hold of these principles, and endeavor to become familiar with them, and a beneficent light will soon enlighten its progress among the forces and elements of nature. In the following pages we shall see how easily Swedenborg explains by means of his theory the difference in proportion of the two constituents of air in different localities and under different circumstances.

The reader will recollect that an air-particle consists of oxygen particles on the surface, and of elementaries within. Swedenborg now says :—

"The surface of the aërial particle may be doubled, tripled, or variously multiplied interiorly, and this during a state of *compression;* but the part of the surface which recedes towards the interiors is formed into new spherules and bullules similar to the larger."—Part III., chap. vii., n. 11.

"By this process," says Mr. Beswick, "it is evident the volume of the particle must be considerably reduced. Under it the 'finites' or oxygen particles pressed within are described as 'consuming' the 'elementaries' or nitrogen particles there enclosed, and by that means 'forming new spherules and bullules;' in other words, new substances; for the nitrogen particles, by this 'consuming' or combination, are said to lose their elementary character and become solid and hard; Part III., chap. v., n. 19; or, as is said of an air particle.

"'It likewise follows, that the aërial particle during its highest degree of compression becomes at length entirely occupied by small similar spheres, extending from the surface to the centre, and ceases to be elastic and elementary, growing *hard,* and similar to a material finite.'—*Id.* chap. vii., n. 11.

"As noticed above, the oxygen particles pressed within are said to consume the 'elementaries' or nitrogen particles by the gradual formation of a new class of substances within the particle of air. During this compression of the volume, the 'elementaries' in the interior gradually disappear, whilst the 'finites' pressed into the interior absorb them and generate a new substance; hence the volume of 'finites' or oxygen would, during this compression, gradually occupy a greater portion of the space within, besides forming the whole of its superficies. We should expect to discover the quantity of oxygen, or of these 'fifth finite' substances, varying perceptibly in the interior of continents, and but slightly over the sea; and that, whilst in polar countries, north and south, aërial particles would be compressed, the reverse would result from the action of the sun in tropical climates.* In polar regions, where the particles are compressed, the volume of 'elementaries' within will suffer most; but in tropical climates, the volume of oxygen on the surface will appear to diminish by the expansion of the particles, and consequent increase in volume, of the enclosed 'elementaries.' The extremes of the seasons, summer and winter, will produce a corresponding result, in every locality all over the world. Winter, by the compression of the 'elementals' within aërial particles, will give the *minimum* advantage to their volume, or what is the same, to nitrogen; whilst summer, by the expansion of their volume, will give the *maximum* advantage. Hence, Dr. Turner remarks :—

" ' It is remarkable that this (pure) air is very rich in oxygen. That procured from snow-water by boiling, was found by Gay, Lussac and Humboldt to contain 34.8, and that from rain water 32 per cent. of oxygen gas ; ' whilst ordinary atmospheric air has only 20.8. See 'Elements of Chemistry,' p. 960, and p. 224.

" The expansion, during summer, will cause the oxygen particles forced within to rush back to the surface. Hence Swedenborg says :—

" ' The bullular particles, which during their expansion are interiorly in a state of nitency, become again set at liberty, recede to the surface, and enter into its expanse.' Chap. vii. n. 11.

" From these two physical causes the proportionate volumes of oxygen and nitrogen, or finites and elementals, will be in a constant state of oscillation, the mean of which will also vary according to latitudinal, local, and mensual circumstances. These theoretical considerations have now become matters of empirical certainty. We could quote confirmations from the works of German, French, and even English investigators, if our space would permit and the case demanded : to only one instance shall we refer :—

---

* " We are not overlooking Cavendish's report to the contrary; *Phil. Trans.* 1783 ; nor the more recent experiments of Martin's, see Dumas in the *Annals of Chemistry*, third series, t. iii., 1841, p. 237."

" ' Some observations of Davy render it probable that the quantity of oxygen varies perceptibly, although but slightly, over the sea, and in the interior of continents according to local conditions, or to seasons of the year.' "—*Cosmos*, vol. i., p. 317.

In a subsequent article Mr. Beswick makes the following remarks :—" Another fact affirms, that the proportionate volumes of the two elements entering into the composition of atmospheric air are various in different localities and under different circumstances. This fact has been illustrated from the *Principia*. An additional illustration from the *Observations*, with proofs, shall now be given. In the latter work, as in the former, Swedenborg assumes what is now universally admitted, that in elevated situations, high up in the rarified regions of the aërial envelope of our terraqueous globe, the air-particles will be more expanded and dilated ; and hence, there will be less of the ' fifth finites,' or fire-feeding particles of oxygen, in a given volume, than there will be in the same volume on the terrestrial surface, when the air-particles will be compressed ; or in the depths of the ocean, where the particles will have their greatest compression. His thesis is given as follows :—

" ' Hence, in the highest regions of the atmosphere, on the tops of mountains, and above the clouds, we find that the air is very rare, and scarcely affords matter (fifth finites or oxygen) for supporting fire.

" ' In lower situations, these particles are more compressed, and form a very thick surface or crust to the air particle . . . hence, they are compressed into a narrower space, and a thicker crust (of fire particles or oxygen) is produced.'—(See ' Hypothesis of Fire, etc.')

" In accordance with the general tenor of these propositions, he is at once led to the adoption of the following important conclusion, which the facts of science will justify, that there is less of the fire-supporting element, oxygen, in warm, rarified, and distended air, than in cold, heavy, and compressed air. These are his words :—

" ' There is less fire where the particles of air are more

rarified or distended; but more fire where they are more compressed, as indeed follows from the hypothesis.'

" Or more forcibly and pointedly stated in these words :—

" ' Thus in the same space, there is more fire in compressed particles than in dilated particles.

" ' Thus more fire (or oxygen particles) exists in the bottom of our atmosphere than in its upper parts.'

" In other words, there is more oxygen in a compressed volume of air than in the same volume of uncompressed, dilated, and rarified air. Swedenborg, therefore, lays it down as an invariable rule, that wherever air-particles are more than ordinarily compressed—as at the bottom of the sea—and under whatever circumstances that compression may be produced, it will always be found, on investigation, that in a given volume such compressed air will give forth a greater quantity of the fire-supporting element, *i. e.*, oxygen. So self-evidently true is this rule, that its utterance is but the announcement of a mere truism. But the reader must bear in mind, that these reasonings and announcements were recorded at a period when air was universally believed to be a simple body, and when the utterance of this truism would be regarded as a palpable absurdity."

Mr. Beswick corroborates this theory by eminent authorities, such as Humboldt, Liebig, etc., and then continues :—

" Wherever we apply this beautiful and simple theory, we shall have fresh cause for admiration of the genius which could elaborate such views of the laws and constitution of the universe in which we live, move, and have our being. The wonder is, how his conceptions could be so complete, and so true to the natural principia of things, whilst no experiments existed to guide the conception."

Mr. Beswick, then, gives the following resumé of his investigations with regard to the discovery of the compound nature of atmospheric air: "The *Miscellaneous Observations* were published in 1722, and contain the same theory of fire and of air-particles as the *Principia*, which was subsequently published in 1733–4. Black and Cavendish, in 1766, were the first to proclaim the conjecture that air is a compound body. Up to this period it was believed to be a simple elemental

body. But they had no idea, neither did they offer a conjecture, of the number and nature of its elements.   To
Priestly in 1772–4, Scheele in 1774–5, Lavoisier and Trudaine in 1775, and Cavendish in 1784, we are indebted for
the first announcement of the number of its constituents, and
their nature.   Now, before all these, in 1722, Swedenborg,
as we have seen, in his *Miscellaneous Observations*, and again
in 1733–4, in his *Principia*, propounded a most admirable
theory of the nature and composition of atmospheric air ;
wherein he unmistakably pronounces, and pictorially represents, its binary composition ; and wherein he describes in
detail, and in the most explicit language, the antagonistic
nature of the binary elements, and announces in plain terms,
as well as by implication, the now well-known fact, that the
least in volume of these binary elements of air is the fire-feeding
element, now known under the name of oxygen.   The priority
of claim to this remarkable discovery is without doubt to be
awarded to Swedenborg."—*Intellectual Repository*, for 1850,
pp. 288–301, and pp. 367–376.*

---

* We have inserted Mr. Beswick's argument in full as he gives it in
the *Intellectual Repository*, taking the liberty, however, of condensing
it, and changing its order.   We do not wish it, however, to be under- .
stood that we endorse all his views.

There can be no doubt about the identity of Swedenborg's fifth
finites with oxygen, and of his having recognized the air, and also
water, as compound bodies.   But the identity of nitrogen with Swedenborg's first and second elementaries seems extremely doubtful.   The
first and second elementaries of Swedenborg are the vortical and magnetic elements, and as such penetrate all fixed material substances,
including metals and glass, while nitrogen is so coarse a body that it
can easily be enclosed in metallic bodies or vessels of glass.   Nitrogen
seems to have considerable to do with the effluvia in nature, and to be
the common chemical expression of a great number of them ; it is
possible also that the first and second elementaries combine with these
effluvia and represent nitrogen, in which state they may again combine
with oxygen so as to constitute the common atmospheric air.   Swedenborg's own statements about nitre in the "Principles of Chemistry,"
seem to corroborate this view.   Still all of this is as yet mere conjecture; that much, however, is certain, that the places of nitrogen,
hydrogen and carbon in Swedenborg's system are still undetermined,

5. THE COMPOSITE NATURE OF WATER.

Mr. Beswick says :—" Pure water, as it comes from the chemist's still, is a colorless liquid, having neither scent nor taste. Its binary composition is uniformly designated the grand discovery of modern chemistry. No wonder, then, that the honors thereof have been warmly contested; the rival claimants being Watt, Cavendish and Lavoisier. The severity of this rivalry sprung out of the fact, that each claimant professed to have made the discovery about the same time, during the years 1783–4. . . . . . No claimant has ever come forward, nor has ever been found to have even suggested the composite nature of the aqueous element, water, prior to the year 1783. We can therefore by no means regard it as over-sanguine to affirm, that there is no rival claimant that can come forward, or be put forth by others, to dispute the honor of first announcing this great modern discovery, with EMANUEL SWEDENBORG. To him belongs the indisputable merit of presenting the first suggestion as well as the first exposition of the composite nature of the aqueous envelope. But to place this case clearly before the reader, we shall formally present it under several heads. For him we claim the important theoretical discovery and the first published announcement of the following important fundamental facts :—

" Fundamental Facts.

" *a.* Pure water is a compound substance.

" *b.* Its two constituents are equal in volume when forming water.

" *c.* The atomic weight of the elements being $= 9$.

" *d.* One of its elements is a constituent of both air and water.

---

but we have no doubt in our own mind that a more thorough and profound study of the " Principia," and the " Principles of Chemistry," will enable us to identify them with some of Swedenborg's elementary bodies.

" *c.* Water, like air, is capable of decomposition, and of becoming a constituent of all compound substances.

" We might have enumerated other particulars, but since they are only partially admitted in the scientific world, we have thought it best to omit their enumeration."

" *Proof of the above Fundamental Facts.*

" No ingenuity could guess, *a priori*, that water is a compound body, much less that it is composed of *two* gases, oxygen and hydrogen." — Turner's *Elements of Chemistry*, page 170.

a. " PURE WATER IS A COMPOUND SUBSTANCE.—Upon reading the above, the uninitiated will be inclined to inquire—Why could ' no ingenuity guess it *a priori*'? Had this eminent writer been questioned personally, he would no doubt have replied in these words—Because oxygen is an eminent supporter of combustion, and hydrogen is eminently combustible, yet oxygen and hydrogen form together the compound substance, water, which is eminently useful in putting an end to combustion. Hence the very plausible remark,—

" ' That no ingenuity could guess *a priori*, that water is a compound body,' etc.

" Notwithstanding the general truthfulness of this sentence, there are some individuals who seem to be inclined to believe that Swedenborg guessed *a priori* some of the theoretical announcements claimed for him. We are somewhat curious to know, if this theoretical announcement in the *Principia*, Part III., was a guess of this kind:

" ' That a particle of water is similar to a compressed particle of air (also a compound), in which there remains nothing elementary.'—Chap. ix., n. 1.

" ' The enclosed elementaries are consumed in compounding the particle, and the consequence is, that the particle *cannot* be called elementary.'—*Ibid.*

" This announcement was published, and sent to some of the first institutions in Europe about sixty-three years prior to Watt's suggestion, and two years before he was born. It was, therefore, published and circulated at a time when every one believed in the elemental simplicity of water. Surely this

23*

was something more than simply a lucky reflection of the truth, a mere guessing *a priori*. We who have read and studied the groundwork of the opinion thus anticipatively formed, know for a certainty, that the contrary is the truth. To all such asserters we would respectfully recommend the contents of this article to their calm and steady consideration. But to proceed. It is only recently that the compressibility of water has been proved. The celebrated experiment of the Florentine Academicians seemed to prove that water was compressible to a slight extent; but this matter has been placed beyond all doubt by the excellent researches of Professor Oersted and of Mr. Perkins: for by a pressure of two thousand atmospheres Mr. Perkins reduced a mass of water to eight-ninths of its original volume. Water is, therefore, a compressible fluid. This will enable us to confirm the thesis of the following quotation from the *Principia* :—

" ' That a particle of water is similar to a compressed particle of air, in which there remains nothing elementary, yielding, and elastic, but something hard, consisting of contiguous spherules formed within another larger sphere. . . . That water, consequently, is *not* an elementary particle. . . . . The enclosed " elementaries " are consumed in compounding the particle.'—Part III., chap. ix., n. 1.

" ' So considerable a portion of its extremely large surface is pressed inwards, as to be received by the enclosed " elementaries " and formed into new spherules or particles, which gradually throng the particle (within) and render it hard and resisting, thus urging and keeping it, in the ratio of its weight, near the surface of the earth. The figure of the particle may be seen in Fig. 110.'—*Ibid*.

b. " ITS TWO CONSTITUENTS ARE EQUAL IN VOLUME WHEN FORMING WATER.—In agreement with the law of condensation, water consists of two equal volumes of the vapor of two gases. The scientific world has ventured to broach an hypothesis of the cause of this striking phenomenon, which though allied to the one given above by Swedenborg, is as yet unworthy even of comparison therewith. According to his theory, the ' fifth finites' or oxygen, like as with the air particle so also with the aqueous, occupy the surface and form the crust of the particle, having the other constituent within.

" ' The particles of water belong to the sixth kind of hard particles . . . . that on its surface there are crustals of the fifth kind.'—Part IX., n. 1.

" The above was given in 1721 in his *Principles of Chemistry*. That the two volumes constituting a water particle are equal according to this theory is expressly affirmed, though for the sake of convenience in illustration, the internal space of a particle is spoken of as a cavity, as in the following quotation from this work :—

" ' As in Plate II., Fig. 1, where it may be seen ;—

" ' 1. That a particle of water is round.

" ' 2. That on its surface there are crustals of the fifth kind (oxygen).

" ' 3. In the middle of the particle of water there is a cavity, the space in which is equal to the space of its crustals, or of its superficial parts.'—Part IX., n. 1.

" ' According to the theory of water, n. 1, the internal cavity of the particle is half of the space.'—N. 4.

" . . . . The manner in which Swedenborg proves that the two volumes of matter entering into the composition of a water particle are equal, is as follows :—

" ' If the internal cavity be equal to the space which the crustals occupy, and the diameter of the (whole water) particle be 10, it follows that the diameter of the cavity will be very nearly 8 ; for $8 \times 8 \times 8 = 512$; and $10 \times 10 \times 10 = 1000$.'—N. 1.

" In this computation 512 represents the volume of the internal space, and 1000 the space of the whole particle ; hence $500 + 500 = 1000$, or the volume of the internal space + the volume of the external space = the whole space of the particle. Thus Swedenborg proves himself to have formed a conception of the compound nature of water, its twofold composition, the equality of the volumes constituting it, the identity of one of its elements with one of the elements of air, and other particulars which we cannot now enumerate."

c. " *The atomic weight of water* $= 9$. The proportions

necessary for forming water in 100 parts of its constituents, are as follows :—

	By weight.		By measure.	
Oxygen	88.9 or 8	. .	33.34 or 1	volume.
Hydrogen	11.1 or 1	. .	66.66 or 2	"
Mixed	100.0 9	. .	100.00 3	"
Combined forming water	100.0 9	. .	66.66 2	"

" Hence the gases, when combined to form water, are reduced to the original bulk of hydrogen, the entire bulk of oxygen having completely disappeared. It will make no difference in the present computation, whether we infer that the oxygen has absorbed the other gas, or one-half the bulk of hydrogen has absorbed the oxygen. Of this we are certain, the whole bulk of oxygen has disappeared to such a degree of nicety, that the exact bulk of hydrogen is never in the least disturbed during the combination ; the original bulk of the hydrogen being 66.66 before combination, whilst the bulk of the resultant mass after combination is also exactly 66.66. In agreement with this fact of disappearance Swedenborg says, in the second volume of his Principia,—

" 'The enclosed "elementaries" are consumed in compounding the particle of water.'—Part III., chap. ix., n. 1.

" ' So considerable a portion of its extremely large surface is pressed inwards as to be received by the enclosed "elementaries.' "—*Ibid.*

" It may be seen from the above table, and indeed is now generally admitted, that water is constituted of precisely two volumes of hydrogen combined with one volume of oxygen, or by weight eight out of nine parts are oxygen, and the remaining part is hydrogen ; or, according to the atomic theory, of one atom of each of these elements. The atom of water, therefore, upon the hydrogen scale is = 9. This is the identical number given by Swedenborg in 1721, in his ' *Principles of Chemistry,*' as the equivalent of water ; it was certainly given at a time when water was believed a simple uncompounded substance, and about sixty-three years before the atomic weight of water was known to be represented in the scale of atomic weights by the number 9. We are prepared to combat the idea that this equivalent was assumed by him as a random but lucky guess, *a priori*. By a process of reasoning, the entirety of which we cannot pretend to enumerate, but which may be found in the above-named work, he arrived at the important conclusion that the equivalent of a particle of water = 9. There would be no paucity of means to arrive at this result, according to the line of investigation evidently adopted by him, and inversely introduced in his work on *Chemistry*. There would be no end to the instances inviting him to the adoption of this equivalent for water. Indeed, the line of investigation is so peculiar, so strictly founded upon geometrical data, that we cannot really detect the slightest possibility of his adoption of any other equivalent. We will enter into a brief discussion of the reasons which determined the adoption of this equivalent, with a view to set at rest the idea of guessing.

"The hydrogen scale has this substance as the basis of measurement, because it is the lightest of all known substances. Its equivalent is therefore 1. Since the proportional numbers merely express the relative quantities of different substances which combine together, it is in itself immaterial what figures are employed to express them. The only essential point is, that the relation should be strictly observed. Different chemists have adopted a series of their own, which was considered by them as more simple than any other. For example, Dr. Thomson makes oxygen 1 as the basis of his series. Dr. Wollaston fixes oxygen at 10. The celebrated Berzelius has oxygen at 100. Whilst several other chemists, as Dalton, Davy, Turner, Henry, and others, have oxygen at 8; consequently hydrogen will be given in this scale at 1. Any one of these scales may easily be reduced to the others by an obvious increase or diminution of the corresponding equivalents, as the case may be.

"Now in Part IX., n. 4, *Principles of Chemistry*, where Swedenborg first gives his weight of the water particle, he assumes the volume of fifth finites, or oxygen = 1, which is the same as Dr. Thomson's scale of equivalents. This volume he regards as occupying half the space of the particle of water. Hence he says,—

" ' Let the matter in the particle of water = 1.'

" ' The internal cavity is half of the space.'

" Swedenborg must certainly be considered as having adopted a similar scale to that of Dr. Thomson, in which oxygen = 1, for we have already, in a former article, proved the identity of his ' fifth finites' with oxygen ; but the reason which induced him to adopt the ratio or scale now in general use, first suggested by Dalton, we will endeavor to explain. In this section Swedenborg is attempting to estimate the comparative weights of a water particle and the saline particles filling the interstitial spaces of water. He there develops a statement, involving his method of investigation, his scale of equivalents, and the ground-work of the whole superstructure of his *Principles of Chemistry*. If the reader can only master this paragraph, he may go steadily along with its author through the entire work, without much difficulty and doubt.

" ' *Demonstration.*—Let the matter (fifth finites or oxygen) in the particle of water = 1. According to the theory of water, n. 1, the internal cavity of the particle is half of the space ; consequently if it be filled with the same matter (or the whole particle be oxygen), the weight of the particle will = 2. Since then the weights are as the spaces, viz., $3 : 1 :: 2 : \frac{2}{3}$, the weight of the interstitial matter, compared with the weight of a particle of water assumed as equal to 1, will be as $\frac{2}{3}$ to 1, or as 2 to 3.

" ' If, again, the more subtle hard matter of the fourth kind (or atoms of a particle of oxygen) insinuate itself into the interstices of this matter, I maintain that this interstitial substance, or one cube with two triangles, will then weigh to a particle of water as 10 to 9.

" ' *Demonstration.*—Let the aforesaid matter be as 2 to 3 ; also, let the internal cavities of each of these particles (called " fifth finites " or oxygen) occupying half the space, like the cavity in the particle of water, be filled up ; in which case the weight will be double the foregoing, or as 4 to 3. Now, since the ratio of the weights is according to the ratio of the spaces, it will be as $3 : 1 :: 4 : \frac{4}{3}$; to which, if the 2 be added, it becomes $2 + \frac{4}{3} = \frac{10}{3}$, and thus when compared with the weight of the particle of water, taken as 3, it will be, $\frac{10}{3}$ is to 3 as 10 is to 9.'

" Now, is it not evident, that Swedenborg's adoption of 9 as an equivalent for water, in the scale of atomic weights, originates in a numerical necessity? Strictly speaking, the number was not selected, but forced upon his adoption. It took up the position in his scale, as an equivalent of water, irrespective of everything but arithmetical necessity. Conjecture and lucky guessing can lay no claim to the discovery of this important theoretical principle in Swedenborg's system of chemistry—they can claim no familiar acquaintanceship with geometrical proportions, nor take any part in the practical developments of the golden rule of three. The above quotation is called by the author a 'demonstration;' and it is truly such. For in this demonstration, the volume of the ' fifth finites ' or oxygen, occupying only half the space in a water particle, is taken as the basis of his computation : and after a series of reasonings—too obviously true to be doubted —is induced to adopt the result, that, when the interstitial spaces between particles of water are filled up with particles of oxygen and the smaller atoms of which the former are compounded, then this solid interstitial substance will weigh to a particle of water as $\frac{10}{3}$ is to $\frac{9}{3}$, or as 10 is to 9 ; hence it is clear, the only two whole numbers which could have been adopted, as equivalents, are evidently 10 for the interstitial substance, and 9 for water. Let us not be misunderstood ; we do not say that no other numbers could have been adopted as corresponding equivalents, for that would be asserting what we know to be not true ; but we do say, that no other numbers than 9 for water and 10 for salt can possibly be got out of the computed demonstration given by Swedenborg. These equivalents are therefore assumed by him, not as mere conjectural or even convenient proportions, which may or may not be subsequently confirmed, but as real ratios, arithmetically originating in the geometrical structure of a water particle, and based most extensively upon experimental demonstration.

" The reason why the ' elementaries ' occupying the interior of a particle of water are not referred to and accounted for in the computation, is, because their density is too insignificant to form an item. Swedenborg says :—

" ' The enclosed " elementaries " are consumed in compounding the particle of water.'

"This is obviously correct; for we have already shown that this is equally true of oxygen and hydrogen when forming or compounding water. . . . As we proceed, we shall have many opportunities of making it manifest, that this equivalent of water was extensively confirmed by its *undoubted discoverer* from evidence arising out of extensive experiments, of national importance in his country, and familiarly known to him by reason of his position."

d. "ONE OF ITS ELEMENTS IS A CONSTITUENT OF BOTH AIR AND WATER. We mean the 'fifth finites' or oxygenic particles. But as we have sufficiently proved this point in our article on Air, and indirectly also in the present paper, we deem it unnecessary to add further proof.

e. "WATER, LIKE AIR, IS CAPABLE OF DECOMPOSITION, AND OF BECOMING A CONSTITUENT OF ALL COMPOUND SUBSTANCES. This truth was announced as a principium by Swedenborg, half a century before its acknowledged discovery. . . . . He says in his *Principia*, Part III., chap. ix. :—

" ' We cannot consider the aqueous particle as any other than a certain hard body rendered fluid by an extremely small degree of heat.'—n. 2.

" ' The aqueous volume is perfectly similar to that of a *mineral of any kind* melted into a volume or liquid.'—n. 4.

" . . . With regard to its dissolution and union with other substances, he says in the same place,—

" ' Innumerable, therefore, would be our remarks on the subject of water, were we to enter into all its phenomena. We should have to show, for instance, in what manner and by what causes the connections of its particles could be resolved; in what manner, after the dissolution, the enclosed spherules occupied the interstices between other and aqueous particles; in what manner were hence originated new terrestrial and saline parts; what were the figures of these parts, and their motions between the aqueous particles; in what manner these particles convey them through the fibres, stems, and pores of vegetables; how it is they dispose them into the vegetable form,' etc.

"Most of these particulars have been explained in his *Principles of Chemistry*, and have a charm of such genuine

simplicity about them, that we shall delight ourselves in some
of our subsequent articles by captivating the reader's attention
with their exposition and illustration, by a variety of interesting and familiar phenomena. In Swedenborg's day the above
particulars would appear anomalous; and, however beautiful
and true they may now seem, they would then be silently
regarded as being both learned, ingenious, and ridiculous.
What would be more absurd than to proclaim the dissolution
of an elemental substance into *its parts?* Or that water, by
dissolution, forms salt, and becomes a part of the hard solid
rock, or a part of the earth's minerals, vegetables, and animals?
Yet nothing is more true, than that such is the case. . . ." *

---

* The same remark that we made at the close of the last article, we
have to repeat here, viz., that we do not consider Mr. Beswick's arguments as exhausting the subject. The same elementaries that Mr.
Beswick, in the case of the air, called nitrogen, figure again in Swedenborg's theory of the water, and Mr. Beswick allows us now to infer
that they are identical with, or form, hydrogen. There may be a connection between nitrogen, hydrogen, and Swedenborg's elementaries,
but there is quite a hiatus between the elementaries composing the
vortical and magnetic elements, and the chemical bodies of hydrogen
and nitrogen, which hiatus Mr. Beswick has not yet accounted for.
From the fact that both gases, oxygen and hydrogen, are capable of
assuming the solid shape, as in water, and again of expanding in the
gaseous state, it seems as if both were finites capable of being expanded
by elementaries into the gaseous state, and by the withdrawal of these
elementaries, of being compressed into the solid state. The identity
of Swedenborg's fifth finites with oxygen, however, we think Mr. Beswick has confirmed by his article on water, also the fact that both the
air and water are compound bodies.

24

IV.

SWEDENBORG'S MAGNETIC THEORIES.

1. The Law of Magnetic Intensity.

Of all the laws of magnetism, that of its intensity increasing towards the poles is, on account of the practical uses of the magnetic needle in navigation, unquestionably the most important. The very existence of its variation was scarcely known in the scientific world till the time of Humboldt, who was the first to bring it into notice ; on which subject he says, in his *Relation Historique* (p. 615) : "The observations on the variation of terrestrial magnetism, to which I have devoted myself for thirty-two years, by means of instruments which admit of comparison with one another, in America, Europe and Asia, embrace an area extending over 188 degrees of longitude, from the frontier of Chinese Dzoungarie to the west of the South Sea, bathing the coasts of Mexico and Peru, and reaching from 60° north latitude to 12° south latitude. I regard the discovery of the law of the decrement of the magnetic force from the pole to the equator, as the most important result of my American voyage."

In a note to *Cosmos*, Vol. I., p. 179 (Bohn's edition), he adds : "The first recognition of the law belongs, beyond all question, to Lamauon, the companion of La Perouse (1787) ; but long disregarded or forgotten, the knowledge of the law, that the intensity of the magnetic force of the earth varied with the latitude, did not, I conceive, acquire an existence in science until the publication of my observations from 1798 to 1804."

"Now," Mr. Beswick observes, "the publication of the very same law, announced in nearly the same terms, took place in Swedenborg's *Principia* in 1733, being sixty-five years in priority of publication, thirty-six years before Humboldt was born, and fifty-two years before the time of La Perouse's expedition, which was commenced in 1785. But let the reader judge for himself. The following is Humboldt's announcement of this law :—

" ' That the intensity of the magnetic force of the earth varied with the latitude.'—*Cosmos*, Vol. I., p. 180, note.

" ' The law of the decrement of magnetic force from the pole to the equator.'—p. 180.

" ' The law that the intensity of the force increases (in general) with the magnetic latitude.'—p. 179.

" ' The intensity of the total force increases from the equator towards the pole.'—p. 179.

" Here also is Swedenborg's announcement :—

" ' There is, therefore, an action upon the particles of this element, according to the arcs in distances from the poles.'— *Principia*, Part II., chap. xv., n. 8.

" ' The force is according to the arc of distance from the poles.'—*Ibid.*

" ' The pressure at a less distance from the pole must be different from the pressure at a greater distance, and *vice versa.*'—*Ibid.*

" ' The magnetic element exercises a pressure according to its altitude ; that its altitude is to be estimated in the direction from one pole to the other.'—*Ibid.*

" Indeed, this force formed one of the data by which Swedenborg endeavored to compute the declination at several places for different years. Hence he remarks, Part II., chap. xv., n. 4 :—' Nevertheless this force, small as it is, must be taken into consideration ; for without it, we shall by no means be enabled to arrive at the true knowledge of the declination.' Though it must be admitted, that his estimation of this force for different latitudes was erroneous ; yet this will not alter the fact, nor detract from the merit, of his having obtained a knowledge of the general law of the variation of the horizontal force all over the earth."—*Intellectual Repository* for 1849, pp. 220–223.

2. MEAN LATITUDINAL POSITIONS OF THE TWO MAGNETIC POLES AND EQUATOR.

"The first individual," says Mr. Beswick, "who appears to have instituted a series of consecutive magnetic experiments, with a view to ascertain whether the same needle varied its dip in different latitudes, was an English navigator of the seventeenth century. The experiments are inserted in *Phil. Transactions*, n. 117. They were written by a navigator in 1684, who crossed the equator to a latitude of 35° 25′ south. But the experiments led to no theoretical results. Although he discovered that the force of each magnetic pole was commonly in equilibrio from a south latitude of 0° 52′ to 8° 17′, which was indicative of his position as being then on the magnetic equator, yet this idea never occurred to him; and it was not until the close of another century (Swedenborg excepted) that it was observed that the geographical and magnetic equators were not identical. Muschenbroek, in his *Experimental and Geometrical Physics*, says of this navigator, 'I have never met with any other person who has instituted similar experiments.' All investigations of the magnetic dip, by which the position of the magnetic equator is ascertained, began, properly speaking, with Graham, in 1720. But no one up to the time of Cook and Fourneaux, in 1773–77, Lamauon and Perouse, in 1785, Rossel, in 1791–94, and of Humboldt and Bonpland, from 1798 to 1804, even ventured an opinion.*

"Swedenborg was the first who announced, not only their non-identity, but also the mean latitudinal position of the magnetic equator. During his day, and even until the close of the eighteenth century, it was believed that the position of the two equators was identical. Humboldt, speaking of the seventeenth century, at the close of which (1688) Swedenborg was born, says *Cosmos*, Vol. II., p. 718 :—

" ' The position of the magnetic equator, which was believed

---

* See Duperrey, *On the Configuration of the Magnetic Equator* in the *Annals of Time*, t. 45, pp. 371, 379; also Morlet, in the *Memoirs of different Savans of the Roy. Acad. of Sciences*, t. iii., p. 132; also Sabine's *Contributions to Terrestrial Magnetism*, 1825, 1837, 1840–41, and part 2, 1849, in the *Phil. Transactions*.

to be identical with the geographical equator, remained un-investigated. Observations were only carried on in a few of the capital cities of western and southern Europe.'

" And it was not until the close of the eighteenth century that this fallacy was removed. Hence the same writer observes, *Cosmos*, Vol. I., p. 176 :—

" ' The position of this line, and its secular change of configuration, have been made an object of careful investigation in modern times.'

" Yet Swedenborg, at the beginning of the eighteenth century (1734), affirmed this fact of non-identity, by assuming as one of the fundamental principles of his theory, that the magnetic poles follow the mean latitudinal position of the poles of the ecliptic, and the magnetic equator the mean latitudinal position of the ecliptic. And in Part II., chap. xiv., n. 5, there is a beautiful diagram, expressly introduced by Swedenborg as descriptive of the relative positions of the two equators and poles. The mean latitudinal positions of the magnetic poles and magnetic equator are stated by Swedenborg in the following extract :—

" ' Since, therefore, there are two poles, we may next inquire what is the distance between the poles of the earth or world. Now they cannot be the same with the poles of the earth, but are the same with the poles of the vortex (or magnetic sphere). For as the vortex by its spiral motion forms ecliptics, so these poles (the magnetic) must be the same with the poles of the ecliptics ; that is to say, they will be at the same distance from the poles of the earth as the poles of the ecliptic, or 22° 30′. Nor can there be any other magnetic poles than those of the ecliptics of the (magnetic) vortex ; that is to say, they must be poles at a distance of 22° 30′ on each side from the poles of the earth.'—Part II., chap. xv., n. 3.

" This extract, coupled with the diagram referred to above, will confirm what we have stated, that one of the fundamental principles of his theory was the non-identity of the magnetic and terrestrial poles and equators. And that the mean latitudinal positions of the magnetic poles and equator are identical with those of the earth's ecliptical poles and ecliptic, will be evident to any one who will take the trouble of tracing the course of each. The position of the nodes of the magnetic equator and ecliptic are almost identical, as affirmed by Swedenborg, and the nodes of each have a backward movement or precession in the same direction, and is implied in the theory of Swedenborg. For the recent observations of Sabine (*Contributions to Terrestrial Magnetism*, 1840, p. 134) have shown, that the magnetic node of island of St. Thomas has moved 4° from east to west, between 1825 and 1837, and the opposite node in the South Sea, near Gilbert Islands, has approached the Carolinas in a westerly direction. And the magnetic poles, though now situated in a higher latitude than the poles of the ecliptic, are nevertheless found, by tracing back their course for the last three centuries, to oscillate above and below the mean latitudinal positions of the ecliptical poles; as affirmed by this philosopher.*

"The merit of first propounding the non-identity of the magnetic and terrestrial equators, and the mean latitudinal positions of the magnetic poles and equator, belongs unquestionably to the Swedish philosopher, Emanuel Swedenborg."— "*Intellectual Repository*" for 1850, pp. 129–131.

3. SOUTHERN MAGNETIC AXIS LONGER THAN THE NORTHERN.

"It is a matter of singular interest in the science of terrestrial magnetism," says Mr. Beswick, "that the southern magnetic pole has a longer axis from the centre of the magnetic equator than the northern, and hence occupies a higher latitudinal position. Their positions are as follows :—.

South Magnetic Pole, 75° 5′ south latitude.
North Magnetic Pole, 70° 0′ north latitude.

"But even this fact, which was not even suspected before the investigations of Professor Hansteen, published in 1819,† who was the first among scientific men to conjecture this fact,

---

* *Professor Hansteen's* observations on the position and revolution of the magnetic poles, Edin. Journal of Science, Vol. V., 9, p. 65; also *Grover's* Memoir, Orbital Motion of the Magnetic Pole, read at the annual meeting of the British Association, 1849; also *Beswick's* Illustrations, &c., Phil. Mag., vol. 36, n. 242, p. 183.

† Researches into the Magnetism of the Earth, Christiania, 1819.

was published by Swedenborg nearly a century (85 years) previous. The confirmation of this fact has been so recent as the memorable Antarctic Expedition of Sir James Clarke Ross (1839–43), who determined empirically the position of the magnetic south pole. When Swedenborg declared this fact in 1734, the affirmation was not conjectural, for it is expressly declared to be the result of experiment, and the application of theory. It was announced in these words :—

" ' Both from experiment, and from our first principles, it is evident that the north magnetic pole moves round the north tellurian pole sooner than the south magnetic pole moves round the south tellurian ; and this because the distance of the two from the centre of the vortex (magnetic sphere) is not similar.' —Part II., chap. xv., n. 6.

" And this suggestion of the physical cause must appear self-evidently true to every theoretical magnetician who considers that the north magnetic axis, being shortest, would perform its revolution in a shorter time. The reverse would be the case with the opposite axis. Swedenborg, therefore, announced this fact eighty-five years before Professor Hansteen first conjectured it, and one hundred and seven years before it was confirmed by actual observation."—"*Intellectual Repository*" for 1850, pp. 131, 132.

4. The Revolution of the North Magnetic Pole speedier than that of the South Magnetic Pole.

" It would appear, from this case and the following," says Mr. Beswick, " that one discovery led the way and gave the initiament to others, all forming one chain of fundamental facts, dependent upon what the author terms his ' experiments and our first principles.' For, as stated in the last case, it is clear that if two axes, the northern being shorter than the southern, be moved by a force acting equally upon each, the shorter or northern axis will revolve with greater speed and velocity than the longer or southern axis. Accordingly we find that such is the case. Although it was suspected that the magnetic poles had a translatory revolution, yet Swedenborg was the first and the only individual during the eighteenth century who held the opinion that the north magnetic pole had a much quicker revolution than the southern. For from the publication of the *Principia* to the time of Hansteen, the idea was never broached; and this involves an interval of eighty-five years.* The following are the words in which this fact was first announced (Part II., chap. xv., n. 6) :—

" ' But both from experiment and from our first principles, it is evident that the north magnetic pole moves round the north tellurian pole sooner than the south magnetic pole moves round the south tellurian.

" ' In the same theory we shall have to demonstrate that these magnetic poles move round the poles of the earth continually from west to east, but with uneven progress.'

" And although he estimates their relative annual velocities at 56' for the north magnetic pole, and 20' for the southern, which is more than four times too much in either case for that epoch, yet it is worthy of notice that though the estimate is considerably wrong, the theoretical principle involved is perfectly correct, namely, the velocity of the northern is about twice as great, and somewhat above that of the southern. I have made this particular fact a subject of proof in two articles, entitled, *Illustrations of a New Method for computing Magnetic Declination, on the Principle proposed by Professor Gauss* (Philosophical Magazine, No. 239, vol. 35, p. 511) ; also, *Further Illustrations*, etc. 242, vol. 36, p. 183).

" The following estimate is given by Prof. Hansteen :—

Period of revolution of North Magnetic Pole . 1890 years.
Mean annual motion . . . . 11'·425.
Period of revolution of South Magnetic Pole . 4605 years.
Mean annual motion . . . . 4·69.

" Now this ratio is the same as given by Swedenborg, as may appear from the following proportion :—

$$4' : 11' :: 20' : 55';$$

the two first being the velocities given by Hansteen, and the two latter, or rather 20' and 56', being the velocities given by Swedenborg."—*Intellectual Repository* for 1850, pp. 132–133.

---

* " The time of the publication of the second volume of the *Principia* (1734) is here alluded to."

5. The Attractive Force of the South Magnetic Pole greater than that of the North Magnetic Pole.

" The following, like the last case," Mr. Beswick continues, " is an instance of forming a correct conception of important fundamental facts, when the first principles of a theory are grounded in the nature of things. Like the former, the present instance depends on the principle assumed in No. 3. For, as a consequence of the south magnetic pole having a longer axis, and therefore containing a greater quantity of the magnetic element, Swedenborg was compelled to assume, as a subordinate principle in this theory, that this pole must be stronger, and the more intensely attractive of the two magnetic poles. Hence he says :—

" ' As the magnetic element tends with a certain tacit current from the south pole to the north (through the earth's interior), its force is greatest at the south pole, and becomes gradually less towards the north. The nearer to the south pole the greater is the force.'—Part II., chap. xvi., n. 5.

" From the recent experiments and researches of Sabine, Ross, Gauss, and others, this statement has received a remarkable confirmation. Humboldt says, *Cosmos*, vol. 1., p. 181 :—

" ' If the intensity near the magnetic south pole be expressed by 2.052, Sabine found it was only 1.624 at the magnetic north pole.'

" It would, therefore, appear from the observations hitherto collected, that the attractive force of the south magnetic pole bears the same ratio to the attractive force of the opposite pole as 1.624 is to 2.052. Swedenborg's ratio is also about the same. (Part II, chap. xvi., n. 5.) We have already proved his discovery of the law of intensity, or its increased force and tension in the direction of each pole (our No. 1). Now it is somewhat remarkable, and indicative of a distinguishing feature in his genius, in possessing the highest order of anticipative originality, that he should predict not only the law of intensity—that it varied all over the world—fifty-two years before it was conjectured * ; but also that he should proclaim the greater intensity of the southern magnetic pole compared with the northern fifty-two years before a single experiment had been undertaken which could lead to such an idea; and 107 years before it was proved."—*Intellectual Repository* for 1850, p. 135-36.

6. IDENTITY OF THE MAGNETIC STREAMS FORMING THE AURORA, AND THOSE INFLUENCING THE MAGNETIC NEEDLE.

Mr. Beswick says, " Humboldt attributes, erroneously, the discovery of the simultaneity of the perturbations and influence of the magnetic streams (which are visible even to the unassisted eye during an auroral display) to the French astronomer Arago.† For the simultaneity at distant points had already been suggested and distinctly ascertained by Celsius and Graham in 1741, whilst residing the one at Upsala and the other in London. The identity of the streams forming the earth's magnetic vortex, and those directing the needle, was also clearly established by the Swedish observers, Celsius, Hiorter, and Wargentin, between 1740–1750, in a number of special cases, the details of which are recorded in Prof. Kämtz's *Meteorology* (iii. 494, etc.,), and recorded, too, in the very part of that work cited by Humboldt himself in his *Cosmos* (vol. 1, note, p. 188). They must, therefore, I should imagine, have passed under his observation. Why he should think proper to pass over them in favor of his personal friend, the French royal astronomer, is a matter we cannot explain. . . . . . It is somewhat remarkable in the present instance that Swedenborg, in 1734, and Celsius, Hiorter, and Wargentin, between 1740 and 1750 ‡ —the only individuals who have a rightful claim to the merit of this discovery—should all be Swedish philosophers, and living at the same time, and all alike passed over . . . by this greatest of all scientific travellers and writers of the present era.

" The theory of Swedenborg affirms that the earth is enveloped in a vortex of magnetic streams, which give a direc-

---

* Cosmos, vol. 1, p. 179.

† Cosmos, vol. 1, p. 179.

‡ Wargentin, and others, *Trans. of the Swedish Academy, vol.* 15.

tion to the magnetic needle according to their situation, whether near or remote from the magnetic poles. Or, as he himself expresses it, Part II, chap. xv., n. 2,—

" ' The vortex, therefore, of our earth consists of particles of the magnetic element, for it is known that there is a vortex which surrounds the earth, and within which, like a nucleus, the earth is revolved, or is enfolded as an infant in the arms of its nurse.'

" The fact of such a magnetic vortex was already known, and indeed was suggested by the celebrated Kepler, in 1619. This is admitted ; but no one prior to Swedenborg had suggested (what every aurora now exhibits as a self-evident fact), that this vortex is formed of progressive streams flowing out of the northern magnetic pole, and into the southern, and in their course deflecting the needles wherever they may be situated, and irresistibly impelling them in the same direction as themselves. The following is Swedenborg's announcement :—

" ' Such as is the situation of the particles of the magnetic element, such will be the situation of the magnet when left to itself. For this element directs the sphere, and at the same time the body of the magnet into a parallelism and similarity of situation with its own ; or more clearly thus—such as is the situation of the particles of the magnetic element, such also is the declination of the needle. As for example :—At Paris, in the year 1727, where the declination was observed to be 14° west, then in the same place the very particles of the element declined themselves at an angle of 14° from the north pole of the earth toward the west, and consequently so also did the needle.'—*Ibid*, n. 8.

" Side by side with Swedenborg we place the theory of M. Biot, which expresses the general opinion of the scientific world ; speaking of which Dr. Lardner observes (*Cabinet Cyclopædia*—Magnetism, vol. ii., p. 232–33) ' that it appears most entitled to attention.' We are disposed to ask—What difference is there between the theory of Swedenborg, as given above, 117 years ago, which affirms that the streams of ' this (magnetic) element direct the sphere and body of the magnet into a parallelism and similarity of situation with their own,' and the following theory of the French observer, M. Biot, given in 1818?

" ' The fact that the rays or columns of light (magnetic streams of the vortex forming an aurora) are always parallel to the dipping needle, and always symmetrically placed with respect to the magnetic meridian, demonstrates that the cause, whatever it be, has an intimate relation with that of terrestrial magnetism.

" ' He considers that the phenomenon is produced by an infinite number of luminous columns (or streams) parallel to the dipping needle and to each other, arranged side by side.'

" To the list of observers of this parallelism and similarity in situation of the magnetic streams and the direction of the needle, we can add the testimonies of Parry, Franklin, Richardson, Ross, and Hearne, explorers near the north pole ; Gieseke in Greenland ; Henderson and Thienemann in Iceland ; Sabine, Scoresby, Lottin, and Bravais, in the region of Spitzbergen and North Cape ; lastly, Back, Anjou, Cook, and Wrangel in the region of Behring's Strait. Every one of whose reports we have taken the trouble to examine in the order here given, and we find that they successfully corroborate this fact. The most striking instances of confirmation are the following, to which we direct the attention of the scientific inquirer." *—*Intellectual Repository*, pp. 134–137.

7. THE NORTHERN LIGHT AND MAGNETIC STORMS.

In his next article (*Intellect. Repos.* pp. 168–175), Mr. Beswick proceeds a step further, and applies Swedenborg's *Principia* to the elucidation of the *aurora borealis*. This he attempts by means of Swedenborg's doctrine of spiral motion ; wherein he states (and to a certain extent proves) the now

---

* *Edin. Phil. Journal*, vol. 5, p. 85, 1826 ; Humboldt, Pogg. *Annals* bd. xix., s. 357, part 1-3 ; Gauss and Weber, *Magnetic Results*, 1839, s. 128 ; Sabine's important work, *Observations on Days of Unusual Magnetic Disturbances*, 1843, part 14, pp. 78, 85, and 87 ; Thienemann, *Edin. Phil. Journal*, vol. xx., p. 366 ; Lottin and Bravais, *Martin's Meteorology*, 1843, pp. 117 and 453 ; Sir D. Brewster, *Treatise on Magnetism*, p. 280 ; Professor Challis, *Athenaeum*, Oct. 31, 1847 ; *British Association Report*, 1842, section 5.

well-known fact that the magnetic needle receives its direction, dip, and intensity from the direction, dip, and intensity of the magnetic stream during their flow in a tacit and profound current from one pole to the other; and he additionally affirms, what might be anticipated from the above as a correlative, that the declinations or spiral windings of the streams in their fluxion must so impel and carry the needle, as to place it pointing in the direction of the spire, and thus give it an equal amount of declination as themselves, so that the increased spirality of the streams will be clearly indicated by the increased declination of the needle, and the reverse by a diminished spirality.

This thesis, he says, is beautifully illustrated by Swedenborg in chap. xiv., on *The Declinations of the Magnet;* and in chap. xv., on *The Causes of Magnetic Declination,* and as instances quotes the passage in Part II., chap. xv., n. 8, which will be found in the preceding article, and also the following :—

" When therefore the magnet or needle in its declination is urged by the situation of the particles of the magnetic element, then the needle evidently receives a direction in the element according with the position of the particles . . . . for the current of the particles acts directly upon the sphere of the needle; but if the particles of the element are in an oblique position, as in the following figure (here follows diagram), then the particles are obliquely upon the sphere of the needle, and urge it further downwards rather than in the polar direction."—Part II., chap. xiv., n. 5.

Mr. B. also proved, by a number of instances, that the spirality of the streams increases or diminishes with the increased or diminished intensity of their fluxion; and hence, when speaking of the use of certain magnetic instruments in the experiment he proposes for the demonstration of Swedenborg's Magnetic Theory of the Earth, he is led to remark—"The declination needle tests the spirality of the streams—its increase or diminution; whilst the isodynamic force needle tests their rate or intensity of fluxion—its increase or diminution."

He therefore, as he observes, simply stated a correlative

fact, which presented itself on the very surface of Swedenborg's thesis of the spiral fluxion of these streams, when he wrote out the following :—

"*Deduction.*—It will, therefore, be a uniform law of magnetic storms that their commencement is indicated by a diminishing intensity and decreased declination from the earth's pole ; and their cessation and abatement by a reversion."

The whole philosophy of which, he says, Swedenborg gives in the following short sentence :—

" The more intense the motion the greater the declination of the spires."—Part II., chap. i., n. 8.

As an additional confirmation of his theory, Mr. Beswick mentions (p. 211), that a scientific friend called his attention to the striking confirmation which the wires and needles of the electric telegraph present of the above uniform law of magnetic storms, as directly deduced from Swedenborg's Theory of Magnetic Spiral Motion :—

" *Magnetic Storms.*

" Did any doubt remain of the electrical character of the *aurora borealis*, it would be removed by the phenomena presented by the needles of the telegraph, and often by the bells during the prevalence of this meteor. At such times the needles move just as if a good working current were pursuing its ordinary course along the wires ; they are deflected this way or that, at times with a quick motion, and changing rapidly from side to side many times in a few seconds ; and at other times moving more slowly and remaining deflected for many minutes, with greater or less intensity, their motion being inconstant and uncertain. These phenomena have occurred less frequently on the part of the line between Reigate and Dover, which runs nearly east and west, than on the part between London and Reigate, which is nearly north and south. When, however, they do make their appearance on the telegraph in those parts, we are prepared to expect auroral manifestations when night arrives ; and we are rarely disappointed." —*Electric Telegraph Manipulations, by Charles V. Walker.*

8. Professor Gauss's Theory Identical in Principle
with Swedenborg's Magnetic Theory.

"My honored friend, the great mathematician, Frederick
Gauss, has succeeded in establishing the first general theory of
terrestrial magnestism."—Humboldt's *Cosmos*, vol, ii., p. 720.

"I think also that you will find that . . . is entirely
superseded by the more general theory of magnetic attraction
to and repulsion from every part of the earth. This theory
was first explained in the *Theory of Terrestial Magnetism* of
Gauss and Weber, to which I would beg leave to refer you,
etc."—*Royal Astronomer*, in a letter to S. B., Sept. 24, 1849.

On the strength of these quotations Mr. Beswick observes:
"The Gaussian theory is therefore the first and only one acknowledged by the scientific world, capable of explaining the
varied phenomena exhibited in the geographical distribution of
the earth's magnetism; but we now propose to prove that its
fundamental principle was enunciated by Swedenborg (1734)
104 years before the* publication of the Gaussian theory
(1838). The following is submitted for the reader's inspection :—

<table>
<tr><td>Gauss in 1838.</td><td>Swedenborg in 1734.</td></tr>
<tr><td>After the geometrical representation of the relations of the horizontal force, we proceed to develop the mode of submitting them to calculation. On the surface of the earth, V, (which represents the whole of the earth's magnetic force,) becomes a simple function of two variable magnitudes, for which we will take geographical longitude reckoned eastward from an arbitrary first meridian, and the distance (in latitude) from the north pole of the earth.—Taylor's Scientific Memoirs, Article V., p. 205.</td><td>We thus obtain the situation of the particles (or declination) in every place, provided there be given the distances (in latitude) or arcs from the poles, and the angles formed by each with a given meridian (or longitude).—Part II., chap. xv., n. 8.</td></tr>
</table>

"It will be almost superfluous to affirm that the method invented by each for the expressed purpose of obtaining magnetic declination is founded upon the same principle. The
particulars of each method, we admit, are in every respect
unlike each other, but the principle is indisputably identical.
In the same page as the above the principle is again stated by
Gauss in another form, thus :—

"'Resolving the horizontal magnetic force into two portions, one of which, X, acts in the direction of the geographical

meridian, and the other, Y, perpendicularly to that meridian.'
—p. 205.

"So, indeed, does Swedenborg; and if the reader will take
the trouble he will discover that the enunciation of this identical principle, and its exposition, occupies the whole of chap.
xv., vol. ii. What could be more evidently identical than the
following?—

Gauss in 1838.	*Swedenborg in* 1734.
It is clear that the knowledge of Y on the whole earth, combined with the knowledge of X at all points of a line running from one side of the earth to the other, is sufficient for the foundation of the complete theory of the magnetism of the earth.—p. 206.	We thus obtain the situation of the particles (or declination) in every place, provided there be given the distances or arcs (of latitude, or Y) from the poles, and the angles (or X) formed by each with a given meridian.—Part II., chap. xv., n. 8.

"Swedenborg, in his formula, affirms that we obtain the
declination of the earth's magnetism ' in every place,' provided
we have a trigonometrical value of the arcs of latitude and
angles of longitude which the two magnetic poles make with
the earth's poles, and a given meridian; for then we can obtain
the value of the magnetic force for the whole earth, represented by V, as it operates in the twofold direction of latitude
and longitude at the place of observation. The precise value
of this force in each direction Gauss represents by Y and X;
the knowledge of which, both he and Swedenborg affirm, is
sufficient for a complete theory of terrestrial magnetism. The
principle assumed by each is, therefore, without doubt, strictly
identical. Hence the values of the latus calculi and angulus
calculi, given in Swedenborg's method, Vol. II., pp. 160–61, are
identical with the values of X and Y in Gauss's method. For
in both they simply mean the value of V, or the whole earth's
magnetic force in the twofold direction of latitude and longitude. Now in all the great mass of calculations from p. 166
to p. 225, Vol. II., as well as in all the diagrams, p. 368, the
sides *b c* and *g c*, in Swedenborg's method, are equivalent
values for Y in the two hemispheres, as given in every case by
Gauss's method. The whole of Swedenborg's remarks from
p. 158 to 161, are explanatory of the corrections to be made
for the rotundity of the earth in latitude and longitude, and
the gradual variation of the magnetic force in this twofold
direction; in other words, to obtain the clear or net values of

the sides and angles in Swedenborg's formula, or of X and Y in the Professor's formula.

"But there is not only an identity in principle—which is but a simple principle in mechanics—we also find, upon strict investigation, that it pervades all his methods, and is the fundamental condition of all his problems and solutions. In every instance given in the Professor's profound essay to investigate some special feature of the terrestrial magnetic forces, the following remark of the Swedish philosopher receives a singular fulfilment :—

" ' That we can find no other proportion than the one existing between the distances and angles.'—p. 149.

" The following is an instance, amongst many, of a striking identity in fundamental problems :—

<table>
<tr><td>Gauss in 1838.</td><td>Swedenborg in 1734.</td></tr>
<tr><td>We must consider the problem in all its generality. We select for the purpose the distance r (or Swedenborg's b) from the centre of the earth, the angle u (or Swedenborg's ba) which r makes with the northern part of the earth's axis, and the angle l! which a plane passing through r and the axis of the earth makes with a first meridian.— p. 202.</td><td>Let the place of observation be in c (fig. 89). Let the meridian of this place be in ah; the magnetic north pole in b; magnetic south pole in g; distance from one pole to the place of observation be bc, &c.—Part II., chap. xv., n. 8.</td></tr>
</table>

"Now the same diagram will represent the conditions of both. Indeed the Professor's conditions, as given above, referring as they do, and as himself states, to the problem of magnetic distribution in its widest generality, embody only the values of the angles and sides to which we have so often referred, as the fundamental conditions of Swedenborg's method, for the northern hemisphere only. We cannot further analyze the above quotations, from the want of a diagram as the means of illustrating our remarks, but we at once refer the reader to fig. 89 in the *Principia*. In fact there is not one essential feature in the Gaussian theory and method, respecting declination, but can be found in detail, and extensively confirmed and illustrated both by argument and experiment, in the profound work of the Swedish philosopher, Emanuel Swedenborg. And this work (*Principia*), so full of research, and superabounding in germs of philosophical discovery, was published to the world, containing the fundamental *principium*

25*

of the Gaussian theory of terrestrial magnetism, and of the method for computing magnetic declination, one hundred and four years before the work containing the latter came into being ! "—*Intellectual Repository* for 1850, pp. 213–216.

We shall close here our extracts from Mr. Beswick's interesting series of papers on Swedenborg's principles of magnetism ; but in doing so we must direct the attention of our readers to one additional paper of Mr. Beswick in the *Intellectual Repository*, pp. 216–220, in which he shows that Swedenborg not only anticipated in full all the modern theories about magnetism, but also that " his method improved is the only one capable of computing magnetic declination for all places and times—past, present, and to come."

V.

SWEDENBORG'S ASTRONOMICAL THEORIES.

1. Introductory Notes.

Before entering upon a discussion in detail of the astronomical theories promulgated by Swedenborg, and before comparing them with those that have since been adopted by science, we think it best to give to our readers an insight into the grounds on which the whole of Swedenborg's astronomical system is based, using his own words for this purpose. He says :—

"The magnetic sphere with its vorticles is a type and small effigy of the starry heaven; there is the same kind of motion in small things as in great; for the same element which is moved in a vortical direction, is in both."—*Principia*, Part II., chap. 1, n. 22.

In order to understand Swedenborg's system of the starry heavens, we must therefore have an idea of his theory of the magnet. This theory we shall present for the sake of convenient reference, in the following numbers :—

1. The magnetic element, inasmuch as it is most subtile, and prior, permeates with a current perfectly uninterrupted, the interstices of every succeeding and grosser element. Thus it is capable of flowing freely not only through volumes of the elements, such as air and ether, but also through water and matter; as in like manner through hard bodies, whether of wood or of stone. It presents to our view its phenomena and natural mechanism, more especially in the case of magnets, although it acts likewise upon the particles of ether, air, and other elements, which, without an orderly sequence, and series of smaller and greater particles, could not subsist.—*Principia*, Part. II., chap. viii., n. 1 ; chap. xv., n. 1.

(295)

2.   Every particle of this element spontaneously endeavors to enter into a vortical motion, if there be only an active centre round which they can gyrate. There may be as many spiral gyrations or vorticles as there are centres of motion ; and the vorticles may be conjoined one with another in a manner conformable to their figure and motion. If the vorticles are conjoined as to their spires, and as to the harmony of their motions, they are also as it were naturally colligated by their conjunctions ; and tend to remain in that state of conjunction. Vorticles, or spiral gyrations of this kind, have a greater tendency to conjunction and colligation with each other, the nearer they are to the centre, or the greater the curvature of the spires by which they are conjoined.—*Ibid.*, chap. 1, nos. 1, 7–9.

3.   There are corpuscles so small as to emanate and exhale from hard bodies in the form of effluvia ; of this kind are the smallest corpuscles or effluvia proceeding from magnets and iron. Corpuscles of every form are magnetic ; provided the elementary magnetic particles can pass through their pores, and the connectives of their structure, and do not open wide enough for particles of a grosser element. Corpuscles of this kind, or effluvia, when free, cannot be quiescent ; but gyrate continually round their centre conformably to the situation of the elementary particles.   They constitute, therefore, active centres, and form around themselves spiral gyrations or vorticles.—*Ibid.*, chap. 1, nos. 10, 11.

4.   Accordingly, such as is the number of magnetic effluvia, such is the number of vorticles formed round the magnet. The greater the quantity of these effluvia round a magnet, the greater is the number of centres and vorticles ; also the more nearly and closely may they be conjoined and colligated by their interior spires, and *vice versa.* The colligation of the effluvia or vorticles is closer at a less than at a greater distance from the mass ; and closest at its confines or boundaries, or nearest to the mass. The vorticles surround this mass by a continually connected line from one polar wall to the other ; and thus connect and enclose each wall and pole by means of a kind of sphere. By this sphere, therefore, is formed a figure similar to the oval, conformably to whose curvature or

surface the axes of the vorticles are inflected. By reason of
the connection between the vorticles which extend from one
pole to the other, and of the formation of the sphere, there
exist poles one on each side of the magnet; there exist in like
manner polar axes extending in the sphere to a distance from
the magnet; and these axes do not receive their determination
from the magnet, but from the sphere and its figure.—*Ibid.*,
chap. 1, nos. 12, 13, 17–19.

5. The axes of the vorticles are not in one parallelism and
situation with the axis of the sphere; but are inflected according to the figure of the sphere; and this inflection begins
at the polar axis of the sphere. The whole motion in the
vorticle is according to the situation of its axis; or the axis
has a flexure conformable to the motion. If the axes are in
a right line, the motions in the vorticle are concentric; if the
axes are inflected, the motions are eccentric; if several vorticles
are in the vicinity of each other, according to whose motion
and application the axes are to be curved, then is there at
different distances from the centre or effluvium a different
eccentricity.—*Ibid.*, nos. 20, 22.

6. The axes of the vorticles and the axes of the elementary particles round the magnet are in the same parallelism;
and the elementary particles are disposed by the motion of
the vorticles into the same situation, and the same figure of
situation with the sphere. The axis of the sphere, or the
common axis of the vorticles, lies parallel with the common
axis of the magnetic element itself, so as to be exactly accommodated to it; but, nevertheless, it may be easily diverted from
this into any other direction. When free, however, it will always be directed and relapse into the situation of the common
axis.—*Ibid.*, nos. 21, 23.

7. Two or more magnetic spheres may be combined.
Their conjunction will be most close and direct at the poles,
but between the poles is slighter and obliquer.—*Ibid.*, n. 26, 27.

8. Without influxes and effluxes of particles, there can be
no continuous spiral motion; therefore at the magnetic poles
of our earth there are made apertures in the magnetic sphere
in the form of cones, through which the magnetic element can
flow in, and also flow out on the opposite side. The influx of

the particles of this element is at the south pole, and hence it tends to the north; not like a stream and torrent, but like a tranquil and tacit current, which gradually, and without any sensible motion, pursues its course from one haven to another. —*Ibid.*, Part II., chap. xv., nos. 2–4.

9.   All things are similar one to the other; because in small things as well as in large, nature preserves the greatest similarity to herself.   Thus, in the magnet and its sphere there is a type and effigy of the heaven; a mundane system in miniature, and accommodated to our senses.   In the sphere of the magnet are spiral gyrations or vorticles; in like manner, in the sidereal heavens there are spiral gyrations and vortices. In every vorticle round the magnet there is an active centre; in every vortex in the heaven there is also an active centre. In every vorticle round the magnet the motion is quicker near the centre than it is at a distance from it; the same is the case in every vortex in the heaven.   In every vorticle round the magnet the spiral gyration is of greater curvature in proportion to its nearness to the centre; the same is the case in every vortex in the heaven.   In every vorticle round the magnet there are, in all probability, corpuscles fluent round the centre and revolving round an axis; such also is the case with every vortex in the heaven.   The vorticles round the magnet mutually colligate themselves by means of their spiral motions, and, thus colligated, form a larger sphere; the same is the case in the sidereal heaven—not to mention other points of agreement of which we shall speak in the sequel.—*Principia*, Part III., chap. 1, Introduction.

We shall now investigate the extent to which the astronomical theories advocated by Swedenborg have been confirmed by modern science, taking Mr. Beswick for our guide.

2. The Cosmical Structure of the Starry Heavens.

" One vortex or solar system, with its active centre, constitutes one heaven of itself, or one mundane system; several vortices, with their centres, form together a certain sidereal sphere.   A sphere, consisting of many vortices of the same kind, has its own proper figure." — *Principia*, Part III., chap. i., n. 4.

" The whole visible sidereal heaven is one large sphere, and its suns or stars, together with their vortices, are parts of a sphere connected one with the other in the manner we have mentioned."—*Ibid.*, n. 5.

" There may be innumerable spheres or sidereal heavens in the finite universe. The whole sidereal heaven is perhaps but a point in respect to the universe. The sidereal heaven, stupendous as it is, forms perhaps but a single sphere of which our solar vortex constitutes only a part. Possibly there may be innumerable other spheres, and innumerable other heavens similar to those we behold ; so many indeed, and so mighty, that our own may be respectively only a point."—*Ibid.*, n. 11.

" By the joint labors of the two Herschel's, and the Earl of Rosse," says Mr. Beswick, " the heavens have been gauged above, below, on all sides, with their gigantic telescopes ; and the result has been, that these theoretical suggestions, so loftily and sublimely elevating, have now to be regarded as matters of fact."

The history of this discovery as recorded by science, is as follows :—

" The ingenious Mr. Mitchell, more than fifty years ago, started the idea of the stars being formed into groups or systems, which are entirely detached from one another, and have no immediate connection."—*Dick's Sidereal Heavens*, p. 210.

" The next object alluded to was the systematic arrangement of the stars. It was an Englishman, named Mitchell, who first observed this systematic arrangement."—*Prof. Nichol's Lect. on Astron.*, see *Manchester Guardian*, May 15, 1847.

" Mr. Herschel improved on Mitchell's idea of the fixed stars being collected into groups."—*Encyclopædia Britannica*, Vol. II., Part ii., p. 472, Astronomy.

" Another doctrine published at Venice in the year 1763, by M. Boscovich, said to have been first thought of by Mr. Mitchell," etc.—*Young's Essay on the Power and Mechanism of Nature*, p. 64.

" It would appear from the above quotations," says Mr. Beswick, " that Mitchell was the first, in the history of hypothesis, to propose a true conception of the cosmical structure of the starry heavens. He suggested, that gravitation might cause the stars to cluster together into distinct systems ; that as planets are parts of solar systems, so are solar systems parts of what may be called star systems. Mitchell's proposition, given in 1767 (Phil. Trans. 1767 and 1783), contains, according to the unanimous opinion of the scientific world, as shown above, the first suggestion on record of the grouping of stars into separate and distinct systems.

" But the true history of the matter stands thus : Kant, the celebrated German transcendentalist, was the first who published a true conception of the distribution of matter in space. The work was called, *On the Theory and Structure of the Heavens*, and published at Königsberg in 1755. About this time Mitchell was revolving the matter in his mind, but had not published anything thereon. Lambert, in 1757, followed Kant in his *Letters on Cosmogony*. Two years subsequently (1759) Boscovich published his celebrated theory of the *Constitution of the Universe*. All advocating similar views of the arrangement and distribution of matter in space. In 1767 Mitchell presented his views, but, differently from all previous theorists, gave certain illustrations which brought the theory at once before the attention of observers, so as to be capable of demonstration. On this account, I suppose, he is regarded as being the first who presented a true theory of the starry heavens, the former being entirely overlooked or unknown. In 1780, Herschel gauges the heavens, and literally beholds what had hitherto been only theoretical, and to some absolutely impossible."

This statement of Mr. Beswick is confirmed by Humboldt : " The purely speculative conclusions arrived at by Wright, Kant, and Lambert, concerning the general structural arrangement of the universe, and of the distribution of matter in space, have been confirmed by Sir William Herschel on the more certain path of observation and measurement."—*Cosmos*, vol. i., p. 71.

" Yet preceding all these," continues Mr. B., " and when Kant was only ten years of age, Swedenborg had formally given the same ideas and views of creation—expressly calling his Essay—' The Theory of the Sidereal Heavens '—in his immortal *Principia*, published in 1733,—being twenty-two years before Kant, twenty-four years before Lambert, twenty-six years before Boscovich, thirty-four years before Mitchell, and forty-seven years before Herschel. This work, which preceded all others in the suggestion of true views regarding the clustering of stars, and their arrangement and distribution in space, was published under royal auspices, and at the expense of the then reigning Duke of Brunswick. Considerable extracts, with brief notices, were inserted in the ' *Acta Eruditorum*' of Leipzig . . . These extracts could not fail to strike the attention of the German astronomers, and give rise to certain general considerations ; to plant the germs of more universal and enlarged views of creation, and to be suggestive of a most rational and comprehensive theory of the sidereal heavens."

3. Translatory Motion of the Stars along the Milky Way.

" One vortex or solar system, with its active centre, constitutes one heaven of itself, or one mundane system. Several solar systems, with their centres, form together a certain sidereal sphere. This sphere, which consists of many solar systems of this kind, has its own proper figure, and the figure of the sphere its axes. The solar systems inflect and bend themselves from the axis in every direction, till towards the other axis ; around this other axis they inflect and bend themselves in a like manner, and by the colligation of its systems the sphere again passes over (transeat) to the other axis. The sphere is thus colligated with its axes, so that all the systems in the whole sphere have reference to the axes."—*Principia*, Part III., chap. i., n. 5.

" The common axis of the sphere or sidereal heaven seems to be the milky way, where there is the largest gathering of stars. Along the milky way all systems are in a rectilinear position and series, in which direction the poles cohere. The systems are likewise connected there more intimately, and by spirals of sharper curves. The remaining solar or stellar systems afterwards proceed (prodeant) from the axis, and inflect themselves in different directions ; yet they have all reference to this axis."—*Ibid.*, n. 8.

" The striking fact of the sun's translatory motion amongst the stars, first distinctly observed by Sir W. Herschel," says Mr. Beswick, " has now received instrumental demonstration. The perfection of our astronomical instruments of measurement, the admirable exactitude and extreme nicety with which they can be used, on account of considerable improvements in the art of observing, have enabled us to reduce our advance towards remote stars, in the opposite region of the heavens, to visual perceptibility, like an approximation towards remote objects in apparent motion on a distant shore.

" Bessel, the Königsberg astronomer, has solved the grand problem of stellar remoteness. His investigations were made upon the star 61 Cygni, in the wing of the Swan; they commenced in the year 1834, and were completed in 1838; and during the whole of this period, he ordinarily took observations sixteen times every night. At length the long sought-for desideratum—the determination of the annular parallax of a star, was complete. He gives it $= 0''.3136$, or somewhat less than one-third of a second,[*] which places this star at the astonishing distance from us of 657,700 times the radius of the earth's orbit, or nearly $62\frac{1}{2}$ billions of miles. The distance is obtained as follows :—When the angle or parallax is secured, the distance of the star is then determined by an easy process in trigonometry, thus :—

Radius ; sine of angle : : diameter of the earth's orbit : distance of the star.

" The parallaxes and distances of thirty-five stars, ascertained by M. Peters, and of two other stars, have been most satisfactorily completed within the last few years. The measurements by Maclear, Meadows, and Henderson, of the double star in Centauri,[†] was completed in 1840, with a probable mean error of only $0''.0640$, and those by Professor Struve in

---

[*] Bessel. Schum. Jahrb. 1830, s. 47; and Schum. Astron. Nachr. bd. xviii., s. 401, 402, where the probable mean error is given $= 0''.0141$; also Dick's Sidereal Heavens, p. 80.

[†] Maclear, Results from 1839 to 1840, Trans. Astron. Soc., vol. xii., p 370; also Henderson and Lieut. Meadows, Monthly Notices, 1842, vol. v., p. 223.

1842.* From these distinct and perfectly independent measurements, it appears there is now the possibility of actually
measuring the velocity and direction of our solar system
amongst the stars, and of the stars in their progressions along
the milky way. Bessel informs us, that from his measurement
of the relative velocity of our solar system, and the star
61 Cygni, after allowing each its proper motion, there will be
a velocity for our planetary system, in space, of nearly three
and a half millions of miles in one day (3,336,000) ; which is
rather more than double the earth's velocity in its orbit in the
same time, or about 2,316 miles per minute. The direction
in which the system is moving, is also mathematically defined.
From a comparison of Professor Struve's measurements with
the admirable and exact researches of Argelander,† we have
the mean direction of the sun's motion = 259° 9′ R. A., multiplied by 34° 36′ Decl. The calculations of Sir W. Herschel,
and of four of the most eminent astronomers, concur in establishing this direction from the stars of the northern hemisphere ; and it has further been confirmed by the researches
of Galloway, who came to the same conclusion, from the
proper motions of the stars in the southern hemisphere. The
parallaxes of thirty-five stars, ascertained by M. Peters, give
the same direction. We are, therefore, moving in a direction
towards a point in the constellation of Hercules. . . . . .

" Having shown the astronomical grounds for believing in
a translatory motion of all the stars of the visible heaven
along the galaxy, we have now a clear way by which to proceed, in order to present a satisfactory confirmation of Swedenborg's *Theory of the Magnetic Course of the Sidereal
Heavens.*

" In the year 1733 this theory was given to the world. At
that time the translatory motion of the fixed stars had not
been conjectured : the idea of a proper motion belonging to

---

* Struve. Bulletin of Acad. of St. Petersburgh, 1842, t. x. No. 9.
pp. 137–139.

† Argelander. Schum. Astron. Nachr. No. 363–64, 398; also his
Treatise *On the Proper Motion of the Solar System*, 1837, s. 33.

the solar system had, however, been adopted by Halley, and other of Swedenborg's contemporaries.* No sooner had the latter opinion gained ground by the subsequent researches of Argelander, Struve, Peters, Mayer, Herschel, and others, than it became evident from their observations that there was a general rush, or local fluxion, along the galaxy, of all the stars of the firmament. Let the reader bear in mind, we are referring to sidereal measurements in the starry ring made within the last thirty years.† We prefer presenting the results of these measurements and researches, for many reasons, in the words of Baron Humboldt, *Cosmos*, vol. i., p. 139 :—

"'These data give us some idea of the extent of the motions which, divided into infinitely small portions of time, proceed without intermission in the great chronometer of time. If for a moment we could yield to the power of fancy, and imagine the acuteness of our visual organs to be made equal to the extremest bounds of telescopic vision, and bring together that which is now divided by long periods of time, the apparent rest that reigns in space would suddenly disappear. We should see the countless host of fixed stars moving in thronged groups in different directions; the veil of the milky way separated and broken up into many parts, and motion ruling in every portion of the vault of heaven.'

"But the main object of this article has yet to be shown. In what direction do the stars move in space. Do they move along the milky way? Echo answers, 'They do.' The theory of Swedenborg, and the theory of observation, both echo, 'They do.'

"Recently this theory of sidereal observation has had its exposition in an introductory lecture delivered at the opening

---

* Respecting the opinions of Bradley, Mayer, Lambert, Lalande, and Sir W. Herschel, on the motion of the solar system, see Arago, in the *Annuaire*, 1842, pp. 338–399.

† *Phil. Trans.* 1803, p. 225; Sir J. Herschel, *Mem. Astron. Soc.*, vol. v., p. 171; Mädler, *Astron.* s. 476; Bessel in *Schum. Jahrb.*, 1839, s. 53; also Mädler in ditto, s. 95; Encke, in Berlin. *Jahrb.*, 1832, s. 253, &c.; Arago, *Annuaire*, 1834, pp. 260, 295; also for 1842, p. 375; Savary in the *Connaissance des Temps.*, 1830, pp. 56, 163.

of the Corfu University Session, 1839, by O. F. Mossatti, Professor of Mathematics in the University of the Ionian Islands. The following striking contrast between the theory of Swedenborg, when the scientific world, without exception, had not even conjectured the general fluxion of the starry heavens, and the theory of Mossatti, as expressive of that fact when completely and satisfactorily established, solicits the reader's examination :—

Swedenborg in 1733, before even conjectured.	*Professor Mossatti in 1839, after empirically determined.*

The common axis of the sphere, or sidereal heaven, seems to be the milky way, where there is the largest gathering of stars . . . The solar or stellar systems afterwards proceed from the axis, and inflect themselves in different directions; yet they have all reference to this axis . . . the largest congeries is in the milky way . . . here lies the chain and magnetic course of the whole of our sidereal heaven. — *Principia,* Part III., chap. 1, n. 8.

The countless stars of the milky way may therefore constitute an unchangeable system, circulating in an annular space to which they are always limited . . . The solar system revolves, therefore, in the milky way from west to east, exactly in the direction in which all the bodies of this system revolve.

To give, in a few words, a clear image of what has been said, consider a cluster of countless stars in the immensity of space, all placed along a ring of enormous dimensions, and all moving in it in periods which only myriads of centuries can measure: following them in their long and slow courses, imagine them to approach promiscuously, but alternately, the outer and inner edge of the ring, and you will have an idea of the sidereal system in which we are placed.—*Phil. Mag.,* vol. xvii., No. 143, Feb., 1843, pp. 88–89.

"But our confirmation is not complete. We have shown the progressive fluxion of the stars along the milky way, but not their divergence from the axis or pole. . . . . Swedenborg says,—'That the star systems inflect their course in every direction from one axis or end of the milky way, and curve it towards the other.'—Part III., chap. i., n. 5.

"The northern pole, or axis, is always the pole of emergence, and the southern of influx; in other words, the magnetic element flows out of the northern end, and in at the southern [consult our 'Introductory Note' No. 8, prefixed to section 1 of our present chapter]. So also with the milky stream. One end is in the northern hemisphere, in the region of Cepheus and Cassiopea; this we must call the northern pole of the milky way. The other end is in the southern hemisphere, in the vicinity of Scorpio and Sagittarius; and this we must call the southern pole of the milky way. Now let us compare the application of Swedenborg's theory with the theory of observation.

NORTH POLE OF THE GALAXY.

*Swedenborg's Theory Applied.**	*Humboldt's Theory of Observation.†*
The stars, in diverging their course in opposite directions from the northern axis, will present an appearance of the stream as if it was breaking up or splitting into branches. So that we may expect to see that appearance where the northern axis is located, in the region of Cepheus, etc.	The two brilliant nodes (or poles) in which the branches of the zone unite in the region of Cepheus and Cassiopea, and (the other) Sagittarius, appear to exercise a powerful attraction on the contiguous stars: in the most brilliant part, however (of the northern axis), between B and z Cygni, one-half of the 330,000 stars that have been discovered in a breadth of 5°, are directed towards one side, and the remainder to the other. It is in this part that Herschel supposes the layer to be broken up.

"And well might Herschel suppose a breaking up in that part, for in the constellation of Cygni is the very point of divergence where the stars stream out of the northern axis, so that there must necessarily be an appearance of breaking up in the layer. We say necessarily, as to appearance, because there really is a splitting of the stream at the northern axis, where the streams, as Humboldt expresses it, 'are directed towards one side, and the remainder to the other.' . . . .

"At the southern pole, on the other hand, where the stars are coming from all points of the heavens, and crowding into the galaxy, we are to expect the phenomena of clustering, crowding together, and grouping, to be characteristic of this pole.

---

* Principia, Part III., chap. i., n. 8.
† Cosmos, vol. i., p. 140.

SOUTH POLE OF THE GALAXY.

Swedenborg's Theory Applied.	*Theory of Observation.*

On the contrary. The stars, in bending their course from different quarters towards the southern axis, will present the phenomenon of agglomeration, concentration, or clustering—the very reverse to that of the northern axis. So that we may expect this phenomenon about the southern axis, in the region of Scorpio and Sagittarius, where, as a consequence of the crowding together by the influx of stars into the southern pole, it will have a superior brilliancy and larger development, compared with the northern pole. The stars will therefore appear as if scattered in countless myriads, with a more bountiful and flowing hand than about the northern pole of this starry bed. The region of greatest brilliancy, and where the stars are crowded with greatest density, will, of course, be in the immediate vicinity of the southern end of the galaxy, or in the region of Scorpio and Sagittarius.

The general aspect of the southern circumpolar region, is in a high degree rich and magnificent, owing to the superior brilliancy and larger development of the milky way; which, from the constellation of Orion to that of Antinous, is a blaze of light; while to the north it fades away pale and dim, and is in comparison hardly traceable.—SIR J. HERSCHEL.

The southern stream maintains an unbroken course of extreme brilliancy, forming some of the most glorious clusters of stars in the heavens.

The telescopic structure of the milky way is in the highest degree complex and magnificent in the body and tail of Scorpio, the hand and bow of Sagittarius, and the following leg of Ophiucus. No region of the heavens is fuller of objects, beautiful and remarkable in themselves, and rendered still more so by their mode of association, and by the peculiar features assumed by the milky way, which are without a parallel in any other part of the heavens.

In Scorpio and Sagittarius the milky way is composed of definite clouds of light, running into clusters; the stars forming them are like sand, not strewn evenly as with a sieve, but as if thrown in handfuls, and both hands at once, leaving dark intervals. In this astonishing profusion the stars are of all sizes, from the 14th to the 20th magnitude, and even down to nebulosity. After an interval the same appearance is renewed, the stars being inconceivably minute, and numerous beyond description: they are in millions and millions—each is a sun, possibly surrounded by encircling worlds.—*Recent Discoveries in Astronomy.*—Frazer's Mag., No. 221, May, 1848, p. 504.

"Thus it appears, that on examining our own galaxy, we find action and translatory motion to be the characteristics of all the groups composing it. Upon a comparative examination of its two extremities, we find that the stars of its northern extremity are emerging therefrom in opposite directions, and thereby widening their distances; whilst on looking at the stars of its southern extremity, and comparing them with the observations made by old astronomers, we find they are coming more closely together, and pressing onwards into the main stream or axis of the galaxy.

"Never did a theory receive so full and yet so striking a confirmation. These amazing discoveries in the translatory motion of the whole starry heavens, coupled with the equally surprising one, which will be referred to in the next article — the discovery without a parallel — of the exact situation of our solar system among the stars, will alone stamp immortality on this work of genius, which will ever be regarded as going hand in hand with its brother *Principia* (Sir I. Newton's), each helping the other, — and whilst the one is occupied in pointing out causes and their phenomena, and giving them exposition in the doctrines of form, order and degrees, the other will assist in subjecting them to rule and measurement. Newton, at no distant period, will be seen in the studio of Swedenborg, the two in mutual converse with each other, on the destined uses of his pendulum and calculus, and the reciprocal bearing of their respective *Principia*.

" This striking agreement between Swedenborg's theoretical Principia, and the facts of observation, are not mere coincidences, but are the positive results flowing from the application of the new formula he invented, and which he based on actual experiment and geometry. And these results flow as directly from his formula, as the revolutionary motions of the planetary system from Newton's formula of gravitation, or the situation and velocity of a new planet from the formula of Le Verrier or Adams. The confirmation of his formula on so extensive a scale, and yet so complete, displays the profound correctness of his conception, the gigantic character of his philosophic and mathematical genius, the deeply penetrating sagacity which could anticipate so many, and so varied, but wonderful phenomena, aided, likewise, by an indefatigable power of analytic thought, which never ceased until it had sounded and explored the universe on all sides, and in all its depths."

4. THE SUN'S POSITION AMONG THE STARS.

Swedenborg says, " Our solar vortex or system is not in the axis of the sphere, but is near the axis where there is a considerable incurvation or inflection."—*Principia*, Part III., chap. i., n. 7.

This result, according to Mr. Beswick, was obtained by Swedenborg from the following formula : " From a given number of planetary orbits, the eccentricity and mean distance of each from their centre or sun, the skilful geometrician may infer the relative situation of neighboring star systems ; also the inflections and divergencies of solar systems from the milky way, according to their situation therein ; and from this again (as data), he may discover in the system of each star what will be the circular or elliptical character of the planetary orbits around each star, at different distances therefrom, with various other particulars." — See *Principia*, Part III., chap. i., n. 8, also Nos. 6 and 7 ; compare also our " *Introductory Note*," 5.

" Five years subsequently," says Mr. Beswick, " Herschel is born (1738).   In the year 1789 he directs his monster telescope to the sides and surfaces of the galaxy, and without knowing of Swedenborg's announcement of the sun's position therein, conjectures the identical spot, seeks for evidence of its truth by a species of star-gauging, and a few efforts reward his labors with the most abundant confirmation of the reality of his conjecture.   Certainly, never did a more bold assertion receive a more striking confirmation ! "

In order to show that Swedenborg has assigned the true and exact position of our solar system amongst the stars, and in order to present the comparison in the most striking manner, Mr. B., in the following extracts, selected only the particular words in which the fact is given :—

" Swedenborg. — ' Near the axis where there is a considerable inflection.'

" Sir. J. Herschel. — ' Near the point where it subdivides into two principal laminae.' — *Astron.*, n. 586.

" Sir W. Herschel. — ' Not far from the place where some smaller stratum branches out.' — Phil. Trans., vol. 75.

" There is no mistaking the exact spot here indicated by each.   All affirm the situation of our system to be at one end of the milky axis or stream, and near the point of divergence into two main branches.   So says Humboldt, *Cosmos*, Vol. I., p. 72 : —

" ' We are near this division.'

" Indeed so exactly has Swedenborg described this position of the sun's system, that his declaration contains this positive statement : —

" ' Our solar vortex is not in the axis, but is near the axis,' or main stream.

" So say the two Herschels, Rosse, Mädler, and other astronomers.   Or as the ' *Vestiges* ' has given it : —

" ' Our sun is believed to be placed in the southern portion of the ring (milky zone), near its inner edge.' — p. 2.

" Or as Sir J. Herschel remarks, after visiting the southern hemisphere, Phil. Trans. 1833, Part II., p. 479, fig. 25 : —

" ' Our system is placed eccentrically, so as to be much nearer to the parts about the cross, than to that diametrically opposed to it.'

" This confirms the wonderful exactness of Swedenborg's statement." — *Intellectual Repository*, Jan. 1850.

5.   THE STABILITY OF THE SOLAR SYSTEM.

Swedenborg, according to Mr. Beswick, develops the following proposition : " As the solar system is carried along the milky path, and afterwards compelled to diverge therefrom, the planetary orbits will change their form and eccentricity to a certain amount, and then return to their original condition, when they will again change, and again return, and so on to eternity."—*Principia*, Part III., chap. i, n. 5, 6.

Mr. B. continues : " The beautiful demonstration by La Grange* of the stability of the solar system, is a direct proof of Swedenborg's theorem.   The changes in the character of the planetary orbits, spoken of in the proposition, were already known and seen at work undermining the present form of the system, and fears were entertained that they might become exorbitantly great, so as to subvert those relations which render it habitable to man.   This was a difficulty which appeared insurmountable to the astronomers of Swedenborg's day, and for some time afterwards.   Theologians everywhere accepted it as an obvious demonstration of their doctrine of the final

---

* Memoirs of the Royal Academy of Berlin, 1777.

destruction of all things. Newton and Leibnitz had both bowed with submission to the order of things, which was winding up the operations of the great whole, and bringing on an inevitable doom. Geometers, philosophers, and theologians, accepted the fact as evidence of the common declaration, ' that the end of all things,' if not at hand, was at least certain. Everywhere the profoundest mathematical resources were employed to their utmost limits, but the equation on one side always equalled nothing, and the quantities only seemed to converge without the slightest possibility of their opening out, and again returning to a new development of being. Only one bright, refreshing spot existed like an oasis, where weary man, had he known it, might have refreshed himself; and that was the *Principia* of Swedenborg. There alone, amongst all the works of his period, is shown the now accepted doctrine of a cyclar return. At length, La Grange appears with a demonstration, grounded on the discovery of a certain relation which prevails in the system, between the masses, orbital axes, and eccentricities ; by which the doctrine is completely established, that though the solar system is liable to certain mutations in the form and eccentricity of its orbits, of very long periods, yet its orbits return again exactly to what they originally were, oscillating between very narrow limits. The same matter has been recently investigated by Le Verrier, with the same successful results.* So that the doctrine of a cyclar return in the form of the solar system, first propounded by Swedenborg, is now received as one of the most beautiful conceptions of man, under the name of La Grange's Theory of the Stability of the Solar System.†

" There is, however, this superiority in Swedenborg's theory, it not only explains the doctrine of a cyclar return, but also most satisfactorily exhibits the reason why it is so, bringing

---

* Taylor's Scientific Memoirs, Part 18.

† "After Newton's discovery," says Professor Playfair, " of the elliptical orbits of the planets, *La Grange's* discovery of their periodical (or cyclar) inequalities is without doubt the noblest truth in physical astronomy."

the philosophy down to the very senses, by telling you, *Principia*, Part. III., chap. i., n. 1 :—

" ' In the magnet and its sphere there is a type of the heavens : a mundane system in miniature presented to our senses ;'— the philosophy being stated where it is referred to in the proposition to these remarks ; this proposition declaring, that this doctrine of cyclar return is grounded on the changes and mutations in the form of the whole system, considered as a unit or globular vortex, in being bent in various directions, and again unfolding itself, according as it happens to be either passing in or out, or along the stream of the milky way ; the latter being considered in the light of a magnetic axis. . . . Nothing now remains but to establish, that these secular outstanding changes are dependent on, and due to, the translatory motion of the solar system.

" Hitherto, astronomers have admitted only the doctrine that quantity of matter is the only standard of the amount of attractive force : but now, another is added to their formula. Specific forces of attraction, coming from adjacent and surrounding systems, which act additionally to those belonging to, and arising out of the system itself, thereby causing additional and unaccountable changes in the form and situation of the system, producing translatory motions in space,—these specific forces are now, for the first time, taken into consideration. *Bessel*, the great Königsberg astronomer, was ' the first to conjecture,' *Cosmos*, vol. i., page 137, and practically apply this idea to the solution of planetary disturbances. The solution is similar in character to that given by Laplace to solve the discovery of Halley, in regard to the secular acceleration of the moon's mean motion, at the rate of eleven seconds in a century. Every change in the form of the earth's orbit, causes one in the distance and periodic time of the moon. So also with the sun and its system ; every change in the form of the orbit of the sun, causes a change in the distances and forms of orbits throughout its system. Accordingly, Bessel has proved, in an article entitled ' An Investigation of the Planetary Disturbances depending on the Motion of the Sun,' Abh. der Berlin Acad., 1824, S. 2–6, that secular inequalities are produced by this motion, and are due solely to its influence ; therefore, they change with the relative situation of the solar system among the stars ; and that, with the return of the whole solar system to the same position in its orbit, and amongst the same stars, the whole planetary system will be brought to its original form and condition. . . . See also *Mayer* in Comment. Soc. Reg. Gotting., 1804–1808, vol. xvi., pp. 31–68, and *Arago* in the Annuaire, 1842, pp. 388 399.

" Thus the whole theory of Swedenborg is capable of actual demonstration."—*Intellectual Repository*, for Jan. 1850.

6. Nebular Theories of Swedenborg and La Place.

" After the suggestions of Newton upon this subject, with the existence of which I know not whether La Place was acquainted, it was asserted by the latter that Buffon was the first writer whom he knew, who, since the discovery of the true system of the world, had attempted to investigate the origin of the planets and satellites. Now Swedenborg published his Principia in the year 1734 ; that is to say, ten years before Buffon published his theory, and Buffon himself had read Swedenborg's Principia, as may be concluded from the circumstance that a copy of the Principia was not very long since sold by an eminent bookseller in London, (Bohn, of Henrietta street, Covent Garden,) containing Buffon's own autograph ; therefore, if La Place himself was not acquainted with Swedenborg's treatise, it is reasonable to presume that Buffon was. Ten years, then, before Buffon published his theory, and about thirty years before La Place offered his own to the public, Swedenborg had propounded his theory in the Principia, in the year 1734 ; and again in his treatise on the Worship and Love of God, in the year 1745, or about twenty years before La Place's theory." — *Introduction to the Principia, by the Translator.*

" This notable piece of history," says Mr. Beswick, "is, I think, somewhat incorrectly stated as to dates : nevertheless the error is in favor of Swedenborg, and enhances the value of the comparison. It is to be regretted, however, that the error should have crept into biographies, lectures, reviews, tracts, and periodicals, both in America and Europe, without ever once being

27

detected. Swedenborg's *Principia* was published in 1734, Buffon's *Théorie de la Terre* in 1749, and La Place's *Système de Monde* in 1809; therefore *fifteen* (not *ten*) years before Buffon, and *seventy-five* (not *thirty*) years before La Place, Swedenborg had propounded his Nebular Theory in the Principia, 1734. We should bear in mind that La Place's hypothesis is only an extension of the idea proposed by the elder Herschel in 1802, and was of course published subsequently. . . .

" The honor of conceiving and publishing the first crude notion of heavenly bodies being formed from nebulous vapors, belongs unquestionably to Tycho Brahe and Kepler ; (see Arago in the *Annuaire* 1842, p. 434,) therefore, long antecedent to the time of Swedenborg. The hypothesis appears to have remained latent, through the insufficiency of well observed data, until Halley came forward in 1677, Swedenborg in 1734 (*Principia*), La Caille in 1750–1752 (*Mem. de l'Acad. des Sciences*, 1755), Kant in 1755 (*Structure of the Heavens*), Lambert in 1757 (*Cosmogony*), Herschel in 1799–1802 (*Phil. Trans.* vol. 92), and lastly La Place in 1809 (*Système de Monde*), who gave to the Nebular Hypothesis its present elaborate structure. The idea of heavenly bodies being formed from nebulous vapors, therefore, preceded Swedenborg, and upon this one point Swedenborg is merely one in the foremost rank of its brilliant advocates.

" Hence the crude idea out of which the Nebular Hypothesis has sprung, was not originally suggested by the elder Herschel, as it is sometimes thought, but it was developed and embodied by him. He gathered together the material, and laid the foundations. In the irresolvable class of nebulæ, he thought he had discovered evidence of the existence of nebulous matter : and by classifying his objects, and thus marshalling them under the old nebulous hypothesis, was led to believe that primordial matter, scattered over space, underwent a process of condensation or aggregation into masses, by the power of attraction. Hence, in reviewing the then irresolvable nebulæ, the progressive character in the shapes of the extraordinary objects which his researches disclosed, seemed to demonstrate the old hypothesis of star-formation from cosmical vapor. At this point La Place took up the matter; and suggested such an extension of the original idea, as to constitute what is now popularly known as the *Nebular Hypothesis.* A marked distinction must, therefore, be made, entirely separating the original idea as propounded by Tycho, Kepler, Halley, Swedenborg, and the elder Herschel, from the extensions proposed by La Place. Insomuch so has this necessity been seen, that the younger Herschel has entered his protest against the proposed alliance. (*Athenæum,* June, 1845, p. 615.) Sir J. Herschel is in fact an advocate of the original hypothesis, which, so far as it goes, is identical with Swedenborg's theory. Yea, more; the extensions proposed by Swedenborg are not only agreeable, and consort with the ideas of the younger Herschel, Rosse, Humboldt, and others, but are also being confirmed by recent discoveries in sidereal astronomy, and by other considerations to which we shall refer hereafter. Whilst the extensions proposed by La Place, as we shall have occasion to show, have not a single illustration, yea, not a single fact to rest upon within the range of our ordinary experience, nor within the far mightier range of our best instruments. But it is sufficient for our purpose at this stage of the inquiry to record the fact, that four years before Herschel was born (1738), fifteen years before Buffon's theory (1749), and seventy-five years before La Place's hypothesis (1809), Swedenborg had published illustrations of the formation of belts and zones, their disruption and ultimate formation into revolving spheroids and cometary bodies ; and had distributed the immortal work (*Principia*) in which the Hypothesis is given, over the whole of Europe, and had presented copies of it to the most important institutions and savans.

" We now proceed to place the two theories side by side, and afterwards to form a comparative estimate of the probable truthfulness of each, and of their scientific value as aids to Theoretic Astronomy.

NEBULAR THEORIES.

| *Swedenborg in 1734.* | *La Place in 1809.* |

Swedenborg in 1734.

That the second elementary particles are most highly compressed near the Solar active space . . . . In this manner the number and quantity more and more increase by reason of the successive compression of the elementaries; and also condense themselves round the solar space. That the finites thus concrete into an immense volume, and crowd around and enclose the sun in such a manner as to form an incrustation . . . . That nevertheless this crust which is formed around the sun, is rotated in a certain gyre. . . . That this crustaceous matter being endowed with a continual gyratory motion round the sun, in the course of time removes itself farther and farther from the active space; and, in so removing itself, occupies a larger circle of space, and consequently becomes gradually attenuated, till it can no longer contiguously cohere, but bursts in some part or other . . . . That the solar crust being somewhere disrupted on the admission of the vortical volume, collapses upon itself; and this towards the zodiacal circle of the vortex; so that it surrounds the sun like a belt or broad circle; that this belt, which is formed by the collapse of the crustaceous expanse, gyrates in a like manner; removes itself to a farther distance; and by its removal becomes attenuated till it bursts and forms into larger and smaller globes; that is to say, forms planets and satellites of various dimensions, but of a spherical figure . . . . That this crustaceous expanse may subside partly into itself: that it may partly subside inwardly, or toward the solar space, and thus revolve itself round some active space; that it partly subsides exteriorly or toward the vortex. Thus that there may exist bodies of three different kinds, namely planets, satellites, and erratic bodies straying round the sun, such as we are accustomed to denominate solar spots . . . . That these bodies, separated into globes, direct their course into the vortical current, according to their magnitude and weight; that they continue more and more to elongate their distances from the sun, until they arrive at their destined periphery or orbit in the Solar Vortex, where they are in equilibrium with the volume of the vortex.

La Place in 1809.

Whatever be its nature, since it has produced or directed the motion of the planets and their satellites, it (the sun) must have embraced all these bodies, and considering the prodigious distance which separates them, they can only be a fluid of immense extent. To have given, in the same direction, a motion nearly circular round the sun, this fluid must have surrounded the luminary like an atmosphere (incrustation). This view, therefore, of planetary motion, leads us to think, that in consequence of excessive heat, the atmosphere of the sun originally extended beyond the orbits of all the planets, and that it has gradually contracted itself to its present limits . . . But how has it determined the motions of revolution and rotation of the planets? If these bodies had penetrated this fluid, its resistance would have caused them to fall into the sun. We may then conjecture, that they have been formed at the successive bounds of this atmosphere, by the condensation of zones, which it must have abandoned in the plane of its equator, and in becoming cold have condensed themselves towards the surface of this luminary. One may likewise conjecture, that the satellites have been formed in a similar way by the atmosphere of the planets.—*Systeme de Monde,* vol. ii., p. 362.

La Place conjectures that in the original condition of the solar system, the sun revolved upon his axis surrounded by an atmosphere which, in virtue of an excessive heat, extended far beyond the orbits of all the planets, the planets as yet having no existence. The heat gradually diminished, and as the solar atmosphere contracted by cooling, the rapidity of rotation increased by the laws of rotatory motion, and an exterior zone of vapor was detached from the rest, the central attraction being no longer able to overcome the increased centrifugal force. This zone of vapor might in some cases retain its form, as we see it in Saturn's ring; but more usually the ring of vapor would break into several masses, and these would coalesce into one mass, which would revolve about the sun. Such portions of the solar atmosphere, abandoned successively at different distances, would form planets in a state of vapor. These masses of vapor, it appears from mechanical considerations, would each have a rotatory motion, and as the cooling of the vapor went on, would each produce a planet, which might have satellites and rings, formed from the planet in the same manner as the planets were formed from the atmosphere of the sun.—*Whewell's Bridgewater Treatise,* p. 181.

" Now the essential distinction between these two theories consists in the difference between the two preponderating cosmical forces employed to effect the genetic development of planetary and solar systems. Swedenborg adopts the centrifugal force, and La Place the centripetal. Swedenborg expands his system from the centre to the circumference, and La Place contracts his system from the circumference to the centre. With these exceptions, the main features of the two theories are alike. Both begin with atmospheric incrustation of cooler and denser materials around the solar surface; its greater accumulation from the polar to the equatorial plane, forming a belt or zone: the separation of the central body from its zone by the rotary or centrifugal force of the former; and the disruption of zones into planetary bodies. Thus the main features of the two systems are alike: planetary bodies are affirmed to have their genetic development from the condensation of solar superficial matter into zones: thus, that both classes of bodies have an identical origin, and formed one mass. We now proceed to a critical examination of the two theories.

La Place's Theory.

" *Origin of Rotary Motion.*— It is affirmed by the advocates of this theory to be a well-known law in physics, ' that when gaseous or fluid matter collects towards or meets in a centre, it establishes a rotation.' Upon this mechanical law the whole theory is based, and hence the necessity of giving it the most comprehensive and obvious demonstration from well-known matters of fact. We are reminded, by a glance at our books, of the many eminent names that have been recorded on the list of those who advocate it with more than ordinary acquirements. Yet we have no hesitation in giving this fundamental principle of the Nebular Theory the most unqualified denial : there is no such a law of physics in existence, nor a single fact in nature upon which it can be based, or by which it can be illustrated. We are more than astonished at the profound talents of La Place, as a physical philosopher, establishing his theory on so questionable a foundation as the law cited above. Whirlwinds and whirlpools, eddies and

27*

dimples, are no proofs of such a law, although commonly cited as illustrations : air and water in these cases do not collect from every point to a centre. There is no resemblance in the two cases : the nebulous case supposes that the cosmical vapor collects from all quarters, as if it came from the surface of a sphere or globe. In our astronomical and meteorological observation we have oftentimes had occasion to watch with intense interest the formation of vapory clouds by condensation, or by collecting together from all sides towards a centre : we have condensed gaseous vapor of some of the most important substances : we have compressed water so uniformly from every side, as to bring the central point of resistance to the centre of the mass ; and in every case, we have found it a well-known physical law, ' that when fluid or gaseous matter collects towards or meets in a centre,' it establishes not rotation, but perfect immobility. Indeed there is no single physical cause that would so effectually put an end to rotation if it existed, as the concentration or collecting together of the particles, from all sides of the general mass, towards its centre. There is not the slightest resemblance between the examples generally adduced in support of this theory, and the nebulous case they are intended to illustrate. And ' the well-known physical law ' said to originate the rotation, is the very best ' well-known law ' that could be cited to prove that rotation cannot result from the case supposed.

" The formation of common clouds has the greatest resemblance of anything in nature to the formation of cosmical clouds as held by the theory : yet, who ever saw rotary motion in a condensing cloud ? Let us examine this point more minutely. Every particle is supposed to be drawn together by attraction, and the radial forces in this case cannot be otherwise than equal on all sides, and in a state of equilibrium, since it acts according to the square of the distance. Whirlwinds and whirlpools, and other similar instances, are proofs that only two or more radial forces have met or collected together ; but where radial forces are converging from every direction to a common focus or centre, then rotation cannot result. The merest tyro in physical science might successfully undertake to demonstrate, that where rotation really exists from impact or confluence of radial forces, such impact at the focus of confluence is not in the direction of the centre of gravity of the mass, thus brought together by attraction as affirmed by this theory, since then their radial force would have been in the direction of the centre of gravity. There is emphatically no such law in physics as that upon which this theory is based. All the examples are cases wherein gaseous or fluid matter is supposed to move in one and the same general plane ; as from two or more points of the periphery of a circle to its centre : whilst the theory itself supposes a case where gaseous matter comes from every possible direction — above, below, and on all sides. Our objection constitutes a dilemma, from which there is no escape. The first horn affirms, that there is no instance in nature of rotation resulting from the convergence of radial forces in every direction, and that the examples upon which it is based have no resemblance to the nebulous case itself. The second horn affirms, that rotation cannot possibly result from a convergence of radial forces coming in every direction from a periphery to a centre.

" The Hypothesis supposes the existence of spheroidal masses of vapor aggregating or consolidating themselves to a centre by virtue of attraction. This was the original hypothesis of Herschel, and here he left it. But La Place extended it by adding a ' well-known law,' and basing it upon examples which have no more connection with the original hypothesis than a flat circular plate has with a globe or sphere. For whilst it is obvious that Herschel considered he was dealing with spheroidal masses of nebulous vapor, it is equally obvious that La Place and followers considered they were dealing with flat planes of vapor. We have no hesitation in affirming, that the origin of motion, according to the Nebular Theory of La Place, is a mathematical and physical impossibility. Beyond the question of origin we need not go, since the whole superstructure falls with it.

SWEDENBORG'S THEORY.

" With Swedenborg's Theory the case is otherwise. We have seen that rotary motion must spring from an inherent force in the nebulous matter itself, since it cannot possibly arise from a radial force originating from without. Accordingly, this philosopher holds the theory, that nebulous matter consists of substances or elements having an inherent vortical tendency, force, or activity; which causes it, whilst aggregating, to be impressed with a vortical tendency throughout its mass, and a general consent to move vortically in a mass. This necessarily gives rise to poles and axes : thus to rotary motion about an axis. We now proceed to consider the Swedenborgian Theory more in detail.

" In looking at the Solar System as a whole, the sun is seen to have both a central position and a central force ; and the attendant luminaries forming its system are seen to increase the velocity of their orbital fluxion as they are nearer the body in which resides this central force.

" This clearly proves that planetary motion literally depends on solar motion ; that the sun's axillary force originates all orbital motion in the system : and that the origin of motion in a revolving unsolid mass must be more active than the mass itself.

		Days.			Days.
Sun	. . . .	25.34000	Asteroids	. .	1618.00000
Mercury	. . .	87.96928	Jupiter	. . .	4332.58480
Venus	. . . .	224.70078	Saturn	. . .	10759.21981
Earth	. . . .	365.25637	Uranus	. . .	30686.82051
Mars	. . . .	686.99964	Neptune	. .	60126.70000

" The origin of motion having the greatest force, must have the greatest velocity. So universal is this physical condition, that it is equally applicable to revolving masses whose origins of motion are some in the centre, and others in the circumference. If the motion begin in the circumference, the centre will have the least velocity ; but if it begin in the centre, the circumference will have the least velocity. This simple physical law is alone sufficient to set aside the Nebular Theory of La Place, and establish the theory proposed by Swedenborg. If the former were true, then the central body, the sun, ought to have had the least velocity of rotation, which is the reverse of the fact. The graduation of motion from the centre to the circumference, or the reverse, determines the origin of motion to be in or not in the centre of the revolving mass. If there be diminished velocity, then the origin of motion is within, but if there be an increasing velocity from the centre, then the origin is extraneous. In the Solar System the centre has the greatest velocity; therefore the motion is from a central force in the Sun. The Laplacian Theory is demolished by this simple law, and the Swedenborgian Theory established thereby. We cannot here enter into an exposition of this central origin of planetary fluxion ; this will be done when we come to speak of the physical condition of the sun. Sufficient for our present purpose is the elicitation of the fact, that the origin of orbital fluxion is in the sun itself; and that the primal force from which all motion is derived, including axillary motion, is in the sun ; that it has, therefore, the cause of its own motion, and of the motion of its system, dwelling in itself. Or as Swedenborg expresses it : ' The Solar Ocean existing in the middle of the vortex is the fountain of all the motions which take place between the parts constituent of the world.' — *Principia*, Part I., chap. x., n. 1.

" Nothing is more certain as a law of being than this ; that the forces which sustain this mighty piece of mechanism are the same as those which brought it into being. Herein lies the great theoretic problem, What are these forces? We have already shown that centrifugal force is obviously only an outward development of an indwelling force in the solar mass ; and gravitating force is not a formative force, since it would permit of the system being any shape, structure, number of parts, or kind of motion. For instance: As all the planets move in nearly the same plane with the sun, the gravitating force had nothing to do with this. It had nothing to do with distributing cometary orbits there and planetary orbits here : making the first extra-zodiacal, and the latter zodiacal. Planetary orbits are circular, but cometary orbits are eccentric ; gravitation had nothing to do with this, since it would have allowed planetary motion in any kind of ellipse, however elongated. The planets all revolve round the sun in the same direction; and what is most strange, they rotate on their axis in the same direction as that in which they revolve in their orbits. Now Gravitation had nothing to do with all this uniformity of fluxion : this came from a formative or directive force, since gravitation would have permitted them to have followed any and even the most diverse directions. These different facts, comprising the essential features of the system, were totally irrespective of the operation of this force : and to account for them the Laplacian Hypothesis was originally proposed. It was suggested that the different orbs had come into their present condition and location by the condensation of the solar mass, which is supposed to have originally extended to the extremities of the system, and to have filled in volume the whole solar region : but that during condensation, rings or belts of solar matter were successively abandoned in the plane of the zodiac, which, on breaking up, collapsed, and formed globes or planets. But one important condition is overlooked in this hypothesis, that the mass is in a progressive state of collapse and condensation upon the centre. Now we think that this is the best possible conservative condition for a ring to be in ; for every tendency to breakage would be removed and compensated by the parts being brought closer together, or what is the same, by the condensation and collapse into a less circle, and consequent fall upon the centre. On the contrary, how very simple and natural is the Swedenborgian Theory ! The belts are supposed to expand and enlarge, thereby increasing their diameter, until they must break by attenuation alone. We now proceed to consider this Hypothesis under the three following phases :—

I. Formation of the Solar Mass or Sun from Nebulous Matter.

II. Formation of the Solar Crust, and its disruption into Planetary Bodies.

III. The Distribution of Orbs into a Solar System.

I. *Formation of the Solar Mass or Sun from Nebulous Matter.* —" The original Nebular Theory, referred to above as being held by Tycho Brahe, Kepler, Halley, and Herschel, is precisely similar to Swedenborg's, so far as it goes. And even the younger Herschel, whilst he protests against the extensions of La Place, and admits the resolving power of Rosse's mighty instrument, yet affirms his belief in the original theory ; and thus so far agrees with the fundamental idea of the Swedenborgian Hypothesis, which affirms the existence of primordial elements and nebulous matter aggregating into a solar mass, and becoming a sun or nebulous star.   He observes :—

" ' The existence of a luminous matter disseminated through wide regions of space in a vaporous or cloud-like state, undergoing or awaiting the slow process of aggregation into masses by the power of gravitation, was originally suggested to the late Sir W. Herschel in his reviews of the nebulæ by those extraordinary objects his researches have disclosed. . . . This part of my father's general views of the construction of the heavens, therefore, being entirely distinct from what has of late been called " the nebulous hypothesis," will still subsist as a matter of rational and philosophical speculation,—and perhaps all the better for being separated from the other.'— *Athenæum*, June 21, 1845, p. 615.

" Swedenborg also advocated the existence of nebulous vapor from elements [?], which by aggregation formed a vortex ; but that they formed a vortex, when aggregating, by virtue of their own inherent vortical motions, which dispose them to fall into a motion in one common direction.   He says :—

" ' That in the state of the formation of the vortex among the elements, as they are growing by accretion into an immense sphere or volume, no other form was needed than a certain active centre ; moreover, that the elements themselves would spontaneously dispose themselves into a general motion conformable to the figure of the parts ; and that by means of the action which takes place in the centre, they would perpetually continue this motion both as to each particle, and also as to the whole volume.   If in a sphere of elements there be a centre of motion, or an active centre, the parts which are nearest the centre come into a state of greater compression (through the central action on them) than the parts which are more remote ; consequently there is an attempt of each particle to flow into a gyre produced by its compression ; the degree of

which is proportioned to the distance from the centre . . . .
Hence if there be a centre, and a force of activity in the centre,
the elementary particles dispose themselves, by a mechanical
necessity, into gyres conformable to their distance from the
centre ; that is to say, into a vortical motion.'—*Principia*,
Part I., chap. x., n. 6.

" Hence when the nebulous matter is in its first period, or
when being formed into a solar mass, ... the grosser
or least active would obviously form a vortical sphere of
increasing density towards the centre, where the greatest
density would prevail, consequent on compression or closer
contact from the greater velocity and force of the active
space within. Thus the matter of the sun had then, and must
have now, a vortical motion, having the greatest velocity in
the centre and least at its surface. When we come to speak
of the Physical Constitution of the sun, we shall show from
well-established data, and from recent observations, that such
a vortical motion in the sun's bodily substance does really
exist, and can be presented as a well-sustained fact."

II. *Formation of the Solar Crust, and its disruption into
Planetary Bodies.*—" The action of the Solar Mass being superior to the aggregate re-action of the elements surrounding it,
the former would force the latter into a more compact and
dense arrangement : their surfaces being forced together, the
capability of expansion and fluxion would be reduced in a like
ratio, and a compact and comparative inert mass would accu-
mulate like unto a dense elementary crust or cloud-envelope,
which would cover the whole solar superficies. The compression would be greater near the solar force than in any other
part of the envelope, because there the solar action would be
greatest. Now to form a correct idea of the formation of this
crustaceous envelope, the reader need only conceive that in
the vortex surrounding the solar mass the elements become
individually more passive by compression from within ; hence
they flow more densely around the active centre, and so form
a crustaceous instead of a diffused expanse on the solar face.

" ' That in this manner the number and quantity of finites
(passive elements) more and more increase, by reason of the
successive compression of the elementaries ; and also condense

themselves round the solar space. That the finites (passive substances) thus concrete into an immense volume, and crowd around and enclose the sun's in such a manner as to form an incrustation ; nor do they cease to act till the vortex be fully formed . . . . In this manner finites will be added in crowds, and press closely upon the active spaces, and, like an extremely dense crust or cloud, will interpose themselves between the vortex which has to be formed and the solar space ; thus also will they intercept the immediate force of the spaces, and its operation upon their vortex ; and consequently will throw into shadow the whole of the mundane system, darkening it as by an extremely opaque cloud, and super-inducing upon it another and different state.' — *Principia*, Part III., chap. iv., n. 3.

" And as the internal activity continues supreme, even after the vaporous crust or cloud-envelope is formed, it follows that the envelope is compelled to expand from, and at the same time to aggregate around, the active solar force ; because it is formed in this very motion itself, or this motion is going on while it is being formed. The consequences of this expansion must obviously be attenuation of the crust, and ultimate disruption.

" ' This crustaceous matter, being endowed with a continual gyratory motion round the sun, in the course of time removes itself farther and farther from the active spaces ; and, in so removing itself, occupies a larger circle of space, and consequently becomes gradually attenuated, till it can no longer contiguously cohere, but bursts in some part or other . . . . The space within is continually active, and incessantly acts upon the walls and barriers of its prison : and it is evident that the heavy bodies in the solar vortex tend from the centre to the circumference . . . . Now if the tendency of this crust is to fly off to a greater distance, it follows that it must become gradually attenuated, because the same volume occupies a larger circle. That the expanse becomes attenuated in consequence of forming a larger circle, is a purely geometrical fact ; as also, that if it becomes attenuated and be in perpetual motion, it in some part or other becomes disrupted.'—*Ibid.*, n. 5.

" Seeing that the cloud-envelope encloses the sun on all

sides, it becomes an interesting point of inquiry as to where the first disruption exists, and whether sufficient uniformity prevails in such vortical masses as to predict with certainty the exact spot where it may be definitely expected. The problem of disruptive location, or the precise place where it first occurs, is easily solved. The locale is not accidental, not first in one place and then in another, but is definitely determined by a physical law from which there is no exception ; it must and can only occur at the poles, north and south. Polar compression in the bodily mass of every planet in the system is caused by axillary rotation : from centrifugal action alone the polar parts of the sun have sunk, and the zodiacal and equatorial parts expanded or bulged out, thereby causing the polar diameter to be less than the equatorial. This law of axillary projection of the equatorial parts, and a rushing of the polar parts to the same location, would obviously effect the first disruption at the poles, from the effects of attenuation, and a collapse upon the equatorial diameter of the crust.

" ' That the solar crust being somewhere disrupted, collapses upon itself on the admission of the vortical volume ; and this toward the zodiacal circle of the vortex ; so that it surrounds the sun like a belt or broad circle ; that this belt gyrates in a similar manner ; removes itself to a farther distance, and by its removal becomes attenuated till it bursts, and forms into larger and smaller globes ; that is to say, forms planets and satellites of various dimensions, but of a spherical figure.'— *Ibid.*, n. 5.

III. *The Distribution of Orbs into a Solar System.*—" According to the Swedenborgian Theory, the planetary bodies originated near the solar equatorial surface, by the disruption of a crustaceous belt, as stated above. After the disruption, the crustaceous pieces, as planets, launched out and extended their excursions from the sun to various distances in the zodiacal plane of the great vortex or system. In this respect it essentially differs from the Laplacian Hypothesis, which affirms that planets have been left at their respective distances by the contraction of the solar mass, which originally extended to the successive distances of the planetary orbits.

" ' Hence it follows, that these bodies direct their **course**

into the vortical current according to their magnitude and
weight; that they continue more and more to elongate their
distance from the sun, until they arrive at their destined
periphery or orbit in the solar vortex, where they are in
equilibrium with the volume of the vortex.'—*Ibid.*, n. 7.

" ' That the earth perpetually revolves round its axis spontaneously; that is to say, by reason of the nitency of its individual parts constituting its central globe; and thus that it
begins to measure the intervals of day and night the moment
of its making its exit from the sun; at which moment also
it seems to perform its axillary revolutions more rapidly than
it does at a farther distance from the sun, when a considerable
portion of it is consumed in the formation of ether, air, water,
and terrestrial matter, and the parts of the earth become more
closely bound and connected with each other by means of a
solid incrustation.'—*Ibid.*, chap. xi., n. 2.

" The question now arises, What is the direct physical cause
which compelled each planet to select or settle down in the
exact locality it now occupies, and which compels them to
remain in that locality and not to encroach upon each other's
domain? The answer is unique, and peculiar to the Swedenborgian Theory. The axillary motion of each planet arises
from an inherent force derived from the sun, whose motion is
in itself. This self-motion necessarily forms a vortex around
each planet, which consists of the elements of the general vortex in which they float or gyrate orbitally. The axillary motion forms a vortex of its own, and the precise velocity of this
axillary vortex determines the orbital location in the general
vortex. If it be greater or swifter, then a slower locality of
the general vortex would be selected; and if slower, then a
swifter location would be preferred. Equilibrium between
the individual or planetary vortex and the general or solar
vortex, determines the position or location of the planets. This
simple relation subsisting between the velocities of the planetary vortex and general solar vortex, is the physical cause of
the location and distribution of orbs in the Solar System.
Hence Swedenborg says :—

" ' The vortex formed round the earth aims at an equilibrium in the solar vortex, that is to say, occupies the place

where it can be in a state of equilibrium. That were the vortical motion greater or swifter, it would seek a different locality from what it would were the motion less, or slower.'—*Ibid.*, Part III., chap. xi., n. 5.

" Now the extraordinary result from this simple law is one of the most remarkable of all the facts belonging to the Solar System. We should expect the nearest planets to the sun to have the least axillary motion and the greatest orbital velocity : and the farthest planets to have the quickest axillary motion and the least orbital velocity. And as a general rule this is actually the case. Humboldt says, ' The rotation is most rapid in the case of the exterior planets, which have at the same time a longer period of revolution ; slower in the case of the smaller interior planets, which are nearer the sun.'—(*Cosmos*, vol. iv., p. 449.)

" We regard Swedenborg's Theory as capable of explaining all the main facts of the System, and as constituting the widest and most comprehensive generalization of all the fundamental features of the Solar Region, that Theoretic Astronomy has ever yet recorded."—*New Church Repository* for 1855, pp. 301–307, and 428–434.

INDEX.